MW01128123

A NOTE FROM THE AUTHOR

O ur universe is a big place. Statistically, it's foolish to assume that there's no life beyond Earth. But assuming there *is* life out there, is any of it highly intelligent? Intelligent enough to conquer the daunting challenges of traveling through deep space? Such a task requires technologies and phenomena we can only theorize and place into fictional scenarios at the present; and according to the current laws of physics, such travel may be impossible altogether within any reasonable timeframe, such as a human being's lifespan.

To date, no concrete evidence has been presented that is compelling enough to prove, beyond reasonable doubt, that Earth has been visited by extraterrestrials. There are numerous records of mysterious occurrences, convincing testimonies, blurry video clips, and tangible artifacts (some of them thousands of years old) that suggest it *could* be true, but irrefutable proof of any "First Contact" has yet to surface. Despite that, I am convinced that aliens *have* been to Earth.

Years ago, a personal experience led me to

realize that we are most certainly not alone, and that aliens not only exist, but have been visiting Earth. No, I have never met an alien face-to-face, but while flying in a small, private plane, I did see something that I believe was of alien origin. The thing I saw was no recognizable aircraft, and it defied the laws of physics that our present technology must adhere to. Simply put, there is nothing from Earth like what I experienced. That exhilarating encounter has remained with me ever since, and has played a significant role in my developing and writing this story. This story is, of course, fictional, but my imagination was spurred to new levels at that moment, and these following chapters of fantasy are all connected back to how I felt that day and the reality of what I saw… and, perhaps, also by the fact that I have always loved science fiction, especially that which includes aliens.

Science often needs to explain and micro-analyze everything it theorizes, limiting itself to known parameters within its field of vision. Science *fiction*, however, allows us to move beyond those boundaries… beyond what we can actually see in the furthest points of the Universe, or in the minute world of quantum physics from our own corner of space. But, beyond that, who's to say what is or isn't possible? There's still plenty of the unknown out there to be exploited by active imaginations. It is in this spirit of imagination without boundaries that I present you this story, the tale of Dewey the Alien. This is the first in a series of unfolding adventures that I hope you will enjoy reading as much as I have enjoyed writing them.

It's fun to imagine what's out there, isn't it?

—Marshall Lefferts

FOREWORD

In a distant galaxy, there is a binary star system where there orbits a planet with lavender-colored oceans and a bright purple atmosphere. Like Earth, it is endowed with life-sustaining elements (although the elements are quite different from those on Earth), and it orbits in its system's "Goldilocks zone," exactly the right distance from its twin stars to be at the proper temperature for liquid water to exist — and therefore, the proper temperature for supporting life.

The Purple Planet is home to many living things, and at the top of the evolutionary chain is a sentient, highly-intelligent species that has endured in its current form for many millions of years. These Aliens originated as squid-like, aquatic creatures, evolving mostly in the planet's oceans. To escape growing numbers of ravenous sea predators, they eventually crawled onto dry land and adapted to living outside of their former liquid environment, utilizing the elements of their new, dry world to build vast cities and develop incredible technologies.

Within several thousand years of leaving the

oceans, the Aliens developed the means to travel into space, where they discovered and achieved amazing things. At first, they explored every corner of their own solar system and then their home galaxy; but within a few million years they were venturing deeper and deeper into the Universe, exploring countless other galaxies and solar systems far beyond their own.

The Aliens found millions of living planets, containing countless species to study and ogle at. But all life they discovered was classified somewhere between primordial and primitive. None proved intelligent enough to communicate or interact with. The Aliens began to wonder if they would ever find another species whose intellect and understanding of the Cosmos could rival their own.

Then, about seventy million years ago, they discovered a solar system near the edge of a mid-sized spiral galaxy, and in it a water-covered blue planet containing abundant life. There was no sentient life there yet, but of all the inhabited worlds they had come across, this one proved to be the most intriguing. It had the most diverse variety of species they had ever encountered on any single planet, including their own. Studying the Blue Planet became a top priority. They began visiting regularly, monitoring its ecological and evolutionary developments with great interest.

Through thousands of generations, Alien scientists kept a keen eye on the Blue Planet and its occupants. They observed with great sadness as a massive asteroid strike decimated most of the planet's life-forms, including a promising reptilian species that had begun making stone tools, and then watched with fascination as life rebounded and thrived again. They witnessed small mammals evolve into primates, and eventually into hominids, then into several species of Humans that began to use fire and, in time, build structured societies. The species of Human that won out and colonized nearly all their world began calling the Blue Planet Earth, which the Aliens found amusing. When the Humans started to show promise of becoming advanced enough to communicate with, the Aliens considered contacting them.

But as the Humans' societies developed, they became too diverse and unpredictable. Many of them were quite peaceful, but equally as many were cruel and violent towards each other. It was decided by the Alien Council that exposing themselves to the Humans was too risky and might compromise the balance of their cultures. The Aliens had no interest in changing or trying to police the path of Human cultural progress, whether they agreed with it or not. Instead, the Aliens decided to continue study-ing Earth, but to remain unseen by the Humans.

At least, that was the plan.

For a great while after that decision was made, the Humans remained the most fascinating thing in the Universe to the Aliens. That was, until an expedition to Earth's solar system discovered something buried on the lifeless fourth planet the Humans called Mars: an ancient, massive structure of unknown origin. So astonishing was this discovery that it brought a whole new perspective to the Aliens' place in the Universe. Soon afterwards, the Aliens found a *second* structure, identical to the one on Mars — only this one was on Earth itself, hidden in one of the planet's deepest oceans. How they could have missed these gargantuan objects over thousands of missions to Earth was most puzzling, and the origin and purpose of them was a complete mystery. With these new developments, it became more important than ever to continue sending exploratory missions to the Milky Way in general, and Earth in particular.

CHAPTER 1

THE UNITED STATES OF AMERICA
PLANET EARTH

It was 8 am in a suburban neighborhood of Raleigh, North Carolina. The sun's warmth was just beginning to disperse the mist that bathed a small, public park's grassy field, where a Human mother sat on a bench, sipping her nutmeg-laced Vente cappuccino. As the espresso kicked in, she smiled as she watched her two young children play in the dew-covered grass with the family's new puppy, a chocolate lab of two months.

The children laughed and giggled uncontrollably as they rolled around in the damp grass, taking turns letting the puppy jump on them to lick their noses. Their mother teared up, savoring the moment and wishing kids and puppies could stay this age forever.

She had no way of knowing that, at that very moment, an eerily similar thing was happening fifty million light-years away, in a galaxy of the Virgo Cluster.

CHAPTER 2

THE PURPLE PLANET
PRIME CITY

It was late afternoon at the Intergalactic Zoo Complex, a massive campus in the heart of Prime City. Oblivious of their true origins, two juvenile Human clones were rolling on their backs in a field of too-green artificial grass, happily playing with a young canine specimen. The German Shephard puppy was a recent addition to this particular Earth exhibit, and was proving to be a big hit with the younger Human specimens.

The Human children were seven and four years of age, the elder an Asian male and the younger an African female. At the edge of the field, a adult female Caucasian sat cross-legged, observing the noisy ordeal. She was smiling as she looked on, feeling great joy from watching the youngsters and their pet, but wasn't exactly sure why she felt this way. The three Humans were disparately clothed, each sporting garments that the Aliens had designed to resemble the native dress of their respective cultures on Earth.

The dialects spoken by the Humans were mixed as well. The adult female spoke English with a thick British accent, while the Asian boy responded in Mandarin and the little black girl babbled in fluent French. Yet they all understood each other perfectly.

The frivolous activities between the Human children and the dog puzzled the male Alien who was observing them from a distance through the ecosystem's one-way viewing wall. This particular Alien was in his twentieth season as an Apprentice of Universal Sciences. As his name is impossible to pronounce in any Human tongue, we will, for now, just call him *the Apprentice*. The Apprentice was 164 years old, about one-third of his life expectancy. His physical attributes were quite different from those of the Humans, or any other Earth creatures for that matter. He possessed tentacle-like arms and legs, four of each around the upper and lower portions of his pear-shaped torso, each hand and foot bearing seven long, flexible digits. He had no neck; nor was his skull separate from his shoulders, so he could not turn his bulbous head like a Human could. But that did not impair his constant field of vision while standing still; his four eye-stalks, each topped with a pair of eyes, could contort into any position needed, giving him a full 360° scope. Upright, with his eye stalks fully extended above his head, he stood nine feet tall.

The Apprentice wore no clothing. He needed

none, as the Aliens' bodies were composed of robust elements, incredibly strong and resilient compared to those of Humans. Nor did the Aliens care for anything ornamental. The only item that adorned an Alien's flesh was a wide alloy belt around its lower torso. These bands were permanently attached to all Aliens at an early age and served as a dock for the four holo-discs each Alien was assigned for life, one for each of their four brains. The holo-discs were paired with microchips implanted in each brain at birth, and they served many purposes — from communications to controlling any number of devices, and tapping the vast information networks the Aliens had amassed over many millions of years.

Physically, Aliens and Humans shared little in common. But the Aliens *had* found one very intriguing similarity between themselves and the bipeds: emotion. No other species they had discovered in the Cosmos had displayed it as much, or as dramatically, as the Humans did. The Aliens were emotional creatures as well, although they considered themselves to be far more rational in how they dealt with it. It was this aspect of Human nature that intrigued the Apprentice most, and he enjoyed studying them more than any other species.

There were thousands of different Earth life-forms at the Intergalactic Zoo, including many of the smaller creatures, real examples brought back alive or bred in captivity; but most of the larger mammals, and all of the Humans, were clones, grown from

DNA harvested during collection missions. Long ago, there had briefly been wild-born Human specimens at the Zoo, but no longer. The abducted Humans had all gone mad with fear and anxiety, and it was deemed cruel to continue the practice. The collection of real Humans, as well as other more-evolved species, was abolished in favor of harvesting their DNA and cloning specimens instead.

The clones, knowing no other existence, were peaceful and secure in their lives, living them out with no knowledge of their origins or their Alien captors. But despite having happy and comfortable specimens to study rather than frightened and insane ones, for the Alien scientists, cloning had significant disadvantages. Studying a cloned Human or other animal raised in an artificial environment was not ideal as far as sociological study was concerned. It did not offer a true representation of the creature's natural behavior.

But it was better than nothing.

Hidden behind the viewing wall, the Apprentice was 400 meters from where the children and puppy were playing, but even from that distance, he could study them in great detail. His telescopic eyes could zoom in on objects up to a kilometer away with amazing clarity. He pondered how, under the same circumstances, the behavior of Human children on Earth would differ from that of these young clones. In recent years, he had grown extremely fond of studying the Humans in the Zoo, and soon, he hoped, he might get to observe real ones in their natural habitat... on Earth itself.

The young Apprentice had recently been assigned his first intergalactic research mission, and he was elated that of all the possible planets he might be assigned to study, his freshman adventure would be to Earth. For a budding Alien scientist, Earth was the Holy Grail, and very few Apprentices were chosen to go there. During the next several decades, if all went well during this first trip, additional missions to Earth would become a routine part of his responsibilities. But first he had to prove himself worthy of the privilege, completing his first mission without flaw.

His orders were to gather samples of as-yet-uncatalogued species in an isolated section of rainforest, in a place the Humans called the Amazon Basin. This remote ecosystem, and others like it, provided plentiful species for the Alien apprentices to study, in places far from where any Humans lived. As happy and grateful as he was to have been chosen for Earth study, the Apprentice was deeply disappointed he would not get to see real Humans on this trip.

But this was his reality; first-time expeditions to Earth were always sent to areas devoid of Humans. That way, there would be less risk of being detected while the Apprentice honed his exploration skills. There were some Human villages near where he was going, but they did not possess technology that would alert them to his presence. He was under strict orders to keep his distance and to avoid detection at all costs. In due time, he would get his chance to study Humans up close and perhaps even gather their DNA, but the thought of waiting for years was agonizing.

The Apprentice squatted quietly, studying the Humans in the habitat with four eyes while the other four were focused on projections from one of his holo-discs — training manuals he was reviewing for the mission. His attention was diverted when another Alien entered the viewing chamber, appearing head-first from a portal in the ceiling. The arriving Alien gripped metal handles that surrounded the portal, and then flipped upright and dropped to the floor, landing on all four feet.

This Alien was a four-hundred-fifty-year-old female, her skin lighter colored than the Apprentice's and mottled with age. She was his Mentor, a decorated explorer and one of the most highly-respected elders of the Science and Exploration Ministries. She had guided him and many Apprentices before him through their early years of training. She approached the Apprentice, and the two greeted each other by intertwining their fingers like a nest of snakes. "You are troubled?" the Mentor inquired of her student, vocalizing in a sequence of sounds from her communication bladders.

The Apprentice realized he was broadcasting his frustration, and tried to cover the fact. "No, I am fine, Mentor. I am observing while these Humans interact with a young canine. The episode is puzzling; the Humans are pleased and greatly entertained, yet there is no apparent purpose to their activity. I am struggling to understand it."

Two of the Mentor's eyes narrowed smugly as they peered at her apprentice, then shifted in color from bright blue to dark yellow. She scolded him, "Yes, that has always puzzled us. But you are not that concerned with these clones! It serves you no purpose to conceal your true thoughts from me. I know why you are upset."

The reply that came from the Apprentice's comb-bladders was not a pleasant sound, nor did it mean anything in their language. It was purely an exclamation of disgust. He was embarrassed he could not hide his emotions from her. The Mentor was forgiving, however, having been in his situation herself hundreds of years prior. She understood completely the burning desire to advance prematurely into tasks reserved for older, more experienced scientists.

"I share your eagerness, Apprentice, but patience is what you must express, regardless of your true feelings," she quietly puffed. "The Ministry will not show the compassion that I do. Do not jeopardize your future chances of studying real Humans on Earth. Follow protocol and do a professional job. You will be rewarded if you do so."

In a more subdued tone, the Apprentice snorted and bleeped back, "Yes, yes, I know. Thank you for not being overly angry with me. I am vexed with myself for feeling this way. But it seems impossible for me *not* to think about it, and I will be so close to them on their own planet. I just wish I could take a brief look. I am so fascinated by them!"

"We all are, and the time will come to get closer... if you stay focused on your duties."

"Yes, perhaps in thirty years or more," sighed the Apprentice.

The Mentor continued her pep-talk. "There is no shame in your given task, Apprentice. Perhaps you think it is less exciting than studying the more intelligent species, but it is no less important. In order for us to fully understand the Humans' world, we must know all there is to know about every species we can find on their planet. Earth's rainforests still contain plentiful new specimens for us to study. But the Human impact on these ecosystems is eradicating much of the life there at an alarming rate, so it is imperative that we collect samples before they become extinct. It is meaningful work, and I guarantee you will find the experience fulfilling."

"I'm sure I will, and I *am* grateful to be in this position. I just fear that before I am qualified to study real Humans, the Ministry will end the Earth expeditions, and I will get assigned to worlds that do not harbor such fascinating creatures."

"You know as well as I do that will not be the case. We are not about to abandon our research on Earth."

"No, of course not," he sighed. "I am merely

impatient. Do not worry, Mentor, I will focus on my duties and collect as many new rainforest specimens as possible. I will make you proud."

"Good! Now go home to your family and get some rest. You have a big day tomorrow."

"Yes ma'am, I will."

Mentor and Apprentice bid each other farewell by touching the other's chest with the spread finger-tips of one hand. Then the elder reached above her head with all four hands and pulled her body up into the passage from whence she had come, and disappeared into it.

The Apprentice remained motionless for a few more moments, watching the Human children at play and trying to absorb what the Mentor had said. He purged his minds of negative thoughts and concentrated on how lucky he truly was. Few of his kind would ever have the privilege of visiting Earth, and he was fortunate to have been chosen. He admonished himself silently for losing focus, and thanked the Creator for his Mentor being so patient with him.

CHAPTER 3

The transportation chamber of the Intergalactic Zoo was a cavernous, elliptical room. At any given time, it was filled with dozens of intraplanetary transports, departing to and arriving from every point on the Purple Planet. The Apprentice requested one of the smaller ships with a holo-disc, and when one was assigned, he scurried to its docking platform and boarded it.

From outside the transport, one could not see inside through the polished alloy surface. But from the inside, the external viewer displayed a 360° panoramic view of the ship's surroundings on the inner walls, giving the impression it had no outer hull. The Apprentice used three of his hands and all four feet to firmly grasp metal loops protruding from the floor and ceiling, then used a holo-disk to beam destination coordinates to the onboard computer.

As the craft exited the building, its mirror-like surface reflected the purple and orange sunset that was developing above sprawling Prime City. Slowly and gracefully, it maneuvered to avoid colliding with other vehicles in the city's traffic lanes; then, once clear of the lanes and several miles high, it shot off at a blistering pace towards the southern horizon. Within seconds the Apprentice was travelling at six times the speed of sound. He would arrive at his home in the southern hemisphere in seventeen minutes.

By the time he was thirty seconds from home, he had reviewed the complete procedural manuals for his mission to Earth twice. He was cautiously confident that he was well-prepared, ready to face the final testing before the Prime Council of the Exploration Ministry tomorrow. But now, as his home grew near in the viewer, it was time to leave work behind and focus on his family. As the transport descended, however, his thoughts migrated back to Earth and the Humans momentarily. He pondered what the real Humans' private homes on Earth might be like on the inside, and how families interacted with each other in privacy, away from the public eye. Of this much was speculated, but little was known.

The clones in the Zoo offered a great deal of insight, as they did conduct themselves differently in the privacy of their dwellings than they did in public areas. But for the most part, the clones had always managed to live harmoniously with each other. Humans on Earth, on the other hand, although they were often seen being loving, tolerant, and kind to one another, were also frequently observed in conflict. When at odds over anything they felt was important, some of them could be extremely cruel to each other on many levels. *Are they always kind and loving to each other within their family units,* the Apprentice wondered, *or does this periodic public cruelty transgress into family life as well?*

The Apprentice could not imagine cruelty within the family home of any intelligent species. He cared deeply for his mate and children, and loved their life together. The cohesiveness of the family unit was cherished above all thing by the Aliens, and he, his mate, and their children had never once been unkind or ill-willed to each other, regardless of any conflicting opinions. The Apprentice and his mate had pledged themselves to each other over a century ago, and since had conceived two offspring, a male now twenty-five years old and a female of forty-nine who was nearing the age of Occupational Selection.

At fifty years of age, each adolescent Alien reported to the Ministry of Occupations for a series of aptitude tests, and an occupation best suited to each individual was chosen. The outcome was permanent and non-negotiable. His daughter wished to become a scientist like her father, and would be very disappointed if that did not happen, but she would gracefully accept whatever decision the Ministry made. The Apprentice's male offspring was not yet concerned with his ultimate job, and did not show the passion for Universal Sciences his sister did. Both, however, were very excited that their father would be going on a mission to Earth. It was an honorable and prestigious assignment, and a proud accomplishment for any Alien family.

The Apprentice was seconds from home now. The transport slowed as it descended and made final approach to the dwelling, which resembled the ship itself: a shiny metal sphere, only much larger. It stood 150 feet in circumference, protruding from the side of a jagged hill covered in bluish-purple foliage and ledges of pink sedimentary rock. The structure was ablaze with the colors of the sunset, its curved, mirror-like surface reflecting each nuance of the evening sky. On the external viewer, the Apprentice saw his mate and female offspring sitting motionless on top of the house. The two had scaled the sides of the building to perch atop its highest point, a common activity for female Aliens at the end of each day. Unless it was pouring rain or the dense blue fog common to the region was too thick to see anything, meditating atop their home during sunset was a daily evening ritual for females.

The males weren't as passionate about this ritual, but they did, on occasion, join in the experience. On this evening, the Apprentice was eager to join his mate and daughter. In a few days he would be millions of light-years away from them, and he wanted to meditate with them tonight. The transport glided through the open portal of the docking chamber, and he quickly disembarked, scrambled outside through the portal before it closed, and scaled the smooth, curved surface of the house. There were no hand or foot grips on the building's exterior, so he morphed his fingers and toes into small suction cups to grip the metal surface and effortlessly pull himself up the side of the structure. As he approached the crest of the sphere, his mate and daughter each took a pair of eyes off the sunset and swung them about on their stalks towards him. "Welcome home," his mate greeted him softly, with a short burst of faint whistles and breathy sounds.

"Father, it is good that you joined us tonight!" declared his daughter. "The sunset is powerful. The Creator has given us a beautiful end to this day."

"Yes, that the Creator has, and I am grateful to have this moment with both of you," he responded. "Where is my son?"

"He is in the learning chamber," the mother said with a sarcastic tone. "He received a new learning module today, and he cannot get enough of it. It is about the reproductive process, so he finds it most fascinating."

"As do I," snorted the Apprentice, in an equally sarcastic tone. "But wait until he learns how the Humans do it! It is utterly disgusting."

"Tell me, Father!" the high-pitched sounds came from below. The Apprentice's son was clambering up the side of the home towards him. "Is the Human reproductive process more interesting than ours?"

"You will learn that in time," the Apprentice replied. "Have you completed your studies for the day?"

"No, but I will. I heard your transport arrive, but you never came inside, so I came to find you." The youngster approached his father and squatted in a sitting position next to him. "Are you well today, Father? Are you anxious about your trip?"

"I am well, thank you. And I do feel some anxiety over my trip to Earth, but I will be fine."

"I am so proud that you are going to Earth! My classmates are asking me so many questions about it."

The two females were becoming annoyed at the escalating conversation between the males. Meditation at sunset was serious business. Beyond brief interruptions to greet anyone joining the event, ongoing distractions were most unwelcome. "Can you two continue this conversation elsewhere, please? We are meditating here!" said the Mother.

"We apologize!" exclaimed the Apprentice. He did not believe the conversation between he and his son was lengthy or inappropriate, but there were times and places that he could effectively argue a point with a female. This was neither. "We will stay to share the sunset with you, and we will be quiet."

"Good."

The Alien family huddled close together on the domed roof of their home, their legs tucked in tightly and their arms folded flat against their bulbous chests, resembling four upside-down pears lined up in a row. In silence, they focused all eyes on the iridescent streaks of the fading sunset as it painted its final mosaic on the horizon. Scattered across the surrounding hills were numerous other homes of various sizes, most of which also had their female occupants perched atop them, meditating and staring at the sunset. Here they would sit, still and silent, until the last slivers of light disappeared.

As the blanket of night arrived, so did the endless myriad of stars in the sky, as well as the prominent glow of two of the planet's seven moons. The family's gaze shifted to the moons, and then the Apprentice's daughter broke the silence. "Father, which way is Earth?"

The Apprentice raised one of his arms, unfolding a finger towards the sky, pointing it in the direction of the Milky Way's current position. "Of course, it is not visible from here, but it is in that direction at the moment." His family's eyes followed his extended digit, staring in the direction he was pointing. "In just a few days, that is where I will be."

CHAPTER 4

"Rrrrrruff! Burrruurruurr! Oof! Urrrrrf!" The aggravating sounds had begun fifteen minutes prior, piercing the peaceful silence of daybreak in a most unwelcome way. Nathan and Tracie Johnston attempted to find refuge from the offender, staying hidden under their covers and remaining perfectly still, barely breathing so as to not offer any clues that they were already awake. But they knew this charade was doomed to fail. It always did.

"Rrrroof! Owoooo!" Another squeal of displeasure arose from the floor beneath the bed, this time sounding more desperate than the last.

"Oh, Deweyyyy!" Tracie whined, pulling a pillow over her face. "Can't we just have another 30 minutes of peace, you little turd!"

"RRRRRRRUUUUF!" Dewey answered, increasing his volume. The King of the House was seven pounds of alpha wolf, subspecies dog, a puffy tidbit of tan fur prancing on delicate, spindly legs, with a pointy snout and beady eyes. True to his pure-bred Pomeranian lineage, he was neither patient nor forgiving. And he was spoiled rotten. "Doo-Doo" was his nickname when he was being a little angel, Tracie's little bundle of joy... but that name had yet to be mentioned this morning.

Dewey carried on with his demands while his Human staff continued their futile attempt to ignore him. He could sense their frustration building, and he knew it was only a matter of moments before he would push them to the brink and he'd get his breakfast.

Then Nate's cell phone rang, and Dewey went ballistic.

Ringing phones, regardless of the ringtone selected, always sent Dewey into a frenzy. But Nate's phone always irritated him the most, as it repeatedly played the opening passage of the song *Limelight* by Rush, a Canadian rock band Tracy had never warmed up to but that Nate worshiped as the best music on Earth. Apparently, Dewey didn't like Rush either, as the sound of it caused him to spin in a frenzy, snarling and screeching at the top of his tiny lungs. Tracie chuckled despite herself.

"You two have no taste in fine music!" Nate scolded as he groped for his phone on the nightstand.

"Who friggin' calls this early on a Sunday!?" Tracie moaned under the pillow that covered her face.

"Honey, it's not that early. Normal people are usually up by now. It's probably your mother wondering if we're coming down tonight. You never got back to her yesterday, so now she's after me for an answer."

"Well, we're *not* normal people! You think she'd know *that* by now," Tracie sneered as Dewey continued spinning in circles and snarling. She threw the pillow off her head in his direction and sat up. "Dewey! Shut it!" she hissed with her lips curled tight, her eyes glaring at the tiny beast.

Dewey abruptly stopped barking. He let out a final disgruntled squeal and sat down, staring up at Tracie forlornly. He knew that tone of voice, the one that meant he had driven her to the brink and he'd better be quiet or get escorted to the garage for a timeout. No matter; he had succeeded in getting her awake and her attention focused on him. Time now for the sad puppy-eyes strategy... that usually did the trick.

Meanwhile, Nate had finally secured his phone after dropping it off the edge of the nightstand. "Hellooo!" he said playfully, but then quickly sat up, his tone changing to serious. He hadn't bothered to check the caller ID, assuming it was his mother-in-law. It wasn't. "Yes, yes, Jason. Of course this is a good time, we were already up," Nate fibbed politely. "Yes... of course... no way! Really?... REALLY!?... *Holy crap!* Jason, are you serious? You're not punking me?"

Tracie sat up and looked at Nate with a puzzled look. "What is it?" she mouthed, holding her hands out to her sides in an inquisitive gesture. Nate shook his head without looking at her, waving her off with his hand. Then he took the phone and walked into the bathroom, closing the door behind him. For a moment she was angry; she *hated* being waved off like that. But then she realized that she did the same thing to him all the time, and she shrugged it off. She pulled the pillow back over her head and drifted back to sleep, letting out a muffled snore that prompted an angry squeal from Dewey.

In the bathroom, Professor Nathan Johnston could hardly believe his luck. The person on the phone was Jason O'Rourke, Chief Director at ARCA headquarters in London. ARCA stood for Amazon Research Center Associates, with whom Nate had been volunteering as a research contributor for years now. Jason had called to tell Nate that his bid to be selected for a fully-funded, two-week expedition into the heart of the Amazon had been approved. Several times each year, ARCA funded and equipped expeditions to conduct research in the deepest forests of Asia, Africa, and South America, and although there were numerous other organizations doing so as well, none had the deep pockets and resources that ARCA did.

ARCA was funded by a small group of some of the wealthiest individuals on the planet, a New York-based board of anonymous moguls who had deep passions for the sciences, particularly biology and astronomy. Nobody in the scientific community fully understood why these mysterious philanthropists were so interested in rainforest research, or why they sank such incredible amounts of their resources into ARCA. But Nate didn't question such wonderful gifts; he was elated to put the funding and ARCA's state-of-the-art equipment to good use.

ARCA spared no expense in equipping their researchers with technology that made surviving in the rainforests quite easy, even in the most extreme conditions. But the funding wasn't endless, so not everyone who wanted to go could. Thousands of candidates volunteered, but only a few were chosen each year. This was a great honor and opportunity for Nate.

"Unbelievable!" Nate shouted out loud as he ended the call and walked back into the bedroom. Tracie stirred back to life, casting the pillow aside and sitting up on her elbows, squinting at the obnoxious sunlight that snuck past the bottom of the window shades. "What's so exciting?" she asked. "Did one of your geeky buddies discover a new species of slug in their backyard?"

"Not quite." Nate smirked at her attempted humor. "*That*, my dear, was Jason O'Rourke at ARCA. He just called to tell they want me to go do a little extra research for them." Nate spoke casually, doing his best to sound like it was no big deal.

Tracie absorbed the information for a moment,

then sat up abruptly on the edge of the bed. "You got it? They're sending *you* this time?"

"Yep!" Nate grinned widely, barely able to contain his excitement.

"Oh my God! That's awesome, baby! *When!?*" Tracie jumped off the bed and hugged him.

"I fly to London the first week of next month to train on ARCA's equipment, then I go to São Paulo the following week to put the expedition together."

"How long will you be gone?"

"Seven weeks — one in London, one in São Paulo, a whole month in my little heaven, then a week to get it all packed up and get home."

"Great," Tracie sighed, "you'll miss our anniversary."

"I'm sorry, sweetie, I'll make it up to you, I promise. You know I can't pass on this." Nate stroked her hair and gently kissed her cheek.

"Darn right you'll make it up to me," she replied, drawing him in and kissing him hard on the lips. "Congratulations, Professor, you finally got your big break. Doo-Doo and I will miss you."

Dewey snorted in disgust as he watched Nate and Tracie. He was getting frustrated with all this nonsense, and he hated being ignored.

"You could come with me," Nate said. He knew this was out of the question, but he wanted to see Tracie's reaction anyway.

She pulled away from the embrace with a wrinkled face. "Me, sleep in the jungle with a zillion

creepy things crawling all around me? Uhhhhh…
no."

"You should see the campsite equipment ARCA
has. It's designed to keep everything with more
than two legs outside the camp."

"It won't work. The bugs will find a way in. They
always find a way in!"

Nate grinned, amused by her repulsed look.
Odd, he thought, since as a marine biologist she
was perfectly at home with bizarre, slimy creatures
discovered in the ocean's depths. She could spend
weeks on research ships at sea and be in her own
heaven, yet somehow, spending a week in the rainforest amidst bugs and spiders creeped her out.
He didn't care; she looked stunning in her pajamas
and bedhead, and her silliness turned him on. He
pulled her close, grinding his body into hers and
softly kissing her neck.

"Well, in that case, Mrs. Dr. Johnston," Nate
sneered in his best British accent, "you'd best give
the fearless entomologist a proper shagging before
he's shipped off to the Amazon to meet his fate
amongst those dreadful, maniacal creatures."

Tracie laughed. "Why, Professor, is that a micro-
scope in your pocket?" she said playfully, pulling
Nate back towards the bed. "Just what kind of research are you planning to do with *that*?"

Dewey snorted in disgust. He'd seen this before, and it meant that today, continuing his morning tantrum routine would be a wasted effort. His

Humans were not going to get out of bed and cater to his whims, at least not for the next hour or so. He let out a sigh, curled up in a ball on his bed in the corner of the room, and drifted back to sleep.

CHAPTER 5

At the center of the Exploration Ministry's main briefing chamber, a three-dimensional holo-image of Earth rotated several feet above the floor. Around the rest of the chamber floated images of the other planets in Earth's solar system, as well as various waypoints in the Milky Way that were relevant to the Apprentice's first mission there.

The Mentor, Chief Administrator, and several Directors of the Ministry followed the Apprentice as he moved amongst the images, discussing the relevance of each to the mission. The Chief Administrator asked the Apprentice many questions, and he responded to all of them without hesitation.

"Unless there are gravity tunnel complications, I will arrive at the galaxy's Primary Station in three days," The Apprentice said, pointing at the holo-image of the station at the center of the Milky Way, orbiting its massive black hole. "I will complete a thorough check of the station's systems and perform any necessary updates, and download any new data it has gathered into my transport's databases," he continued. "Then, assuming all is in order, I will program a passage to Earth's solar system and dock with Earth Station... here." He pointed at the image of the small station, hidden behind Jupiter.

For millions of years, this station had been in close orbit around the Earth itself. But when Humans developed the means to detect objects in near space using primitive telescopes, about six hundred years ago, it had become necessary to hide it from view behind the Moon. Then, when Humans began visiting the Moon less than a century ago, the station's orbit was moved further out into space, directly behind Mars. But the Humans eventually went to Mars as well, and so the station was again relocated, this time behind Jupiter. There it would be safe for at least several more decades, as the Humans had no technology in the works that would take them that far out any time soon, other than unmanned probes the station could easily avoid.

The Apprentice went on with his mission review. "Once I have updated Earth Station, I will gather the necessary research equipment and specimen containers from its storage chambers and then program the transport for descent to Earth. I will double-check the stealth systems to be sure I cannot be detected, and then I will enter Earth's atmosphere here," he pointed to the highlighted area just above the South American continent. "Next, I will find a suitable landing site in this region," he said, circling his finger around the middle of the Amazon Basin.

This formality was a blatantly redundant exercise. Moments after first receiving the mission's digital parameter files, which had been years prior, the Apprentice had memorized the entire plan. He was highly adept at operating Alien technology of any kind, including the sophisticated research equipment stowed at Earth Station. The Directors all knew this, as did his Mentor, but it was standard for them to repeatedly put rookie explorers through this last-minute inquiry, no matter how tedious and pointless it seemed. There was no room for error in these missions. Once he had departed, there would be no communication with home; he would be completely alone, with no one to help him if anything went wrong. So, despite the redundancy, the questioning continued until the Council was satisfied he was ready.

Finally, the Chief Administrator stated, "I am satisfied, Apprentice. You are well-prepared for your mission, as we all knew long ago. You will forgive the tediousness of this protocol; we realize it is monotonous to you and all other cadets, but you know it is necessary, given the risks."

"Yes, Director, I do understand," the Apprentice replied, hiding his impatience. He did in fact comprehend the purpose of the protocols for novice explorers leaving the system for the first time, especially when their first mission was to Earth. But quietly, he thought that his abilities were beyond such repeated scrutiny, and his exemplary track record should have allowed him more benefit of the doubt — and that it should have pre-qualified him to go on a more meaningful expedition than to simply collect insect, bird, and reptile specimens, far from any Humans. But the orders to maintain distance from Humans had been very explicit, and the most repeated of any other during the mission training. In fact, it had already been mentioned several times on this very day. But apparently it was not yet enough, as the Director felt the need to say it once more.

"And again, I cannot emphasize to you enough that you absolutely must avoid contact with Humans. Where you are going there should be none present for many miles, so I doubt it will be a factor, but if anything goes wrong, you *must* follow protocol. It is imperative! Are we clear on this?"

"Yes, quite clear, Director."

"And in the event that all attempts to avoid contact fail, you are able and willing to do what you must?"

The Apprentice nodded two eye stalks in silent acknowledgement. Protocols for dealing with un-planned Human encounters on Earth were complicated and varied depending on the degree of exposure, but the general concept was clear; Humans must not become aware of the Aliens presence. If any Human was to discover an Alien during a mission, drastic measures were approved to prevent further exposure.

Having survived the final review and being approved to proceed with the mission, the Apprentice was dismissed from the Ministry Complex. He bid farewell to the Mentor and Chief Administrator, and then he headed home to enjoy one last evening with his family. As the transport whisked him away from Prime City and across the purple sky, his emotions were mixed. He loved his family dearly and would miss them while he was gone, so incredibly far from home. But he was also tingling with anticipation, eager to depart on his first mission. Several days from now he would be millions of light-years away, on a fascinating world full of new things to discover.

CHAPTER 6

Nate Johnston was busy making final preparations to head for the Amazon Basin. He had arrived in São Paulo a week ago from London, where he'd spent four intense days at ARCA headquarters training on their latest jungle survival gear and research equipment. Their new technology was incredible, light years beyond Nate's wildest dreams, and he felt more like James Bond being equipped to save the world than a bug scientist on his way into the rainforest.

With ARCA's approval, Nate had chosen a mostly unexplored spot in the Amazon Basin, far from any known villages or tribes. Tribes in the Amazon were often semi-nomadic, so there was always the chance of an encounter; but ideally, Nate would end up where he could have complete solitude for the duration of his stay. But the area was very remote, and that meant that getting himself and all the gear there would be a long, arduous task. Fortunately, as well as spending millions on the high-tech gear, ARCA spared no expenses on logistics either, giving Nate a healthy budget to work with.

When the gear arrived in São Paulo on ARCA's 747-800F freighter, Nate supervised as it was carefully loaded onto the truck he had hired, along with two drivers so that one could drive while the other slept. Nate also hired a well-armed security guard to ride along. If the gear were stolen, the expedition would be over before it even began.

It was early evening on the second day out of São Paolo when the truck reached the outskirts of Porto Velho, a small city in the heart of Brazil that served as a launching point for many rainforest expeditions. Nate directed the driver to the hotel he had booked for the night, where they were to meet up with Pedro Escoval, a seasoned river-guide whom ARCA used frequently for their Amazon expeditions.

Escoval was waiting in the hotel's parking lot when the truck pulled in. He was leaning up against an old, rusted pickup and casually smoking a cigarette. At first approach, Nate found the veteran river-boat skipper a bit intimidating. Escoval was a robust man, six feet two with a muscular build, chiseled jaw, piercing brown eyes, and short grayish-black hair. He wore faded brown khakis and a dark gray muscle-shirt, and around his neck was a thick silver chain on which hung what appeared to be a set of piranha's jaws. Escoval was in his late-thirties, but Nate thought he looked ten years older from the weathered skin on his face and neck, a testament to his countless hours spent in the strong Amazon sun.

"You are Professor Nathan Johnston?" Escoval inquired politely in a thick accent, blowing smoke through his nose as he spoke.

"Pedro? It's good to finally meet you!"

"And you, my friend. I have been looking forward to this. You must be hungry and ready for a beer, yes?" Escoval said, slapping Nate on the shoulders with two firm hands.

"You read my mind, and a shower for dessert, please!" Nate responded, grinning. He was relieved at Pedro's warmth and welcoming demeanor. Until that moment, he had only spoken with Pedro by phone a few times, and the connections had never been all that good, so the conversations had been short and to the point. In person, he seemed much friendlier.

Nate bid the truck drivers and security guard a good evening, shoring up plans for the next morning, and then climbed into Escoval's pickup. They drove a few miles to a small roadside cantina on the edge of town, where Escoval was greeted with cheers in Portuguese from several inebriated locals hanging out in the parking lot. He joked and laughed with them for a few minutes, and although Nate couldn't understand a word Pedro was saying, he laughed along with the drunk men anyway. Then Escoval escorted Nate inside the establishment through its rickety front door, weaving between tables of festive diners to a secluded wooden booth at the back of the bar area.

A middle-aged woman emerged from behind the bar and came up to the table, her brown, wrinkled face beaming with a semi-toothless grin. She seemed happy to see Escoval as he stood to embrace her and kiss her cheek, and Nate began to get the impression that his host was somewhat of a celebrity in these parts.

"This, my friend, is Yitsi!" Pedro introduced the woman to Nate. "She and her family have run this place for twenty years. Her sister is the best cook in all of Brazil!"

"My pleasure, ma'am." Nate said, shaking Yitsi's hand. "I'm starving. What would you recommend?"

"She doesn't speak English, so I'll order for you," Pedro said cheerfully.

Escoval rattled off the order, and Yitsi retreated behind the bar. She returned a moment later with two unmarked bottles of clear, brownish liquid that had some strange-looking sediment swirling at the bottom, which made Nate wince. Then she disappeared through the open door behind the bar into the kitchen, yelling out to her sister behind the stove, shouting loudly to overcome the clatter of pans and dishes. Nate leaned over to get a better view into the kitchen. It looked old and greasy. Nothing about it appeared remotely sanitary.

"Do not worry, my friend," Escoval said, noticing Nate's wrinkled brow. "I know it looks like a shithole in here compared to restaurants back in the city, but the food is fantastic… very fresh."

Nate laughed and relaxed. He was starving, and would have eaten whatever Yitsi brought without any such reassurance, but he was glad that Pedro had put him at ease.

"And *this*… this is the good stuff," Escoval said, winking as he opened one of the bottles and poured the fizzy brown brew into a tall glass for Nate. "It's a local recipe. It's not legal, per se, but it's the best beer in all of Brazil."

"Yeah? What's it made from?" Nate asked, looking apprehensively at the swirling sediment in his glass.

"You don't want to know, my friend. Just trust me, it's good. It will put hair on your balls, get you really messed up. and won't give you the runs."

Nate laughed again, then took a big swig. It *was* good, and he nodded at Pedro in approval as he took another gulp. Two beers later, dinner arrived, and the meal of grilled fish, yucca, and vegetables was also delicious, incredibly fresh and expertly prepared, just as Pedro had predicted. As the alcohol and food buzz kicked in, the entire scene felt perfectly cozy and satisfying to Nate, like something out of one of those TV shows where the host has traveled the globe to find the most unique and coveted dining experiences off the world's beaten paths.

After dinner, Escoval ordered another round of drinks, and then pulled a folded map out of his rear pants pocket and spread it out on the table. "Okay. Tomorrow morning, we drive your truck to here." Escoval pointed to Labrea, a small town on the banks of the Madeira River, six hours drive northeast of Porto Velho. "My boat and crew will meet us there, and we can depart as soon as we get your gear loaded up. A few hundred kilometers up the river, I know where there are plenty of uncharted tributaries. We can pick one big enough for the boat to get into and find a suitable landing area to unload the equipment." Then Escoval cracked a wide grin and spoke softly, "And then, may God be with you, my friend."

"How will you be able to find me again in two weeks?" Nate inquired.

"Oh, we will find you... or whatever is left of you!" Escoval laughed out loud, then leaned forward and spoke in a more serious tone. "Not to worry, just a joke. If an onca or crocodile gets you, there won't *be* anything left to find." He looked into Nate's eyes and tried to keep a straight face, but he could not, and more laughter burst through his pursed lips.

"What the hell is an onca?"

"You Americans call them jaguars... big, bad pussy *gato*.»

"Okay," Nate chuckled. "Assuming I haven't been eaten, will you be able to find the same spot again without any problems?"

"Absolutely. I know these rivers and tributaries better than anyone. My father and grandfather were among the best rivermen that ever lived. I sailed with them since I was very young, and they taught me everything they knew. My crew and I will stay in Labrea, so if you notify ARCA on the satellite-phone that you need help, they can call for me. My boat is fast, so I will not be more than eight to ten hours away, depending on how deep into the jungle you decide to go. And if things get really bad, we can call in a chopper, if we can find one. There aren't too many in these parts. 'Nother beer?"

After a few more beers, Nate paid for the meal, leaving a generous tip that caused Yitsi to squeal with delight and hug him on his way out the door. The two men stumbled to Escoval's pickup, and Nate briefly thought that perhaps Pedro was too drunk to drive, but he quickly dismissed his apprehension. Pedro didn't look anywhere near as shit-faced as Nate felt, and besides, there was no traffic at this hour and the hotel was just a few blocks away. On the way, they finalized plans to depart for Labrea in the morning.

They pulled into Labrea just before noon the next day, and followed Escoval's pickup through town to one of the city's riverboat ports, where they parked near one of the rickety piers that extended out over the swirling brown water. The port seemed overly large to Nate for a town of this size, which was comprised mostly of simple, tin-roofed shacks painted in bright pastel colors. There were riverboats of many shapes and sizes lined up along the piers, and Nate was relieved to see that Escoval's vessel was one of the more seaworthy-looking of the bunch.

As Pedro had promised, his crew was ready to get to work the moment they arrived, and three barefoot, bronze-skinned, wiry men immediately opened the back of the truck and started carefully moving the crates down the pier on makeshift carts, then onto the boat. The *Juanita Linda* was 150 feet long, with a large, two-story cabin at the front and a sizeable open-aired deck at the rear. The crew secured the crates to the aft deck as Escoval scurried about the boat, making final preparations for departure. Once most of the crates were onboard, he paused for a moment, hands on his hips, gazing at the space-age looking containers. He had guided many rainforest expeditions into remote parts of the Amazon before, including for ARCA, but he had never seen as much equipment as this, nor anything so modern and expensive looking.

"ARCA doesn't mess around, do they?" Pedro shouted to Nate, who was standing on the pier while the deckhands loaded the last two crates.

"Nope!" Nate shouted back, cracking a grin. "This is my first time on a research mission for them, but from what I understand, this is double the gear they've sent out on past expeditions.

Some new state-of-the-art stuff they're having me try out."

"What kind of *stuff*?" Escoval asked.

"Well, there's all of the usual research and specimen-collecting equipment, but a lot of it is a new line of jungle survival gear, super high-tech stuff designed to make living in the rainforest a breeze. ARCA designed it for whiny-ass pussies like me."

Escoval smirked and nodded in moderate approval. "Good. You're gonna need all the help you can get. The Amazon will eat you alive if you let your guard down. I told ARCA they are crazy to send you out there alone!"

"Well they normally *do* send out teams," Nate admitted. "But I requested it this way. I work best on my own, so I insisted on it, and they're certain this gear will keep me safe."

"Careful what you wish for, my friend. You might just regret it."

"I'll be fine, Pedro. But I do appreciate the concern."

"Okay then, it's your charter. We should be ready to leave in twenty minutes."

Nate watched the gear being loaded for a few more minutes, then walked back up the pier and down the river bank a hundred yards to the port's marine supply store to take a piss and try to reach Tracie, assuming this would be his last chance at getting a cell signal for a while until his camp gear was unloaded and the sat-phone was powered up.

After several attempts to connect, he managed to get through to her.

"Yellooo," Tracie answered sarcastically. She suspected it was Nate from the strange sequence of numbers on her caller ID.

"Hey hon, whatcha up to?"

"Oh, I just got home and Doo-Doo's having a cow. I've been at work all day, and he's going bat-shit, so I'm leashing him up for a walk."

Nate could hear Dewey yapping relentlessly in the background. The mere mention of the word "walk" always sent him ballistic.

"So, how was London?" Tracie inquired.

"Wet and dreary, but I didn't get out much, so it didn't matter."

"Are you in Labrea yet?"

"Yep, got here an hour ago. My butt's killing me from riding in that damn truck for four days."

Tracie sneered, "You mean ARCA paid for all that gear and airfare, but didn't spring for the stretch limo?"

"I know, right?" Nate laughed. Tracie always made him laugh with her sarcastic pokes; he loved that about her. "Anyway, I just wanted to call and tell you I'm here and we head upriver in a few minutes."

"Are you excited?"

"Oh, honey, it's so beautiful. Every time I see the Amazon in real life again, it takes my breath away. It's good to be back. This is my happy place."

"I know, sweetheart. I'm glad for you. When will I hear from you again?"

"I'll call you on the sat-phone at nine your time every other night, starting the day after tomorrow, but only for a few minutes. I have to conserve the battery for emergencies in case the power generator fails."

"Please be careful."

"Okay, I promise. I love you."

"I love you too. Talk to you in a few days."

Nate shut down and pocketed his phone then glanced down towards the boat. Escoval was waving to him, shouting that it was time to depart. Nate waved back and yelled out, "Two minutes!" He ducked into the store and bought a cold bottle of orange soda, then walked briskly back to the pier and jumped aboard the *Juanita Linda*.

Escoval revved the twin diesel motors and shouted commands in Portuguese to the deckhands, who untied the mooring lines and used their bare feet to push the boat away from the pier. Then Escoval engaged the props, churning the brown water to a boil as the *Juanita Linda* pushed northeast against the river's robust current.

Nate broke into a wide grin as the Amazon's warm afternoon breeze kissed his face and ruffled his hair. He found his way forward to the boat's pointed bow and struck a pose, leaning forward into the wind and raising the bottle of orange soda to his lips. The ominous presence of the rainforest surrounded him, overtaking all his senses and sending them into overdrive. He took a long, thirsty gulp, then belched the words "Yeah baby!"

He felt alive and vibrant. He loved this place.

CHAPTER 7

It was well past midnight on the Purple Planet's western hemisphere, where the Apprentice and his family lived. All four were suspended in their dwelling's spherical sleeping chamber, hanging up-side-down like four-legged bats as their feet gripped the metal rings that lined the ceiling. In the morning, the Apprentice would leave for Earth, and although three of his brains had managed to find sleep, one remained wide awake, on fire with anticipation. He was exhilarated to go, yet terrified of being so far away for the first time. He worried about his family and how they might suffer if something went wrong and he did not return.

With one set of eyes, he silently observed his mate and offspring as they slept. The room was pitch-black, but he could see them just fine, his eyes picking up images from the micro-pulses they sent out when no light source was present. *What if*, he thought, *this is the last time I will ever see them*? As concern manifested into unbearable anxiety, he unfolded all four of his arms and began to fidget with his hands, twenty-eight long, jointless fingers intertwining, writhing like nervous snakes.

"Father, why are you not completely asleep?" The words came silently into his lone active brain through its corresponding holo-disc. It was his daughter.

"I am sorry I woke you," he replied. "I am happy to be leaving for Earth tomorrow, yet I am afraid to leave you three behind. I seem to have become fearful that I might not return."

"You will return safely, and we will be proud and happy to see you when you arrive." His daughter's confident response was soothing. She continued, "You are one of the best Apprentices the Ministry has ever trained, and well prepared for this mission. The Mentor told you this herself. And you must trust the Ministry's technologies. No explorers have been lost for thousands of years now. You *must* get some sleep."

"I am sleeping three brains; I will be fine."

"It is far better that all four brains are well rested for this mission. This you know," she scolded. "If I am ever fortunate enough to go to Earth, you would say the same to me."

"Of course. I cannot argue with you on that. You are wise beyond your years, daughter."

"Good night, then. I am very proud of you, Father. We all are."

"And I of you. Good night."

She will make a fine scientist, the Apprentice thought, *if the Creator is willing and she is fortunate enough to have that opportunity*. He relaxed and stopped his fidgeting, folding his arms back around his chest and hanging completely motionless until he was sure she had continued her sleep cycle. But contrary to her good advice, his fourth brain stayed wide awake, unable to squelch the overwhelming euphoria and terror that were fighting each other within.

CHAPTER 8

The Apprentice had, eventually, managed to calm himself enough to shut his fourth brain down, giving it a few hours' rest before the waking signal came. As consciousness stirred, his eye-stalks emerged from their retracted position within his skull, and he scanned the sleeping chamber for signs of activity. Everyone else was still sound asleep.

He lowered himself to the ground silently and stealthily exited the room, pulling himself through the home's tunnel network towards the feeding chamber. The curved outer wall of the chamber was made of transparent alloy, offering a panoramic view of the valley below and the sunrise on the horizon. The sun was just starting to peek above the distant mountains, bathing the sky and the feeding chamber in a welcoming lavender glow.

The inner walls of the chamber were peppered with cubbyholes, each stacked with a variety of nourishment rods. The Aliens could not taste; they chose nourishment rods solely on the benefits of their composition, so as the Apprentice stood motionless at the room's center, a holo-disc scanned his body, analyzing which nutrients were presently required. He chose two appropriate rods and placed them into the recessed spot on the floor near the window-wall, and then settled his bottom into the recess, sitting directly on the rods. After three minutes, he lifted his bottom out of the indentation on the floor, leaving it as clean and bare as it had been before he'd sat down, having absorbed his breakfast.

Rested and nourished, the Apprentice felt robust and full of life. The angst he had suffered overnight was, for the moment, subdued, and now he was delirious with excitement to depart for Earth. He returned to the sleeping chamber to wake his family, and they followed him to the transport deck to bid him an emotional farewell.

CHAPTER 9

The Exploration Ministry's Orbital Station Complex was the largest single structure ever built by the Aliens. It was oval in shape and the size of a small moon, set in a permanent orbit six hundred miles above the planet's surface. Its flat, concave profile followed the curvature of the planet's surface, like an enormous contact lens floating above an even more enormous purple eyeball. It was here that the Aliens plotted courses to distant galaxies and generated the gravity tunnels used to travel vast distances through space. It had taken many generations thousands of years to build it.

The small transport that had collected the Apprentice from his home that morning slowed as it approached the underside of the Complex, becoming a tiny speck in the shadows of the behemoth satellite. When it was within range of the docking computers, a laser shot out from the tip of an entry tube, interfaced with the transport's computers, and guided it through the mile-long passage into one of the Complex's numerous docking bays. Before the Apprentice could exit the craft, a small football-shaped object floated into the cabin: a sterilization module, used to kill any microbes that might have come uninvited from the planet's surface.

The Apprentice kept still as the module's pulsating fan of blue light spread out in every direction, sweeping his body and every surface of the transport's interior. When the module was finished, the Apprentice pulled himself out onto the deck, where he was greeted by several launch technicians, as well as his Mentor. The Mentor had not attended an intergalactic launch in many decades, and it pleased the Apprentice to see her there.

"I wasn't sure if you would be here today. I am glad you came." The Apprentice spoke audibly to his teacher, using the Complex's gas atmosphere to make sounds through his communication bladders. All four of his holo-discs, meanwhile, were busy in conversations with the launch technicians.

The elder extended her fingers and intertwined them into his, addressing him in low guttural noises. "I would not dare miss this. I have not been in the practice of coming up here to see off missions as of late, but for you I have made an exception."

"I am honored. But there are Apprentice missions launching every day; why did you choose this one?"

"You know why I am here. Rarely is an Apprentice mission assigned to Earth. Normally, it would be decades before you would be allowed to go there. This is an extraordinary event."

"You were the first," he reminded her. "And I have your teachings to thank for allowing me to qualify for the same opportunity."

"My teachings are only part of the equation. I gave you knowledge and direction, but in the end, you had to make this happen. You have been an exemplary student, and you earned it. I am very proud of what you have accomplished."

"I will do my best to please the Ministry, and continue to make you proud."

"Of course you will!" she snorted, "And this is just the beginning of many such adventures for you."

One of the launch technicians beckoned for everyone to move on to the tube-shuttle stop, and to board the awaiting shuttle that would take them to one of the station's many Launching Chambers, fifty miles away at the center of the Complex.

In the Launching Chamber, dozens of technicians scurried about, attending to holographic controls that lined the perimeter of the room. At the center of the chamber's ceiling was a huge appendage that tapered down to a circular opening 100 feet off the floor, like a giant funnel. Directly below the opening, nestled in its cradle, was the transport that would take the Apprentice to the Milky Way.

The ship was just over a hundred feet in length and shaped like a football, fat in the middle and tapering to a conical point at either end. Its featureless alloy surface was bright and polished, reflecting images of everything around it like a giant, convex mirror. When he arrived at the Launching Chamber, the Apprentice took in the spectacular scene through one set of eyes, while using the rest to continue engaging with the Mentor and his escort technicians. They reviewed with him the final procedures before launch, then led him to the medical station, where a physician scanned him and transmitted his vital signs to the medicomp onboard the ship.

"You are in excellent physical condition," the physician said after reviewing the scan. "But how is your mental state? You seem anxious, and your heart rates are a bit accelerated."

"I am a bit excited," the Apprentice admitted. "But I feel well. I am ready."

"Your excitement is typical for an Apprentice mission. But aside from that, I agree that you are ready. I see no concerning data. Relax your minds; you will be fine."

"Thank you. I will try."

The physician continued with a personal note. "I am also excited. I will greatly enjoy seeing what new specimens you bring back. It has been many years since we sent a gathering mission into this particular rainforest, and I find the creatures there more fascinating than anywhere else on the planet, even more so than the Humans."

The Apprentice's eyes pulled backwards on their stalk, changing color from green to pale yellow. "You would rather see new rainforest specimens than learn more about the Humans?"

"Don't misunderstand; I do find Humans fascinating, and their intellect is, of course, remarkable, but physically they are boring! Two legs, two arms, no natural defense mechanisms. I find Earth's less intelligent life to have much more interesting designs. *Especially* the insects and arachnids."

"I have never thought of it that way, but you make a good point," the Apprentice said. He had always placed the Humans above all other species on the planet. In fact, he considered the importance of studying Humans to be above *all* other species discovered in the universe so far. "Insects and spiders *are* quite interesting compared to Humans, when you put them in that context," the Apprentice continued. "And I am sure I will find new varieties of them on this trip for you to admire when I return. I do also want to study the social structures of any ants I encounter that are indigenous to the Amazon. From what we can tell, ant colonies are among the most efficiently structured societies on Earth."

"Yes, I know!" The medical technician's eyes changed colors from orange to mottled blue. "I love ants! I will be anxious to hear your observations and see the specimens."

"If your medical devices keep me alive throughout this mission, then I promise you shall be one of the first to see them."

"They will, unless you do something foolish. So don't," the Physician said, and then ushered the Apprentice off to the next pre-launch protocol.

After several more stops at various stations in the chamber, the Complex's Chief Technician issued a message to all in the chamber. "Pre-launch sequences are complete," she announced. "All systems are in order, and our Apprentice is cleared for departure. Everyone please monitor your posts and prepare to initiate the gravity tunnel."

"If you are ready, it is time to board," she said silently to the Apprentice.

"I am ready." He stepped up to the front of the ship and paused a moment, standing motionless beneath its open portal. A blue glow was emitting from within, like a spotlight shining on him as he took one final gaze about the chamber. Then, with all four hands, he reached up into the portal, firmly grasped the metal loops that lined the inner wall, and pulled himself up inside. A Launch Technician followed.

The cockpit was spherical, and glowed from numerous holographic displays and control-panels. Unlike most planet-bound transports, this one had a seat, with a deep, pear-shaped cavity that had been custom-fit to the Apprentice's torso. He had to fold two of his legs and arms behind his body in order to fit snugly into the seat cavity, and once he was firmly planted, a trio of restrictor beams shot out of the chair's frame and wrapped themselves around him, holding him securely in place. Then the entire seat levitated off its pedestal and floated to a stationary hovering position at the center of the cockpit. Once all inside the ship was confirmed to be functioning properly, the Launch Technician bid the Apprentice farewell and good luck, and exited the ship. With a whirr, the portal door spiraled shut and the Apprentice was sealed inside.

"Are you ready for launch?" the inaudible message came to one of the Apprentice's holo-discs from the Chief Technician.

"Yes, I am ready." This would be the final exchange he would have with anyone before losing all contact for several weeks, he knew.

With a thunderous electric hum, a thick flood of orangish light rained down from above, completely engulfing the transport as it levitated into the launch funnel's opening. Once the ship was fully inside, five triangular panels slid together beneath it, coming together like slices of a gigantic pizza, sealing the transport inside.

Deep-space transports had no viewports — their alloy hulls were too thick to allow it — but the ship's outer viewers could project a 360° image of all that surrounded it onto its inner walls. This gave the Apprentice the impression that the transport had no hull at all, as if he were floating in his chair surrounded by holographic controls and displays. Looking up, he saw the top of the launch funnel spiral open, exposing the craft to space and offering a view of the enormous curved spikes of the gravity amplifiers that protruded around the opening like a ring of giant teeth. From the tips of these spikes, focused graviton beams emerged, converging in a symmetrical pattern and drawing massive amounts of energy from the Complex's power banks — enough to generate an intergalactic gravity tunnel, a one-way passage to the Milky Way.

A tingling sensation came over the Apprentice as the transport's gravity equalizers created a balance between the forces generated by his own galaxy and the Milky Way's. The tingling intensified until his entire body became numb, and then, in a flash, the vessel seemed to simply disappear from existence as it was sucked out of the funnel and into the passage, sending it into the abyss of deep space at incomprehensible speed.

The Apprentice's minds were racing, his hearts pounding, and his eyes shifted through a rainbow of colors as he watched his solar system, then other systems, and soon his galaxy fall away into the distance. In a matter of minutes, he was hundreds of trillions of miles from home.

CHAPTER 10

The *Juanita Linda* was chugging along at a steady twenty knots, now headed northeast through the brown waters of the Rio Purus. It was dawn on Tuesday morning, a day after launching from Labrea with Nate Johnston and his crates of ARCA gear onboard. Using a pair of powerful spotlights mounted on the bow, two of Pedro Escoval's crew had navigated through the night while everyone else slept. With sunrise came the changing of the guard; Escoval and his remaining deckhand relieved the two weary men, who quickly fell asleep in their hammocks.

It had rained heavily overnight, and thick patches of fog and mist hovered over the river's banks, waiting for the kiss of the sun's warmth to burn them away. The night air had been alive with the noisy routines of countless nocturnal species, but the tones and nuances changed as morning came and the daytime creatures started foraging for their breakfast, sounding different yet equally as vibrant.

Escoval made a brief trip into the *Juanita Linda's* bowels to check on the engines. They were chugging along in their usual clunky symphony. Then he made a pit stop at the galley to re-caffeinate, and climbed the narrow staircase to the wheelhouse to relieve his deckhand at the helm. He slowed the boat to a crawl and began scanning the riverbanks for a glimpse through the fog of any tributaries that might be large enough to get into without running aground.

Nate had still been snoring in his hammock when Escoval got up, which impressed Escoval, as few of his charter guests had ever been able to sleep soundly through the chatter of Amazonian night-life. But Nate had slept like a baby all night. Now Pedro could hear him fumbling around for a coffee cup in the galley cupboards below, and moments later he emerged from the staircase, smiling but looking groggy and struggling not to spill his cup of coffee. "G' morning!" Nate chirped cheerfully. "Are we close?"

"Yes, my friend, *very* close, I think." Escoval chuckled at Nate's child-like exuberance as he pulled a cigarette out of his shirt pocket and lit it with a match, steadying the ship's wheel with a knee. "See those jagged rocks along the edge of those hills out there?" he nodded towards a line of hills that rose in the distance behind the apron of the forest canopy.

"Yes, I see them."

"That's the landmark I told you about. Up ahead are some tributaries that are wide enough for the boat. This is a very remote area, no tribes for miles. That is what you wanted, right?"

Nate nodded and grinned, intoxicated by the Amazon morning. He tingled as the rising sun peeked over the hills in the distance, sending shimmers of green and yellow through the forest canopy. There was no visible movement in the dense foliage, but the chorus coming from within gave vibrant life to the otherwise serene ambiance. The noise was intense, almost deafening. To many it might have seemed intimidating…but this was Nate's *White Album.*

"This is perfect, Pedro, just perfect."

Escoval didn't respond. He stood upright, staring intensely at the north riverbank through the weakening fog. He took a deep draw from his cigarette, casually flicked it through the open window into the river, then used both hands to manipulate the wheel slightly to port. "You really shouldn't do that, it's terrible for the river," Nate scolded Escoval, watching as a fish took a nip at Pedro's discarded cigarette, then spat it out.

"Do what?"

"Your cigarette."

Escoval shrugged but didn't reply; he was fixated on a spot along the left side of the river up ahead, and he guided the *Juanita Linda* in that direction. He pulled the throttle levers back, reducing their speed to a crawl.

"Look right over there. This is where I think we will go in." Escoval pointed towards an approaching break in the riverbank.

As they neared the opening, Nate could see through the mist that it was a large stream that branched off the river at nearly a 90° angle and disappeared deep into the forest. "This tributary is deep, ten, maybe fifteen feet at the opening, so it should be navigable for about a mile into the forest," Escoval said. "We'll have to tow the boat in backwards with the launch; there won't be room to turn her around in there, and I don't want to try to back out." He navigated to the tributary's opening, then shouted orders in Portuguese for the deckhand to drop anchor. Once it was secure, the crewman scrambled up the ladder to the boat's roof and untied the launch from its tether atop the main cabin. The launch was a 15-foot flat-bottomed aluminum job with an outboard motor, and the crewman used a small crane to swing it out over the river and lower it into the water. Escoval secured the launch to the *Juanita Linda's* side with rope.

Nate's adrenalin was at full throttle. He and the gear had made it all the way to the deep Amazon Basin without incident. The weather was perfect, the early-morning buzz of the rainforest was perfect, the tributary Escoval had found was perfect... *everything was perfect*. He couldn't wait to get into the tributary and unloaded to establish his research camp, and for the civilized world to go away and leave him alone in the forest for a while.

"Okay, let's grab some breakfast," Escoval announced nonchalantly, stepping out of the launch and back onto the deck. The deckhand came down from the roof and joined him on his way to the galley.

Nate was stunned. "*Breakfast?*" he protested as he stepped into the galley, where he found the deckhand slicing fruit and Escoval making a fresh pot of coffee. "I'm *way* to excited to eat! Why can't we move the boat into the tributary first, then you guys can have your meal?"

Escoval looked at Nate but didn't respond; he just smiled, shook his head, and helped himself to a plate of fruit and bread, gesturing for Nate to do the same. Nate pushed the issue. "Pedro, why are you stopping to eat? I'm paying you a lot of money, and we have work to do!"

Escoval let out a sigh and looked up from his breakfast. "I understand that, my friend, and I know you are anxious to get your camp established, but I need all three of my men to tow the boat in and unload your gear. Two of them just went to sleep an hour ago. They were up all night getting us to this spot, so let's let them rest a bit first."

Nate felt embarrassed for being so insensitive. "Yes, of course, I'm sorry. Please forgive my ignorance." *You idiot*, Nate chastised himself. *You need to calm down and remember how dangerous this place is.* The river and surrounding forest looked harmless enough, but Nate was well aware that countless perils lurked within the murky waters and thick vegetation. The slightest mistake could be fatal, and everyone needed to be on their toes out here.

"It's okay." Escoval replied. "We all get excited about our passions sometimes, but we do need to be cautious out here and stay alive."

"I know. And I *am* sorry, Pedro."

"Forget it, and don't worry — by this afternoon you will be all alone in your little paradise."

"Perfect... thanks," Nate said sheepishly, then he exhaled deeply and poured himself another cup of coffee, and graciously accepted the plate of fruit and bread the grinning deck-hand set in front of him.

CHAPTER 11

The Apprentice had been travelling through the gravity tunnel for nearly two days now, and would reach the Milky Way within 24 hours. This was a drastic improvement from the intergalactic journeys his ancestors had taken. The first successful trips beyond their own galaxy had taken the Aliens years to complete, and many before that had failed altogether, never returning home. But that was millions of years ago. Current technologies were capable of things beyond his predecessors' wildest dreams, allowing travel to the Milky Way and other distant galaxies in days, not years.

The feat was incredible, but not very comfortable. He could not leave the confines of his floating chair for the duration of the trip. The speed at which his transport was travelling made it far too dangerous not to be strapped in and have the chair levitated at all times. The gravitational equalizers of the floating chair and the energy field that surrounded it protected him from massive acceleration or deceleration forces. Otherwise, if anything were to malfunction and the transport needed to come to a quick stop, he would be completely pulverized against the inner walls of the cabin. How, he wondered, had the first brave explorers managed to survive sitting in that chair for years on end? It must have been a truly miserable experience. After only two days, he was beginning to feel itchy and sore. But this didn't bother him much; it was a small price to pay for the privilege of a trip to Earth.

He had slept all four brains for much of the first day. The second day he passed time viewing recorded episodes of Human media transmissions, four at a time, displayed about the cockpit's curved walls. These recordings, gathered by previous expeditions to Earth, had become a treasured means of research, as well as entertainment, for all Aliens since their discovery over a century ago. Not only were these productions a good resource on how Humans lived and interacted amongst their various cultures, but they also provided a vivid portrayal of the Humans' often bizarre imaginations.

The concept of producing fictional, at times impossible, situations in a transmittable, viewable media for entertainment was beyond the Aliens' comprehension. The documentaries and news programs made sense, as the Aliens had those as well; but the Humans seemed to have an insatiable passion for manufactured drama. The dilemma the Aliens faced when viewing them was that it was not always clear if the subjects and events being represented were real or not, making it difficult to differentiate between fact and fiction sometimes. Nonetheless, the transmissions were fascinating. The Aliens could not get enough of them to satisfy their curiosity, and the Apprentice loved watching them, especially the ones about the little yellow man who lived in a pineapple under the sea.

Midway through the third day it was time to prepare for the first stop, the Milky Way Transfer Station, orbiting a blue giant near the very center of the galaxy. Not far from it was the Milky Way's super-massive central black hole, whose gravitational forces held the galaxy together in its graceful, spiral pattern, and which had played a vital role in pulling the Apprentice's ship through the gravity tunnel to its destination. As the Milky Way drew closer, the Apprentice switched off the Human programs and engaged the outer displays to take a look outside. The walls of the cockpit disappeared, presenting him with a magnificent, panoramic view of the approaching galaxy. It seemed small at first, from the ship's current location of about 500,000 light years away. But it grew quickly, until its shape was no longer discernable, and the vast distances between its hundreds of billions of stars and other celestial objects became apparent, reducing them to mere specks of light far in the distance.

When the ship passed through the galaxy's outer layers, it began the automated process of decelerating as it neared the exit of the gravity tunnel. It took half an hour to slow down to just under light speed, which was necessary to exit the final collapsing segment of the passage. Exiting the tunnel over the speed of light would be disastrous. The Apprentice and the vessel would be ripped apart at the molecular level, then their molecules would come back together randomly as their mass slowed, resulting in a lifeless blob of space debris. Many such blobs were scattered about Universe, permanent shrines to the brave Alien souls who had lost their lives while pioneering the art of intergalactic travel.

The transport exited the tunnel at 150,000 miles per second, automatically transmitting a signal to announce its arrival to the Transfer Station, which responded by sending a homing signal. The ship continued decelerating, and within half an hour the Apprentice saw the station appear in the distance, growing larger upon approach until it dwarfed the ship and took up the entire viewing wall. It looked nearly identical to the massive Orbital Complex from which the Apprentice had departed several days ago, but this facility was much smaller, only a hundred miles across.

The transport slowed to a crawl, approaching the underside of the station where the docking bays were located. Soon, a tractor beam shot out and locked onto the ship, pulling it towards an entry tube. Once securely docked inside the transport deck, the energy field that had surrounded the Apprentice's chair dissipated, and the chair descended, latching firmly into its receptacle on the cockpit floor.

The Apprentice gripped metal loops and agonizingly pulled himself out of the chair, fighting the numbness and stiffness of sitting still for so long. The station's gravity generators hadn't activated yet — that would take a few minutes — so he feebly launched himself off the chair and floated weightlessly towards the portal. He felt dizzy and his sense of balance was awry, causing him to sprawl and roll a few times before the cockpit wall abruptly stopped his progress. There was no atmosphere at the station, so there was no sound when he hit.

He righted himself using the handles that surrounded the portal, then sat motionless for a moment as he regained strength and balance. Then he opened the portal and exited the ship. The portal was several feet off the docking bay's floor, and his balance was not functional enough yet to walk, so he just free-floated, tumbling awkwardly out into the bay without any specific direction. As he floated across the room he stretched and flexed his limbs, waiting for his hearts to pump blood to his tingling extremities and restore his full dexterity. The station's illumination panels had not yet activated; these would come online later, along with the gravity generators, once the energy cells had soaked up enough power from the nearby star. So aside from the faint glow of light coming through the transport's open portal, the docking chamber was pitch-black, so the Apprentice used his radar-vision to look about.

There was nothing unfamiliar about the station's features, as he had seen all of this before in countless holographic simulations. But physically being there, at the *real* Milky Way transfer station, brought a whole new level of exhilaration. The role this place had played in history was monumental! Through this very facility, over millions of years, had passed some of the most famous explorers of his kind, whose data and samples from Earth and other life-bearing planets he had studied with such passion for most of his life.

A few moments later, the illumination panels flickered to life, and then numerous holo-displays showing every system's status about the station. Most were functioning perfectly. The Apprentice had been trained to deal with any critical malfunctions, but for the moment none were detected. When the gravitational stabilizers engaged, pulling him down to the floor, they duplicated the gravity he would encounter on Earth, so he could acclimate to the conditions there. He scurried to a small tube transport at the far end of the docking chamber, boarded a shuttle, and sped off into other sections of the station to get to work. It would take him a full day to update the station's systems and program any needed repairs, and then another full day to prepare for the short trip from here to Earth.

CHAPTER 12

It was 10:45 a.m., and the *Juanita Linda's* crew were all awake now, preparing to tow her backwards into the tributary Escoval had chosen. Nate sat on a bench at the bow, staying out of their way while reviewing journals from previous expeditions on his iPad. He had studied these journals countless times, but wanted to commit to memory as many recent discoveries as possible, so as not to waste valuable time researching them while in the rainforest. This region of the Amazon Basin was still mostly unexplored, so he hoped he could hit the jackpot with a good list of new spider and insect types, but he didn't want to spend his time or ARCA's money duplicating someone else's findings.

When Escoval announced they were ready to enter the tributary, Nate climbed up a level and perched himself at the aft upper deck railing to get a good view. Escoval hopped into the launch, taking position at the tiny boat's bow as a crewman manned the outboard motor. The *Juanita Linda's* anchor was raised and the launch surged gently forward, causing the ropes connecting the two vessels to snap taut and the *Juanita Linda* to follow the launch backwards.

For an intense forty minutes, the launch maneuvered its mothership into the tributary, dragging her deeper and deeper into the forest. Then Escoval turned abruptly and gave the command to kill the launch's motor. The tributary had shallowed beyond his comfort to proceed any further. He picked out a site on the north bank that looked adequate for off-loading Nate's gear, and directed his crew to maneuver the *Juanita Linda* as close to the bank as possible.

With the boat securely anchored and the ramp lowered, all five men walked into the forest in search of a suitable campsite for Nate to set up shop. They located a clearing about ninety yards from the tributary, and the deckhands used machetes to clear the brush from the center of the site, making a space for the shelter to be erected. Then they returned to the boat to start unloading the crates full of ARCA gear.

The crates themselves were too large and awkward to easily maneuver through the dense forest, so the men unpacked them and used wheelbarrows to move the gear to the clearing, hauling some of the larger pieces in on their shoulders. With the exception of Nate's food and water rations, it was all surprisingly light, due to extensive use of carbon-fiber and aluminum, and Escoval and his crew chattered in amazement at its high-tech appearance. They had guided many expeditions into the Amazon, but had never seen anything like this before; it looked more like something ARCA would send to Mars than into a rainforest. Once the last of it was delivered to the clearing, Nate instructed the men on how to help him assemble the camp.

Nate would be the first to test this new ARCA design in the field. It was by far the most advanced of its kind. The octagonal floor was elevated off the ground, supported by a tubular aluminum frame. The interlocking panels that became the walls and roof of the dwelling were curved, forming a spacious, water-tight dome tall enough for Nate to stand in. The shelter could withstand gale-force winds and, according to Jason O'Rourke, was strong enough to protect Nate from any jaguars in the area. The outer surface of the dome was painted with camouflage patterns, and once completed, it blended in quite nicely with the surrounding rainforest.

The shelter's interior was equipped with a desk, a computer, a small refrigerator, a satellite phone, and a collapsible cot. The devices and the dwelling's LED illumination panels were all powered by a compact solar-energy unit mounted to the top of the dome. ARCA had developed a new solar panel and battery that could charge to capacity rapidly in direct sunlight, and store enough electricity to run everything for several days. All of this was quite impressive to Escoval and his men, but what astonished them the most was the sophisticated security-system ARCA had provided for the camp.

With Nate's guidance, the men erected the carbon-fiber frame of the security-field generator: four modular segments of framework that leaned above the shelter to complete a thirty-foot high pyramid. It had its own solar energy panels, keeping its electricity source separate from the one that powered the hut. "What the hell *is* this thing?" Escoval asked Nate.

Nathan grinned and replied, "This is my security dome. I'll show you how it works."

Nate stepped into the hut, booted up the computer, and typed in a few commands. Instantly an audible hum could be heard, and blue sparks started jumping through the air, emanating from the pyramid's legs. Then a thin, blue haze slowly appeared in a dome shape, centered directly above the pyramid and covering the entire campsite, as if a giant translucent bowl had been placed over it. Escoval and his men instinctively hunkered down into a defensive squat as the energy field crackled above and all around them.

Nate chuckled. "Don't worry gentlemen, it's harmless as long as you're inside it. It's only dangerous to anything that tries to enter from the outside. Let me demonstrate; don't move!"

"No worries my friend, *we aren't moving*!" Escoval said, laughing nervously. "We are too busy shitting our pants to move."

Nate collected the camp's remote control unit from his back pocket, then walked to the energy-field's edge and stepped cautiously through the blue haze, so that he was standing outside the glowing bowl. His hair stood straight up as he passed through, causing Escoval and his men to burst out laughing. Then Nate turned and beckoned for them to follow, and the laughter abruptly faded. At first they shook their heads no, but Nate assured them they would not be harmed and, one by one, they reluctantly passed through to join him. As each man stepped through the energy-field, the hair on their heads, arms, and chests stood at attention.

"It's an adjustable energy shield," Nate explained. "The protective dome of energy is generated through the pyramid frame, and I can control its functions either with the computer or this remote control. It's on the lowest setting now, which only bothers insects and birds, but check this out."

Nate pressed a few buttons on the remote, then picked up a small branch from the ground and tossed it at the energy field. Instantly a network of blue sparks converged on the branch, causing a sound like a mosquito being toasted on a bug-zapper. The four Brazilians watched in horror as Nate then moved towards the side of the energy-field and extended his hand towards it. He poked his arm into the blue haze and the same sparks jumped out to his flesh. He winced at the mild shock, but quickly regained his composure and turned, grinning at his stunned entourage while moving his arm about in the sparks.

"Come on, you guys try it." Nate gestured with his other hand for the men to approach.

"No fuckin' way, man," Escoval spoke in English, his crew voicing similar gestures in Portuguese.

"Look, it only hurts a bit, like a mild electric shock. It's not designed to harm an animal, just shock them enough to be scared off. And it's still on one of the lower settings right now."

"You sure about that?"

"Yes, of course. Even at the highest setting it would just stun you a bit but not do you any harm. Pedro, I wouldn't ask you to do it if it were dangerous."

Escoval bravely stepped forward and slowly put his hand into the energy field. At first he jerked it back as the sparks jumped towards his arm, but then slowly inserted his limb in until his elbow was close to the outer edge. He turned to Nate and cracked a wide, toothy grin. "It tickles!" Escoval exclaimed, breaking out in laughter.

Seeing their boss hadn't been fried to a crisp, and not wanting to look unbrave, the three deck-hands reluctantly stuck their hands in, wincing and flinching at first, then grinning and laughing as they felt the prickle of energy. Now that the men were no longer afraid, their fascination with ARCA's new security dome grew, and Escoval asked Nate how it all worked. Nate explained in English, while Escoval translated to his men.

"At the lowest setting, the energy field maintains

a constant low voltage, like what you just experienced. At higher settings, which I'll set when I'm away from camp or at night while I'm sleeping, the system is fully automatic and the sensors will detect any breach. The system can detect the size of the intruder, then regulate the amount of energy needed to repel the animal with a painful but non-fatal blast of electricity. It only delivers a shock to anything trying to enter the camp; the sensors won't activate a pulse if anything's trying to get out, so if I need to evacuate quickly and don't have time to deactivate it, I won't get zapped! *And* here's my favorite feature...»

Nate punched a few commands into the remote before he continued. "No matter what setting it's on, the system projects a mild pulse *into* the entire campsite to aggravate any insects and small animals inside the perimeter, encouraging them to leave!" The effectiveness of this feature could already be seen: ants, beetles, spiders, small frogs, and other small species were rapidly migrating away from the shelter and exiting the energy field as quickly as they could.

Next, Nate took inventory of other items ARCA had provided, basic survival gear far more familiar to the crew. There were cases of freeze-dried food and plastic jugs with funnel-tops to collect rainwater, clothing, a well-equipped first-aid kit, tools, knives, a rifle, a handgun, a flare gun, and crates of small jars for collecting samples. In the electronics case,

Nate found the GPS unit, and he clipped it securely to his belt alongside the security system remote. The advanced GPS unit was linked to the computer through ARCA's satellite network, and served many functions. Most importantly, it could give him his exact location relative to the camp at all times, no matter how deep into the forest he ventured, so he wouldn't get lost and be unable to find his way back. It also allowed Jason O'Rourke and his team in London to track Nate's movements.

Nate double-checked that all the devices and camp's systems were functioning properly; then, before dismissing Escoval and his crew, he pulled one final gadget from the electronics case and handed it to Pedro. "This is how I'll contact you if there's a problem and I need early extraction," Nate said. "If something happens and I can't get back to camp to use the sat-phone, all I have to do is enter a code on the GPS and it will page you to contact Jason. Then you can call Jason and confirm if I'm in trouble, and if I am, he can tell you my exact location. Otherwise, if you don't hear from me or ARCA, then assume I'm fine and I'll just plan on seeing you back here in fourteen days."

Escoval put a firm hand on Nate's shoulder and the two men shook hands. "Okay, my friend, but you be *really careful* out here, understand?"

"Yes, Pedro. I will."

"Even with all this fancy shit you got here, the forest can catch you off-guard and eat you alive, and if you page me I won't be here for at least eight hours... so don't get careless."

"I won't, Pedro, I'll be very careful, I promise. And thanks for everything, you and your men are the best."

"You got that right, and you might just be the stupidest, being out here all alone," Escoval said with a straight face, then cracked a toothy grin.

Nate blushed and chuckled, nodding his head in agreement. "Perhaps I am at that."

Escoval offered one more piece of advice. "If you are in serious trouble and can't get through to anyone on that phone, try to get back to the river and use your flare gun to get the attention of a river-boat. If you don't see any boats, the nearest village is about a day's hike east of the tributary's opening. Just follow the river banks, and watch out for croco-diles and jaguars."

The two finished their goodbyes, and Nate thanked the deckhands for their hard work. Then Escoval and his men returned to the *Juanita Linda*, leaving Nate alone in the depths of the Amazon. His senses were alive, every nerve tingling and vibrant. He loaded and holstered the handgun on his utility belt, sprayed his exposed flesh with the industrial-strength insect-repellant ARCA had provided, and began to explore the area surrounding the camp.

CHAPTER 13

Having completed his checklist at the Transfer Station, the Apprentice slept for several hours to rest up for the trip to Earth. He awoke hungry, and nourished himself by sitting on three sustenance bars before gathering the few pieces of equipment and supplies he'd need from the Transfer Station's storage bays. Most of the gear used for Earth expeditions was stored at Earth Station, so within moments everything was loaded and he boarded the transport, ready to launch.

The journey took just over an hour, and the Apprentice spent the time once again reviewing every previously-discovered Amazonian species. He did not want to waste any time collecting specimens that had already been documented during previous missions. As the ship sped through the gravity tunnel, countless images flashed about his chair in rapid succession, each picture lasting only a fraction of a second. Using all four brains, he kept up effortlessly, re-confirming to memory every creature that had already been discovered in the mission zone.

When the transport neared the outer reaches of

Earth's system, he switched on the external viewer and could make out the sun, still hundreds of millions of miles away, but shining brightly in the distance. Even at full magnification, he couldn't yet see the Earth or the other planets in any great detail, but soon he would pass close enough to Jupiter and Saturn to get some spectacular views. Saturn came first, its rings more impressive in person than any holographic image back home. When he arrived at Jupiter, he took a quick, close orbit around Europa to take some readings. The frozen moon held abundant life in the oceans beneath its thick, icy crust. But nothing on Europa had ever proven to be as interesting as Earth, so no new missions had been sent there after all of its life-forms were catalogued and DNA collected.

Mars was another planet the Apprentice would have enjoyed exploring on his rookie mission. Even though there were no life-forms living there currently, the discovery of an ancient abandoned structure there just a few millennia ago was nothing short of incredible. But Mars was not on this mission's priority list, other than to use long-range sensors to gather any new data on the structure, should there be any. He would save that task for the return trip, as Mars was on the far side of the system currently, and he was anxious to get to Earth.

Leaving Europa, he ship's guidance systems locked in on the Earth Station. The station was in a stable orbit around Jupiter, oriented so that it was never visible from Earth, Mars, or the Deep Space telescopes orbiting both planets. It had originally been placed just a few hundred miles above the Earth's surface, since when the Aliens first discovered Earth tens of millions of years ago, there was no need for stealth — no Earth creature was going to notice it back then. In recent centuries, however, it had been moved further and further out when the Humans developed telescopes, near-space vehicles, and other technologies that might discover it.

The Earth Station was the same shape as most such stations, resembling a shallow, oval bowl, but it was tiny in comparison to the Milky Way Transfer Station or the Alien's Orbital Complex, only 300 feet across and 100 feet thick. Its surface also had a very different appearance, sporting an overall flat-black finish to eliminate reflection and hide it amidst the darkness of space. There was only one docking chamber inside this station; once securely docked, the transport transferred energy from its own reserves into the station's cells, as the non-reflective surface treatment prevented the station from absorbing energy from the Sun, relying instead on power infusions from visiting ships.

To conserve energy, the Apprentice did not engage the station's gravity generators or illumination circuits, so the only source of light was from the holographic interfaces and monitors that came online as he disembarked his ship and floated through the facilities chambers. All systems were in proper order. Within moments of his arrival, the station's computers were automatically updated with system upgrades from his ship, and in turn the transport's computer downloaded all recently gathered Earth data to take back home for study. Once the data transfers were complete, the Apprentice entered the navigation chamber to plot coordinates for his final destination, the Amazon rainforest.

A colorful image of the Earth-Moon system appeared in the middle of the chamber, casting a green and blue glow about the room. Brightly colored symbols and lines appeared, indicating the station's position and the trajectory the transport would take to descend to Earth and land in the Amazon basin. The Apprentice waved a finger and the image zoomed in on the area surrounding the landing spot, showing a detailed topographic view of the region. He could see the mountainous terrain, the nearby river and tributaries that surrounded the site, and a few small Human villages several miles away. The imaging sensors would identify any Human technology being used anywhere near the site. None was detected, so these remote villages were too primitive to be considered a concern.

The landing site itself was marked by a green circle surrounding a red icon. Several yellow dots appeared on the nearby river, moving slowly in both directions. These would be the floating vessels Humans used to navigate aqueous surfaces. The river wasn't near enough to the landing site for the vessels to be of concern… but then, suddenly, a small red dot appeared on the image right next to the landing site! The symbols that appeared next to it read, "Unknown technology, verification required."

The Apprentice swirled two fingers, causing the holo-image to zoom in on the red dot and conduct further analysis. The anomaly was several hundred yards from his landing site, near a large tributary that branched off the river into the forest. The station sent a rapid-pulse beam to the precise spot to try and analyze the source of the technology. After a light-speed lag of over an hour, the findings returned and were displayed in alien symbols beneath the red dot.

- Solar-generated electricity
- Microwave pulses
- Computing device
- Other unidentifiable technology

He was perplexed. *What could the purpose of these technologies possibly be at this remote location? And what could the "unidentifiable technology" be? Have the Humans come up with something new and placed it in the middle of the Amazon?*

He longed to know what this strange Human outpost was all about, assuming it *was* Human. But protocol mandated that in such a situation, he must abort that location and plot a new destination void of any possible Human detection risks. He could go take a look, but he had promised his Mentor to stick to the plan and not take any risks. That was the proper thing to do.

Reluctantly, he commanded the computers to plot a new landing site deeper in the forest, away from the odd readings. But he couldn't shake the curiosity and burning desire to investigate this anomaly further. He wondered if any explorers before him had broken protocol and simply not reported it. It would be fairly easy to do, but risky, as the ship's log would note the detection of the anomaly and any attempt to engage it. If he did make an investigation, he would have to manipulate the log to show he had followed protocol.

He suddenly felt guilty for even considering such an idea, and shook it off.

With the new landing site plotted and entered into the guidance systems, the Apprentice boarded his ship, mounted the floating chair, and initiated the launch sequence. He would reach Earth's outer atmosphere in 40 minutes, then the computer would slow the ship down enough to approach and land without creating any heat-signature that might be detected by the curious Humans.

As the ship passed the Moon, Earth's image grew on the display, until its signature blue, green, and white glow encapsulated the entire cockpit. The Apprentice was thrilled and overcome with joy. It was beautiful, and so thrilling to see the real thing rather than just a hologram or recorded image! But the splendor of it was short-lived, as the ship quickly circled around the planet to line up directly over South American, where it was the middle of the night. This was most unsatisfying — to come all this way and not see more of the planet up close in daylight was a shame. He began to tremble as his minds went to places he knew they should not. But he could not help it. He *had* to see more.

The Apprentice decided to break the automatic sequence and fly the vessel manually. He wanted desperately to see more of the sunlit side of the planet before landing, and reprogramming the guidance computer to plot new trajectories along the way would be tedious. He perceived no real danger in taking a quick spin around the Earth before proceeding to the landing site, so long as he was careful not to be detected. So he disengaged the autopilot and used two hands to work the holographic controls that appeared in front of him. After a quick check of the stealth systems, he guided the ship into a low orbit, about 250 miles up. A new display popped up, showing the position of all satellites the Humans had placed into orbit, as well as the chunks of debris they had discarded or lost during their early space ventures. Steering clear of these obstacles, he broke orbit and manually guided the ship in a spiral pattern across the sunlit hemisphere, and the rich, blue glow of Earth once again lit up the cabin. He saw Asia and Europe for the first time in real life, and his eyes changed colors with joy and exhilaration.

After twenty minutes of spectacular sightseeing,

the Apprentice returned the ship to the dark side of the Earth, and relinquished command to the guidance computer to resume its plotted course. The craft should have immediately slowed and gently descended through the atmosphere, but instead, it suddenly plummeted towards Earth's surface at blistering speed. He was momentarily startled, but soon reacted, shutting off the guidance system and taking back manual control. He decreased speed as quickly as possible, but it was too late: a display was already warning that the outer hull's temperature had far exceeded the required limits to remain stealthy.

Has the transport created a heat-signature that can be seen by the Humans? The Apprentice felt a wave of panic, his hearts pounding. If there had been a heat-signature created, there was nothing he could do about it now; he needed to concentrate on the landing. He slowed the ship to a crawl and used the trajectory-grid display to find the area where he had plotted the secondary landing site. He knew he was close, but with the autopilot off, he had no way of knowing if this was exactly the right spot. The transport moved slowly just above the dense canopy of the forest while a quad of sensor-beams scanned the terrain for a clearing. An adequate area devoid of trees was detected within several hundred feet, and he guided the craft towards it, then maneuvered the ship gently towards the ground. The transport stopped three feet short of the clearing's grassy surface, and he set the gravity-anchors to hold it motionless.

The Apprentice trembled in his chair. He had never experienced such intense fear before. His restraining harness dissipated and the seat descended, latching into its cradle, but he remained implanted in it, needing a moment to unwind before dismounting. The outer hull sensor warned that the ship's exterior was burning-hot. This was not good, as it meant the ship had definitely been visible in the night sky as it entered Earth's atmosphere. But he was happy he had reacted quickly enough to make a safe landing. One moment's hesitation and the ship could have smashed into the planet's surface at high speed, possibly damaging it beyond repair and further risking detection by the Humans.

Several minutes went by, and finally the Apprentice was able to calm his minds and think clearly. He dismounted the seat and moved about, confirming there was no structural damage to the cockpit or cargo bay, nor to any of the research equipment. Everything was fine, but now he had to wait for the ship's exterior to cool down before he could safely exit and take his first steps onto Earth's surface. His skin was very tough — it could withstand up to 400° F without injury — but the hull temperature was still much higher than that.

As he waited, he scanned the surrounding area to see if the strange readings were still present. They were, and he was much closer to them than he had intended to be. In the moments of confusion during the descent, he had failed to steer further away from where the technology was located, and instead had landed relatively close to it, a mere mile and a half away. Hopefully, this was still far away enough that his not-so-stealthy landing had not been noticed by any Humans present there.

While the ship cooled, he ran a diagnostic on the navigation systems. *What had caused the malfunction?* The systems check revealed that there had been a momentary glitch in the holo-interface when he re-engaged the autopilot. The system would fix the problem on its own, but he could not reverse what had happened. If he had been seen, there was nothing he could do but wait and see if any Humans came to investigate. Then, if he were to follow protocol, he should abort the mission and leave quickly. He would also be required to dispatch any Humans who had witnessed his presence, to avoid their passing on any knowledge of the Aliens' presence on Earth. He prayed to the Creator this would not happen. He shuddered at the thought that his mission to Earth could be over before it even began, and that he might be required to kill Humans as a consequence of his actions.

After an hour, the hull cooled below 400°, and the Apprentice anxiously crawled out of the portal. He lowered himself to the ground and squatted, taking a long look at everything surrounding the ship. The soil and plant life surrounding the craft were scorched by the heat, creating a football-shaped patch of smoldering brush around the landing spot. Fortunately, it had begun to rain, which had probably prevented a forest fire from erupting. The rain sizzled and steamed as it struck the ship's hot surface. The clearing itself was about 200 yards in diameter, sloping up at the eastern edge to the base of a rocky cliff. The surrounding forest echoed with the pattering of rain, which blended with the night-calls of millions of nocturnal creatures. The Apprentice had heard insect and amphibian specimens at the Intergalactic Zoo make these kinds of noises before, but never so many at once, or at such a volume. The sensory overload was intoxicating, and for a moment he forgot about the disaster he had barely avoided. He allowed himself a few minutes to relish the sights and sounds, then reluctantly returned to reality, assessing the situation and contemplating any additional fallout he should be prepared for.

He circled the transport, visually inspecting the outer surface for damage. There was none, but it was still quite hot. He used a holo-disc to scan the surrounding area in a mile-wide radius. There were numerous living things all around, but no Humans within the circle. Convinced it was safe to proceed with the mission, the Apprentice began unloading his research equipment. He didn't have to do anything manually; the gear silently levitated itself out of the cargo bay and stacked itself neatly on the ground next to the ship.

The rain had picked up its intensity and was now

a steady downpour. It felt odd on the Apprentice's skin. Rain on the homeworld was hot and purple, composed of elements foreign to Earth. The colorless water falling from Earth's sky was freezing cold in comparison. It had, however, helped to quickly cool the ship's surface, and the steam had now subsided. He had not replenished his body's fluid supply since leaving home, so he sat in a puddle and absorbed some of the water through his digestive skin-patch. Water was not ideal for his body, but his digestive system could adapt to the foreign elements, and it sufficed to hydrate his muscles and blood.

As morning came, the sounds coming from within the forest changed pitch and tone, as nocturnal species yielded to those who thrived in the daylight. The Apprentice selected various-sized specimen containers from the gear piles and began moving into the dense jungle, the containers floating behind him like a string of levitated ducklings following their mother.

Time to get to work.

CHAPTER 14

The deafening drone of the Amazon's night-life didn't bother Nate Johnston one bit. In fact, it was soothing. After Escoval and his men left him alone in the rainforest, he spent the afternoon and evening setting up the smaller details of his camp and preparing to get to work in the morning. He went to bed at around ten-thirty, after a dinner of reconstituted turkey tetrazzini, and was just about to drift off to sleep when a bright streak of light shot across the sky, catching his eye through the shelter's window. *Shooting star! Holy cow, that was a big one!*

Nate ran outside and watched the sky for several minutes to see if he could catch a glimpse of another, thinking there might be some trailing fragments that had broken off the meteor when it hit the upper atmosphere. But none came, so he went back inside to the cot and eventually drifted off to sleep.

An hour later the sat-phone rang. It was just slightly louder than the chorus of insects singing beyond the camp's electric perimeter, but was audible enough to arouse Nate. He groggily sat up and snatched the phone from the desk, cursing at the bulky device as he fumbled to find the button to answer. "Hello?"

"Hallo, Nathan?" It was Jason O'Rourke at ARCA in London, speaking in his thick British accent.

"Jason, hello there. Greetings from the rainforest," Nate half-spoke, half-yawned.

"Glad you got there in one piece! Have the new outfit all set up proper, I gather?"

"Yes, believe it or not, I remembered everything you guys taught me on how to operate this stuff, and it's all working great so far. Dinner was pretty good, too — my compliments to the chef."

"Wonderful, glad to hear it! And I do apologize for the late intrusion. I know you must be exhausted from travel, but this is more than just a courtesy call. Something urgent has come up, and we're hoping you can check it out for us."

Nate was wide awake now. "Yeah? What's up?"

"We got a call from one of our affiliates in Brazil, an astronomer we work with regularly. It seems an observatory there picked up something rather odd right in your area. They were hoping you might have noticed it — an unusually bright streak of light coming down from the upper atmosphere over the Amazon Basin. It appeared to be a large meteor, from the looks of it."

"Yeah, I saw it, big son-of-a-bitch, lit up the whole sky. Brighter than any shooting star I've ever seen." *So what?* Nate thought. *Shooting stars happen all the time. Why call me in the middle of the night to ask if I saw it?* "What does this have to do with me, Jason?"

"Well… my contact thinks a very large meteorite might have survived the atmosphere and impacted the surface. He called us because he knew we had someone doing research in the area this week. Did you hear anything, or perhaps feel an impact tremor? He estimates that if it didn't burn up, it would have hit about a mile or two north of your location."

"No, I saw the thing shoot across the sky through my window, but never heard or felt anything. Pretty loud here from the night bugs and rain, though, so if it made a sound, I probably wouldn't have heard it."

"Right. Well, chances are it didn't get through and burnt to a crisp, but if it did hit ground it may have started a fire, so be on watch."

"Doubt it, been raining pretty hard off and on here, and everything's really wet."

"Jolly good then. Well, if you get the chance to hike due north a-ways, be on the lookout for anything unusual. I'll have the estimated impact point's coordinates downloaded to your computer. Our friends would love to retrieve some fragments if it did make it through. A meteorite that big would make a noticeable impact crater, so if you get close, you should see it."

"Got it. If I happen to notice any stray meteorites that landed in my backyard, you'll be the first to know." Nate chuckled. *I don't have time for this shit!* he thought. His time in the rainforest was precious, and couldn't care less about a meteorite. *The astronomer can do this on his own time!*

"Good man!" Jason replied. "I know this isn't why you're there, Nate, and I apologize for the distraction. But please understand, our financial backers are quite fond of this sort of thing, so anything you come up with will be… well, let's just say they hope you *do* find something."

"Sure, Jason, I understand." Nate suddenly felt guilty for his selfish thoughts. Those financial backers of whom Jason spoke had spent a pretty penny on this trip. He knew he should be more grateful, and do them a favor without question when asked.

"Very well then, give me a shout if you need anything else. I'll check back in a few days."

"Take care, Jason, talk to you soon."

Nate hung up and stepped outside the shelter into the damp air, walking to the edge of the security field. He stared up at the sky beyond the forest canopy, hoping to see another shooting star, but clouds had enveloped the entire area and nothing was visible now. A steady rain began to pick up, creating tiny blue flashes of light as the droplets passed through the pyramid's energy field. Nate pondered Jason's request. He figured it didn't matter which direction he went in his quest for new insect species; due north would be just as good as any. A mile or two was stretching the limits of safe distance from the camp, but not out of the question. He'd get some research done in the immediate area for the next few days, and then, assuming he'd been fruitful in that time, would go looking for more new bugs a mile and a half or so north, and try to find Jason's precious meteorite.

Resolved in the matter, Nate turned to return to the shelter. Just then, a loud rustling noise coming from behind startled him. *Something big was moving in the forest near the clearing!* He turned quickly to try to see what it was, just as the creature came crashing through the brush, sprinting directly towards him. Nate stumbled backwards as its silhouette rapidly approached, but it was too dark to see what it was until it reached the outer edge of the energy field, where the shelter's lights cast a glow on it. *A huge jaguar!* There was no time to retreat into the shelter; the animal would reach Nate in seconds, so he dropped to the ground in a fetal position and put his arms in front of his face to protect himself.

When the big spotted cat leapt through the energy field, a sudden blast of electricity enveloped it in a flash of blue sparks. The big cat produced a howling screech as it crumpled to the ground, flailing as it rolled towards Nate, stopping just short of his position. ARCA's security pyramid had worked flawlessly. The electric jolt didn't harm the animal; it had instantly calculated its mass and only delivered enough of a shock to momentarily stun it. The disoriented predator quickly shook off the cobwebs, stared at Nate with a very confused look for a moment, and then growled irritably as it jumped to its feet and darted back into the forest.

Nate's heart was pounding like a bongo, and sweat was rolling off his forehead. The entire episode had taken only twenty seconds, but he lay there paralyzed with fear for ten minutes before he could move. As he returned to his shelter, he could hear the jaguar growling in the distance as it moved farther away. Hopefully, he thought, the experience would frighten it away from the camp for good. Jaguars were territorial, so he would need to be sure to pack his pistol and keep his guard up as he worked in this section of the forest over the next several days.

It was well past midnight now, and Nate was exhausted. He'd never imagined having so much excitement on his first night in the rainforest. He lay down on the cot and cleared his mind, trying to focus on the things he wanted to accomplish the following day. Comforted by the knowledge that ARCA's space-age security fence was doing its job, he closed his eyes and drifted into a deep sleep.

He dreamed of Tracie and Dewey.

CHAPTER 15

The morning after they arrived in the Amazon, the Apprentice and Nate diligently began conducting the very similar tasks they had come to do. The Apprentice was aware that there was some type of mysterious Human activity occurring nearby, but Nate was completely oblivious to the Alien's presence a mile and a half away. They began their research and sample-collecting, each equipped with the latest gadgets and gizmos their species could provide for the task. Needless to say, the Apprentice had the technological advantage by far.

Within a few days, Nate had collected dozens of specimens. He was thrilled to have found a number of insects, spiders, and small reptiles and frogs that he didn't recognize as previously catalogued species. Some were quite normal in appearance, but others were nothing short of bizarre. He carried a specially-designed backpack with compartments that snugly held specimen jars of various sizes. Once all the jars were filled, he would to return to camp to drop off what he had collected and reload with empty containers.

When Nate was done collecting for the day, he used the special digital camera ARCA had provided to photograph each critter and then upload the pictures into the computer. The computer would cross-reference the features of the photos with its vast archive of previously discovered species. If a specimen Nate collected didn't match anything on file, it was flagged as a potential new species. If an exact match was found, it would alert Nate of the fact and he would discard the specimen so he could re-use the specimen jar. At two a.m. every morning, the computer would automatically uplink to the servers at ARCA via satellite and transfer the data on the new discoveries.

The Apprentice had a much more efficient system. When he found a specimen, a holo-disc would scan the creature and cross-reference it with the Earth database on the spot, identifying whether it was a new species to be collected or one that had already been catalogued. And although he could have easily handled it, his sample containers didn't require the ample strength of his back for transport; they simply floated behind him wherever he roamed, and were hexagonal in profile, allowing them to neatly stack into condensed piles for transport.

Still shaken by his near mishap during descent, the Apprentice was extra careful to follow all protocols to the letter. He went about conducting his research exactly as he had been instructed. He tried to purge all distracting thoughts and concentrate on the mission, but he couldn't help wondering about the strange Human anomaly the sensors had picked up to the south. It ate at him, driving all four brains into a frenzy of burning curiosity. His best judgment told him to forget about it; it would be a blatant disregard of orders to approach anything Human in origin during this mission. But he couldn't shake his desire to take a closer look.

No, I cannot. I must not. I will not, the Apprentice scolded himself repeatedly.

He managed to contain his rebellious urges and get on with his work for the next few days, and by the fourth day, he was well ahead of schedule. Most of the containers were now occupied with new specimens and loaded into the ship's cargo bay — more than enough for the mission to be declared a success back home. With that accomplished, the distraction of his rogue curiosity became difficult to ignore. Once again his moral compass came crashing down, and the notion of spying on the Human outpost crept back into his minds.

The temptation became unbearable, and the Apprentice began to plot how he might get away with it. A few hours was all he would need to venture to the Human anomaly and back, and he would only stay for a few minutes, just long enough see what it was from a safe distance. He could shut down his holo-discs, claiming it was for unscheduled maintenance due to an interface malfunction, so they would not record his insubordination. No one would ever know.

He squatted on the ground beside the ship, his eyes spread out evenly, staring in all directions into the dense foliage of the forest. His body was motionless, but his brains were ablaze with conflicting thoughts. *Am I the only one who has ever considered doing something like this? How could other apprentices who have come before me have resisted such a temptation? If this type of opportunity has ever presented itself before, and it must have at some point over thousands of missions, did they all follow the protocol? How can I resist? I may never be sent back here again. I could die on the trip home, or in an accident after I return. Or the Exploration Ministry could decide to delay further Earth missions beyond my lifetime. I may never get another chance! I have to go see what it is!*

His pear-shaped body began to quiver. No matter how much he tried to talk himself out of this ridiculous plan, he knew he was too weak to resist putting it into motion. His curiosity had won. He *had* to take a closer look at this Human outpost in the middle of the rainforest. He was embarrassed by his weakness, but with none of his kind around to witness it, his excitement quickly overshadowed the shame.

The Apprentice plotted out every detail of his plan, contemplating the best methods of keeping this a secret when he returned home. He had already collected plenty of specimens, so there would be no questions as to his use of time, or any lost productivity. He would never mention any of this to anyone, except perhaps his mate. He trusted her to keep a secret, and would not feel comfortable lying to her for the remainder of their lives. *But what about my offspring... and my Mentor?*

His children might be displeased by what he was contemplating, and although he didn't believe they would ever betray him, he didn't want to burden them with knowledge of their father's sins. And the Mentor... well, she would be thoroughly disgusted and might put an end to his career. He couldn't possibly tell her directly, but she had an uncanny ability to read his thoughts. How could he hide this from her? He had never been able to hide *anything* from her. He would have to find a way to mask his emotions from her and live with the shame of lying. *So be it. It is worth the shame to experience real Humans first-hand. I must do this.*

While the Apprentice battled his demons and prepared to go off-grid and find the Human outpost, he had no way of knowing that a similar plan was developing just a mile and a half away.

It was early morning now, and Nate was on his second cup of coffee, waiting for his instant oatmeal to cool off a bit. He too was well ahead of schedule, and quite pleased with the number of potential new species he'd gathered. He had been up most of the night, reconsidering his thoughts on the significance of the meteorite. Even though he had begrudgingly committed to Jason that he would try to find the meteorite's impact location, he had continued to think it a useless, unproductive exercise, not worthy of his precious time in the Amazon. But now, since he could relax in the satisfaction of a successful mission, Nate put himself in the shoes of the astronomer who had called Jason to ask for help. A new meteorite impact probably meant as much to them as a new species of bug meant to himself. He felt foolish for poo-pooing Jason's request so brazenly, and decided to be a team player and take it more seriously now. Today he would make an honest effort to find the impact site.

Nate pulled up a map of the area on the monitor, plugged in the coordinates Jason had sent, and a flashing red dot appeared a mile and a half north of camp. He synced up the hand-held GPS so he could use it to navigate to the exact spot. It would take a little over two hours to hike there through the dense jungle, and probably an hour or two to scour the area for evidence of a meteorite strike. If he left soon, he'd have plenty of time to get back to camp before dark.

He packed some food and water, as well as a few specimen jars into the backpack in case he found something unusual along the way, then hefted the pack onto his shoulders and put on his utility belt, attaching the GPS to its clip. What he failed to check was the pistol holster; it was snapped shut, and he assumed the gun was inside. It wasn't. He'd forgotten that he had removed it and put it under his cot the night before, in case the jaguar came back and the pyramid failed to stop it this time. Unarmed, Nate left camp and headed north into the forest.

Almost simultaneously, the Apprentice left the sanctuary of his camp and headed south in search of the Human outpost. With his holo-discs shut off, he would have to navigate using his senses, reading the Earth's magnetic field like a compass to find the coordinates he had memorized. He also would have to make do without the holo-discs' bio-scanners, which would have alerted him to all life-forms within a few mile's radius along the way. He was aware of many creatures in the area as he scurried through the forest, but he did not notice Nate as they passed each other, just a few hundred yards apart.

CHAPTER 16

Guided only by his ample sensory system and Earth's magnetic field, the Apprentice found he was able to navigate through the rainforest nearly as well as if he had done so with his holo-discs active. At first he was apprehensive, never before having relinquished the technology of the discs in any such situation, but soon he felt liberated, free of his dependence on them for the first time in as long as he could remember. He tingled with the excitement of being completely on his own — a vagabond explorer roughing it without technology in this wonderful alien environment. It was dangerous, rebellious, and *fun*. He made good progress, pushing through the dense foliage of the forest floor or climbing trees and moving through the canopy in order to avoid larger obstacles below.

Within an hour, the Apprentice was several hundred feet from his target. A tingle in his skin alerted him to a mild disturbance in the Earth's magnetic field up ahead. The anomaly was emitting a pulsing electrical charge! He climbed into the trees and nimbly moved through the highest branches, approaching from a high vantage point. His skin changed colors, transforming from its usual hue to a mottled mix of browns and bright greens, blending in perfectly with the forest canopy. As he drew nearer to the clearing, the Apprentice caught a glimpse of Nate Johnston's camp for the first time. He froze in place and perched motionless on a large branch, all eight eyes focused intently on the strange-looking Human outpost. Through the wavering leaves, he studied the camp with intense curiosity.

There was a hemispherical structure, what appeared to be a dwelling of some sort, at the center of the clearing. It was mostly opaque, but there were two transparent sections among the faceted panels that formed its domed shape. The opaque sections were colored in patches of brown and green like he was, apparently an attempt to camouflage the odd structure. There were contraptions protruding from its top — what appeared to be an antenna of sorts, and a dish like the ones Humans used to communicate via their satellites. Oddest, though, was the tubular carbon-fibre framework that formed a pyramid around and above the entire outpost.

The periodic blue sparks that were dancing across the pyramid's frame suggested that it was the source of electrical interference that was making the Apprentice's skin tingle. *What could that be? A security device?* That theory made the most sense. After all, the rainforest was a dangerous place for fragile Humans. But the forest-dwelling Humans were not known to have anything this technologically advanced, and there had been no records of previous expeditions finding anything like this in the rainforests of Earth. This outpost had clearly been erected by advanced members of the species, most likely not indigenous to the area. Its modular design suggested it was portable. *Perhaps a temporary research site?*

The Apprentice wanted to see what was inside the structure, but he couldn't make out anything through its windows from his current perch, so he carefully moved through the canopy to a closer treetop near the edge of the clearing. From this improved position, he still could not see clearly inside the dome, and he dared not move any closer until he knew where the occupants might be; but at least he now had a better view of the entire campsite. He could see that it was surrounded by several piles of articles, some of which were small, clear cylindrical containers with bronze-colored metal lids. *Sample containers! How ironic!* He had travelled millions of light-years to collect biologic samples in the Amazon, and he had just discovered Humans doing exactly the same thing in their own backyard.

Now the Apprentice really wished he had his holo-discs, so he could scan the area for life-forms and find the Humans. He assumed they were probably out in the forest, collecting samples, but didn't want to be discovered by any coming out of the structure. He remained perfectly still except for slight adjustments of his eye stalks. He listened intently, scanning every inch of his surroundings with both visual and pulse-radar senses, to identify any possible living thing larger than a bug, reptile, or bird, of which there were many. If there were any Humans nearby, he couldn't see or hear them.

Were there Humans inside the dome? The Apprentice's minds were racing, his body tingling euphorically at the thought of seeing of a real Human at any moment. He wanted terribly to get even closer and peer into the structure, but he dared not. He decided he would stay put no matter how long it took, until a Human either came out of the dome or returned to the camp from an expedition in the forest. Sooner or later, he figured, one or the other *had* to happen.

An hour lapsed... still no Humans, but a large family of capuchin monkeys passed through the trees around him, offering some entertainment to pass the time. The monkeys looked at him cautiously and then screeched furiously, trying to scare him off. He remained perfectly still as the dominant male came right up to him, sniffed his skin, and then backed off in puzzlement. The smell of his flesh was completely foreign to the monkey, who snorted and chattered angrily in protest of his unwelcome presence. But it seemed to realize that the Apprentice was of no real threat to his harem or offspring, and didn't make any aggressive moves. Eventually the monkeys lost interest and moved on, leaving him alone again in the tree.

Another half-hour passed without any Human sighting, and the Apprentice became impatient. At this point he was fairly certain there were no Humans inside the dwelling, so he decided to take a slight risk and move to a different vantage point where he could get a clearer look inside the dome. He proceeded stealthily, using all eight limbs to nimbly navigate the canopy in a circle around the site, and then descend to some lower branches right up at the edge of the clearing, directly across from the structure's window.

The Apprentice focused one set of eyes on the window, keeping the other sets in a spread to watch for any approaching Humans. Using his telescopic vision to study the dwelling's contents, he saw a Human bed and some simple furniture, as well as several interesting gadgets whose nature he was unsure of; one looked like a small refrigerator and another like a telephonic communications device. And then he saw a primitive display monitor sitting on a desk. *A liquid-crystal visual display! How deliciously archaic!*

The Apprentice zoomed in on the monitor. It was active, and he instantly recognized the image: a map of the surrounding area. He studied it for a few seconds, and then a shiver ran through his limbs. There was a flashing red spot on the map, north of the Human outpost's location, very close to where his transport was located! Worse, approaching the red spot on the monitor was a flashing yellow spot!

Panic spread like wildfire through the Apprentice's brains. He'd been so concerned with not being detected by the Humans that he hadn't considered that they might *already* have detected his presence and were out looking for him! The Humans must have detected the ship's heat signature and calculated its trajectory to the landing site! And now it seemed likely they were on the brink of discovering it!

The Apprentice abandoned his perch, switched on his holo-discs, and made haste back towards the transport. As the discs came online, a quick scan of the landing site confirmed his worst fears: there were two large biologics within several hundred feet of his ship. Based on their size and weight, they were likely the Humans from the outpost. Curiously, they were several hundred feet apart from each other, but were moving uniformly, circling the landing site in a spiral pattern and closing in rapidly. Scampering and leaping through the forest at top speed, the Apprentice was still twenty minutes away. If the Humans progressed at their current pace, he feared he would not get there in time to take off and avoid an encounter.

As he traveled, the Apprentice silently admonished himself for his irresponsibility. The rules he had broken to satisfy his curiosity would now all be recorded by the holo-discs, as well as the ship's sensor logs. His carelessness was going to seriously jeopardize the entire mission, and his future with the Exploration Ministry. He contemplated how he might erase or modify the data, but this was not something he had planned for and would be incredibly risky. There was little he could do about it now, as the damage was about to be done; these two Humans would likely find his ship, and that meant he would have to kill them. The thought made him cringe, but protocol in such matters was clear: under no circumstances could Humans be allowed to know of his presence on Earth, or acquire any Alien technology.

The Apprentice intently monitored the status of the two Humans as he made progress. They were remaining a good distance apart from each other, which did seem odd, but was of little concern now. He watched in horror as one of them reached the landing site, entered the clearing, and stopped in its tracks a hundred feet from the transport. It stood perfectly still for a few moments, then slowly circled the ship. Then it moved closer, coming within several yards before halting abruptly and jumping back. *It had come in contact with the transport's security field!* The blip cautiously circled the vessel again, keeping its distance this time, then stopping at the exact spot where the Apprentice had left a stack of his sample containers.

He was close now. He abandoned the trees, leaping to the ground and scampering towards his ship, circling to the east to stay clear of the second

Human, who was still hidden in the forest and keeping its distance from the clearing. The Apprentice was only a few hundred feet from the edge of the landing site when a holo-disc alerted him that the Human by the ship had suddenly exited the clearing back into the forest...and was now coming straight toward him. The Apprentice stood fast a moment, contemplating what to do, then quickly scaled some thick vines back up into the trees. He flipped upside down and used his feet to grip a large branch forty feet above the forest floor, his skin morphing into the colors and patterns of the tree's bark and leaves. He blended into the canopy above like a large, camouflaged bat, his eye stalks hanging beneath him, watching the forest floor intently for the Human to come through. He heard rustling, intensifying as the Human moved closer and then came into view.

It appeared to be a male. It was dressed in brown, baggy garments with lots of pockets. It wore a large brimmed hat on its head, blocking its face from the Alien's curious eyes, and it carried what looked like a soft-sided storage container on its back. It moved frantically and clumsily through the underbrush, breathing heavily and dripping wet from perspiration, while nervously turning to look over its shoulder every few seconds, as if to see what might be following it through the forest.

The Apprentice remained perfectly still as the anxious Human passed directly beneath his position. This was not how he had envisioned his first encounter with a real Human. Instead of joy and ful-fillment, he felt panic... and he felt sorry for the man, who was obviously under a considerable amount of anguish. He checked a holo-disc for the second Human's location. It was two hundred feet to the west, pacing this one's progress on a parallel path. *Why aren't they together, or at least communicating with each other?* The Apprentice was puzzled. He remained motionless as the man moved on through the brush, out of sight, heading south towards its outpost.

The Apprentice waited until the Human was far enough away to not detect him, and then descended from the tree and made haste towards the ship. He needed to access the damage and figure out what he must do to rectify it. When he reached the clear-ing, he wasted no time interfacing with the ship's records, and a visual display of the Human's activ-ity appeared on the side of the vessel's hull. When the man discovered the transport, he had stood in his tracks for a few moments, just gazing at it. Then he had circled the vessel at a distance before ap-proaching it and getting a mild energy jolt from the security field. The Human had then pulled a small device from its belt, and appeared to use it to record images of the ship. Then the man had approached the pile of specimen containers, and the Apprentice shook with dismay as he observed him putting one of the smaller containers into the storage pack on his back. The Apprentice would have to retrieve the container, as well as destroy the images the man had recorded. He would also have to kill both of the Humans; of that he was now sadly convinced. The second one had apparently not seen the ship or taken anything from the landing site, but surely its partner would tell it about all that he had seen there.

All life in the Universe was precious to the Aliens. They were not a cruel, hostile, or capricious race. Yet it had been determined and mandated that, under certain circumstances, the loss of one Human's life would be far less tragic than what might happen on Earth should all Humans discover they were being frequently visited by extraterrestrials. There had been much debate on this, the opposing side declaring it nothing short of barbaric. But the overwhelming conclusion was that it was far too important to continue visiting Earth and studying the Humans, yet far too dangerous to let them know of the Aliens' presence — at least for now. The idea of ending any Human life in the name of science, however, was not taken lightly, and much training was conducted to insure avoiding it on any mission to Earth. Now the Apprentice faced the reality that he had failed his training, and might have to follow through with this protocol.

He squatted on the ground beside his transport, quivering, plotting what he must do. He was ashamed, furious with himself, and very sad. But he could not reverse what had happened, and his new objective was clear. He stood, scampered to the forest's edge, and leapt effortlessly up into the trees. He moved through the branches at a deliberate pace towards the Human outpost. One thing was still puzzling him: Why had the second Human not approached the ship? Why were the two Humans not working side by side? It made no sense.

CHAPTER 17

On his way to search for the meteorite, Nate discovered several unusual insects he didn't recognize, and collected them in the specimen jars he'd packed just in case. This made him feel better about this side-trip, as he was getting some work done along the way. As he pushed ahead in the direction the GPS was guiding him, he began to notice a pungent odor. *Smoke!*

Nate couldn't see any smoke around him, and it had rained a lot over the past two days; so if there had been a fire, it probably wasn't still burning. But there was no mistaking the odor of freshly scorched wood and brush; there had definitely been a fire in the area recently, and he presumed this easily could have been caused by a meteorite impact. He pushed forward, then stopped when the yellow dot on the GPS indicating his position sat directly on top of the red dot, where the meteorite should be. There was no sign of any impact here, but the strong odor of smoke fueled Nate's confidence that there had, in fact, been one nearby. Then, suddenly, the GPS screen went haywire, the clear image becoming a garbled mess of dancing green, red, and yellow patterns. "Crap, now what?" Nate muttered, tapping on the screen. The tapping had no effect. The display was still gibberish. "Well that's just great. What kind of junk did you give me, Jason?" Nate spoke towards the sky, as if he could somehow bounce his voice off ARCA's satellite to Jason O'Rourke, halfway around the world.

He continued another hundred meters in the direction he'd been going, stopping for a moment when the smoky odor began to fade. Then, just as suddenly as it had malfunctioned, the GPS came to life and the screen returned to its normal display. He turned and retraced his steps back towards the red dot on the screen, and the display went awry again.

Could a magnetic field from a meteorite cause this? Do meteorites even generate magnetic fields? Nate knew little about astronomy, but it was the most logical explanation he could think of. He wondered if he could use his compass to navigate, but assumed a magnetic anomaly would affect that as well. This was confirmed when he unclipped the compass from his belt and held it out flat. He knew he was facing due south, so the needle should be pointing directly at his chest, but instead it was slowly moving back and forth ninety degrees between the S and the W on the dial.

Now Nate was getting excited. There was *definitely* something unusual going on here. The smoky odor, malfunctioning GPS, and screwy compass couldn't all just be a coincidence. He was sure they must be related somehow. He advanced cautiously towards the center of the needle's wavering path, he assumed southwest, meticulously scanning every inch of the forest with his curious eyes. As he made progress, the compass needle's path narrowed, until it just quivered, pointing straight in front of his position. He stopped and stood completely still for a moment, staring straight ahead. There was nothing out of the ordinary there that he could detect.

Then the needle went AWOL again, wavering between the E and N this time. Nate cursed, unable to decipher any logical pattern to follow in the compass's behavior. He pushed ahead; only now he moved in a spiral path, outwards from the original spot the GPS had calculated as the meteorite's impact site. After thirty minutes, he came to the edge of a rocky clearing in the forest that jutted up to a small hillside. The smoky odor was more intense here. *This must be the spot!* He stepped out of the trees and ventured slowly into the clearing, looking in every direction with each step.

The clearing was about two hundred meters across, and scattered with patches of waist-high grass and small bushes. The smoke smell was now quite strong, and a few steps later Nate noticed that some of the vegetation around him looked singed and charred. *The source of the smoky smell!* Then he saw something very peculiar right at the center of the clearing. He couldn't quite make out what it was, but from this distance it looked like a dense group of small, curved trees rising above the grass and bushes… like a miniature patch of forest.

What puzzled Nate was that the trees were curved very oddly, in an un-natural, deformed, yet symmetrical pattern. He pushed through the grass to get a closer look, stepping carefully and watching his feet to avoid stomping on any snakes that might be hiding there. As he neared the center of the clearing, he saw that most of the plant life was singed or completely charred, *except* for those strangely curved trees up ahead; they looked vibrantly green and healthy. And then, when he was close enough to pause and get a better look, he gasped, then held his breath and stood motionless for a moment, unwilling to immediately accept what he was seeing.

A chill ran down Nate's spine, and goosebumps erupted on his exposed forearms. What he thought he saw did not compute; it was too strange to be real, yet *there it was*. He took a deep breath and slowly advanced, keeping his eyes keenly focused directly ahead. A few more paces towards the center of the clearing affirmed that what he was seeing was most certainly real. *Unless,* he thought, *I'm hallucinating*.

But he wasn't. It was clearly an exact image of himself, walking away from the strange trees directly towards him, mimicking his every move, its eyes staring back into his own. But the image appeared bloated, as if he were looking into one of those goofy mirrors at a carnival that adds girth to one's body where it's never wanted. Despite the sweltering Amazon heat, Nate felt chills as his contorted, pudgy doppelganger came closer, copying every move he made. He called out, "Who are you, what are you doing here?" and the image's lips spoke the words as well, in perfect unison but silently. There was no separate reply.

Nate took his eyes away from his unsettling twin for a moment to have a closer look at the odd trees, which now seemed just several yards away. As strange as the fat image of himself had been, now he was seeing even more unbelievable things. He quickly realized the patch of curved trees at the center of the clearing wasn't real, but rather a distorted reflection of the forest behind him! And the portly version of himself was, in fact, also a reflection. The source of the reflections was even more bizarre than the images themselves. It was the shape of a football, a *huge* football, hovering several feet off the ground and completely smooth and shiny, like highly polished chrome.

"What the *fuck*?" Nathan said out loud, trembling with a combination of sheer terror and burning curiosity. He theorized that perhaps he was seeing a mirage of some sort, or just imagining the whole thing, perhaps brought on by heat stroke or some insect's toxic bite. *No, I feel fine, and this is no mirage. This shit is real.*

Nate's heart pounded, and for the first time in

his career, he felt completely befuddled, unable to process any of the information on his plate. He *knew* rainforests, was an expert in *everything* about them, and this thing did not belong. And although he was no trained astronomer, he knew no meteorite could resemble it. His mind was drawing a complete blank, clueless as to what he had come across in the heart of the Amazon. After a few minutes of just staring at it, collecting his wits, he cautiously stepped back a few feet to get a better perspective, then slowly walked the length of the thing and circled behind it. It truly did resemble a giant chrome football, a perfectly round cylinder at the middle, he estimated about thirty feet in diameter and maybe a hundred feet in length, tapering at each end to a perfectly pointed cone. *This is no meteorite, Jason! Just what did you guys send me to find?*

Nate circled the object again, studying its every inch. It had no visible features; its entire surface was completely smooth and reflective of its surroundings. He could see himself, the clearing, the forest behind him, and the sky above, all moving and distorting with the curved surface as he circled. When he reached a position where the reflection of the sun came into view, he was stunned to see that it was just a dull reddish-orange spot, not the blinding globe of radiance one would normally see when viewing the sun in a mirror.

He stared at the sun's reflection; something was very wrong. He shouldn't have been able to stare at it directly, but it wasn't hurting his eyes, and he soon realized that no light was being reflected off the object at all; instead, it was as if it were just a curved viewing screen, like looking at a real-time image of a distorted landscape. His curiosity was intense now, and he mustered enough courage to get a bit closer, perhaps even try to touch the object.

Nate took two steps closer, then paused. There had obviously been some significant heat coming from the object at some point, enough to singe the surrounding vegetation, but he felt no heat now, and there didn't appear to be any imminent danger. He took a few more steps forward, and his skin began to tingle. He stopped, extending his right arm in front of his chest, testing the air. Suddenly, the hair on his forearm stood straight up, and the tingling sensation intensified. He could only extend his hand two feet in front of his chest before it was met by an invisible resistance that he couldn't push through. The sensation reminded him of trying to push two strong magnets together from their common poles: you could push all you wanted, but the resistance would prevent the surfaces from joining.

Nate pushed harder, trying to make progress through whatever was holding him back. In his mind, he knew this was probably quite foolish, but his curiosity had taken complete control. Then, without warning, a narrow beam of blue light shot out of the object and touched Nate's extended hand. He felt a jolt of energy shoot down his arm into his chest, similar to an electric shock but subtler and not painful. Painful or not, it freaked him out plenty. He turned and ran, scampering through the singed brush away from the object, stopping at the edge of the clearing and turning back to look at the thing once more from a distance.

Nate's better judgment was telling him to get the hell away from this place now, to get back to camp and report his discovery to ARCA. After all, it was *their* problem now; he had located it for them, and now he could get back to collecting bugs. But he didn't leave. He stayed at the edge of the clearing, keeping a good distance from the object, too curious now to abandon it. He hated to admit it to himself, but *this* was equally as exciting and mysterious as any new bug he had ever discovered. To satisfy his own curiosity, he felt compelled to learn more about it... and *then* he would go back and report it to Jason.

Nate extracted the digital camera from his backpack and circled the perimeter of the clearing, using the zoom lens to get pictures of the thing from every angle. As he reviewed each photo, something caught his eye that he hadn't noticed before: a pile of objects of some sort, neatly stacked in the singed grass. From their symmetry and how neatly they were stacked, it was obvious that they weren't natural, and Nate wondered how he could have missed them before. *They must have something to do with the chrome football.*

Nate wanted get a closer look, and decided to

leave the safety of the forest's edge again. He approached the mysterious pile cautiously, expecting the same tingling sensation and shock to occur as before if he got too close, but the objects weren't as close to the chrome football as when he received the shock, and apparently they weren't protected by whatever had caused it, so he was able to walk right up to them.

The stacked objects were of varying sizes, but otherwise identical and very modern-looking. They were hexagonal in profile, with clear mid-sections and tops and bottoms made of some kind of bronze-colored metal, and each appeared to be filled with a glowing purple-tinted fluid. "Sample containers. These look like sample containers of some kind," Nate whispered to himself, not really believing it but having no better explanation to offer on the spot.

Without thinking, he instinctively reached out and picked up one of the smaller containers. It felt very strange. The thing felt solid and heavy in his hands, as if it held significant mass, and yet he could pick it up easily, as if someone or something was helping him handle its weight. When he loosened his grip, it floated gently out of his hands, like a helium-filled balloon. He backed away, startled, and let the container gracefully glide through the air on its own trajectory. It floated back to the pile he had plucked it from and placed itself right back where it had been, fitting perfectly into the stack. Nate reclaimed the container, but this time he didn't release his grip. He felt a mild tugging as it attempted once again to go back to its pile, but the force wasn't enough to counter Nate's grip, and he put it in his backpack, securely zipping it shut.

Nate snapped more photos of the mysterious container stack, the singed plant-life surround the center of the clearing, and the chrome football, being sure not to get too close to it this time. Once he was convinced he had enough photos, he just stood still, staring at the thing. He was dying to know what it was he'd found in lieu of a meteorite, which this most definitely was *not*. A theory was lurking in the back of Nate's mind, but he was trying to avoid it. It was too "out there" for him to accept just yet. *Nope, not gonna go there!* He shook his head nervously, trying to purge the idea, searching instead for a more logical answer. *Perhaps*, he thought, *it's some sort of top-secret military experiment*? *Maybe some country's government has lost their new gadget and asked ARCA to have me locate it for them*. But he quickly shrugged off that notion. *No, that can't be it.*

Nate was sure Jason wouldn't say it was a meteorite he was looking for if he knew otherwise. The Brazilian astronomer must have *thought* it was a meteor, but, if this chrome football was what he had seen, then it was something quite unexpected. *But what? A new secret weapon that got lost?* No, if that had been the case, the place would be crawling with some country's soldiers looking for it. *A high-tech research device on a covert assignment?*

Nate quickly dismissed that possibility as well. The stack of containers *could*, as he originally suspected, be some kind of new, high-tech sample jars, but it made no sense that he wouldn't recognize them. The global community of people who researched insects and other wildlife in the rainforests was a rather tight-knit group, and Nate was constantly in contact with all of them. They shared everything with each other, and surely he would have been told about something like this. Besides, nobody he knew of, besides ARCA, had the money or technology to do something like this, and *he* was ARCA's representative in the Amazon. If it this were ARCA's latest line of rainforest research gear, *he* would be the one using it.

No. This had to have come from a source unknown to ARCA and the rest of the scientific community. Nate grimaced and rubbed his chin, then allowed himself to say what he had briefly thought moments ago, but then quickly put back on the shelf. "Could it be a remote probe from another planet?" He didn't want to believe it that this was the explanation, not because he didn't believe in such things — he had always known there must be intelligent life beyond Earth — but because if he reported this kind of news, it would change the entire scope of his presence in the Amazon. The remainder of his expedition would certainly be put on hold, and *this* would become the new priority. If news about it got out to the public, all hell would break loose, putting

him and ARCA under a lot of scrutiny. He wasn't
prepared to deal with that. But having eliminating
all other possibilities, there was little else to with
go with right now. An alien probe of some sort had
landed in the Amazon. There was no other way he
could frame it up for Jason. What to do with that
information would be up to ARCA.

Nate started chuckling nervously. "A remote
alien probe sent to Earth to collect biological samples. And of all people, I have to be the one to find
it." As bizarre as it sounded, he was beginning to
feel impressed with himself for figuring this out, and
was mildly amused by the thought that if this theory
proved correct, he had so much in common with this
thing. It might have the same objective as he did:
to study the Amazon's living bounty and bring some
home for further review. He grinned, mentally patting himself on the back for a moment, but then a
new thought crossed his mind, and the grin disappeared rapidly.

It had suddenly struck Nate that perhaps the
alien probe wasn't unmanned at all. *What if it has
occupants*? He had assumed there couldn't be anything or anyone inside the chrome football, because
he hadn't seen any doors, windows, or portals. But
the specimen containers were *outside* of it. *They
must have come from inside it at one point*! And they
were all empty... *what about any containers that had
specimens in them? Where were they?* Nate concluded that either no samples had been collected

yet, which was unlikely if the alien probe had been there for several days already, or the full containers *had already been put back inside the probe*.

Nate panicked. If there were aliens nearby, he could only hope they were friendly. *But what if they weren't*? They might not be too happy to see him poking around their spaceship. He scared himself batty with the image of little green men coming back from their hike in the forest, only to discover a piddly-ass Human had discovered their ship and was messing with their gear. *Poor, stupid Human, we'll have to vaporize you now.* Nate wiped the sweat from his brow with a sleeve, then looked anxiously all around, looking for anything moving. Nothing; he seemed to still be alone in the clearing, and he didn't want to be there if aliens showed up. *Time to leave!*

Nate's heart pounded as he navigated the forest away from the clearing as fast as he could. He reached for his pistol in case he ran into some aliens on his way back to camp. But when he unsnapped the holster cover and felt for the weapon, he found no gun. *No friggin' way!* Nate whined mentally, remembering that he had put the pistol under his cot the night before, in case the jaguar returned and managed to get through the pyramid's energy field. "What kind of moron goes into a rainforest full of aliens without his fucking gun?!" Nate chastised himself out loud, "Of all the…" then he abruptly shut up, feeling incredibly stupid for the outburst and considering it much wiser to remain quiet and keep his thoughts to himself. *Good thinking there, Einstein, just announce to the aliens that you're here... and unarmed.*

Nate moved through the underbrush as quickly as he could, stumbling on shaky legs. As he made progress away from the clearing, the magnetic interference subsided, and the GPS unit kicked back in, giving him a fix on his camp a mile and a half due south. He pressed on, nervously looking over his shoulder every few seconds. He didn't see anything following him, but swore he heard something large moving in the underbrush to the west, just beyond his sight. *Aliens! There are aliens stalking me!* He had a vision of himself being stuffed into one of the larger specimen containers he had seen back at the clearing.

Nate was more frightened than he'd ever been in his life. He was drenched in sweat. All he wanted now was to get back to camp, back to the security of the pyramid and the pistol under his cot. He would use the sat-phone to contact Pedro Escoval and have him come get his ass out of there ASAP. Screw the gear, he just wanted to hop on the boat and leave. He would notify ARCA and the Brazilian government, and they could come back with a squadron of marines to investigate the spaceship and collect his gear. He was exhausted to the brink of collapse, but with his adrenaline surging, he forced himself to keep going.

He was relieved that whatever was moving in the brush beyond his sight seemed to be keeping its distance. *They're just observing me...maybe they don't want to engage.* He hoped that would remain the case, and if an alien wanted to approach him, it would wait until he was within the safety of the camp and its defenses. Nate figured those defenses might be useless against alien technology, but if there were to be an encounter, it would be better to have it happen at the camp than out here in the open.

Nate kept looking all around him as he trekked towards the safety of his camp, hoping not to see anything coming at him through the brush. It never dawned on him to keep an eye on the trees above as well. He didn't notice the camouflaged body of the Apprentice suspended from a branch forty feet above, his eight eyes looking straight down at Nate as he stumbled onward.

Forty-five agonizing minutes later, Nate saw his camp through the trees up ahead, and he cried a bit, sobbing with joy and relief. He was completely spent, his legs and arms trembling with fatigue. He could still hear the alien moving in the forest, directly behind him now. He knew he had to get inside the perimeter of the pyramid and quickly get the protective field turned up to the highest power, but would that protect him against this creature? Theoretically, at the highest setting, the pyramid could drop any living thing in its tracks. But that assumed it was something from Earth. Who knew what effect it would have on an extraterrestrial? *Hell, they could probably just disable it with their technology, then walk right in and vaporize me.* The pyramid wasn't enough comfort; he desperately wanted the pistol.

Nate was in the camp's clearing now, his wobbly legs moving as fast as they could towards the asylum of the pyramid and hut. He had fifty yards to go. Now something was definitely moving faster in the forest behind him. He could hear loud rustling in the undergrowth. Whatever had been following him was no longer trying to hide its presence, and it was coming towards him in a hurry. A fresh wave of panic gave his legs new life, and he ran into the clearing as fast as he could, not daring to look behind him. He fumbled with his belt as he ran, grasping for the pyramid's remote-control so that he could boost the security field the moment he was through the perimeter.

The pyramid was just feet away now, and Nate heard heavy rustling right behind him —the alien was almost upon him! And then he heard a low, guttural growl as it got closer. *Aliens growl?* Nate was momentarily amused that the last thing he would ever hear before being toasted by a death ray might be an extraterrestrial growling like a jaguar.

Wait, like a jaguar? *Holy shit!*

Instantly, Nate felt very foolish, questioning his conclusion that the chrome football was a spaceship and that aliens were chasing him through the forest. *This* was no alien, just a big, hungry pussycat, with massive claws and fangs! He'd rather face an alien. At least you could try to reason with an alien, and if negotiations failed, being vaporized was likely less painful than being shredded and eaten alive. All these things, as well as thoughts of Tracie and Dewey, passed through Nate's mind in a nanosecond as the world around him decelerated into slow motion. He kept running, but felt like he was in one of those dreams where no matter how fast you try to run, you can't seem to make any progress. Then, with one final surge of reserve strength, Nate lunged forward towards the pyramid's outer edge. *Almost there… move it, Professor, or get eaten!*

Like an exhausted marathon runner crossing the finish line, Nate fell through the perimeter of the pyramid and collapsed in a heap. He had removed the remote-control from his belt so he could boost the security field the moment he got through, but when he fell, the impact knocked it out of his hand and it disappeared into a patch of tall grass. The rustling in the forest ceased, but the growling was getting louder. Nate knew the jaguar was inside the clearing now, probably headed straight towards him. He tried to get up to look for the remote, but the combination of his exhaustion and the heavy pack on his back made the process awkward, and he was out of time. He rolled over onto his side and looked for the approaching predator.

Nate saw the jaguar now, twenty meters away

and bounding towards him as he lay helpless on the ground. He scrambled, trying to get up so he could get to the entrance of the hut, but there was no time: the jaguar was nearly to the edge of the pyramid. All thoughts of aliens and spacecraft quickly exited Nate's mind. Now he was petrified by the image of being mauled to death and ending up as dinner. He briefly imagined how someone would explain his demise to Tracie. "*So sorry, Mrs. Johnston, but this piece of jaguar poo is all that's left of your husband.*"

It was all happening very fast, but it still felt to Nate like it took forever. His peripheral vision blurred as he focused on the big cat coming straight at him, its gleaming white fangs bared. For a brief moment, Nate's eyes met with those of the snarling beast. The jaguar's gaze was emotionless, focused, hungry, and determined. It leapt gracefully and effortlessly into the air, clearing the bottom of the pyramid's frame and soaring towards Nate, its immense claws pivoting forward and reaching out like a fan of curved switchblades. Nate clenched his body into a fetal position and exhaled, the image of Tracie's beautiful face popping into his final thoughts. "I'm sorry, sweetheart... I'm so sorry!" he sobbed out loud, then clenched his eyes shut and waited for the sting of claws and teeth.

Then Nate heard a sound come from behind his position, like a sudden concentrated burst of air. The leaping cat recoiled in mid-air and let out a high-pitched squeal as it dropped to the ground at

Nate's feet. It began writhing in the grass and growling angrily, biting and licking furiously at a spot on its side. Bewildered, Nate sat up and scooted backwards on his butt. The cat was obviously in a great deal of pain from something unexpected. *But what? What was it I heard?* The sound had reminded Nate of the subtle noise made by a blow-dart being expelled from a long tube, a weapon commonly used by the Amazon's native tribes for hunting monkeys, boars, and birds. Had a local villager come to his rescue? He wanted to look behind him to see who had helped him, but he was too afraid to take his eyes off the jaguar, which continued writhing and hissing on the ground.

After a few seconds, it became obvious to Nate that the jaguar wasn't going to attack again. It was more concerned with tending to its injury, so he turned away from the cat to see what the sound had come from. At first he noticed nothing, but then he realized something was coming towards him around the side of the hut. Sweat in his eyes blurred his vision, making it difficult to focus, but whatever it that was coming towards him did not appear human. It looked bigger than a man, and seemed to blend in with trees at the edge of the clearing, as if it were camouflaged. *A soldier perhaps, sent to look for the chrome football!* In full gear, a soldier could look bigger than most men, Nate supposed. He lifted his sunglasses and wiped the sweat out of his eyes with a sleeve, then took another hard look.

Nate's throat tightened up and he froze, holding his breath, petrified by what he saw approaching. This was no soldier, nor an Amazon tribesman with a blow-dart gun… or any other living thing he recognized. Whatever it was, it appeared camouflaged at first, a moving, bulbous shape that blended in with the forest in the background, much like one of the alien hunters in the *Predator* movies; but as it came towards Nate, it began morphing into a uniform, purplish-gray.

Nate counted four pairs of large, black eyes (although he could swear they, too, had been camouflaged a moment ago) atop flexible stalks above the thing's head… assuming that *was* its head. As the creature moved closer, it focused one pair of eyes on the wounded jaguar, while another pair stared directly at Nate, sending chills down his spine and giving him goosebumps. It didn't appear to be wearing any clothing, and as far as Nate could tell, it wasn't brandishing any type of weapon; but as it came closer, Nate saw the metallic band around its midsection with several large discs attached to it. Each of the discs was emitting an eerie, purple glow from its center. *Technology!*

Instantly, thoughts of aliens chasing him through the forest, and of being vaporized or abducted for a rectal probe (or something equally unpleasant) came rushing back to Nate. His bowels began to quiver and he clenched his butt cheeks to keep from crapping his pants. *Oh, this is just fucking great. I survive a jaguar attack only to be vaporized by an alien anyway!* Nate thought, laughing in his mind at the irony. He remained frozen but trembling, waiting for the alien to make its move. It stopped several yards short of his position and did nothing except stare at both him and the jaguar while it fidgeted nervously with its dozens of snake-like fingers.

The presence of this odd creature was obviously agitating the jaguar as well. It stopped tending to its wound and hopped to its feet, taking an aggressive stance and snarling at both Nate and the alien. It began to pace back and forth, growling and hissing as if trying to decide who to be most angry with. *Why doesn't it just leave, run away*? Nate wondered. *I would if I could outrun this thing!* He wasn't sure why he assumed that he couldn't, but it looked like it could move pretty fast if it wanted to — and besides, he was too terrified to move.

The alien's stance shifted, and it appeared to focus all of its eyes — which had turned dark yellow — on the pacing jaguar. Then it slowly moved on its four lanky legs, placing itself between Nate and the predator, its four hands extended in what looked like a defensive posture, with all its fingers pointed directly at the pissed-off cat. Nate realized the alien was trying to protect him.

While the alien confronted the jaguar, Nate took advantage of the moment to shed his backpack and jump to his feet. He bolted for the entrance of the hut and jumped in, diving and rolling like an awkward infantry soldier trying to avoid a volley of gunfire. He scrambled on hands and knees to the cot and grabbed the pistol from under it, and then in an instant he was back outside again, waving the pistol in a shaky hand.

The jaguar was still pacing, snarling and baring its teeth. The alien stood calm and stoic, with the exception of its four pairs of eyes, which were moving on their stalks to follow the motions of the cat. Nate watched in disbelief, trying to stop his pistol-bearing hand from shaking so badly, as the jaguar coiled and pounced towards the alien. The alien's body jerked slightly and Nate heard that sound again, the blow-dart noise. Nate saw nothing to explain the noise or what had caused it, but like before, the predator stopped mid-air with a screech and fell to the ground, writhing in pain. Now Nate saw what was causing the predator's duress: there were what appeared to be several small black spikes protruding from its shoulder. He didn't see that the alien had brandished any type of weapon, but somehow it had shot the jaguar with the spikes.

The jaguar no longer wished to participate in this losing game. After rolling around in agony for a few seconds it jumped to its feet and bounded off into the forest, yowling in pain. With the jaguar out of the picture, the alien shifted its eyes towards Nate. All eight changed to mottled black and purple as it stood, staring at the trembling Human. Nate was shaking even more now, but he managed to feebly point the pistol at the creature and rack the slide.

Great. What do I do now? he wondered, fresh, warm urine soaking his pant leg.

The Apprentice wondered the same thing.

CHAPTER 18

The Apprentice couldn't believe he had let things come to this, and how completely out of control the situation had gotten. When he had followed the Human back to its outpost, he had assumed the other large life-form nearby was a second Human. But he didn't want to lose sight of the man he was following, so he hadn't attempted a look at the other target, nor had he taken the time to do a full bio-scan with a holo-disc to confirm the species. Instead, when the man had reached the clearing where the Human outpost was, he had stayed hidden in the treetops, in a good spot to observe the entire campsite. There he had watched in amazement as the hectic scene unfolded below.

Only when the second biologic burst out of the forest did the Apprentice realize it was not Human, but rather a large, predatory mammal, most likely feline. A quick bio-scan confirmed the species as a jaguar, just like the cloned ones he'd seen many times back home at the zoo while preparing for this mission. When the jaguar attacked the Human, the Apprentice was surprised that the man had not wielded any kind of weapon to defend itself; it would be foolish not to have one in such a hostile environment. It quickly became evident the Human had no means of protection, and was in great peril.

The Apprentice didn't enjoy the thought of watching as this Human was mauled and eaten, so in a sudden flash of compassion, he had decided to intervene. He would, of course, still have to kill the man, but his method would be far less traumatic than the jaguar's. With haste, he had circled to the back side of the clearing and leapt from the trees, scurrying to a position beside the Human's shelter where he had a clear shot. The man had fallen trying to escape the attack and was on his back, looking in the direction of the oncoming jaguar, completely unaware of the Apprentice's presence behind him. He did not see the Apprentice plant himself firmly on all four feet, recoil slightly, and then jerk forward in the direction of the jaguar, launching two small black spikes out of the holes that had opened in his chest. The spikes had hit with pinpoint accuracy, sinking deep into the flesh of the jaguar's shoulder and felling it mid-leap.

The spikes had the desired effect: not permanently harming the big cat, but stopping it from killing the man. It rolled about on the ground, protesting loudly and gnawing desperately at the excruciating pain in its shoulder, trying to extract the spikes. The startled Human stared in disbelief at the neutralized jaguar, then turned and looked towards the Apprentice's position. The jig was up; there was no hiding from the Human now. *It knows I am here,* the Apprentice thought. No longer needing to conceal himself, he stepped out in front of the shelter and approached the man, his camouflaged skin returning to its normal hue.

The man's eyes were open wide, his facial expression and body language suggesting deep fear. He was trembling and babbling a string of nonsense, littered with references to defecation and fornication. The Human languages were numerous, and although the Apprentice was physically incapable of speaking them, he understood many of them quite well, including English, so he *did* understand the man's words, if not his message. As the man continued to utter profanities repeatedly, the Apprentice was momentarily lost in deep fascination. He wanted to study this *real* Human in greater detail. He stood motionless, basking in the moment he had always dreamt of but did not think would become a reality, at least not on this trip. Then the jaguar snarled loudly, drawing him out of his trance.

Despite the searing pain in its shoulder, the jaguar had jumped back to its feet, growling menacingly and pacing back and forth, dividing its attention between the Apprentice and the man. The Apprentice had hoped the two spikes he had delivered would be enough to neutralize the animal and discourage it from further attack, but apparently they had not, and the big cat suddenly leapt towards the Apprentice. The Apprentice quickly expelled two more spikes from its abdomen, firmly planting them into the animal's chest with enough force to cause significant pain, but not enough to penetrate the heart. This proved sufficient, and the jaguar ran off into the forest, yowling in protest.

While the Apprentice was distracted by the jaguar, the man had taken refuge in the shelter. But once the cat was gone he stepped back outside, still trembling with fear but now holding a shiny metal object in his hand. The Apprentice recognized the primitive weapon. *A handgun. So the Human does have a weapon after all!* He did not fear the gun; the worst harm it could do was a little damage to his outer skin or extremities, nothing that wouldn't grow back. But his eyes would be quite vulnerable to the bullets, and even though they too could regenerate, he wanted to keep them all intact for the remainder of the mission, so he remained cautious.

All of this had seemed to happen very quickly to the Apprentice. But now it felt as if time had stopped. He stood motionless, staring at the frightened Human. The man was trembling, trying to hold his gun steady, pointing it in his general direction. He waited for the weapon to fire so he could react quickly and avoid the bullet, but the man did not fire; he just continued babbling gibberish, still referencing defecation, fornication, and other curious things that made little sense to the Apprentice.

This had gone on long enough. The Apprentice

knew he needed to resolve this matter at once and get back to his mission. Protocol dictated that he should kill the Human without further delay, but he hesitated, overcome with guilt and remorse. He *loved* Humans, and it seemed grossly unfair that he should have to kill one because of his own irresponsible actions. He would regret this for the rest of his life, but all other options would have significantly unpleasant consequences back home if discovered. It was time to get it over with. Without moving to alarm the Human, he programmed a holo-disc to euthanize the man with a lethal burst of energy that would stop all biologic functions without trauma or pain.

Just as the Apprentice was about to carry out the execution, Professor Nate Johnston lowered his pistol and collapsed to the ground onto his knees, laying down the pistol at his side. He took a deep breath and, in a shaky but calmer voice, he began to speak again, only this time without the profanity. The Apprentice hesitated in delivering the lethal burst, listening carefully to what Nate was saying.

The Apprentice's eyes shifted to bright purple. Now he could understand the man. It was no longer just ranting irrationally, it was structuring sentences with clear meaning. *It wanted to communicate.*

CHAPTER 19

Nate had wanted to shoot at the terrifying creature the moment he had retrieved his gun, but he just couldn't do it. Instead, he had stood there quivering, uttering a volley of expletives under his breath. He was scared out of his mind and didn't want to die in the middle of the rainforest, but he resisted the urge to fire the pistol.

Nate knew now, beyond all reasonable doubt, that he was having an encounter with an extraterrestrial life-form, one that had come to Earth in a football-shaped spaceship and must possess unimaginable technology. One that could probably end his life in a blink of an eye if it so chose, regardless of the pistol. But it hadn't killed the jaguar... in fact, it had *saved* him from being attacked by it, *so perhaps,* Nate thought, *this is a friendly alien*?

He was still terrified, but Nate's passion for discovering the unknown was stirring, balancing fear with burning curiosity. He had never contemplated the possibility that in his quest for interesting life, he might someday come across a specimen from another world. Searching for the countless undiscovered species on his own planet had always been enough to keep him satisfied, but now, standing in front of him was ET, and suddenly insects, spiders, and reptiles seemed much less fascinating.

Nate's knees buckled. He collapsed and took a deep breath, doing his best to think clearly. He knew that from a *logical* standpoint, instead of shooting at the alien, he should try to learn more about it. Maybe even communicate and interact with it. That, of course, would depend on the alien agreeing to the idea and *not* vaporizing him, or shooting him with those scary little spikes that the poor jaguar had experienced. First things first, he decided, and he laid his pistol down on the deck.

"There, I put my gun down... see?" Nate said, trying to keep his voice from cracking, but failing. "Please don't shoot me. I just want to talk to you."

The alien did not move, but its eyes did change color to bright purple.

Nate continued, "I don't mean you any harm, and I'd like to think maybe you don't mean me any harm either? Any chance we could try to communicate here?" He made gestures with his hands, attempting to imply that a back-and-forth conversation would be welcome. "And by the way, thank you for saving my life."

The Apprentice did not offer any response. He remained perfectly still, staring at Nate with four eyes, the other four scanning the forest in case the jaguar came back.

"My name is Nathan." Nate tapped his chest with a finger and spoke playfully, as one would to a young child. "But you can call me Nate. My friends call me Nate. What is *your* name? Can we be *friends*? I am a scientist, here on a research mission*, just like you*... only I'm guessing you travelled a little farther to get here." Nate chuckled nervously as he realized the silliness of his tone. *I'm talking to a fucking alien, and I sound like Big Bird.* He resumed his appeals, trying to speak in a more normal, less childish tone.

"I suppose you have no idea what I'm saying, but you must be very intelligent, so I hope you understand I'm just trying to be friendly and communicate with you. Right?"

Still, the Apprentice did not respond. He remained stoic, staring at Nate. He tried desperately to convince himself to get on with the execution so he could return to his ship and complete the mission, but his minds were in turmoil and he found himself paralyzed, unable to proceed. Before him was the opportunity he had dreamt of and longed for his entire life. But he was forbidden to communicate with this man, and now was supposed kill him — because for a number of rational reasons, the leaders of his world had decided this was best for all under such circumstances. Awareness of the Aliens' presence on Earth by the Humans must not happen, at least not until the Humans were "ready" for such a leap forward... perhaps within several thousand years, if they hadn't killed each other off by then. But the

Apprentice wouldn't live for several thousand years, and even if the rules changed within his lifetime, there was no guarantee he would ever get back to Earth again. If he was going to abandon protocol and pursue his own agenda, it was now or never.

The Apprentice struggled in silence, his minds heatedly debating both sides of the issue. He tapped into his last shred of reason and convinced himself that he must abandon this fantasy and do what was expected of him. He could never get away with what he wanted to do, and even if he did, he would be miserable for the rest of his life if he had to lie to his superiors, family, and friends to conceal his wrong-doings. *I will do my duty. I will do what is expected of me.* These were his final thoughts on the subject. He would kill the man, but he could not bear to do the deed in close proximity.

The Apprentice broke his motionless stance and began to move. In a knee-jerk reaction, Nate gasped and stumbled backwards, falling to the deck and instinctively grabbing and raising the pistol. He pointed it at the alien and followed it as it walked sideways, like a crab, towards the backpack that was lying in the tall grass. *The specimen container. It wants the specimen container back!*

The Apprentice kept two sets of eyes on Nate while opening the backpack and retrieving the stolen container. Then Nate began speaking again.

"Yeah, I took that from your ship. I'm really, *really* sorry about that. Please, take it. I didn't mean to steal anything... I... I was just curious. Y-you know, *curious*?" Nate was stuttering and had lowered the pistol again. He felt certain the pistol was of little use against this thing, and would only solicit the sting of those nasty spikes if he tried to use it. He abandoned the pistol again and stood up.

"Look, I have sample jars too!" Nate said, walking over to a small pile of his containers and holding one up. Inside was a huge, bright-green beetle with sharp horns on its head. The alien still made no reply.

Now Nate was getting frustrated and angry, his fear giving way to determination to somehow make a connection. "Why aren't you responding?" he shouted. "I said I was sorry for stealing your sample jar, or whatever the hell that thing is!" He pointed at the object in the Apprentice's hand. "This is a pretty unusual situation we have here, me from Earth, you from... wherever the hell you're from. We should be trying to talk, compare biological samples we've collected, build a campfire and sing songs... *something*!»

Nate's sarcasm caught the Apprentice off-guard. He found it fascinating and amusing, and his eyes changed colors again to a mustard-yellow.

It's responding! Nate thought. *But are the changing colors in its eyes a means of communication or just an emotional response?*

"Your eyes, are you trying to tell me something with your eyes?" Nate inquired.

The Apprentice remained silent, his eyes turning jet-black. He let go of the container he had pulled from the backpack, and Nate gasped in amazement as, instead of it crashing to the ground, it stayed exactly where it was, floating in mid-air. Then the Apprentice lifted a holo-disc off his belt and held it out towards Nate. Before Nate could react, a fine beam of blue light shot out of the disc, landing on his bare forearm. He felt a sharp pain, like a bee sting, then the beam disappeared, leaving behind a tiny drop of blood.

"Ouch! What the…!" Nate blurted out, rubbing his tingling arm. "What was *that*?" he yelled, glaring at the Apprentice.

The Apprentice holstered the holo-disc and then abruptly departed, scampering across the clearing towards the forest with the retrieved sample container floating behind him. Nate shouted out angrily after him. "You tagged me didn't you?" he yelled, surprised at his boldness. "You son-of-a-bitch, you tagged me, and now you're just going to *leave*? I have a million questions… *please come back*!»

The thought of being tagged for some kind of study was frightening, but it made perfect sense to Nate. He had tagged many creatures in his lifetime, all in the name of science, but they were unaware of their being tagged and had no idea what was going on. Actually knowing that he might have just become the subject of alien research was a different story. *No biggie,* Nate thought. *I can have the tag removed, and I'm sure ARCA would love to study it!*

Then he considered other possibilities. *Oh my God, maybe it's not a research tag; maybe it's something else! Maybe it's an egg, and an alien will explode from my chest in a few days!* Nate was panicking now, scratching hard at the sore spot on his arm, but the tiny sliver the Apprentice had delivered there was too deep to reach with fingernails. It had already burrowed through his flesh and attached itself to the bone.

Nate looked up from his arm just in time to see the Apprentice reach the edge of the clearing, leap into the trees, and then disappear into the dense forest canopy. He snatched the pager off his belt and began typing a message to Pedro Escoval to come early and extract him from the site. He wondered why he hadn't done so already, and figured that he was just too freaked out to think of it amidst all the mayhem. He finished typing, but then hesitated before pressing Send; and then he deleted the message and put the pager back on his belt.

If he sent the message, Pedro would have to notify ARCA of the early extraction, and then Nate would have a lot of explaining to do — and he wasn't yet sure exactly what to say. He had no proof of his alien encounter aside from pictures of the spaceship, which really didn't look like a spaceship at all. He didn't want to be subject to intense interrogation without *some* solid evidence that he had truly met an extraterrestrial being, and that evidence was now headed rapidly back to its spaceship, presumably to depart Earth very soon. *No! I can't let it end this way,* Nate told himself. *I can't go home without pictures of that thing.* He marched into the forest and headed north, this time not forgetting to bring the pistol.

CHAPTER 20

The setting sun cast orange beams through the forest canopy as the Apprentice leapt through the branches. He would reach the transport in ten minutes, and as soon as it was dark enough, he would take off. From the sky, he would lock onto the microscopic tracking device that he had planted in the Human's arm and send an energy pulse to stop its heart. The pulse would also find the camera in the man's pocket and erase its contents. He would also send a pulse to the man's camp, to seek out and erase any digital evidence of the encounter the man might have recorded on his devices there. As he made haste, the Apprentice fought his conscience, trying to ignore the dread and remorse he felt.

When he reached the ship, the Apprentice wasted no time. Once the remaining sample containers were properly stowed in the cargo bay, he secured himself into the cockpit and sat motionless in the floating chair, trying to calm down as he waited for the cloak of night to come. He engaged the external viewer and the walls of the cockpit disappeared, revealing a panoramic view of the Amazon sunset, ablaze in the sky beyond the dark silhouette of the forest. The launch computer's holo-display indicated forty more minutes before there would be sufficient darkness to depart unseen.

When the countdown reached eight minutes, a warning popped up on the holo-display: the proximity sensors had detected a large biologic approaching from the south. *The feline? Or the Human? Probably the Human*. The sensors locked in and displayed a Human form, confirming it was the man he'd tagged. *He followed me back!*

The image on the holo-display hesitated when it reached the edge of the clearing, but then came abruptly out of the forest and headed straight for the ship. As Nate approached, the Apprentice saw him clearly on the external display. He was not brandishing the pistol, although it was clearly visible, attached to his belt. He held an illumination device — *a flashlight,* the Humans called it — and was pointing it at the ship and appeared to be yelling something. The Apprentice switched on the external audio sensors to hear what Nate was saying.

"I know you're in there! Please, I need to talk to you! What did you put inside me?" Nate was holding his arm out, pointing at the mark where the probe had entered. "Look, I'm not just some bug you can tag and turn loose, we do have doctors you know, I'll have this thing cut out and you won't get any data! You'll learn a lot more about me if you just come out here and *talk to me!*»

The Human thinks the implant is for research. It has no idea of its true purpose. The Apprentice was entranced, completely mesmerized by this curious man's pleas.

"I'm a scientist, damn it, I know why you're here! You're a scientist too! You came here to study us! So come out here and *study me!* And take this stupid thing out of my arm! Think of the things we can learn from each other! I have so many questions to ask you! *Don't you have questions for me!?*»

The Apprentice could not bear to listen any more. So much of what he yearned for was being offered, and he could take none of it. He switched the audio sensors off and proceeded with the launch sequence.

Nate tried to get closer to the ship but again encountered the odd, tingling force field that had halted his progress when he had first discovered it; only this time, the force-field's perimeter was further out. The containers he had found earlier were gone, so he was sure the alien had returned and loaded them up, and was now inside the spaceship. Then Nate felt the ground begin to vibrate under his feet, and a low-pitched hum began coming from the ship. It left its stationary hovering position and slowly began rising farther off the ground. Nate shook a pointed finger towards the craft, shouting even louder as it rose above the clearing.

"Don't leave! You can't just show yourself to me, shoot a probe into my arm, then leave without the courtesy of a hello, or nanu-nanu, or SOMETHING! They're going to lock me up for being a *lunatic* over this, you know! The *least* you could do is make it *worth my while!*»

Nate was angry. He began picking up fist-sized rocks and chucking them up towards the departing ship with all his might. It was a childish thing to do, he realized, but he was quite sure he could cause the ship no harm, and it felt good to release some frustration. As he suspected, the rocks bounced harmlessly off the force-field and fell back to the ground.

Then one rock bounced directly back at him, hitting him square on the forehead and knocking him over backwards.

Nate lay on the ground dazed, blood streaming down his face from the wound above his left eyebrow. The Apprentice saw this and his eyes turned dark yellow with guilt and remorse. He had not intended for the man to suffer any duress or pain beyond the brief sting of the implant. *This is out of control,* he thought. *I must end this now*.

Groggy from the blow, Nate perched himself on one elbow and held a hand to his forehead to gingerly feel the wound. Blood, dirt, and sweat were trickling into his eyes, making them sting so badly that he could hardly see. He stood up on shaky legs and used the sleeves of his shirt to wipe the mess off his face, and then looked back up towards the rising ship. It was very dark now, and he could barely make out the silhouette of the craft about two hundred feet above him. The blow from the falling rock had knocked the flashlight out of his hand, but he quickly located it and pointed it skyward, just in time to see the spaceship shoot silently towards the stars. There didn't seem to be any acceleration; one moment it looked stationary and then it was departing at an incredible speed. Nate shouted again, but this time with sadness instead of anger in his voice. "Please, don't go! I'm sorry I yelled at you, please come back!"

Nate kept pleading at the sky, knowing it was useless but feeling the need anyway. After thirty seconds, he fell silent and let out a deep sigh, but continued to stare up at the spot where the ship had disappeared.

Suddenly, a thin beam of white light shot down from high up in the atmosphere and landed on his forearm, exactly where the implant had entered. Nate froze, staring at the beam of light on his arm for a second; and then he felt a powerful but numbing jolt, like he'd just stuck his finger into a light socket, only there was no sharp pain, just a strong tingling sensation. The numbing quickly spread from his arm to the rest of his body, and the strength in his legs disappeared along with his sense of balance. He tried desperately to extend his hands and break his fall, but could no longer control them, and collapsed to the ground onto his back.

Nate lay motionless, managing only to stare straight up at the stars — and then he felt his heart stop. Images of Tracie and Dewey flashed through his mind, then images of numerous occasions throughout his life, both happy and sad. It seemed to Nate an eternity, but within seconds he felt his conciseness start slipping away. He felt no physical pain, only the emotional duress of deep sadness and confusion.

Just before his vision faded completely, he saw a shooting star streak across the heavens, and he wondered if it was his alien executioner, leaving for home. "Why did you do that?" Nate whispered the words with what little breath he had left. «Why couldn't we have been friends?" Then he stopped breathing, and his body went completely limp.

CHAPTER 21

After a long day's work at the Tampa Aquarium, Tracie Johnston had taken Dewey for a walk, treated herself to Chinese delivery and two glasses of sauvignon blanc, and then gone to bed early. Nate would be calling in on the sat-phone around nine, so she figured she'd get an hour's snooze before talking to him. She placed the phone on the bed next to her pillow so the ring would wake her, and within fifteen minutes she was sound asleep, snoring so loudly that Dewey left the room to find a quieter place to hunker down for the night.

She dreamt of lying in a field of soft grass surrounded by tiny Pomeranian puppies, all yapping gleefully and licking her face and nose. Suddenly the puppies disappeared, and she saw Nate standing naked at the edge of the field, holding Dewey in his arms. At first she cringed and chuckled nervously, trying to decipher the meaning of such a silly and perverse image. Then she noticed Nate's condition, and realized this had nothing to do with sex.

He was covered in dirty sweat, and his forehead was bleeding badly down onto his nose and cheeks.

He looked sad, tears streaming down, creating pink streaks in the bloody grime that coated his face. He leaned forward, kissed Dewey on the top of his head, and then gently set him down. Dewey ran to where Tracie lay and jumped into her arms, whimpering, smelling of sweat and blood. Suddenly a thin streak of white light shot down from above, striking Nate on his forearm, and next a bigger, blinding flash of light caused Tracie to wince. When she reopened her eyes, Nate had disappeared and everything around her was pitch black. The ground beneath her crumbled away into oblivion, and then she was falling into dark nothingness, clutching Dewey to her breast and screaming.

Tracie woke up in a cold sweat, her pillow and sheet soaked. Her heart was pounding. She glanced at the alarm-clock on the nightstand… ten thirty. Had she missed Nate's call? No, she was a very light sleeper… no way could she have slept through a ringing phone right next to her head. She checked the phone to see if she had missed a call or if any messages were waiting. Nate hadn't called. An empty, desperate feeling washed over her. It wasn't like Nate to forget to call when he had promised it… and the weird dream had her seriously freaked out.

She got up and threw on a robe, then called ARCA in London. She got a recording stating that the offices were currently closed, and to please call during normal hours or leave a message. *What time is it in London, anyway?* Then she remembered that Nate had given her Jason O'Rourke's cell phone number, in case of emergencies.

Jason was fast asleep next to his wife, Margaret, who was snoring loudly enough to vibrate the bed, when the sound of the bedroom door opening woke him. He had learned to tune out the frequency of Margaret's chronic snoring over the years, and could sleep through even her most violent episodes, but the high-pitched squeak of the old hinges was a dreadful intrusion at this hour… enough to rouse him and remind him of his continued failure to fix the matter with a simple shot of silicone spray. *I must pick up some bloody lubricant for those damned hinges today,* he thought, waiting to hear which of his children had decided, in the middle of the night, to have a need that couldn't possibly wait until morning.

"Papa?" a tiny voice whispered in the dark.

"What is it, buckaroo?" Jason responded softly to Owen, his seven-year-old son.

"Papa, your mobile has been ringing in the kitchen. It keeps ringing over and over and I can hear it through the floor. It woke me up."

Jason recalled he had left his phone plugged in to charge up on the kitchen counter. He must have forgotten to bring it to bed in case of an emergency call. He glanced over at the clock: 3:42 a.m. *Who the bloody hell is calling at this hour? Perhaps Nathan! Maybe Nathan has found the meteorite and is anxious to make a report!*

Jason stealthily crawled out of bed so as not to disturb Margaret, and tiptoed out into the hallway, gently closing the squeaky door behind him. Margaret stirred briefly and grunted, then resumed sawing logs. Owen followed his father down the hallway as his mobile phone began ringing again, detectable to Jason now without the snoring present. He quickened his pace and scampered down the steps to try and catch the call before it went to voicemail. He snatched the phone off the counter just as it stopped ringing. *"Damn!"* Jason hissed.

"Who was it, Papa?" Owen yawned.

Although the international number looked familiar, Jason didn't recognize it immediately. It certainly wasn't Nate's sat-phone or mobile — he had committed those to memory — but the call had come from the United States. "Some bloody American with no sense of international time-zones, I gather," Jason huffed. "Now back off to bed with you, young man, and don't wake your sister."

Jason watched as Owen disappeared up the stairs, and then he dialed his voicemail. There were three messages waiting, but before he could listen to any of them, the phone began ringing again. Another call from the mysterious American number. "Hallo?" Jason answered with a puzzled tone.

"Jason? Jason O'Rourke?" a female voice came over the line in a neutral American accent. She was audibly distraught, her voice shaking.

"Speaking. Who's calling please?"

"Jason, it's Tracie Johnston, Nate's wife. I'm so sorry to call at this hour, but ARCA is closed and I had to speak to someone."

"Yes, Tracie, of course. Nathan has spoken of you often, but I regret we've never met before. No bother at all. I thought perhaps you were Nathan calling. Is everything all right?"

"I'm not sure, but I'm scared, Jason. Nate was supposed to call me several hours ago from the sat-phone and he didn't. It's not like him to miss a call when he promises one. And..." Tracie fell silent.

"And what?" Jason inquired.

"Well... I don't know how to say this. You'll think I'm crazy."

"Nonsense, please tell me."

"I had a very strange dream. I know this sounds ridiculous, but I think Nate's in trouble."

Jason slumped into a bar-stool at the kitchen counter as Tracie described her dream in detail. *She's delusional,* he thought. *It was just a bloody dream, and missing one call is not a reason to panic*. Nate had missed his call to ARCA the day before as well, but Jason had attributed this to the side-trip he'd asked Nate to take to investigate the possible meteorite. The trip would have taken a good amount of time, and Nate would perhaps have returned to camp exhausted and collapsed for a good sleep. Jason told Tracie about the meteor sighting and Nate's agreeing to look for it, and suggested he might have fallen asleep before he had a chance to call her.

"He has *never* not called me right on schedule," Tracie argued. "And my dream... I just know something's wrong."

"I'm sure he just elected to postpone calls until tomorrow," Jason replied. "He has a gun, top-rank first-aid gear, the latest in rainforest survival equipment, and the best training available. Besides, he carries a GPS locator and a satellite pager with him at all times to signal us and his guide if he runs into trouble. All he has to do is press one button, and help will be on the way to his precise location within hours. I'd wager he got back to camp late and didn't want to wake you. I'm sure he'll call first thing when he gets up."

"Jason, I know my husband. He would have called me last night if he was able, even if it was late. He wouldn't just fall asleep without calling first. And what if something prevented him from pressing the pager button? I know it sounds silly and superstitious, but this dream I had... it was so *real!* I'm really scared, Jason. Can you please try to reach him on the sat-phone? And if he doesn't answer, call the guide and have him check on Nate right away?" Tracie pleaded.

"Of course, of course I will," Jason conceded. The dream seemed preposterous and he was sure Nate was okay, but he could sense the fear in her trembling voice and saw no harm in appeasing her. "I need ARCA's satellite uplink to place the call. I can't do it from my cell, but I'll get washed up and go in to the office right now and look into this, and I'll call you as soon as I find out what's going on. And please call me back if you do hear from him first."

"Thank you, Jason. Please hurry, and call me at any hour."

Jason rinsed off briefly in the shower, then dressed and quietly departed as to not wake anyone. He left a note for Margaret, not wanting to interrupt her symphony of snoring. In route, he began to feel guilty for dismissing Tracie's concerns so quickly. The Amazon was a very dangerous place, and she was right; good men do not simply dismiss phone calls to their wives, and Nate Johnston was a good man. Worry set in, and he let his foot get a bit heavier on the petrol pedal, keeping an eye out for London's finest, who would have little better to do at this hour than issue him a speeding citation.

Forty minutes later, Jason pulled his Range Rover into the gated garage at ARCA Headquarters and hurriedly worked his way through security, up to the Rainforest Research Department, and into the Sat-Com Room. No one else would be there until nine. It was 1 a.m. in the Amazon, so the automatic upload from Nate's field-computer should have been received an hour ago. Jason sat down at a holo-monitor station and fired up the link to Nate's expedition, checking the most recent data. The upload had completed on schedule, but there was nothing new since the previous upload. *Nate had made no new entries at all in 24 hours*. Now Jason was truly

worried. Even if the side-trip to the meteorite location had prevented Nate from collecting any new
specimens, surely he would have had *something* to
report. No way could a scientist go 24 hours in uncharted rainforest without having discovered anything worth sharing.

Jason patched into the sat-phone at Nate's
camp. The computer at the camp was in sleep-mode
at this hour to conserve power, but the incoming call
brought the system to life and sounded the alert.
Nate didn't answer. Jason engaged the remote cameras so he could see the inside of the hut and the
surrounding area in the clearing. The monitor screen
in the shelter cast a dim glow about the space, and
Jason could see the cot at the far end of the room
— but Nate wasn't in it, or anywhere else within the
cameras' fields of vision. Jason let the phone ring for
five minutes, in case Nate had stepped out for a wee
or whatever. But Nate still didn't return to the dome
to get the phone, nor was he answering it remotely
via the GPS unit.

As the phone continued ringing, Jason pulled
up the GPS locator display and looked for the hand-
held unit's location, but after thirty seconds of
"Searching" flashing across the display, the words
"Target Not Found" appeared. "That's not possible,"
Jason scowled as he uttered the words out loud.
ARCA had spared no expense on the GPS unit. It was
top-of-the-line, latest technology, and rugged as a
brick. Even if Nate had tossed it off a cliff into a river,

it could not have malfunctioned. Yet there it was on the screen, "Target Not Found."

Jason made four quick phone calls. The first three were to rouse his senior tech staff and get them into the office early. The fourth call was to Pedro Escoval's mobile phone.

———⫷⬤⫸———

Pedro Escoval was in Labrea, fast asleep on his cousin's sofa, when his phone rang. "*Sim, isto e Pedro,*" Escoval answered groggily.

"Hallo, Pedro? Thank God I got through to you! Jason O'Rourke at ARCA calling from London."

Escoval converted from Portuguese to his Latin-accented English. "Yes, yes, Jason, hello to you. It is early, is everything okay?"

"No, Pedro, I'm afraid not. I need you to go look for Nathan. He's not at the camp, at least not that I can see on the cameras, we can't reach him, and he hasn't checked in on schedule. Has he paged you at all?"

Escoval rolled off the sofa and located the pager Nathan had given him. He checked the screen, but saw no indication that any page had been received. "No, I have not received any pages. Can't you track his GPS on the satellite?"

"Tried that. We can't locate its signal. How fast can you get back to the camp?"

"I will get my men up. They're sleeping on the boat, so it won't take long to get ready, and we'll be off within an hour. We should reach where we set up the camp in about ten hours from now."

"Thanks, Pedro, please hurry. When you get to the camp, your mobile phone won't work, so call me on the sat-phone inside the shelter — there are instructions for use on the housing unit. If you don't find Nathan at the camp, there should be a map in the camp's database of where I think he might be. It's about a mile and a half north of the camp. Once you call me on the sat-phone, I'll walk you through how to pull up the map."

"A mile and a half? What the hell is he doing that far away from the camp? That's very dangerous."

"Yes, I know… I know. I'll explain later, just please get there as fast as you can."

After hanging up with Escoval, Jason called Tracie to update her on the situation. He told her not to worry, that he was sending in the river-guide to find Nathan right away and would get down there himself as well. Regardless of his reassurances, Tracie was, as he had expected, worried sick. He then called the cellphone of Antonio Perron, his friend at the Brazilian Astronomical Society in São Paolo, the one who had asked Jason to send Nate looking for the meteorite in the first place. When Perron answered in a sleepy voice, Jason got right to the point "Tony, I think my man has had an accident looking for your meteorite. He's missing."

"Oh my God, Jason. This is very bad news, I am so sorry...what can I do?"

"I need you to pull some strings and get a chopper and some soldiers with a medic out there to look for him."

"Of course, I'll get right on it. I hope he is all right. I feel terrible about this."

"Me too, my friend. I've never lost anyone on an ARCA expedition before, and I don't care to start now. I just e-mailed you the coordinates of his camp, and you already have the location of where the meteor may have impacted. That's where I sent him. Odds are he's somewhere between the two."

As Jason ended the call, the staff he had called in early began to arrive. He briefed them on the situation and instructed them to monitor the GPS and sat-phone around the clock, and to continue trying to reach Nate. They were to report to him immediately with any news. And then he was on his way to Heathrow to catch the next flight to Brazil.

CHAPTER 22

The Apprentice shuddered with remorse and guilt. It had been only moments since he had sent the energy pulse to terminate Nate's life, and the mandated act was having a far worse effect on him than he had anticipated. It wasn't as if he were eradicating the species, or even compromising it in any way. One less Human was certainly no threat to their existence. But he had felt a connection with Nate in a way he never imagined. Not only had Nate tried to communicate with him, he had expressed things — *emotional* things — that the Apprentice himself could relate to. And Nate's final words kept ringing repeatedly in the Apprentice's minds...

I'm a scientist, damn it, I know why you're here! You're a scientist too, you came here to study us! So come out here and study me! And take this stupid thing out of my arm! Think of the things we can learn from each other! I have so many questions to ask you! I can speak... I can communicate and tell you things that no other life form on this planet can. Don't you have questions for me?

And he *did* have questions. So many questions

that he would love to have asked a real Human, not to mention a scientist from the species. The Apprentice wondered if Nate had left behind a family. He appeared to be of the age when most Human males had a mate, a "wife" as they called them, and perhaps offspring to return to in a village or city somewhere. Did Nate love his mate and offspring as much as the Apprentice did his own? Nate didn't look to the Apprentice to be native to the Amazon rainforest, and the technology he possessed seemed more advanced than what typical Amazon dwellers had, so presumably he had travelled far to be there and conduct his research. As a scientist, Nate probably worked in a similar, albeit very primitive place to the research complexes where the Apprentice himself worked back home. He and this Human came from different corners of the Universe, but were similar in so many ways. *And the Apprentice had just killed him.*

Once again, the Apprentice was torn by the conflict of following orders or following his hearts. It wasn't right. It wasn't right at all that he should have to kill such a fascinating being simply to remain anonymous to the rest of its species, especially when his own mistakes had led to the tragic situation. He was overcome with remorse for following such a cruel directive. He couldn't imagine living the rest of his life harboring such guilt. *No, I cannot leave it this way. I cannot just let that man die because of things I caused through my own neglect!*

The Apprentice could no longer ward off his conscience. He was going to try to undo what he had
done, and would suffer whatever consequences he
must. With any luck, he could resurrect Nate, con-
verse with him for a while (while pleading to Nate to
keep it all in confidence) and then hide all this from
everyone back home. The guilt of living out his life in
such a lie, or being discovered in it, he could learn to
live with. The innocent man's death by his hands, he
decided, he could not.

Nate's heart would have been stopped for a few
minutes now, so while the Apprentice was sure he
could bring him back to life, he would have to act
quickly to prevent damage to Nate's brain and other vital organs. He disengaged the travel computer,
pulled up the manual holo-controls, and turned the
ship around. It was still early night in the Amazon,
and there was thick cloud-cover over much of the
basin; perfect conditions for a stealthy approach. He
sped back to the clearing as fast as the craft could go
without creating a heat-signature.

As soon as the transport was securely gravity-an-
chored, the Apprentice disembarked and scampered
to where Nate lay motionless on his back. A quick
scan with a holo-disc calculated the energy-pulse
needed to start his heart beating again, and additional pulses to other vital organs required to accel-
erate their recovery once blood-flow was restored.

Nate's extremities jerked repeatedly as the
pulses struck. A few seconds later, his chest heaved

upwards and he gasped, drawing in a deep breath. His eyelids fluttered and then slowly opened, and he put his hands to his chest, clutching clumsily at the fabric of his blood-stained shirt. He took several more deep breaths and then sat up abruptly, opening his eyes wide but apparently unable to focus immediately. After a long moment, the Human finally realized he was not alone, and stared up in astonishment at the eight purple eyes looking down at him.

CHAPTER 23

Nate was weak, groggy and disoriented, without a clue where he was or what he had been doing. Everything was dark, and he was lying in tall grass. His chest felt like it had been the target of a well-swung sledgehammer, and his head wasn't much better. A whirlwind of bizarre thoughts swirled haphazardly though his mind as he noticed what looked like eyes, big purple ones, staring down at him from several feet above. But they *couldn't* be eyes... *nothing* had big purple eyes like those... and eight of them, no less. *Think, Nathan.* He forced himself to brainstorm for answers. *Where the hell are you, and what were you doing here?*

As he strained to think, more bizarre thoughts came. *Trees, rainforest, collecting bugs, a jaguar, something strange... strange and alive... strange and from another planet... chrome football... an alien ship... an alien chasing me!* It all came back in a flood and he sat up. He was in the Amazon collecting specimens and Jason O'Rourke had sent him looking for a meteorite but he had found a *spaceship* instead and the ship's occupant had saved his life from a jaguar and then killed him anyway. Had the alien changed its mind and revived him? Was he really still alive, or was this just a dream from beyond life as he knew it?

Nate stared at the alien, who remained still and silent. After a few minutes of staring, Nate began to feel his strength return, and he mustered the energy to try and stand. His legs wobbled, but he managed to get up. "You killed me, didn't you?" Nate said quietly. "Then you came back and brought me back to life. Why? Why did you come back?"

The Apprentice did not respond, but this time, instead of remaining perfectly still, he slowly moved about Nate, studying him up close with all eight eyes as Nate continued to speak.

"What's your name? Where do you come from?"

There was still no response. *Maybe it's trying to talk to me telepathically?* Nate theorized. *It doesn't appear to have a mouth of any kind.* He was sure that it wanted to communicate; they just needed to figure out a common language.

The Apprentice *did* want to communicate with Nate now, but he was unsure how to do it. He could not vocalize in Human speech patterns. All he could do was use the Earth's thin atmosphere to make noises with his communication holes or offer sign language, neither of which the Human would understand. He decided to at least acknowledge Nate's gestures with audible responses. He sucked some air into the blowholes around his torso and volleyed out a brief sequence of Alien words.

"Breet-biuuuu-twooot-prrrrrrft!" Earth's atmosphere was thinner than the Purple Planet's, so the sounds were higher-pitched than they would have been back home.

Nate recoiled slightly as the alien's first sounds came from the small orifices about its mid-section. He had not noticed the holes before — they weren't visible when shut — and Nate's first thought was that they resembled a row of dog butts in a chorus of high-pitched flatulence. "Did you just fart at me, or is that how you talk?" Nate said, then chuckled nervously, figuring this might finally be an attempt at conversation. *Oh my God, maybe they communicate by smell!* If that were the case, Nate was sure he could never decode alien language by smelling their farts, nor did he want to try.

"Seeeurt-hoooorth-whraaaaa-eeeep," The Apprentice responded.

"Okay, I'll assume that *is* how you talk then." Nate replied. "My name is Nathan… Nathan… Nathan." Nate tapped his fingers on his chest.

The Apprentice understood. "Nathan" was the designation of the Human, his name. He needed a better means of responding than using his blowholes, so he studied the small devices that were attached to Nathan's belt. One of them appeared to have an adequately-sized display screen. It was very primitive technology, but he could work with it. He approached Nate and extended a hand, aiming its long, writhing fingers towards Nate's waist, causing Nate to recoil with apprehension.

"What are you doing? You wouldn't hurt me again, would you?" Nate asked nervously. He was terrified, but decided to trust the alien and stopped retreating, firming up his posture in anticipation of the first physical contact. Like seven miniature elephant trunks, the Apprentice's nimble digits gently probed the GPS unit on Nate's belt. Then Nate stiffened even more as the alien firmly grasped and tugged at the device.

"You want to see this?" Nate inquired. He unclipped the GPS from his belt and held it out.

"Nyuuuus-yrtiiiip," the Apprentice chirped as he grasped the GPS from Nate's hand.

"You're welcome."

The Apprentice studied the GPS, and then a thin beam of white light shot out from a holo-disc and encapsulated the unit in a hazy glow. After thirty seconds, the beam vanished and the Apprentice handed the GPS back to Nate. It felt hot in Nate's hand. Nate looked at it, puzzled, then looked into the alien's eyes and shrugged his shoulders inquisitively.

"Laadriiip-dfroooj-beorp," the Apprentice bleated, and pointed a finger at the screen on the GPS.

Nate looked down and gasped in astonishment. There on the display of the unit, in bright green letters, were the words "YOUR NAME IS NAYTHIN." As he read the words, the Apprentice reached out and tapped Nate's chest with a finger, mimicking Nate's gesture when he was introducing himself. Nate felt chills sprint up his spine and his flesh erupted in goosebumps. He wondered if this might truly be the first time any Human being had spoken with an extraterrestrial. *Probably not,* he thought, *but it sure feels like it*!

"Yes… YES!" Nate laughed out loud, holding back tears of joy and triumph. "My name *is* Nathan, but you can call me Nate…my *friends* all call me Nate."

"FOR FRIENDS YOUR NAME IS NAYT." the display on the GPS read, but the Apprentice was no longer vocalizing as the words appeared. "FRIEND NOW IS NAYT."

"You can understand me? How are you doing this?" Nate asked, pointing at the GPS display.

«YES, I UNDERSTAND THE WORDS OF HUMAN LANGUAGE: ENGLISH. BRAINS OF I ARE CONNECTED TO THESE DEVICES." The Apprentice tapped his holo-discs. "THE DEVICES TRANSMIT MY WORDS TO DEVICE OF NAYT.»

«*Brains*? You have more than one?"

"I HAS FOUR BRAINS."

"Well, *that* figures. Amazing! How do you understand English? Have you spoken to people on Earth before?"

"I HAS … HAVE STUDIED HUMANS FOR MUCH TIME. I HAVE NEVER SPOKEN TO HUMANS. I DID NOT COME TO EARTH BEFORE NOW. OTHERS BEFORE I HAVE COME TO EARTH BUT THEY HAVE NOT SPOKEN WITH HUMANS, ONLY SPOKEN TO OCEAN

AIR BREATHERS HUMANS DESIGNATE: CETACEANS.»

Nate paused, chewing on these word a moment before replying. "Your kind has been to Earth before… and they didn't speak to Humans but they spoke to *whales*?"

"YES SPOKE TO WHALES BUT NOT HUMANS."

"I don't understand. Why would you speak to the whales but not to us?"

«SPEAKING TO HUMANS IS VIOLATION. I VIOLATE DIRECTIVE SPEAKING TO NAYT.»

A Prime Directive! Nate thought. His years of watching *Star Trek* as a kid had some educational value after all. The alien wasn't allowed to speak to Humans, but this one was breaking the rules. *Why?*

"So, now you know my name, what is *your* name?"

«HUMANS CANNOT PRONOUNCE NAME OF I.»

"Well, I have to call you *something*. Just *I* is way too boring and impersonal."

"ACCEPTABLE. SOMETHING IS NOW NAME OF I TO NAYT.»

"No, I mean I need to… well… *give* you a name that I can pronounce. *Something* is not a name."

«WHAT NAME NAYT GIVE I?»

Nate rubbed his chin and thought for a moment. *Not every day you get to name an ET!* He smiled and looked at the Alien.

"Dewey. I'll call you Dewey."

«DUE NAME OF I." the Apprentice tapped his torso.

Nate laughed. "I see you understand me perfectly, but you must have flunked spelling. It's D-E-W-E-Y, Dewey. And Nate is spelled N-A-T-E."

«ACKNOWLEDGE CORRECT SPELLING OF DEWEY AND NATE. DEWEY IS NAME OF I WHO IS NOW FRIEND OF NATE. WHAT IS MEANING OF NAME DEWEY? DEWEY IS A NAME WITH SIGNIFICANT MEANING?»

"Yes, yes it is. Dewey is a good name," Nate laughed. "Dewey is the name of a very famous little duckling, a famous organizer of libraries, *and* my wife's little dog."

«YOU SELECT NAME OF INFANT AQUATIC AVIAN AND CANINE COMPANION FOR I?»

"It *is* kind of cheesy, isn't it? I'm sorry." Nate felt embarrassed for what he had just done; he had just named the most intelligent creature ever to walk on the planet after a cartoon duck. "I was just shooting from the hip without thinking. We can choose another more appropriate name for you. Something a bit more sophisticated."

«NOT NECESSARY. NAME DEWEY IS ACCEPTABLE. I IS … AM PLEASED WITH THIS NAME. DEWEY IS NOW NAME OF I … MY NAME TO FRIEND NATE.»

Nate cracked a big, toothy grin. He felt giddy and he tingled all over.

"Well then, it's settled." Nate said "While visiting Earth, you are Dewey. My friend, Dewey... *Dewey the Alien.*»

CHAPTER 24

Jason O'Rourke had managed to book a direct flight out of Heathrow to São Paolo on short notice. He would arrive in ten hours and take a regional flight to Porto Velho, where he would hire a helicopter to take him into the Amazon Basin to hook up with the *Juanita Linda*. He desperately hoped that by the time he arrived, Escoval and his crew would have already located Nate, and he would be fine. But Jason wasn't counting on this, and he feared the worst.

This rescue effort would likely cost ARCA a small fortune, and Jason had not bothered to call its chairman, Alan Mercer, for approval. He was quite sure Mercer would not hesitate to approve; ARCA had deep pockets, and was always very generous when it came to taking care of its affiliates. But Jason didn't want finding Nate to be delayed by red tape, so he'd left London for Brazil immediately and would justify the expense to Mercer and the board later. Besides, he didn't want to report to the Board until he knew for sure what had happened to Nate.

While Jason was in route, Antonio Perron was

running into roadblocks getting any cooperation from the Brazilian military. He had called the army's regional Commanding Officer in Porto Velho, who told him that budget cuts had put tight strings on resources like helicopters and med-evac crews. And there was little sympathy for a vagabond American scientist who had risked the many perils of the Amazon on his own and now needed to be rescued. Who would pay for this? Brazilian taxpayers? The United States government? ARCA was not known to this C.O., and Perron could not convince him that this "ARCA" would gladly cover the expense. But Perron persisted, and he would not allow the C.O. to end the phone call.

Instead, Perron tried a new approach and told the C.O. the potential value of a large meteorite impact to the world's scientific community. He was sure to mention that the area must be carefully searched and guarded, as any surviving fragments of the meteorite would be the property of the Brazilian government, and if found by civilians or ARCA, might end up for sale on the black market for who-knew-how-much money...perhaps tens of thousands of *reales*. That did the trick. The C.O. hesitated, but then told Perron he would dispatch a chopper as soon as one could be made available, probably within several hours, and he himself would go along to help in the search.

Meanwhile, Escoval had arrived at the river port in Labrea just as daylight broke. He roused his crew from their hammocks on the *Juanita Linda* and briefed them on the situation. After quickly fueling up and gathering some supplies, the men untethered the boat and its twin engines churned the brown water, heading upriver at top speed. Escoval perched himself in the wheelhouse, lighting a cigarette and slurping coal-black coffee as he manned the rudder, and he muttered angrily in Portuguese at his first mate. "That idiot, Jason O'Rourke, he sent Nathan a mile and a half from the camp into the forest by himself! And Nathan was a fool to do it. Suicide! You don't *fuck* with the forest. You fuck with the *forest,* it fucks you back!"

As agitated and angry as Escoval was with Jason and Nate for such a risky undertaking, mostly he was frightened for Nate's safety. Normally, he didn't care that much about anything, but the lucrative retainers he received from ARCA... if they got careless and one of their researchers was injured or killed in the rainforest, it would be *their* fault, not his, and he would get paid anyway. But he liked Nate, more so than anyone else ARCA had sent before, and now he feared for the life of his friend.

CHAPTER 25

Now that Nate and Dewey the Alien had figured out how to communicate, they were both anxious to learn as much as they could about each other. They sat on the ground next to Dewey's ship, Nate cross-legged and Dewey squatting, curving his legs into arches that propped his torso upright. A segment of the ship's outer surface cast a beam of soft, blue light on the two, so Nate could see Dewey clearly in the pitch-black of the Amazon night. Dewey had done this for Nate's benefit, since he didn't need light to see, which amazed Nate.

"Where do you come from?" Nate began the conversation.

Dewey replied on the modified GPS screen, "DEWEY COME FROM DIFFERENT GALAXY. SOLAR SYSTEM OF TWELVE PLANETS. WE LIVE ON THE SEVENTH PLANET," he said, pointing a finger down at the ground, indicating that his galaxy was currently off the far side of the Earth.

"A different galaxy? You don't come from within the Milky Way?"

«NOT FROM GALAXY: MILKY WAY. DEWEY IS FROM DIFFERENT GALAXY.»

"How is that possible?" Nate said in disbelief. "Even at the speed of light, wouldn't that take millions of years? *How can you travel that far?*" Nate was no astrophysicist, but he understood the basic principles and obstacles of deep space travel — at least, what had been laid out in layman's terms by the likes of Newton, Einstein, Hawking, and Koiku, *An organic life-form simply couldn't survive traveling that far or that fast. Could it?*

Dewey responded, "MUST USE COMPOUNDED ACCELERATION OF SPACE SEGMENTS THROUGH PASSAGES USING GRAVITATIONAL FORCES TO TRAVEL TO THIS GALAXY.»

"Compounded acceleration of… gravitational what? How does *that* work? Is it like a wormhole, a short-cut through the space-time fabric?" Nate tried to sound as smart as he could on the subject, brainstorming to remember everything he had ever heard from his astrophysicist peers at the University… or the Science Channel.

«NOT IMPORTANT FOR NATE TO UNDERSTAND THIS. NATE AND HUMANS CANNOT DO THIS NOW. TAKE MILLIONS OF YEARS FOR SPECIES OF DEWEY TO LEARN THIS. MANY DIE. HUMANS NOT READY.»

"But I *want* to understand. *We* want to understand! If there are other civilizations out there, we need to know how to reach them someday! What is the basis of your travel technology? What are these space-segments? *How do you propel the ship?*»

"VESSEL TRAVELS NEAR LIGHT SPEED INSIDE SEGMENT OF SPACE. THAT SEGMENT TRAVELS NEAR LIGHT SPEED INSIDE ANOTHER SEGMENT OF SPACE WHICH TRAVELS INSIDE ANOTHER SEGMENT. MILLIONS OF SEGMENTS COLLAPSING AND EXPANDING. VESSEL HAS NO PROPULSION. ALL MOVEMENT CREATED BY GRAVITATIONAL FORCES BETWEEN VESSEL, SEGMENTS OF SPACE, STARS, PLANETS, AND SINGULARITIES."

"Holy crap, I think I get it. So you guys are harnessing the forces of gravity from everything in the Universe to pull yourself around inside segments of space. And those segments can move around within each other, like a giant telescope, at just under the speed of light. And *that* would compound the velocity of the innermost segment, with your ship inside it...to *way faster than light-speed! But,* your ship would actually be travelling *under* the speed of light inside the inner segment!" Nate was amazed at his theory, silently congratulating himself for what he had just said. Not bad for a biology major! "But... how do you get the space segments to collapse and expand?"

Dewey straightened up, perplexed that Nate actually understood the basic principles of his travel method. But he didn't intend to share any additional details, so he changed the subject, commenting instead on Nate's statement that Humans would visit other civilizations *if* they had the technology.

"NOT IMPORTANT FOR HUMANS TO KNOW THIS NOW. HUMANS DO NOT HAVE THE ABILITY YET TO ACHIEVE THIS AND THERE ARE NO OTHER INTELLIGENT CIVILIZATIONS DISCOVERED YET FOR HUMANS TO VISIT, ONLY DEWEY AND NATE SPECIES.»

«*No other civilizations?* You mean you guys are the only other life out there besides us? Come on — there are billions of galaxies, trillions of stars, gazillions of planets, there *has* to more life in the Universe than just your planet and ours!"

"YES THERE IS MUCH LIFE. BUT ALL OTHER LIFE DISCOVERED YET BY SPECIES OF DEWEY IS PRIMITIVE. NO CIVILIZATIONS. NO TECHNOLOGY.»

Nate was stunned as he read the words on the GPS screen.

"Dewey, I just don't understand." Nate looked up at the stars as he spoke. "You're telling me that with all that's out there, your people and mine are the only intelligent species in the Universe?"

"NO NATE DEWEY DID NOT SAY THAT THERE ARE NO OTHER INTELLIGENT SPECIES. WE EXPLORE MANY STARS IN MANY GALAXIES BUT NOT ALL YET, THERE ARE MANY LEFT TO INVESTIGATE. NO OTHER INTELLIGENT SPECIES EXCEPT HUMANS HAS BEEN FOUND YET. DEWEY SPECIES HAS SEARCHED FOR 75 MILLION YEARS."

"Seventy-five million —! But there *is* more life out there, you said?"

«YES MUCH LIFE.»

"Here in the Milky Way?"

"SO FAR 483,974,008 SPECIES FOUND IN MILKY WAY BUT NOT ALL PLANETS EXPLORED YET.»

"What, 484 million! Holy crap! Man, would I *love* to see some of them. It's what I do, you know — I'm a biologist. I look for and study new life forms, mostly insects and spiders. So far you're the coolest one I've found."

«IS SAME FOR DEWEY. DEWEY IS APPRENTICE BIOLOGIC SCIENTIST SENT TO EARTH TO COLLECT NEW SPECIMENS.»

"Including Human specimens?"

«NOT COLLECT HUMAN SPECIMENS. APPRENTICE, NOT QUALIFIED YET FOR HUMAN STUDY. DEWEY ONLY STUDIES LIVING HUMANS ON PLANET OF DEWEY. PERHAPS ON ANOTHER MISSION DEWEY WILL BE ALLOWED TO STUDY HUMANS ON EARTH.»

Nate read the words twice, then a third time before replying. "You… have living Humans on *your* planet?"

«CLONES OF HUMANS CULTURED FROM HARVESTED DNA." Dewey immediately questioned himself for telling Nate this. He was so far beyond the boundaries of protocol he was dizzy with internal conflict. But he had come this far. There was no turning back now unless he killed Nate, and that was not going to happen… again.

Nate fell silent for a moment, pondering Dewey's shocking disclosure. *Dewey's race has been cloning Humans from DNA, in another galaxy millions of light years away. How are they getting the DNA? They had to be abducting, maybe even killing Humans to harvest it! Or worse yet, were they taking the captured Earthlings with them?* Nate shuddered at the thought of how this whole business was going down. And he worried perhaps that Dewey's hospitality was a ruse and he was actually being seduced as a DNA donor. *Nonsense! If this creature wanted to abduct me, it would just do it; there would be no need to mess around like this. And he already killed me once; if he wanted only my DNA, he would have it by now.*

Nate asked, "Dewey, how do you get the DNA for the clones?"

Dewey was afraid to answer. Bugs and fish don't ask for an explanation of how they are harvested for research, so he had no prepared statement for such a question. What Nate was asking about might be very unsettling to him. Dewey did not want to create a rift in this new relationship, but he decided that if he was going to trust Nate, then he must get Nate to trust him as well. He decided he would answer honestly, but he would have to lay some ground rules first.

«NATE FRIEND, DEWEY WILL ANSWER YOUR QUESTIONS BUT MUST FIRST SECURE TRUST. THIS INFORMATION IS NOT FOR ALL HUMANS. THIS IN-FORMATION IS ONLY FOR NATE.»

"I understand, Dewey. You do not want me to share anything you say with anyone."

«YES IT IS VERY IMPORTANT. DEWEY SHOULD END LIFE OF NATE TO MAINTAIN PROTOCOL. DEWEY DOES NOT WISH FOR LIFE OF NATE TO END. DEWEY LIKES HUMANS AND ENJOYS FRIENDSHIP WITH NATE. DEWEY WISHES TO ANSWER ALL QUES-TIONS AND ALSO ASK MANY. DEWEY MUST TRUST NATE AND NATE MUST TRUST DEWEY IN ORDER TO PROCEED.»

"Dewey, I promise, I will not tell anyone of our meeting or anything you tell me. Except perhaps my wife. Is it okay if I tell my wife?"

"NO OTHERS MAY KNOW WHAT DEWEY TELLS NATE. DEWEY CANNOT TRUST OTHERS BESIDES NATE.»

"But I have to live with her, you know, and it's difficult to live with someone you love while keeping secrets from them. She trusts me to tell the truth, and I'm not sure I could ever lie to her about this."

«WIFE IS MATE OF NATE ALWAYS FOR LIFE OF BOTH?"

"Yes, that's the plan. Not all Humans are able to stay together that long, but Tracie and I… well, we are very much in love, and we trust each other. I can't lie to her about this, Dewey." Nate began to wonder if he was playing with his own life. If Dewey didn't like this answer, perhaps he would decide to follow protocol after all.

«DEWEY UNDERSTANDS TRUST OF MATE. DEWEY UNDERTSTANDS LOVE. DEWEY HAS MATE AND DEWEY TRUSTS MATE. CAN NATE TRUST MATE

CALLED TRAYCE?"

"It's T-R-A-C-I-E, and yes, I can trust her."

«DEWEY WOULD ENJOY MEETING TRACIE."

Nate laughed out loud. "I'm sure she would just love it if I brought *you* home for dinner. You have too many legs and eyes — she'd probably puke on the spot! She's more into fish; she's a marine biologist."

Dewey didn't completely understand why Tracie would "puke" at the sight of an Alien, but he deduced from Nate's laughter that the comment was mostly meant to entertain, and perhaps was exaggerated to achieve that end. This pleased Dewey immensely, that this Human was comfortable enough to speak so openly and casually, and he *was* entertained. His eyes shifted between several colors as he relaxed and took unparalleled pleasure in opening up his own inner thoughts to Nate.

"DEWEY LIKES HUMANS. DEWEY STUDIES HUMAN CLONES BUT LIKES EARTH HUMANS MORE. DEWEY HAPPY TO HAVE NATE AS A FRIEND."

"Well, you could have fooled me, the way you stuck that thing in my arm and then zapped the shit out of me!"

«OBJECT IN ARM OF NATE WAS FOR LOCATING NATE TO KILL ONLY. DEWEY ONLY KILLED NATE FOR PROTOCOL. DEWEY WAS NOT HAPPY TO DO THIS. DEWEY RETURNED AND GAVE LIFE BACK TO NATE. DEWEY APOLOGIZES.»

"Apology accepted. I am very grateful that you came back and saved my life. Now tell me about these Human clones. How did you get the DNA? How often have you guys been here?"

Dewey explained how the Aliens had discovered Earth and its abundant life millions of years ago, and had been visiting ever since to gather specimens for study at the Intergalactic Zoo. Nate was thrilled to learn that this included many species now extinct on Earth, including dinosaurs (!) though they apparently hadn't managed to collect DNA from any of the hominids that preceded *Homo sapiens.* Dewey went on to explain that larger creatures had always almost always been cloned from DNA samples, as they were simply too big to transport efficiently; but smaller examples, say anything smaller than a buffalo, were captured and taken back alive. Over time, however, it became apparent that to the more intelligent mammal species such as dolphins, primates, and Humans, the experience was quite traumatic, rendering them mentally unstable and unsuitable for study. So the Aliens abolished the practice and had begun cloning all but the lesser species such as insects, birds, and fish ever since.

Dewey also mentioned that although this cloning-only policy was far more compassionate to the subjects, it also made it difficult for scientists to study certain species accurately, as the clones never acted quite the same as their DNA donors in their natural environments. This downside was especially problematic with the cetaceans and Humans, as these were the species the Aliens found the most intriguing of any they had ever encountered. Thus, research trips to Earth were still a hot priority to the Aliens' scientific community, and every Alien scientist yearned to be chosen to come here.

Nate listened with an open mind, fully understanding the scientific reasoning behind the methods of study. But the thought of Aliens stealing DNA samples to clone Humans was unsettling, not to mention that these clones would live in a zoo, millions of light years from Earth. Nor did he like that these Humans were probably completely unaware of their true origins, or their purpose as inter-galactic lab rats. But he wasn't sure what he could possibly do about it. As the far superior creature, Dewey had the upper hand here, and Nate did not think it wise to stage an impromptu Human rights protest under such unbalanced circumstances. So he shelved the subject for the moment, and moved on to other topics.

The conversation went on through the night, Nate and Dewey learning of each other's homes, lives, and routines, and the relationships they had with family, friends, and colleagues. They discussed the amazing similarities between Human and Alien culture, as well as the vast differences. Nate listened with amazement as Dewey described different life-forms on his own planet and many others the Aliens had discovered across the Universe. Dewey showed Nate three-dimensional images of the creatures, projected from a holo-disc.

Having no such technology, Nate could use only words and hand gestures to paint his pictures, except for the laminated photo of Tracie and Dewey the Pomeranian, which he always carried in his shirt pocket on expeditions. Dewey was fascinated by the image, intently studying the features of Tracie's face and her tiny dog whose name he now shared.

Suddenly, without warning, one of Dewey's holo-discs projected an image that looked like a radar screen. There was an ominous red dot on the floating display, flashing and moving slowly in a wide circle around the center of the image. Dewey stood abruptly and scanned the sky with three pairs of black eyes, his fourth pair turning yellow and remaining affixed on the red dot in the holo-image.

"What is it, Dewey?" Nate was alarmed.

«NATE FRIEND, DEWEY MUST NOW LEAVE EARTH." Without any further fanfare or explanation, Dewey scurried towards the transport and Nate saw a circular portal appear in the side of the ship.

"But why? I still have more questions, you can't just leave now!"

«OTHER HUMANS COME WITH ATMOSPHERE TRANSPORT DESIGNATED: HELICOPTER. IT IS SEARCHING THIS AREA.»

Nate stood up, alarmed. "They found you? I thought you told me we can't find your ships with our technology, that you had some gizmo or something to make you invisible to radar?"

«NOT POSSIBLE TO DETECT TRANSPORT OF

DEWEY WITH RADAR BUT PERHAPS OTHER HUMANS SAW HEAT TRAIL OF ORIGINAL ENTRY INTO ATMOSPHERE. OR PERHAPS OTHER HUMANS ARE SEARCHING FOR NATE."

Nate gasped, realizing that Dewey was right. In his bewilderment of the past twenty-four hours, he had completely neglected to communicate with the outside world. He hadn't called ARCA or Tracie as scheduled, and they would both be extremely worried. "*Shit!* It's Jason!" Nate exclaimed. "Someone *did* see your heat-trail, Dewey. Jason sent me to look for a meteorite, which turned out to be a spaceship... *your* spaceship! When I didn't touch base, Jason must have gotten worried and sent someone looking for me!"

Dewey didn't reply; he was circling the transport, quickly inspecting it for departure while continuing to monitor the approaching object on the holo-image.

"Dewey, take me with you!" Nate blurted.

Dewey stopped in his tracks, astonished at what he had just heard. Then he resumed preparing for his departure while responding to Nate's odd request. "FOR WHAT PURPOSE DOES NATE WISH TO GO WITH DEWEY?»

"I want to talk to you some more. I still have a million questions. Besides, I need time to figure out what to say to everyone — I can't deal with other people right now. I need to think this through."

«NOT POSSIBLE FOR NATE TO TRAVEL WITH

DEWEY TO HOME OF DEWEY.»

"Not *home* with you, just… just take me some-where else for a while. So I can come up with a story they'll believe."

"CANNOT DO THIS. DEWEY MUST LEAVE EARTH ATMOSPHERE TO ESCAPE HUMANS NOW. DEPARTING WHILE SUN IS ILLUMINATING THIS SIDE OF EARTH MEANS THERE WILL BE VISUAL DETECTION AND HUMAN TRANSPORTS WILL FOLLOW DEWEY IF DEWEY STAYS IN ATMOSPHERE."

"Okay, so we have to leave Earth for a while. Maybe you can show me some life on other planets or something, *then* bring me back at night?" Nate could hardly believe the words coming out of his mouth. *Had he really just asked an ET to take him for a little spin around the galaxy?* But as insane as it seemed, the request was legitimate. He *was* a bi-ologist, and the thought of joining Dewey on an in-terstellar field trip was exciting. And he wasn't lying about not wanting to face anyone just yet, either. If he was going to conceal this episode from Jason or anyone else, he needed some time to get his act together and come up with a very convincing story.

«NOT POSSIBLE. NATE CANNOT SURVIVE IN TRANSPORT BEYOND EARTH ATMOSPHERE. NO OXYGEN. TOO COLD. NO GRAVITY. TRAVEL TOO FAST FOR HUMAN TO ENDURE. NATE WOULD DIE.»

Of course, you moron, you forgot to pack your spacesuit, Nate silently chastised himself, fuming in frustration as the red blip on Dewey's holo-disc image got closer. Then he remembered the specimen containers that Dewey had been using to collect small creatures. "So, you're telling me that with all the technology you have on this ship to bring home live specimens, you have no way of giving me a ride and keeping me alive?"

"TRANSPORT NOT EQUIPPED TO SUSTAIN ANYTHING AS LARGE AS HUMANS. PERHAPS YES CAN MODIFY BUT NOT HAVE TIME NOW. DEWEY MUST LEAVE IMMEDIATELY. DEWEY VIOLATE ENOUGH PROTOCOL ALREADY. DEWEY CANNOT TAKE NATE FROM EARTH.»

"Okay, I understand," Nate conceded, letting out a big sigh of disappointment. "So then, I guess this is it. Will I ever see you again?"

The thumping of the helicopter was getting louder now, cutting through the sounds of the forest and causing Nate to nervously scan the sky. Dewey stepped over to where Nate was standing and met his eyes with two of his own, which turned deep lavender.

«DEWEY GO NOW BUT HAPPY TO HAVE BECOME FRIEND OF NATE. DEWEY THANKS NATE FOR INFORMATION ON HUMANS AND EARTH. DEWEY WILL REMEMBER NATE WITH GREAT JOY.»

"You too, my friend."

«PLEASE CONFIRM THAT DEWEY CAN TRUST NATE. NATE MUST NOT TELL HUMANS OF DEWEY. EXCEPT FOR TRACIE WIFE.»

"You got it, pal, I promise. Don't forget to write."

«WHAT SHOULD DEWEY WRITE?"

Nate laughed out loud at Dewey's gullibility. The helicopter was very close now, causing birds in the forest canopy to become agitated and raucous.

"Never mind that." Nate shouted over the nervous chatter of the birds. "It's just a silly Human expression. You'd better go! Goodbye, Dewey!"

«GOODBYE NATE MAY THE CREATOR BE FAVORABLE WITH YOU.»

The Creator? Nate thought about the farewell message as he watched Dewey reach into the transport's portal and pull himself through. Then the portal closed and resealed itself. *What did he mean by "The Creator?"* Nate had expected something along the lines of Spock's infamous "Live long and prosper," or Obi-Wan's "May the Force be with you." Something like that. *But instead. it's «May the Creator be favorable with you?"* Did Dewey's people believe in a Creator... in God?

Their conversation hadn't had time to hit upon religious beliefs, nor had Nate even considered bringing up the topic. Nate had assumed that Dewey's species would have a more scientific approach to things than the notion of a universal Supreme Being. The word "Creator," however, could only imply that there was something or someone that Dewey's species recognized as superior to themselves. But Dewey's last words were inconclusive, and now he was leaving.

The low-frequency hum of the ship's gravity

amplifiers rattled Nate's bones as the transport abandoned its hovering position, rising into the afternoon Amazon sky. The thumping of the helicopter was getting louder by the second, and then the helicopter suddenly appeared, racing towards the hovering spacecraft.

"Oh crap, they've seen the ship." Nate muttered.

CHAPTER 26

It had been earlier that evening when the *Juanita Linda* arrived at the tributary where Escoval and his men had escorted Nate into the forest. They anchored near the riverbank and used the launch to navigate up the tributary to the spot where they had unloaded the gear, then quickly made their way towards Nate's camp, shouting out for him along the way; but there was no reply. When they reached the clearing, everything appeared intact and in good order, but Nate wasn't there to greet them. The men spread out, frantically searching for signs of him or what might have happened to him.

Nate was nowhere to be found, not in the shelter nor anywhere near the clearing or in the surrounding forest. Upon closer inspection of the camp, it became evident that something had gone wrong. Nate's backpack was found lying on the ground just outside the shelter, and there was evidence of a struggle in the grass and mud. A closer look revealed Nate's footprints and the tracks of a large animal. A jaguar had been there, inside the pyramid! But there was something else: in the mud were odd impressions, patterns of seven dimples, as if something with large, seven-toed feet had been walking on the tips of its toes. The marks were too big to have been from Nate's hands, and were unlike any animal tracks they had ever seen before.

Escoval and his men were puzzled. Despite their vast experience in the rainforest, none of them could explain what had happened here, other than perhaps the jaguar had killed Nate and dragged him off. But there was neither blood nor dragging marks in the mud or grass to support that theory, so they remained hopeful that Nate was still alive and had just left camp, without his backpack, to pursue the meteorite impact site.

Escoval went back into the hut and moved the computer's mouse to activate the monitor screen. As Jason O'Rourke had promised, it was displaying a map of the area, and there was a flashing red dot about a mile and a half to the north. That would be the location where Jason wanted the men to search for Nate if they didn't find him at the camp.

The sound of an approaching helicopter drew Escoval back outside, where he found his men waving and shouting as the chopper came into view. It appeared above the trees to the south, then flew directly to the clearing and slowed down to a hover above the camp. Escoval recognized the craft: it was a Brazilian reconnaissance unit, equipped to extract fallen soldiers from conflict, and endowed with significant firepower for self-defense. A soldier wearing a white helmet and dark sunglasses leaned out the open side-door, brandishing a bullhorn.

"Professor Nathan Johnston—is he there?" the soldier shouted down in Portuguese to Escoval and his men through the bullhorn.

Escoval waved at him, shaking his head no and pointing north. The soldier nodded in acknowledgement, and then the chopper departed rapidly in the direction Escoval had pointed. Escoval rallied his crew and led them into the forest to follow. *Hopefully*, he thought, *the chopper can find Nate and extract him before we can*. But he wanted to be there as well, in case Nate was invisible under the canopy somewhere, or not near anywhere that the chopper could safely land.

CHAPTER 27

Colonel Enrico Santos had been skeptical about going on a wild-goose chase after a lost American scientist. It was quite foolish, he felt, for this "ARCA," whoever the hell they were, to have sent anyone into the Amazon alone, regardless of how much survival gear they were packing. Santos had only recently been promoted to Field Commander, and at the core of his new duties was managing the Brazilian military's assets in the Amazon Basin on a shoestring budget.

His first reaction to the call from Professor Antonio Perron at the Brazilian Astronomy Institute was to brush it off. No way was he going to spend taxpayer's money to hunt down this vagabond biologist. *An American fool! He is on his own!* he had told Perron. But when Perron had explained the possible meteorite impact and its significance to science, as well as the potential monetary gains for anyone who discovered pieces of such a meteorite, he had changed his attitude.

If there *was* a meteorite impact and fragments had survived, it would serve him well politically to put Brazil in the spotlight of such a discovery. And if there was some money to be had on the side from the sale of any fragments he pocketed, all the better… he could certainly use a financial windfall. Santos was a good and honorable man, but recent economic setbacks had hit his family very hard, and he could not pass on any opportunity — no matter how underhanded — to improve their lives, so long as nobody was harmed. And he was sure no one could be harmed by his covertly collecting a few fragments of space rock and selling them on the black market. If the meteorite was as large as Perron had estimated, there should be plenty left for the government to seize without them noticing anything missing.

Santos commandeered a medevac-equipped recon-assault helicopter that had been doing live-ammo training near Porto Velho. He instructed its crew to meet him at the airbase near his office, and after refueling, the chopper took off with Santos onboard, headed towards the coordinates ARCA had provided to Perron. They would first survey the missing American's campsite to see if perhaps he was still there, injured or even dead. Then they would fly north to the area where Perron had said the meteorite might have hit.

When the chopper arrived at Nate Johnston's camp, Santos and the crew marveled momentarily at the security pyramid surrounding the most modern-looking rainforest research outpost they had ever seen. There was no one who re-sembled an American scientist visible in the clear-ing, but there were several local men waving up at them, one pointing frantically to the north. *The American's river-guide and his men,* Santos assumed, and he shouted down to them with a bullhorn, confirming that none of the men were Professor Nathan Johnston. When the man in charge shook his head "no," Santos acknowledged with a thumbs-up and then instructed the pilot to head north in the direction the guide was pointing.

"The American must have gone in search of the meteorite, exactly as Professor Perron pre-dicted," Santos told the crew. "It will take the riv-er-guide over an hour to get there. Let's find the American first, in case he is injured." In reality, he wanted to find the meteorite, if it existed, before Escoval did.

Two minutes later, the chopper reached the coordinates Perron had suggested, and Santos in-structed his crew to slowly cover the area in a grid pattern. After five minutes of scouring the forest with binoculars, one of the crew shouted out that he had spotted something up ahead. As the chop-per closed in on where the crewman was pointing, a strange distorted image seemed to rise above the treetops out of a large clearing. The distor-tion was shaped like a curved, prolate mirror, re-flecting the images of the trees below and the sky above, but oddly it was not reflecting any blinding light where the direct sun hit it; rather, the image of the sun on the object appeared as a dull orange ball. "What the hell is *that*?" Santos shouted.

"I don't know, sir," was the response from all three crewmen, adrenaline surging as they shouted back and forth through their helmet com units.

"I've never seen anything like that before!"

"Unknown aircraft, no wings or rotors, there doesn't appear to be any propulsion mechanism, it's just floating up out of the clearing!"

"It must be a balloon of some kind, then," Santo reasoned.

"I don't think so, sir. I've never seen a balloon like that way out here, and its surface is too perfect to be fabric or Mylar. It must be made out of some kind of polished metal."

"Then it has to be a foreign aircraft of some type that is here unauthorized, something new we haven't seen before. Probably looking for the meteorite. Try to hail it!"

The co-pilot called out on all open frequencies, "Unidentified aircraft, you are in violation of restricted Brazilian airspace, acknowledge and identify!" No answer. The co-pilot repeated the message twice more. Still no reply.

"Arm weapons!" Santos shouted. He wasn't sure this thing was a threat, but he didn't want to take any chances.

As the chopper's side-mounted machine-guns and rocket-launchers came online, a beam of bright-blue light suddenly shot out from the shiny object and touched the helicopter's nose. The four men panicked as a network of tiny blue sparks started spreading throughout the cabin. When the terrifying sparks reached their feet and began to spread up their legs, their panic became all-out hysteria. "We're under attack!" the pilot screamed in horror as the co-pilot targeted the strange object on the missile guidance system. The third crewman manned a machine-gun mounted in the cabin and swung the barrel of the weapon out the open side-door in the direction of the odd craft.

"Get us out of here!" Santos yelled.

"I can't! I've lost control! It's not responding!" The pilot was fighting the stick as it shook violently in his hand.

"Fire, fire, shoot it down!" Santos screamed.

In a frenzy, the crew threw everything the helicopter had at the UFO. The side-mounted machine-guns and air-to-air rockets, as well as the manual machine-gun in the cabin, all fired simultaneously in a massive burst of flashes and smoke. But before any bullets or missiles could get more than a few meters from the chopper, the beam of light touching the aircraft's nose expanded into a giant globe of glowing energy, encapsulating the chopper and all the ordinance it had just fired. The rounds hit the inside wall of the bubble, either detonating instantly or ricocheting back towards the helicopter, creating a fiery holocaust of explosions inside the globe that instantly disintegrated the chopper and its crew. But no debris fell to the ground; rather, it was all contained within the ball of energy, which began to constrict around the flaming mass.

CHAPTER 28

Nate watched with horror as the spectacular scene unfolded right above him. The Brazilian military helicopter had arrived just as Dewey's transport was lifting off, roaring straight at it. Nate saw the beam of light shoot from the Dewey's ship to the nose of the chopper, and then the chopper's weapons swivel to take aim at the ship and fire. Instantly, a giant bubble of crackling energy surrounded the chopper, causing the rockets and bullets to ricochet and explode, engulfing the hapless helicopter in an inferno within the bubble.

The bubble now resembled a small sun floating above the clearing, radiating intense heat and glowing bright orange. As Nate stared in disbelief, the bubble began to contract, getting smaller and smaller, squeezing the chopper's flaming remnants into a smoldering, globular mass. When the bubble had squished the incinerated debris down to the size of a beach-ball, the globe of energy and the thin beam from Dewey's ship disappeared. The white-hot ball of compacted material plummeted to the ground in the middle of the clearing, exactly where Dewey's transport had been hovering just moments ago, the impact creating a shower of hot dirt and rocks that rained down on Nate. A large rock struck him directly on the forehead, knocking him to the ground. "Not again," he moaned.

Nate picked himself up and brushed the dirt and blood off his face and forehead, but the wound quickly covered his face with blood again. He could feel intense heat coming from the spherical mass, formerly the helicopter, that lay in the shallow crater it had created. The heat was enough that the new grass surrounding the crater was smoldering and turning black, blending in with the grass that had already been singed by the overheated hull of Dewey's ship several days previously. Nate looked up to check on Dewey, and saw that his ship was still hovering above the scene. *Why hasn't he left yet?* Then Dewey sent a message to his GPS screen.

"IS NATE OKAY?"

"Yes... yes, I think so." Nate shouted up towards the ship. "Just a cut on my head."

"DEWEY CAN FIX INJURY."

Before Nate could respond, a small metallic sphere descended from the ship to where he stood and hovered in front of him. A beam of light came off the sphere's surface and passed over the wound on his forehead. Nate felt a tingling sensation, then a slight sting as the gash on his head closed and cauterized.

"What happened, Dewey? Why did you destroy

the helicopter?"

«DEWEY IS SORRY FOR HARMING HUMANS IN HELICOPTER. NOT ABLE TO PREVENT PROTOCOL: AUTOMATED DEFENSE SYSTEM DETECTED WEAPONRY ENABLED BY HELICOPTER AND NEUTRALIZED IT. DEWEY MAKE NEUTRALIZED HELICOPTER SMALLER SO NATE WOULD NOT BE INJURED WHEN IT FELL TO GROUND. DEWEY HOPES NATE IS SAFE. DEWEY MUST GO NOW. GOODBYE NATE FRIEND.»

Without further delay, the ship shot skyward at an insane speed and disappeared into the clouds. Nate just stood there, staring back and forth at the sky and the demolished helicopter in a blank daze for the next hour, unable to come to grips with what he had just witnessed. His emotions were off the charts, ranging from the exhilaration of having just befriended an extraterrestrial to deep remorse for the men who had died in the helicopter. He was unsure how to feel about Dewey's killing them in order to protect himself from the chopper's weapons. Yes, it *had* been self-defense, but the helicopter was probably sent by ARCA to look for Nate... to *save* him from whatever trouble he had fallen into. There was no way those men had any idea they would be confronted by an alien spaceship on their fateful rescue mission. *It wasn't their fault! They didn't deserve to die!*

Then Nate heard someone shouting in the distance behind him, and turned to see Pedro Escoval and his deckhands come crashing through the forest into the clearing. They began running towards him. Then Nate heard the thumping of another helicopter approaching, and seconds later it arrived over the clearing and slowly descended to land in the grass nearby. This one wasn't a military unit; it had civilian markings and lacked any weaponry.

Just as Escoval and his men reached the spot where Nate was standing, the door of the helicopter flew open and out stepped Jason O'Rourke. Jason, Escoval, and the men surrounded Nate, cheering, high-fiving and hugging him and patting him on the back, relieved that he was still alive and that he didn't appear too critically injured.

"My friend, you scared the *shit* out of us!" yelled Escoval over the roar of the idling chopper.

"Am I ever glad to see you, old chap!" exclaimed Jason. "What the bloody hell happened here?" He was now looking around at the smoldering grass and small crater with the glowing-hot globule at its center. "Looks like there was a meteorite after all!"

"Yeah... a meteorite." Nate nodded his head as he spoke, frantically concocting a quick narrative on how to explain the scene. "Your astronomer friend was right, Jason, there *was* a meteorite after all. Still hasn't cooled off. I was checking it out, and I guess I got too close and got dizzy from the heat. I slipped and fell and hit my head on a rock pretty hard. I must have I passed out... I don't remember much after that."

Nate was lying about what happened, but he

didn't have to fake being groggy from a blow to the head. He felt like crap, looked like he had been rolling around on the ground, smelled awful, and the blood that covered his face and shirt from the wound on his forehead helped him sell the concept quite well.

Then Jason looked a bit puzzled and inquired, "But why is the meteorite still so bloody hot? Shouldn't it have cooled off after 72 hours?"

Nate shrugged. "No idea. I wondered that too, but not my expertise."

"Not mine either, but it seems very unusual. Oh well, we'll let Antonio and his astronomer pals figure that one out. You're in no shape to continue your expedition. Let's get you out of here and fixed up, shall we?"

"Yes, please!"

Before departing, Jason asked Escoval if he and his men could pack up the campsite and bring ARCA's gear and the specimens Nate had collected back to Porto Velho. "Yeah, no problem," Escoval replied cheerfully. "By the way, has anyone seen the other helicopter?"

Jason and his pilot shook their heads. "Nope," the pilot said. "ATC lost radio contact with them an hour ago. They must have gone searching in the wrong area far from here, or else we'd have seen them for sure. Their radio must have quit or something, and they were probably flying too low for radar to pick them up way out here."

Nate pondered for a moment how he could ever

rationally explain that the white-hot, smoldering mass lying in the charred dirt at the center of the clearing was *not* a meteorite, but the missing helicopter. He hated lying. *But what choice do I have?*

"What other helicopter?" Nate said, manifesting his best puzzled expression.

CHAPTER 29

Nate called Tracie two hours after arriving in Porto Velho. He had wanted to call her as soon as the chopper landed, but Jason had insisted on a visit to the local hospital first for a look at Nate's head wound. The doctor was dumfounded that the gashes on Nate's forehead seemed to have closed themselves without stiches, and aside from some surface grime and dried blood, seemed quite clean. It would never cross his mind that an extraterrestrial had been Nate's field medic, and Nate did not volunteer this information.

He did have a mild concussion from the rock hitting his head, and a variety of minor cuts and bruises; but aside from that, Nate seemed to be in perfect health, and the doctor quickly dismissed him from the Emergency Room. Jason secured a two-bedroom suite at a nearby hotel, where Nate quickly showered before using the privacy of his bedroom to call Tracie on Jason's cell, while Jason made travel arrangements for Nate to get back home.

At first, Tracie broke down with tears of joy, telling Nate how happy she was that he was okay. But then she became coy and slightly angry, and scolded him for neglecting to keep in touch and worrying her so much. Nate didn't mind the lecture; he was just happy to hear her voice. He could hear little Dewey the Pom yapping angrily in the background, and he laughed with glee, realizing that he missed that little shit almost as much as he missed his wife. He was comforted by the familiar ruckus of Tracie's admonishing tone and Dewey spazzing out over whatever at the top of his tiny lungs. Twenty-four hours of facing death and interacting with an alien had changed his perspective on life, and now he appreciated these things more than ever.

"I'm really sorry, Hon. I screwed up. A lot happened here these past few days. I'll tell you about it when I get home," Nate said apologetically. "I love you and the Dew-poof so much. I can't wait to get home and snuggle up on the sofa with you guys."

Tracie's tone softened to a playful sneer at Nate's candor. "Well, I could just strangle you for worrying me so much... but we love you too, and we can't wait for you to get back. But I'm not done being pissed, so when you get home I'll probably have to torture you for a while yet. And Doo-Doo wants to bite your leg and poop in your shoes."

Nate laughed gleefully at Tracie's sarcasm. It was one of her traits he adored most, and welcome therapy for the angst he was feeling. He told her again that he loved her and was looking forward to his punishment, and then said goodbye and hung up the phone.

Meanwhile, Jason had finished booking Nate's flights, and was now arranging for ARCA's gear to be shipped back to London. Nate emerged from the bedroom and collapsed on the sofa, letting out a big sigh. "Everything good?" Jason inquired.

"Yeah... everything is really good, all things considered. I just want to be home now."

"Well, it's all set, then!" Jason exclaimed as he shut down the laptop. "You leave for São Paolo in the morning, and your flight to the States departs the following morning. You'll be home in time for supper with your wife the day after tomorrow. I'll stay here and oversee getting the gear shipped back to London."

"Thanks, Jason, I really appreciate it. I'm sorry again for all the trouble I've caused you. This can't be cheap."

"Nonsense, all in a day's work for ARCA, old chap. Besides, it was *my* idea to send you on that silly meteorite hunt; I should have told Perron to forget it and get someone else. I'll explain it to the board and all will be fine, I'm sure. Besides, they will be thrilled we actually did find a meteorite... and a rather odd one at that. They love this kind of thing, you know. And from what Escoval tells me, you managed to gather a decent collection of new samples before all this mayhem started."

"Yes, I did. I'm pretty sure there are a few new ones we haven't seen before. But I wish I had found more… I feel terrible that I lost so much time after hitting my head."

"We'll check them out back at the labs in London and let you know, and if you want any of them, I'll send them back to your office for you after we catalog them. Now off to bed with you, and get some sleep. Long travel day tomorrow."

Nate thanked Jason again and retreated into his bedroom. He was exhausted, unable to remember exactly how long it had been since he had slept soundly. Within minutes he was out, dreaming of Dewey the Alien. He imagined amazing adventures for Dewey and other Aliens of his kind, exploring the Universe many light-years from home, in search of new life. What a cool life *that* would be.

CHAPTER 30

Dewey piloted his ship at top speed to the Earth Station behind Jupiter. He couldn't stop thinking of Nate and everything that had happened in the rainforest. He *had* managed to fulfil his lifelong dream, to interact and communicate with a real Human, and it had been every bit as satisfying as he had imagined... but at what cost? He had violated so many protocols that he was afraid to go home, and the loss of Human life on the helicopter was beyond tragic, the remorse unbearable. *Will the Creator punish me for this?*

He hoped not. The deed was done, and there was nothing he could do about it now but beg the Creator for forgiveness, and do whatever he must to conceal his insubordination when he returned home. *In fact*, he contemplated, *now that I have already violated so much protocol, why stop now? What difference will it make if I continue?* He was instantly ashamed of himself for thinking such things again after the consequences of his first escapade, but he couldn't help it. He had learned so much about real Humans during his brief encounter with

Nate, and he longed desperately for more.

As he docked with the station, Dewey vibrated with excitement at the thought of spending more time with Nate. He had left the Amazon prematurely because of the helicopter, so he still had another week before he was due back home. He had already gathered enough specimens in the rainforest to justify the trip, so there was no need to go back and gather more. He desperately wished to seek Nate's company again. How could he resist? He knew now that he couldn't. *But how would he do it*?

Dewey's conscience tortured him mercilessly as he scampered about the station, plotting how he might go back to Earth and find Nate. He felt out of control, as though he were watching himself doing something reckless, desperately trying to talk himself out of it... knowing full well it was pointless, and that the defiant plan would continue despite all reason and logic against it.

He took inventory of all resources he had available between his transport's supplies and the equipment in the station's storage bays, and then he worked for three days building the contraption he needed to carry out his new plan. When the device was complete, he pulled up a holo-image of Earth and initiated a long-range scan to search for Nate's current location. He had never removed the implant from Nate's arm, so he could easily track it anywhere on the planet. After a while a tiny red blip appeared, far from where he had left Nate in the Amazon. It was on the large peninsula that stretched south off the east side of the North American continent.

He moved the specimens he had collected in the Amazon from the ship's cargo bay to the station's storage area, making space on the ship for his newly constructed device before departing the station on a course back to Earth. Once there he orbited the planet several times, waiting until it was completely dark over North America.

After an uneventful descent, the ship slowed to a halt as it neared Nate's location, and then hovered two miles directly above the signal. The area was reasonably remote and void of Human aircraft traffic, much to Dewey's relief, and appeared to contain mostly personal dwellings that were arranged in rows amidst pockets of forestation. It was what the Humans called a "subdivision," according to the database, several miles north of the large city of Tampa.

This was far closer to any Human city than Dewey had been authorized to get on this mission. From this height, he could see a great deal of Tampa and its outlying areas, and he was mesmerized by the panoramic image, the countless twinkling lights creating a soft glow about the cockpit. The rivers of flowing white and red lights from the Humans' wheeled transports gave organic life to the scene, swirling around the city's fixed structures like the lifeblood of a massive, living thing. Back home he had only seen holo-images of such things… and it was far more thrilling in person. What must New York or, better yet, Hong Kong seem like from this height?

After allowing himself another moment to gaze at Tampa, Dewey shifted his focus back to Nate's signal, directly below. Zooming in the display to get a closer look at the coordinates, it appeared Nate was inside one of the small structures... *this must be Nate's home!* It was one of numerous similar structures that were built in a row and backed up to a thickly wooded area. There were fewer lights here than in the big city, and there were no moving vehicles nearby; all seemed quiet and asleep. *Perfect!* Dewey scanned the woods behind Nate's dwelling and located a grassy clearing 200 yards into the trees, large enough to land the ship. Then, after a quick check to see if any Human aircraft were nearby, he manually navigated down to the clearing and brought the ship to a stationary hover several feet off the ground.

Dewey quickly disembarked and scampered through the woods, coming up behind Nate's home. The back of the house was about one hundred feet from the edge of the woods, and the nearly-full moon cast a revealing bath of light across the manicured grass; but there were several large trees in the yard as well, offering deep shadows that Dewey could hide in. He scanned for any life forms nearby. There were numerous Humans inside the neighboring homes, but none outside. Convinced there were no witnesses around, Dewey scampered across the yard up to the rear of Nate's house and crouched down in a tree's shadow.

Dewey scanned and mapped out the interior of the house, revealing a two-level structure with multiple chambers. There were three life-forms inside, one of them being Nate, all in a chamber of the upper level. Nate was lying on an elevated platform next to another Human... a female. *Nate's mate, Tracie!* The third reading was a small canine, lying motionless on the floor below Nate and Tracie. This, Dewey presumed, would be the little dog after which he had been named. *Dewey the canine! And I am Dewey the Alien!* This was far more thrilling than any day Dewey had ever spent studying Humans at the Zoo. And the fact he was doing so against practically every protocol of his training made it even more thrilling — though taxing on his moral compass.

Dewey left the safety of the tree's shadow and crept cautiously up to the back of the home. The lower level was not illuminated, so he used his radar vision to look through the windows, marveling at his first glimpse of a real Human habitat. Directly above him was a blue, pulsating glow coming from the window of the chamber where Nate was. *A television! Nate and Tracie must be watching a transmission on a television!* Dewey contorted the tips of his fingers and toes into suction cups, and he nimbly scaled the side of the house up to the bedroom window. He saw Nate and Tracie lying next to each other on their bed, facing away from the window so they couldn't see him gazing in. The tiny dog was curled up on the floor next to the bed, his snout tucked into his furry belly.

Dewey could not see Nate's eyes from this angle, and Tracie's head was covered by a pillow she had draped over her face, so he couldn't determine if they were awake or asleep. They were motionless, but their heads were facing the direction of the television mounted on the far wall, on which two Humans were sitting at a desk describing some current event. *A newscast,* Dewey concluded, recalling many recordings of these Human informational broadcasts he had studied. Unsure of how to make his entrance without being too shocking, Dewey decided the television could be useful in announcing his arrival. He removed a holo-disc from his belt and placed it flat against the window glass.

CHAPTER 31

N ate had not yet told Tracie about his wild adventure of meeting an alien in the Amazon, let alone that he had named it after their pet. He was still trying to figure out just how to present such a tale without sounding like a complete basket case. He *would* tell her, in time, but for the moment was content to just get back into his daily groove and reflect a bit on the things that had happened without having to do a lot of explaining.

The first night home was rough. Nate had been fidgety and unable to sleep at all, but tonight he was beginning to feel a bit more relaxed. He made love to Tracie, and soon afterwards they were both sound asleep in each other's embrace; but then Tracie woke up at midnight with an odd tingle in her abdomen and found herself unable to get back to sleep. She gently untangled herself from Nate and switched on the TV. The overnight news was on, and the anchors were describing some protest that had taken place in France... something to do with labor unions.

An hour passed and Tracie couldn't fall back

to sleep, but her eyes were fatigued from the TV's glare in the dark room, so she covered her face with a pillow and resumed listening to the news without watching it. She didn't see the thin beam of light that shot through the window behind her and landed on the TV. Nor did Nate, who had remained fast asleep through her brush with insomnia.

When the babble of the news anchor abruptly stopped and was replaced by static, Tracie figured it was just a glitch in the cable service, and the dialogue would resume in a few seconds — but it didn't. After a few minutes, she lifted the pillow off her face and peered towards the TV to see what had happened. For a moment, she lay motionless as she stared in disbelief at what was on the screen. The screen was completely black, save for the large white letters that stretched across it.

"NATE FRIEND DEWEY IS HERE. DEWEY HAS RETURNED TO VISIT NATE AND TRACIE. I AM HERE NOW."

"What the fuhhh..." Tracie mumbled under her breath, and sat up straight in the bed. As she stared in disbelief, the message on the screen changed.

«NATE FRIEND DEWEY WISHES TO RESUME INTERACTION. DEWEY REQUESTS PERMISSION TO ENTER HOME OF NATE.»

Now Tracie became panicked. Her heart was racing, and she felt chills. She reached for Nate and shook him. "Nate, wake up! Wake up *now*!»

"What! What is it?" Nate protested with a

groggy voice, his baggy eyes mere slits.

Tracie pointed at the TV. "Look at the TV! This is really freaking me out! What the hell is this?"

Nate stared at the TV, the impact of what was on the screen taking a moment to settle into his semi-conscious mind. Then, in an instant, he felt chills and became fully awake as adrenaline shot through his system. He sat up abruptly. "Oh my God, he came back. He's *here*!»

«*Who* came back? *Who's here*?"

Doo-Doo began growling on the floor. The commotion had aroused him, but it wasn't the odd image on the TV nor Nate and Tracie's babbling that was irritating him; he was acutely aware of an unfamiliar presence outside the bedroom window. His keen little eyes had spotted something just beyond the pane that was definitely out of place, something large, alive, and unsettling. He jumped to his feet and started growling more intensely, then broke out in a volley of snarls and barked angrily at the window. Tracie and Nate turned their attention to the Dewster, then to the window he seemed to be so pissed at.

The glow of the white letters on the TV screen projected just enough light through the window to see that there was *something* out there. An odd-shaped figure hovered just beyond the glass, vaguely visible, and Tracie thought she recognized a pair of large, black eyes, but no face. She screamed and jumped out of bed, retreating backwards until her back hit the wall.

"Nate, there's somebody out there! *Looking at us through the window!*" she shrieked.

Tracie's scream startled Dewey the Alien. He released his grip and dropped to the ground, landing firmly on the stone-paved patio. *Perhaps this was not a good idea*, he thought. *Has Nate seen the message? Has he not informed his mate of our encounter? Why was she so startled? Why did she make that loud noise? Why did Dewey the canine make all those loud noises? Will Nate be pleased that I have returned for more interaction?*

Dewey retreated to a tree's shadow and stood there motionless, wondering what he should do next. He contemplated aborting his plan and returning to the ship to head home, to be done with this reckless idea. Meanwhile, Nate had gone to the bedroom window to look for Dewey. He cupped his hands to the glass and scanned the back yard, but it was too dark to see anything. He turned towards his frightened wife and approached her, putting his hands on her shoulders.

"Who's out there? What did you see?" Tracie half-whispered, wanting to shriek it out but worried that whoever was outside would hear her.

"Hon, I have to tell you something that's going to sound... well, really crazy."

"Yes, this *is* crazy! Why are you so calm? *Go call the police!*»

"No, there's no need for that. Everything is fine."

«*Fine*? Nathan!" Tracie gritted her teeth, glaring at Nate. "There's someone outside our *fucking second-floor bedroom window! Go call 911*!»

"I... I can't do that. I *know* what... I mean, *who* it is... and that would *not* be a good idea."

«*Not a good idea?* What are you talking about? Who is it? Why would they climb up to our bedroom window in the middle of the night? And what's with this... *stuff* on the TV? *What's going on here*?"

"Honey, I met someone in the rainforest, someone... kind of different. Okay, really different. I thought he went home, but... well, I guess he's come back to visit me. Please calm down, and I'll explain."

"Nate, I can't be calm when someone is looking in our bedroom window in the middle of the night! You met him in the Amazon? That's a little far from home for a midnight social call!"

"He's not from South America. He's from..." Nate paused, completely unsure of how to put this. There simply was no other way than to just blurt out the truth. "He's from another planet."

"I'll say! This is bullshit, peeking in our window like that, scaring the crap out of me and Doo-Doo. And how the hell did he get up there, with a ladder?"

"No, you don't understand, honey. He really *is* from another planet. From another galaxy, in fact."

Tracie stared at Nate in silent shock. She had

heard the words, but they weren't registering. *Nate has lost his mind*, she decided.

Doo-Doo was still snarling at the window. Tracie pulled away from Nate's grasp and ran to grab her cell phone from the nightstand. Nate followed her, and as she began dialing 911, he grabbed the phone from her hand before she could complete the call.

"Nathan! *What's wrong with you*?" She was angry now.

Nate looked deep into his wife's eyes and held her hand firmly. "Tracie, my beautiful, *understanding* wife, please, I'm not making this up. When I was in the Amazon, I met an alien from another planet in a different galaxy. He came to Earth to explore and conduct research. He's a scientist like me... *like us!* His name... well I can't pronounce his real name, so I named him Dewey. We became friends, then he left before Jason found me. I thought he went home, but he's back. He's outside and wants to talk to me."

Tracie felt paralyzed for a moment, like a deer in the headlights, and then she became dizzy. But she managed a response, speaking very slowly, as if to someone who was heavily sedated — or mentally deficient. "There's an ET... Outside our home... That *you* met and named after our dog in the Amazon... and now he's looking into our bedroom in the middle of the night, and he... *it*... wants to *talk* to you?"

Nate nodded with a distant, forlorn look on his

face, then looked her in the eyes. "Yeah, I guess that about sums it up." He grinned sheepishly. "Pretty nutty, huh?"

"Baby, listen to yourself… *are you insane*? What you just described is impossible!"

"Maybe I *am* insane, but I am *not* making this up. I'm dead serious. I think Dewey the *Alien* is out there. And I need you to calm down for a minute while I go talk to him."

Tracie stood trembling, staring at Nate with wide, confused eyes. Doo-Doo, having heard his given name mentioned a few times in the tense conversation, had stopped barking and was looking at Tracie with his head cocked, confused as to what his role in all this excitement was.

"Now, honey," Nate said softly, holding Tracie's shoulders with gentle but firm hands and placing his forehead on hers, "I'm gonna go out there and find out what he wants. I know how ridiculous this all sounds, but everything will be fine, I promise."

"Sure, you go talk to Dewey the Alien." Her voice was laden with sarcasm. "I'll just go back to bed and not worry about a thing!" Her voice rose. *"You're scaring the shit out of me, Nate! What's really going on here?"*

"Sweetheart, if I didn't know better, *I'd* think I was insane. But come on, honey, you *know* me, I'm not crazy. Why would I make up something like this? Just trust me, I'll be back in a few minutes. Don't call anyone! I mean it!" He cautiously gave her back her cell phone, trusting she would refrain from using it until he could prove his case.

Not knowing what else he could possible say to make Tracie understand, Nate left the bedroom and ran downstairs to the kitchen. Tracie and Doo-Doo were right behind him; she wasn't going to miss this.

«*The rock!"* Tracie blurted out as she kept pace. «Honey, the concussion from hitting your head on the rock in the forest, that's what's causing this!"

Nate ignored her, switching on the kitchen lights and stepping up to the sliding glass door that led to the rear patio. He considered turning on the floodlights that would light up the whole back-yard, but opted not to, as he didn't want to startle Dewey… or his neighbors, lest they too discovered an alien in his backyard. He pressed his hands and face to the glass and scanned the yard, looking for signs of Dewey.

There was a full moon out, and aside from the shadows being cast by the house and trees, the pa-tio and backyard were bathed in a dim silver-blue glow. Nate didn't see Dewey out in the open, so he strained to see what was in the shadows. At first, he saw nothing; but then a familiar shape rose into the moonlight. Dewey had been crouching in the shadow of the big magnolia tree at the far corner of the yard. When he saw Nate appear at the glass door, he rose and stepped out into the moonlight, then scampered up to the stone steps at the back of the patio. Nate stiffened. For days he had been questioning his own sanity, trying to come to grips with the bizarre events in the Amazon. As Tracie had suggested, he had already considered on several occasions that the blow to his head was, perhaps, causing him to hallucinate, that he only *believed* that he'd met an alien. But now, Dewey... Dewey the *Alien*, whether a figment of his imagination or not, was standing right there in his back yard.

"Sweetheart, come here," Nate said, beckoning to her behind his back. "He's here. You've got to see this."

Tracie was too scared to approach the glass door. She did not for one moment believe that there was an alien out there, but there was *someone* out there, and she didn't trust whoever it was to be a friend, as Nate insisted. She stood quivering by the kitchen counter, strategically poised next to the block of kitchen knives and clutching her cell phone tightly, 911 re-entered and ready to send on cue. From this position she couldn't see past Nate, to where Dewey was now stepping up onto the patio. Doo-Doo sensed something very unusual, though, and he whimpered nervously at Tracie's feet. She reached down to pick him up, cradling him in one arm while keeping her other hand poised near the handle of a big carving knife.

"So, who's really out there?" Tracie said coyly. "Little gray dude with big eyes?"

"I already told you, it's Dewey… I mean, the alien I met and *named* Dewey. He's right here on the deck waiting for me. I'm going out there to talk to him. You wait here. I'll be right back."

Tracie's patience with the whole ET thing was waning. Now she was more terrified of Nate's lunatic ranting than she was of whoever was out there in the middle of the night. She began to sob and shouted angrily, "Nate, this is not right! It's one-thirty in the morning and you're talking about visiting with a man from outer space on our back deck… in your underwear. *Newsflash… NOT NORMAL*!»

Nate's patience with Tracie's skepticism was also wearing thin. He gritted his teeth and grunted in frustration, turning to her with an angry, piercing stare. Tracie's gaze fell away from his to the floor, her head shaking in disgust. "I just can't believe this," she said, sighing. "You've completely lost it."

"Honey, look at me!" Nate raised his voice, and Tracie complied, lifting her confused gaze to meet his glaring eyes. "I know how ridiculous this all sounds, but you're just going to have to trust me. In just a few minutes, you'll see… everything *will* be fine. Now sit down and *wait* for me. I'll be right back. Do *not* dial that phone, no matter what!"

Tracie could tell she wasn't getting through to Nate. He was too hell-bent on this impossible alien story to realize just how irrational he was being. But this *was* Professor Nathan Johnston, the man she dearly loved and had vowed to put up with 'til death, or in this case, commitment to an insane asylum, did them part. So she let out another sigh, lowered her tone, and conceded… but she couldn't help throwing in another dash of sarcasm

"All right. Go talk to your spaceman friend. Invite him in for a beer while you're at it. I'll make sandwiches. But the second he misbehaves, I'm calling the Men in Black."

Nate couldn't help but lose his anger and crack a grin. His wife's warped sense of humor never failed to amuse him. "Thanks, love, now just sit tight."

"Let's just get this over with, and then we're getting you in for an MRI first thing tomorrow to see what's wrong with your brain."

Ignoring her last statement, Nate slid open the glass door and stepped out into the night, closing the door behind him. He walked towards the far edge of the patio, just beyond the reach of the kitchen light, and stopped ten feet in front of Dewey. "Dewey? What are you doing here? I thought you had to go back home?"

As there was no TV out on the deck for Dewey to send a message to, he could only suck in some air and respond audibly with his communication holes.

"Sdrooolup… gryuuud. Pheeeeep… frooooogh."

"I'm sorry, you know I can't understand you."

"Wweeerty… aaoooos-wheeeef?"

"Okay, look. You sent a message to our TV

upstairs. We have a TV in the kitchen. Why don't you come inside and you can talk to me through it?"

"Jeeelufsuuuu!"

Nate assumed this to be a "yes" from Dewey, and he returned to the door with Dewey scampering close behind. Tracie was going to lay an egg when Dewey came in the house, he just knew it. But she *had* suggested that he invite Dewey in for a beer. Nate chuckled at the irony and the explosive reaction he knew he was about to witness. *Careful what you wish for, honey!*

"Wait here for a moment, I'll be right back," Nate said to Dewey, stopping a few paces short of where the kitchen light illuminated the patio. Dewey waited as Nate stepped into the kitchen. Tracie was still seated at the kitchen counter holding Doo-Doo and her phone. "Well, where's your little Martian friend?" Tracie's demeanor seemed a bit less frazzled now, and her signature wit was still firing on all cylinders.

"Honey," Nate said softly and confidently, "I need you to take a deep breath. I'm going to bring him in, and it's going to freak you out a little. Well, maybe a lot. But I promise, *he won't hurt you*.»

"What?" Tracie lost her momentary calm and regressed back to a nervous panic. "He *won't hurt me*? What's *that* supposed to mean?»

"He's big, and he isn't human or even human-like. Please, just *shut up* for one minute and open your mind a bit."

"Okay…. okay." Tracie shook her head in disgust. "I'm sorry. Bring in your 'alien friend'."

Doo-Doo had detected an unfamiliar, pungent smell coming in from the patio when Nate had re-entered. He began to quiver uncontrollably in the sling of Tracie's forearm, and growled nervously. "It's okay, sweetheart, Mommy's got you." Tracie comforted the dog, putting on her best skeptical face and watching closely as Nate went to the open door and motioned to Dewey to come forward. Dewey emerged from the shadows and scampered across the deck, and then reached for the opening of the sliding door with two arms, his snake-like fingers writhing as they extended outwards and wrapped around the doorframe.

Tracie's eyes widened, and her jaw fell open as the Alien revealed itself to her for the first time. She gasped repeatedly, then screamed when the pear-shaped body squatted down on four lithe legs to squeeze through, four pairs of large eyes on four flat, flexible stalks ducking as well to get under the inadequate height of the door. One pair of the Alien's black eyes swiveled in Tracie's direction, their cold gaze sending shivers down her spine. Then his eyes took on a warmer appearance, shifting to mottled orange and blue, which momentarily fascinated Tracie before she quickly reverted to sheer terror. She shrieked again and tried to grab for a knife with her shaking hand, letting Doo-Doo fall from her embrace. He bounced off her lap before hitting the floor in a snarling fit.

Tracie found herself paralyzed with fear, unable to breathe or move, but not little Doo-Doo. After picking himself up from where she had dropped him, he boldly ran right up to Dewey the Alien, jumping and snarling at him. Tracie watched in horror as the Alien abruptly reached down with one arm and wrapped seven lithe fingers around the little pooch, causing Doo-Doo to squeal with alarm. He struggled uselessly in the Alien's firm grip as Dewey lifted him to eye-level to get a closer look at the tiny creature he had been named after. Realizing he had no chance of escape, Doo-Doo stopped his writhing, went limp, and started whimpering submissively.

Tracie wanted to scream some more, and run to save her dog. But she had lost all function other than clenching her butt-cheeks as tightly as she could to avert disaster. She opened her mouth to yell at the Alien to put Doo-Doo down, but all that came out was a high-pitched screech as she trembled uncontrollably, leaning back against the counter to avoid collapsing altogether.

Dewey notice Tracie's anguish over his holding Doo-Doo captive, and gently set Doo-Doo back down unharmed. Doo-Doo wasted no time retreating to a safe distance from the Alien, but once out of reach, he re-copped his big-dog attitude and resumed snarling and barking at the top of his miniscule lungs. "Doo-Doo, stop that!" Nate shouted crossly. "He's a friend!"

Doo-Doo did tone down his ruckus, snorted in protest at being scolded, and ran back to where Tracie was leaning on the counter. He sat down on the floor in front of her quivering bare feet, growling softly towards Dewey. Tracie managed to lean over to pick Doo-Doo up again, not taking her eyes off Dewey for one second. She held Doo-Doo firmly to her chest and struggled to croak out a few shaky words.

"Nnnnate... h-h-honey... what the hell *is* this thing?"

"Sweetheart, I'd like you to meet Dewey. *Dewey the Alien*," Nate stated proudly, grinning from ear to ear.

"Ah... ah... ah," Tracie tried, but couldn't form any complete words.

Nate continued "Dewey, I'd like you to meet my wife, Tracie."

"Guuuuurg bleeet fraaaaap," Dewey greeted Tracie audibly, his eyes turning dark yellow.

Tracie got a perplexed look on her face as the sounds coming from Dewey reverberated through the room. The whimsical noises he was making amused her, momentarily alleviated her locked jaw. "Did he just fart at me?" Tracie said, surprised that all of a sudden she was able to speak legibly.

"That's how he communicates audibly."

"He farts at you to speak?"

Nate laughed. "Noooo… he sucks air into those little holes around his mid-section and blows it back out to create words. He doesn't breathe; he doesn't have lungs."

"And you know what he's saying?"

"No, but watch this!" Nate pointed towards the small flat-screen TV mounted on the kitchen wall. "Dewey, can you communicate to us on that?"

Dewey responded immediately, a thin white beam of light shooting out from a holo-disc to the TV. The set turned itself on, and after a moment of static, displayed a message:

«YES DEWEY CAN USE TELEVISION TO DISPLAY CONVERSATION.»

Tracie let out a nervous shriek, then broke into a half-cry/half-laugh, shaking her head in disbelief as Nate shuffled about the kitchen in a victory dance. He pointed both index fingers at her, jabbing them back and forth to taunt her, then pointing them at Dewey.

"Well, Mrs. Dr. Johnston… Do you still think I'm insane? How's *this* for a new biological specimen?"

Dewey did not understand Nate's actions, but he found them very amusing, and undulated with glee. Then he flashed a new message on the TV. "DEWEY ENJOYS KNOWING NATHAN. DEWEY WILL ENJOY KNOWING TRACIE WIFE OF NATHAN."

"How sweet," Tracie responded, managing to settle down enough to find her sarcastic side again. "We just met, and your friend from Pluto is flirting with me already." She was in a daze, her screaming mind trying to navigate towards logic as quickly as possible, but this was too much, too fast. It would take a few minutes.

"THERE IS NO LIFE ON PLUTO. I AM FROM ELSEWHERE," declared the TV screen.

"I'm dreaming," Tracie concluded out loud. "This is all just a freaky dream, and we're still asleep upstairs."

"Oh for God's sake, sweetheart, *you're not dreaming*. Dewey is real! He's standing right here! And he's *not* flirting with you."

"How can you be so sure? He's looking at me funny."

"In the Amazon, he told me how they reproduce on his planet, and believe me, he has *no* interest in your body."

"Well, this is just too weird. I'm just not sure... I'm just going to go upstairs, and you two can catch up."

"Now come on, sweetheart!" Nate scolded. "Take advantage of this! I doubt he's going to stay very long, and what are the odds you'll ever get another chance to visit with a real alien? Besides, his ancestors were aquatic! Your specialty!"

"Nate, I'm scared. You don't know what he's capable of. How do you know we're safe here? If he really *is* from another planet, then how do you know his true intensions? How do you know he didn't bring some deadly bacteria with him!?"

"Stop talking like he's not even here. He *can* understand you, you know."

Dewey interrupted with a new message. "ALL BACTERIA FROM HOME OF DEWEY ELIMINATED BEFORE COMING TO EARTH. DEWEY IS NOT DANGER TO TRACIE OR NATE OR DOO-DOO."

"See?" Nate gloated. "His people are pretty damn smart! They have all the bases covered. Stop worrying and enjoy this moment with me!"

Tracie stood silent, staring at Nate and trembling. Her mind was a flip-flopping mess, but she knew now that this was not a dream, and that Nate had been telling the truth all along...and she needed to come to grips with the situation. Fear and panic still gripped her to the core, but as she forced her way through the paralyzing angst into a more sensible frame of mind, she couldn't deny the significance of this; it was potentially the greatest scientific discovery of all time. And in her own kitchen, of all places! *I'm a scientist*, she scolded herself silently. *Time to start acting like one!* She took a few deep breaths and looked into Dewey's eyes.

"Nice to meet you, Dewey. I am sorry for being so rude. Please forgive me. Welcome to our home."

Nate grinned from ear to ear, approaching Tracie to give her a big bear hug.

For the next two hours, Dewey, Nate, and Tracie conversed about many subjects while Doo-Doo added a few growls and barks to the conversation that basically translated to, *My Humans! Bite you!* Dewey's holo-discs transformed the living room into a three-dimensional theatre, projecting life-like images into mid-air while messages on the TV narrated each scene. Tracie's passion for marine biology led to pictures illustrating how Dewey's species had evolved from sea creatures to land-dwellers over millions of years, and he showed her images of countless bizarre aquatic creatures the Aliens had discovered about the Universe, including under the ice on Jupiter's moon Europa. He also showed Nate and Tracie his family home, as well as Alien cities, the orbiting launch station from where his journey had begun, and even the Intergalactic Zoo where he was trained and had conducted his biologic research. But he did not volunteer images of the Human clones that were his favorite subjects there.

In return, Dewey asked many questions about Human nature, and he insisted on a complete tour of Nate and Tracie's home. He was fascinated by every little detail of how they lived, and all the functions of each item in the house. Every new discovery was an adventure to his senses, and he felt like a young adolescent scientist again, learning exciting things for the first time. When the tour was finished, Dewey flashed a new subject on the TV.

«IN RAINFOREST NATE REQUESTED TO TRAVEL IN TRANSPORT OF DEWEY. DEWEY CAN NOW COMPLY.»

Stunned, Nate replied, "Wait...*what*? But... I thought you said that was impossible; that a Human couldn't survive on your ship?"

«DEWEY HAS USED TECHNOLOGY TO DEVELOP LIFE SUPPORT FOR HUMANS IN SPACE. DEWEY HAS MANUFACTURED A DEVICE FOR PROTECTION AND LIFE SUPPORT OF NATE DURING TRANSPORT.»

"Holy shit, are you *kidding me*? Where would we go?" Nate's face had lit up like a light bulb.

"DEWEY CAN SHOW NATE OTHER LIFE IN THIS GALAXY. MANY PLANETS TO CHOOSE FROM."

Tracie jumped in "Wait a minute, *wait a minute*! What are you talking about? Nate, you are *not* going *anywhere* on a spaceship!"

"Yes the hell I *am*!»

«*No you are not*!" Tracie growled in anger, but managed to grin nervously at Dewey.

Nate ignored his wife and addressed Dewey. "You want to take *me* on a trip to see life on other planets? And you can do this without hurting me?"

"YES."

Nate pumped his fists and hooted like a deranged soccer hooligan whose team had just scored a goal, but then he stopped and got a puzzled look. "Wait... how long will we be gone? I mean, these other planets have to be *light-years* away. I can't just disappear never to come back."

"Thank you!" Tracie said victoriously, with a smirk.

«NOT FAR FOR TRANSPORT OF DEWEY. CAN

TRAVEL TO ANY PART OF THIS GALAXY AND RETURN IN A FEW EARTH DAYS.»

"Oh my God, this is awesome!" Nate squealed in a high-pitched, childlike voice, raising his hands into the air and collapsing backwards onto the old beanbag chair he had kept since his bachelor days. But his euphoric bubble was promptly burst by vocal outrage from across the room.

"Nathan Johnston!" Tracie proclaimed, "you are *not* doing this! You cannot just leave the planet on a whim in an Alien spaceship! It's too dangerous — you will *die* out there!" She turned to Dewey. "Dewey, with all due respect, this has been an amazing moment in my life... in *our* lives. You are an amazing creature and I can't begin to put into words how incredible meeting you has been. But you are *not* taking my husband with you on some joy-ride in space and leaving me here alone."

«DEWEY APOLOGIZES. DEWEY WOULD TAKE TRACIE ON JOURNEY ALSO BUT ONLY MANUFAC-TURED ONE DEVICE SPECIFIED TO PHYSIOLOGY OF NATE.»

Tracie laughed sarcastically. "Oh no, you misunderstand me. I'm not envious of him going, I'm *scared shitless*. I don't want to lose my husband. What if something happens out there and he never returns? No... no, I can't let him go."

"Don't listen to her, Dewey. I'm going."

"Nathan! *No!*" Tracie screamed at Nate, furious at his defiance.

"Honey, stop, you'll wake the neighbors. *Please* let me do this."

"No fucking way!"

"Dewey, can you *guarantee* me you can keep me alive and bring me back to Earth, back to my wife, in one piece?"

"THE ODDS ARE GOOD FOR SUCCESS."

"Oh, that's just fucking great!" Tracie blurted, throwing her hands up and collapsing on the sofa. "The *odds are good!*" She started crying.

Nate sat down next to her and spoke calmly. "Honey, I understand you're scared, this is all happening very fast and it's… I know it's just completely nuts. But it's *real*! It's not some cheesy sci-fi movie, it's *all real! Think* about this for a second. I *have* to do this. Anyone offered this opportunity should take it. You're a scientist, so *you* of all people must understand that. No other Human being has *ever* been given this chance, and it may never happen again in our lifetime… or *ever*. How can I pass it up? My whole life I've devoted myself to studying new life forms, and he wants to show me life forms on *another planet!* How can I possibly say no? How could anyone? How could *you?*»

Tracie's sobbing escalated to a complete bawl.

Dewey approached Tracie and extended an arm, wrapping several fingers around her shoulder. Tracie gasped and recoiled; Dewey had not touched her before now. For a moment, the Alien grip felt bizarre and eerie, but the stroke was gentle and caring. Dewey's eyes turned bright purple and a new message scrolled onto the TV:

«TRACIE FRIEND, DEWEY WILL RETURN NATE TO EARTH SAFELY. DEWEY PROMISES THIS TO TRACIE.»

"Oh Dewey, how can you be so sure? I don't care how advanced you are and how much technology you have. Space is *dangerous;* you can't tell me it isn't. How can you possibly guarantee that something bad won't happen out there, something dangerous to Nate?"

Dewey paused for a moment.

«TRACIE IS CORRECT. DEWEY CANNOT GUARANTEE THIS. TOO MANY VARIABLES TO GUARANTEE THIS. DEWEY CAN ONLY GUARANTEE THAT DEWEY WILL DO ALL POSSIBLE TO PROTECT NATE. DEWEY DOES NOT WISH ANY HARM TO COME TO NATE. DEWEY DOES NOT WISH TO CAUSE CONCERN AND SADNESS TO TRACIE. DEWEY LIKES NATE. DEWEY LIKES TRACIE. DEWEY LIKES DEWEY.»

"Call him Doo-Doo," Tracie interjected. "His name *is* Dewey, but we call him Doo-Doo. Let's not make all this any more confusing than it is already."

"THEN DEWEY LIKES DOO-DOO." Dewey replied, extending a hand to gently pet Doo-Doo, who had been following the entourage about the house and was now sitting nervously in Tracie's lap.

Doo-Doo was apprehensive about letting this odd creature touch him again, and he growled and whined softly in protest. But this time the Alien's touch was gentle and soothing, and Tracie seemed at ease with it, so he quickly relaxed and took pleasure in the attention. In fact, he liked it so much that he reached up with his pointy little snout and gently licked Dewey's odd fingers. They tasted unlike anything he had ever licked before.

Tracie cooed in approval at the momentary distraction from her concerns. "Well, I'll be damned. Two hours ago, all the little shit wanted to do was rip your tentacles off, and look at him now." But the distraction was short-lived, as Dewey put up a new message.

"NATE MUST DECIDE NOW. SUN WILL RISE SOON. DEWEY MUST DEPART EARTH IN DARKNESS."

Tracie glared at Nate and addressed him through clenched teeth. "Don't you do it!"

Nate whined, "Honey, I *need* to do this. I'll never get another chance like this. Nobody will!"

"Yeah, and *so what*? And even if you did go, then what? From what he's told us, you can't ever share it with anyone except me. You can't go tell the world about it. You can't write about it or give lectures about it. Can you live with that? Is that what you want?"

"No, I don't like lying to people, but we already have to lie. We've already seen him, talked to him, he's already told us about so much out there that we never knew existed... there's no turning back now! We're just talking about adding a few more sticks to the pile. And you know what would be worse than just living with the lies? Wondering what I *might* have seen if I didn't go!"

Tracie couldn't argue with that. The scientist in her knew fully well how special the opportunity was that Dewey had laid at her husband's feet. It was the stuff of dreams for any scientist, the chance to see and discover new things nobody had ever encountered before, and she knew he couldn't possibly resist. Had she been offered the chance, she wasn't sure she could have turned it down. She broke down sobbing.

"I'm just really scared, okay? Last night we were a normal, dysfunctional married couple, two geek scientists who loved fish and bugs and doing stupid-crazy shit together. A few hours later, you're fraternizing with an Alien and about to go bopping around outer space with him in his flying saucer. No big deal, huh? I'm just... *so* scared you guys won't come back." Tears streamed down her cheeks. "I'm glad you're getting this chance, really I am, but there's nothing in it for me if you don't make it back... my life will be ruined forever."

Nate wrapped his arms around Tracie and let out a deep sigh, and then he turned to Dewey. "Are you sure this piece of technology you have can keep me safe?"

«YES DEWEY IS CONFIDENT IT WILL FUNCTION.»

"You promise you will do everything you can to bring me back here alive and well?"

«YES.»

Tracie knew what was coming next. She had

lost the battle.

"I'll do it," Nate said confidently. Then he held Tracie's face in his hands and softly kissed the tears from her cheeks as he whispered in her ear. "I love you, baby. I love you *so* much. And I'll be back in a few days to prove it to you, you'll see."

Tracie just nodded silently and wrapped her arms around Nate's neck, whispering into his ear. "I love you too, asshole. Just… be careful and get back here in one piece, damn it."

Nate turned to Dewey and asked, "What do I need to do?"

«NATE MUST REMOVE ALL CLOTHING AND FOLLOW DEWEY TO TRANSPORT.»

"Naked? I have to go naked… into the swamp?"

Tracy chuckled through her tears. "Now, this I have to see."

CHAPTER 32

J ason O'Rourke had spent three frantic days mop-
ping up the mess in Brazil. Nate had insisted that
he stay and help, but Jason wouldn't allow it. He
felt responsible for Nate's injuries and quite guilty
for having asked him to venture so far from the safety of the base camp, so he put Nate on a plane back
home and stayed behind to wait for Pedro Escoval
to deliver ARCA's gear back to Porto Velho. Then he
hired a truck to get the crates back to São Paolo and
onto a British Airways 747-800F freighter back to
London. He also notified Antonio Perron of the location of the alleged meteorite, so he could arrange
for its extraction from the rainforest for study back
at the Brazilian Astronomical Institute.

Throughout the process, Jason had been fielding
intense questioning from the Brazilian authorities as
to the possible whereabouts of their missing helicopter and its crew. No flight plan had been filed,
and radar coverage was practically nonexistent in
the depths of the rainforest, so after it had left Porto
Velho there was no record of its activity other than
the brief sighting by Pedro Escoval and his men.

Jason, quite honestly, repeatedly stated that ARCA was not trying to cover anything up, and that he truly knew nothing of the helicopter's whereabouts. This was met with great skepticism, but lacking any evidence of foul play, the interrogation eventually subsided and the chopper was presumed to have gotten far off course and crashed somewhere in the forest. Numerous search aircraft were sent into the Amazon looking for the wreckage… but none was found.

With Nate safely home, the campsite packed up, the meteorite in the care of Antonio Perron, and the Brazilian authorities finally off his back, Jason was happy to be relaxing with a Guinness at the São Paolo airport. He had two hours before boarding his flight to London.

The TV behind the airport's bar was on the local news channel, which was running a feature on the discovery of the meteorite. Jason couldn't fully understand the Portuguese dialogue, but the images told all. There were aerial shots of the impact site, footage of the meteorite being lifted out by helicopter (a rather large helicopter, Jason thought… overkill) and old file photos of Nathan Johnston and ARCA's headquarters flashing on the screen behind the glamorous female anchor. *Where the bloody hell did they get those pictures?* Jason wondered.

Then, pictures of the crewmen from the missing helicopter were put up, causing Jason to frown. He felt terrible for their loss. So far, he had managed to dodge the Brazilian press on the whole episode, although he was sure they would catch up to him in London if the missing chopper wasn't found soon. He would, of course, cooperate fully if asked to, but he truly had already told the authorities everything he knew. For now, he was quite content to stay under the radar and unwind from the stress of the past few days. He ordered another Guinness, and as he poured the frothy brew, his cell-phone rang. It was Antonio Perron.

Jason answered the call, "Tony, old chap, I'm fresh out of scientists today, hope you haven't found another meteorite."

Perron chuckled, then sighed before replying, "No, Jason. No more meteorites. *This* one will be enough trouble for now. And Jason, I cannot begin to apologize enough for what has happened. I was so excited about finding a new meteorite that I lost my senses and didn't think of the dangers I was asking your man to endure. He is all right, yes?"

"Yes, yes, he's fine. Back home shagging the wife by now, I imagine. She was worried sick. And no need to apologize; I was just as excited about finding a meteorite as you were. You know how ARCA's financiers love that kind of stuff, especially Mercer — he went batshit over this."

"Yes, I know. He's been calling me non-stop, wants to buy the meteorite, but our government won't sell it. It is a magnificent find, but I still do feel responsible for Nate's trauma."

"Well, don't. Like I said, he's fine. Besides, I'm the one who actually sent the poor bastard out there to look for it. You didn't have to twist my arm too much."

"Well, I am very relieved to hear that he will be okay. I can't say the same for the crew of the lost helicopter. I'm catching a lot of heat for that one."

"I regret that too. We all do. But I can't understand what might have happened to them. I'm told the crew was well-trained in navigating the basin, and there was no history of any maintenance issues with that particular aircraft. Escoval said he saw them hovering above Nathan's campsite, and then they headed straight for the impact area. It was only a mile and a half north of there; how could they get that far off course and just disappear?"

"Well..." Perron hesitated and sighed, as if unable to continue.

«Well what?"

«Jason, that is why I have called you. I'm not sure they *did* get off course. I think I may have found them. But... I cannot be sure."

Jason's brow wrinkled. He slurped some stout before he responded, "You can't be sure? What the bloody hell does *that* mean?"

"Are you alone?" Perron inquired.

"Yes."

"There are some very strange things about the meteorite we found, *very* strange things."

"Go on."

"Well, for starters, the impact crater, it was only four feet deep and about fifteen feet wide. *Much* too small for a meteorite of this size and weight. And the weight and composition of it; now, *that* is what's really puzzling. It is incredibly dense and heavy, more so than any other meteorite of this size on record. We had to get a heavy-lift helicopter out there just to lift it."

"You're kidding. I saw that beast of a chopper on the news, big enough to lift a tank... I thought maybe it was all they had available for the job or something."

"No, it's no joke. The damn thing weighs over fifteen thousand pounds."

«*Fifteen thousand!* That's not possible. I *saw* it, Tony, it was only about two meters in diameter!"

"Smaller than that, and nearly a perfect sphere, highly irregular as far as meteorites go. But it gets even stranger."

"Stranger?"

"Like I said, the impact crater for something that heavy should have been much larger — about a hundred times larger, in fact. It's as if it only fell about a *hundred meters* or so, not shot in from outer space at high speed. But it's the physical nature and the composition of it that is the most puzzling. It's mostly aluminum and titanium alloys... along with some glass and carbonized rubber and plastic compounds."

"Impossible!"

"Impossible for a meteorite, yes. These elements didn't come from space, or anywhere in nature for that matter. They are not naturally occurring substances. *We* manufactured them. "

"But how...?"

"I don't know how it happened, but I can only conclude that our meteorite is actually what's left of the missing chopper. All the elements are there; this is the stuff we use to make aircraft. And I checked the weight on the missing helicopter: twelve thousand, eight hundred pounds before fuel, ordinance and crew. It all adds up."

Jason stiffened and felt chills. "Oh come on, Tony, now that's bloody ridiculous. What could reduce a helicopter to a bloody two-meter ball? And what about the crew? If that's the helicopter, then where is the crew?"

Perron fell silent for a moment, then said sternly, "I think they are inside the sphere."

"Oh, go on now!" Jason refused to believe what he was hearing.

"Jason, I'm not messing with you. There is a considerable amount of ash blended into the metal. Most of it seems purely organic in origin. We are running some tests."

Jason was now speechless. He chugged the rest of his beer, and motioned to the bartender to bring another. "Jason?" Perron inquired after a moment of silence "Are you still there?"

"Yes, Tony, I'm here."

"Jason, something very odd happened out there. I think you need to speak further with Professor Nathan Johnston about what he might have seen."

"Yes, I agree — and Tony, please keep this between us for now, would you, until I can get some answers from Nate?"

"Okay, but hurry, please. If my suspicions are true, I owe it to my government and the families of that helicopter crew to let them know as soon as possible."

"Understood."

CHAPTER 33

Nate had convinced Dewey to at least let him stay clothed until they reached the ship in the woods. It would be difficult to explain to a nosy neighbor why he was creeping into the woods naked in the middle of the night, not to mention with a creature from another galaxy. Besides, the woods behind the house were mostly a swampy cypress forest with thick, spiny underbrush that would be torture to navigate in bare skin. He kissed Tracie goodbye, her lips not reacting to his but rather just accepting the kiss inanimately. Nate gripped her hands and tried to reassure her. "I *will* be back. I love you."

Tracie didn't reply. She was in a state of shock. She understood Nate's desire to do this, but was devastated that he was going through with it despite her pleas to the contrary. She had elected not to follow Nate and Dewey to the ship; it was all just too bizarre to process, and she felt dizzy — so much so that she didn't think she could walk through the woods without collapsing. She stood in the kitchen, rocking nervously on her feet as the two slipped out the back door and snuck off through the shadows into the trees. When they disappeared from sight, she collapsed into a chair and began weeping. Doo-Doo jumped into her lap and licked the tears from her cheeks, whining.

Nate trailed Dewey into the prickly undergrowth of the cypress trees, grateful he had insisted on remaining clothed; otherwise he might have ended up a punctured, bloody mess. Dewey's tough skin was unaffected, his eight limbs working in fluid rhythm as he efficiently pressed forward, clearing a path in the brush for Nate to follow. Within several minutes they arrived at the small clearing where Dewey had landed, and Nate once again saw the shiny, football-shaped craft, hovering a few feet off the ground just as it had in the Amazon.

«NATE MUST NOW REMOVE ALL CLOTHING." Dewey's message appeared on the side of the ship.

Nate disrobed, then stood nervously, covering his crotch with both hands while the ship's cargo bay opened up to reveal a large, globular object that slowly floated out into the moonlight. It reminded Nate of big fishbowl. It was glass-like in appearance, and seemed to be filled completely with a clear, purplish liquid. At the top of the object was a shiny metal cylinder, making the whole thing look sort of like a giant Christmas-tree ornament.

«What is that?" Nate inquired.

"THIS IS A LIFE SUSTENANCE HABITAT. NATE WILL TRAVEL INSIDE HABITAT. HABITAT WILL

SUSTAIN LIFE OF NATE.»

"You're kidding! That thing's full of liquid, I'll drown in there!"

«LIQUID YES. DROWN NO. LIQUID SUSTAIN LIFE OF NATE. IS NATE READY TO ENTER HABITAT?"

Fear and panic set in. "Dewey I can't *breathe* in liquid! Maybe this wasn't such a good idea. Maybe I shouldn't go."

«NATE WILL SURVIVE IN LIQUID. NATE BREATH LIQUID. NATE EAT LIQUID.»

Nate was not unfamiliar with this concept, only completely unprepared mentally to try it on himself. He knew that the technology of Humans breathing liquid was being developed with great success for deep-sea divers and astronauts, and he recalled one of his favorite scenes from that old movie, *The Abyss*, where Ed Harris had so bravely sucked liquid into his lungs for the first time. In fact, in the real world, ARCA was a leader in developing this technology for practical use. But Nate was neither a trained deep-sea diver nor an astronaut, or Ed Harris's brave, fictitious character, and he was scared out of his skull to try it. He trembled with fear.

"Dewey, I'm not sure I can go through with this. I *do* trust you, but I'm very frightened."

«DEWEY UNDERSTANDS FEAR OF NATE. IF NATE NO LONGER WISHES TO TRAVEL WITH DEWEY, DEWEY WILL UNDERSTAND. BUT DEWEY MUST LEAVE NOW. NATE MUST DECIDE NOW.»

Nate closed his eyes, took a deep breath, and bit

his lower lip while silently trying to motivate himself. *I have to do this. I have to do this*. Exhaling, he opened his eyes, looked up at Dewey, and declared, "I'll be fine, this is just… well, it's terrifying… but I want to do it. I *need* to do it. I *will* do it. Okay, let's go. What do you need me to do?"

«NATE MUST STAND STILL NOW.»

Nate stood up straight, his arms draped to either side, and a fan of blue light shot out from one of Dewey's holo-discs, scanning his naked body from head to toe.

"ALL HARMFUL MICROBES MUST NOW BE REMOVED FROM BODY OF NATE."

The fan of light changed to bright green, and suddenly Nate was engulfed in a crackling sphere of energy. He felt an intense tingling sensation all over, and every hair on his body stood straight out, as if straining to leave his skin. "Whoa! That tickles!" Nate protested, wriggling like a child whose sensitive ribs were being assaulted.

«NATE MUST REMAIN STILL.»

"Okay, I'll try, but this *really* tickles!"

Nate remained as still as he could, and then he felt his feet leave the ground. *He was levitating*. The bright green orb of energy that engulfed him floated purposefully to the top of the habitat, with Nate suspended inside. He began flailing impulsively, as if trying to keep his balance, although the energy field was holding him upright quite securely. It stopped above the globe and positioned Nate directly over its metallic cap, and then a spiral hatch opened under his feet and he was slowly lowered into the fluid.

The viscous liquid felt soothing and comfortable on his feet and legs, like a lukewarm bath of thick oil. He grinned and sighed, forgetting his fear for a moment. When the goo engulfed his genitals, he laughed nervously and exclaimed, "Now *that* was exciting!" But as he continued to go deeper into the fluid, the reality set in that he was about to be completely submerged — sheer panic.

"Oh shit, oh shit, oh shit!" Nate babbled, until his chin touched the fluid, and then he shut up and took a huge gulp of air, holding it as his face slipped beneath the surface.

Nate stopped sinking with his feet several feet off the floor of the habitat. He felt a tingling around his torso, as if the liquid had come alive, molding to his body and holding him in place at the container's center. Through the clear wall he could see Dewey peering in, studying him closely with three sets of eyes while monitoring a display from a holo-disc with the fourth. Then a message appeared inside the habitat right in front of Nate.

«NATE MUST NOW BREATHE THE LIQUID. NATE MUST EXPEL ALL AIR IN HIS LUNGS AND BREATHE THE LIQUID.»

Still holding his breath, Nate shook his head no and instinctively tried to swim to the surface to get a fresh gulp of air. His mind raced in panic. *What was I thinking? I can't breathe this shit!* But no matter how hard he paddled, he was unable to surface from his position in the middle of the habitat. The tingling sensation around his midriff intensified as he struggled to surface, holding him firmly in place.

«NATE MUST NOT LEAVE CENTER OF HABITAT. NATE MUST EXPEL AIR AND BREATHE THE LIQUID.»

Nate stopped struggling and looked at Dewey. His lungs were on fire, and he was getting dizzy from holding his breath. He realized he had to take the leap of faith now or give up and go home. He closed his eyes and opened his mouth, pushing all the air from his lungs into the goop, creating a big bubble that slowly rose to the surface. Then he counted to three and sucked in hard, taking a deep breath of the fluid. His body convulsed as his lungs instinctively tried to expel the intruding substance. The gasping and coughing only drew more of the stuff in, forcing Nate into a frenzy. Dewey watched from outside the globe, carefully monitoring Nate's life-signs on the holo-disc display.

"NATE WILL BE FINE SOON. TRUST DEWEY."

After several minutes of struggling, Nate's lungs began to adapt to the oddness of the fluid. His heart rate returned to a less-frantic pace, and he calmed with Dewey's reassurance that he wasn't going to drown. Several more deep breaths of the liquid, and he felt secure enough to give a thumbs-up to Dewey, and opened his mouth to speak. Then he realized he couldn't... the fluid wouldn't work as a substitute for air on his vocal chords. He pointed at his throat and looked at Dewey inquisitively. *How am I supposed to talk to you now?* He mouthed the words.

«NATE WILL HAVE TO ENTER THOUGHTS ON INTERFACE.»

Right on cue, a three-dimensional image appeared directly in front of Nate. *It was a holographic keyboard!* Dewey had programmed it in the same configuration as the qwerty keyboards familiar to most Humans, and it was now at Nate's fingertips on which to type messages. He gave it a try. At first it was awkward, as there was no resistance to stop his fingers; they just went right through the image. But with a few seconds' practice he was able to create coherent messages.

"This is weird," Nate typed.

«IS NATE SATISFACTORY IN HABITAT?»

Nate typed back, "I am fine, very impressive. I have a few more questions before we go anywhere."

«DEWEY WILL ANSWER QUESTIONS BUT WE MUST LEAVE SOON.»

"How do I eat? You said I should also eat the liquid?"

«YES. LIQUID HAS OXYGEN FOR LUNGS AND SUSTENANCE FOR STOMACH TO DIGEST. BREATHE THE LIQUID. INGEST THE LIQUID WHEN NATE IS HUNGRY.»

"Okay, then what do I do when I have to take a piss or a crap?"

«DEWEY DOES NOT UNDERSTAND PISS OR CRAP.»

"Defecate, urinate."

Dewey understood now. He did not answer with words. Instead he pointed upwards to the cylinder that capped the habitat. Nate looked above his head and noticed a black snake-like tube descending from the ceiling. As it came down behind him, the end of the tube began to stretch out into an oblong bowl shape, and then it clamped itself onto his bottom and began to stretch about his pelvis. The entire end of the tube expanded and molded itself around his waist, forming a soft, rubbery cradle like an over-sized form-fitted diaper. The thought of relieving himself into this thing that gripped his privates was embarrassing and even a bit humiliating, but Nate figured that when the time came, he would have no choice, and he would go through with it just like he had with breathing the liquid. All good.

"Okay, that was the weirdest thing yet." Nate grinned as he typed. "I'm glad no one can see this!"

"IT IS TIME TO DEPART. SUN WILL ILLUMINATE THIS AREA SOON. MUST LEAVE IN DARKNESS.»

"Okay, let's do it!"

The habitat floated back into the ship's cargo bay, which looked dark and cold. This disappointed Nate; he had hoped to be in the cockpit with Dewey, but obviously the habitat was too big for that option. Once the cargo bay door spiraled shut, the habitat was surrounded by complete darkness, with only the glow of the holographic keyboard illuminating the purple liquid. "I can't see anything outside,"

Nate complained with keystrokes.

«DEWEY WILL ACTIVATE VISUALS WHEN SYS-TEMS ARE READY.»

Dewey climbed into the cockpit and secured himself in the floating chair. Nate could hear various clicks, whirrs, and other odd noises about him as the transport went through its pre-launch sequence. A few moments later, Dewey switched on the viewer system and patched it into the cargo bay's walls, causing Nate to gasp liquid as the scene unfolded around him. It was as if the ship's outer hull had become completely transparent, offering a 360° panoramic view of the vessel's surroundings. Despite the wall between the cargo bay and the cockpit, Nate could now see the back of Dewey's chair ahead of him, and Dewey's busy hands working an array of holographic control panels.

Next, Nate felt a tingling sensation in his head, and he could hear a low-frequency hum all around him. He saw the ground move away beneath his feet as the ship levitated into the sky. His heart was pounding. At first the ascent was slow, but then in an instant, the craft shot through the sky away from Earth's surface. *I should be ripped apart by the G-forces*, Nate thought. But he had felt nothing more than slight variations in the tingling he was feeling all over.

Nate watched in complete awe as the lights of Tampa and its sister-cities, St. Petersburg and Clearwater, rapidly fell away. Within seconds he could see the sprawling lights of Orlando to the east, then Miami to the south and other cities across the state. Soon the entire moonlit peninsula of Florida came into view, then the United States, South America, and finally all of the Earth itself, with the glow of the Sun peering over the eastern crest of the planet.

A few seconds later, the Earth became a mere orb in the distance, and then the moon whizzed by and Dewey navigated the ship in a curved trajectory, doubling back past the Earth and moon and headed directly towards the Sun. As the full view of the Sun came directly in front of the ship, Nate instinctively put up his hands to shield his eyes, but he noticed quickly that the burning sensation he had expected in his eyes wasn't there. In fact, he found he could look directly at the Sun without his eyes straining at all. As if reading Nate's mind, Dewey explained.

"IT IS SAFE FOR NATE TO VIEW SUN STAR DIRECTLY. HARMFUL RAYS ARE FILTERED BY VIEWER SYSTEM."

The Earth and Moon quickly became small dots fading into the tapestry of stars behind the ship. Nate wanted to shout with joy but he couldn't. He could only type out his jubilance.

"Dewey, this is incredible. I had no idea how beautiful space really was until now."

«YES IT IS BEAUTIFUL. NATE WILL SEE MANY BEAUTIFUL THINGS TODAY.»

CHAPTER 34

Nate was in a euphoric trance. No images of space he had ever seen on television, the Internet, or in books could compare to what he was looking at now. Before heading to other parts of the Milky Way, Dewey decided to first take him on a tour of his own solar system.

When the ship approached Venus, Dewey navigated through the sulfuric-acid clouds down into the valleys of the molten planet, where Nate saw massive lava flows and volcanic eruptions. Mercury, void of any protective atmosphere, was equally fascinating but less exciting visually, its barren, cratered surface blistering in the Sun's heat on one side and frozen solid by the vacuum of space on the other.

Then Dewey piloted the ship even closer to the Sun, which gradually became so large in the viewing system that it seemed to completely surround the craft. Nate could see the undulations of the star's glowing, boiling surface and magnificent loops of flame shooting out thousands of miles into space. He began to wonder just how much punishment Dewey's vessel could take. "Dewey, how can we withstand the heat here? Or the radiation? Shouldn't we be burning up or dying of radiation poisoning?"

«SURFACE OF TRANSPORT CONVERTS HEAT, RADIATION, AND LIGHT INTO ENERGY. EXCESS IS REFLECTED AWAY. WE CANNOT BE HARMED BY HEAT OR RADIATION INSIDE TRANSPORT.»

"Of course, how silly of me," Nate typed, grinning in amusement at himself for doubting Dewey. *Of course he wouldn't bring us here if we were in danger*. He continued typing, "This is awesome; I just really hope your air conditioner doesn't break down!" Nate nervously considered the fact that outside the ship, the temperature had to be hundreds of thousands of degrees. If the ship malfunctioned and he and Dewey were exposed to it, they would vaporize in a fraction of a second.

After circling the Sun once, evading several enormous loops of flame that protruded from the surface, Dewey navigated back out of the inner solar-system towards the outer planets. He dipped into the swirling, stormy atmosphere of Jupiter, dodging bolts of lightning thousands of times bigger than any Earth storm could produce. After a quick fly-by of Jupiter's volcanic moon Io, Dewey navigated towards the gas-giant's ice-covered moon, Europa.

«DEWEY WILL NOW SHOW NATE ONLY OTHER HOME OF LIFE IN SOLAR SYSTEM OF EARTH.»

Nate responded, "On Europa? Our scientists have suspected there might be life there under the ice."

«THEY ARE CORRECT.»

Europa's frozen surface looked to Nate like a huge snowball that had been cracked into thousands of segments, the dark lines of the cracks stretching into a framework around the entire moon. As they neared the surface, Nate could see that the cracks were actually massive crevasses, immensely deep and dark. The transport slowed down to a few hundred miles per hour and headed straight into one of the larger crevasses.

As Dewey piloted into the depths of the crevasse, he engaged the exterior illumination so that Nate could see their surroundings. The crevasse's walls were massive sheets of ice, and once the ship was several miles down, Nate saw an undulating, swirling surface approach below —*liquid water!* With a tremendous splash, the ship's pointed nose penetrated the strip of churning water and Nate stiffened, expecting to feel a jarring jolt when they hit… but he felt nothing except a brief vibration.

"Dewey, isn't it too cold for liquid water to exist so close to the surface?"

«GRAVITY OF JUPITER CAUSES CRACKS TO OPEN IN SURFACE ICE OF EUROPA. WARM WATER UNDER ICE SURFACE TAKES TIME TO FREEZE AGAIN. THIS WATER WILL BE FROZEN SOON. WILL NEED TO FIND NEW CRACK TO EXIT."

The ship continued downward through the water-filled crack in the ice, and Nate estimated they descended another four or five miles before the crack's walls opened up to a pitch-black ocean beneath Europa's thick, frozen crust. The light emanating from the ship now seemed to disappear into nothing as the craft surged forward into the inky depths. After several more minutes of black nothingness, Nate saw rocky terrain begin to appear far beneath them, and then he movement in the lights ahead. *Something large was moving towards them! Something alive!*

From a distance, the approaching creature slightly resembled the giant manta rays Nate and Tracie had swum with in Hawaii two summers prior. It was "flying" through the water, gracefully using the outer portions of its flat, oval body like wings. The ship came to a halt, hovering stationary as the animal swam without hesitation right up to it. It was huge, easily half the size of the ship. It had several appendages dangling from its underbelly, with a quad of sharp talons at the end of each. There was a semi-circle of dark spots around the snout... *Eyes!* Nate theorized, but then rescinded the thought. *No, there's no light here...perhaps they're sensory organs of some other kind.*

The animal circled the ship twice, and then flipped itself around to present its underside, and Nate saw its massive, toothy mouth, resembling that of a lamprey, only much larger. The creature wrapped its body around the mid-section of the ship and clamped on like a giant suction cup, its appendages folding flat against its belly to allow for the maneuver. Circular rows of jagged teeth chomped vigorously at the alloy surface, desperately trying to gain access to whatever was inside, but to no avail. Nate was both fascinated and horrified by the grotesque mouth in action up close, imagining a painful fate had there not been the impenetrable hull of the ship between him and the hungry Europan beast.

Dewey commented, "DO NOT WORRY. IT CANNOT HARM US.»

Nate wasn't worried. He'd hate to run into this thing in the open water, but he certainly felt quite safe inside Dewey's ship, even as several more of the creatures showed up to investigate. Dewey sent a mild jolt of energy through the ship's surface, causing the one that was trying to have them for lunch to promptly disengage, writhing for a moment to shake off the sting of the shock. Noticing this, the others seemed to realize the futility of attacking the ship and didn't bother to try. Instead, they flapped their wings and headed towards a school of strange red creatures that had come into view in the ship's lights.

The new arrivals were roughly conical in shape, with numerous rounded fins symmetrically placed about their middles, looking like a swarm of boat-propellers that gyrated and spun in synchronized patterns. The giant predators assaulted them mercilessly, folding their bodies around them like enormous Venus Flytraps, encasing them in inescapable prisons to be quickly devoured. Seconds later, when the predators' bodies unfolded, all that remained was floating bits of fleshy debris, which were quickly gobbled up by a throng of small scavengers that had amassed during the massacre. Nate thought of Tracie and how fascinated she would be to see this, much like the feeding frenzies of Earth's oceans she so loved to study, only with a very different and bizarre cast of characters.

Dewey showed Nate a few more examples of life in Europa's ocean. and then headed for the surface. He located a newly developed crack in the icy crust, and the transport was soon clear of the moon and shooting through space again. Nate was perplexed at how little time had actually passed since they'd left Earth, in relation how much he had seen already. He suddenly felt very primitive and incompetent, almost ashamed to be Human. It would have taken humanity years, perhaps decades, to have accomplished the same trip with any current technology available on Earth. Or, perhaps even more likely, Humans would never be intelligent enough to conceive and develop the technologies needed to do what he had just experienced with Dewey in a matter of hours.

After leaving the Jupiter system, Dewey circled the ship around Saturn and gave Nate a close-up look at the planet's rings for a few minutes, then shot out to the most distant regions of the solar system to show Nate Neptune, Uranus, Pluto, and Eris. They had toured billions of miles of space, and it hadn't even been eight hours since they'd left Earth.

"Dewey, how can we go so far in such a short time? Can you tell me more about the technologies you use to travel? How do you harness the gravity? How are we surviving the gravitational forces of going so fast? Is time changing as we go? Will more or less time have passed on Earth when I get back? How do..."

Nate was not allowed to finish. "PERHAPS IN MILLIONS OF YEARS THE DESCENDENTS OF NATE WILL UNDERSTAND THESE THINGS. NO MORE QUESTIONS ON THESE SUBJECTS. DEWEY CANNOT EXPLAIN IN TERMS NATE WILL UNDERSTAND. DO NOT BE CONCERNED WITH TIMELINE. TIMELINE WILL BE IDENTICAL ON EARTH AS IN OUR TRAVELS."

"Fair enough," Nate conceded. He wanted desperately to understand how it was possible to be doing things that had always been touted as physically impossible by Earth's most renowned physicists, but he didn't want to push the matter; he was grateful enough just to be here. "So where are we going now?"

«NOW WE GO TO EARTH STATION. EARTH STATION WILL GENERATE A GRAVITY TUNNEL. A GRAVITY TUNNEL IS NEEDED TO TRAVEL BEYOND

THIS SOLAR SYSTEM.»

"Sounds good! Why didn't we see Mars?"

«WE WILL SEE MARS BEFORE WE RETURN TO EARTH. THERE IS SOMETHING ON MARS DEWEY WANTS NATE TO SEE LAST.»

"What is it?"

«DIFFICULT TO EXPLAIN. BETTER FOR NATE TO SEE IT.»

"Okay, I like surprises!"

Nate couldn't imagine what on the desolate red planet might possibly be any more surprising or interesting than what he had already seen. But he trusted his tour guide, and was fine just going along with whatever Dewey wished to do.

Several minutes later, the transport slowed to approach the Earth Station. Nate marveled at the Alien outpost as it came into view, amazed to learn from Dewey that it had been there, supporting missions to Earth's solar system, for millions of years... and until relatively recently it had been in a low orbit around the Earth itself, and then located behind the Moon for a while before being moved behind Jupiter.

Dewey docked with the station manually, modifying the interface protocols so that no record of what he had been up to would be uploaded into the station's data banks. Then he programmed the station to create a gravity tunnel to a distant solar system in a far corner of the Milky Way. He chose that system because it contained a planet that he himself had often studied, one he was sure would be most fascinating for Nate to see. There was an Earth-like planet there with abundant surface and oceanic life. Of course, Dewey had previously been to all of the places he was taking Nate in holographic training sessions, but since it would be his first real visit there, he was just as excited as Nate to go see it.

Nate watched eagerly as the weave of light strands came together above the station to form the gravity tunnel. He saw the tunnel expand and then shoot off into the depths of space, stretching as far as he could see. He wondered how this wasn't detectable from Earth, but figured that Dewey's kind had addressed that in their stealth procedures and he didn't bother to ask about it. Then Dewey put up a new message.

«NATE SHOULD CONSUME NUTRITION AND SLEEP NOW. TRAVEL THROUGH THIS GRAVITY TUNNEL WILL TAKE 2 HOURS.»

Nate couldn't conceive sleeping and missing anything. But he *was* hungry. Dewey had said the liquid would provide his sustenance, but he hadn't swallowed any yet. He reluctantly took a gulp into his stomach. Other than the odd sensation of drinking and breathing the same substance, he felt no ill effects; and despite the bland flavor, the fluid satisfied his hunger.

"So, what's for dessert?"

«EXPLAIN DESSERT.»

"Never mind. But I'm too excited to sleep, I'd rather just…" Nate hadn't even finished typing before he felt his consciousness fading. He looked up towards Dewey for a moment, then all went black. Dewey waited for the sedative to fully take hold, and then checked Nate's vital signs. They were stable, so he initiated the launch sequence, and the transport disappeared into the gravity tunnel.

CHAPTER 35

It was late Saturday afternoon in London. Jason O'Rourke had arrived at Heathrow several hours earlier, made a brief stop by the house to kiss his wife and kids and freshen up, and then immediately drove to ARCA headquarters. He wanted to be there when the crates carrying Nate's gear were opened. The crates had arrived the previous day, but Jason had given strict instructions that they not be opened until he was there.

Jason and ARCA's Chief Tech Systems Manager, Toby Wickham, spent hours going through the contents of the crates. There were dozens of specimen jars loaded with the subjects Nate had collected. These, once catalogued for ARCA's archives, would later be shipped off to various museums and universities for study. The computer system, shelter components, security pyramid, and survival gear were all accounted for and appeared undamaged, save for the hand-held GPS unit, which had supposedly been smashed when Nate fell on the rocks. It was a cracked mess, and the screen was shattered.

Once the computer system was unpacked,

booted, and interfaced to a holo-display, Jason hovered impatiently over Wickham's shoulder as he extracted information from it. All the data Nate had entered about his research seemed routine, nothing out of the ordinary, and there was nothing logged about the meteorite beyond Jason's messages with the coordinates of the impact site. Nor was there any mention of the missing helicopter, but that was to be expected since Nate had never returned to the camp after going in search of the meteorite. There were, however, some rather interesting events chronicled in the security system's electromagnetic auto-log.

The computer was programmed to record every episode involving breaches in the pyramid's energy field, and the day Nate failed to check in, two large objects other than Nate had passed through the perimeter from opposite sides, just moments apart. Wickham was able to pull up rough images of the objects' shapes on the monitor screen.

"This one's definitely a big cat," Wickham exclaimed as Jason leaned over his shoulder for a close look. "See the long body, four legs, and tail?"

"Yes, I do see it," Jason confirmed.

"Must have been the same jaguar that Nate reported on his first day there. Here it looks like Nate passed through the field just before it, and either he didn't know it was behind him or he didn't have time to react. Otherwise he could have used the remote-control to turn up the field's power and give it a good shock."

"He didn't mention any second encounter with a jaguar."

"Why would he leave something like that out of his report? If it followed him into the camp, then he must have seen it."

"Agreed; he should have told me about it."

"Yes, you would think so, and here's where it gets really strange," Wickham went on. "This next thing to come through the field is bloody weird. It came in through the opposite side of the pyramid just a few seconds after the jaguar... and it's *big*, much bigger than a man. It looks like... well, *look* at it, what do *you* think that is?"

Jason studied the image, his brow rippling as he struggled to associate the silhouette with any creature known to the Amazon. "Well, I haven't a clue, but it *looks* like a giant frog standing on its hind legs... sort of."

Wickham chuckled. "I'm glad you said that, and not me. Last I checked, frogs in South America are a mite smaller, but that *is* what it looks like."

"Well, we know it wasn't a bloody giant frog, now don't we?" Jason said. "Go on, then, was there any more on the log that can help identify it?"

Wickham scrolled to the next recorded episode and pulled up the information. "According to this, a few minutes later the jaguar passed back through the field on its way out. Then the giant frog, or whatever the hell it was, left as well. Then Nate left a few minutes after that. That's the final entry. Nate never came back to the camp after that."

"Bloody hell!" Jason spat in frustration. "This static imagery tells us almost nothing. Alan told me to put video cameras around the campsite. I should have listened."

"I told you to as well," Wickham reminded him.

"Right. Well, Nathan didn't want it, felt it too intrusive on his privacy. Bloody hell. I want to know what that *thing* was out there! There has to be a simple explanation. Maybe a local tribesman with some strange outfit on, or maybe two of them walking close together."

"If that's what it was, then maybe they chased off the jaguar?"

"Perhaps, but I still don't get why Nate wouldn't have mentioned any of this."

"Beats me, chief, I just put the gear together and fix it when your blokes in the field break it, which they always do. It's up to you and your rich American chaps what they actually *do* out there in the jungles. But if you ask me, that is *not* a local tribesman. Look closely at those appendages...they look like curved arms with hands and long, curved fingers, but nothing like a man's fingers. It *still* looks like a frog to me."

Jason changed the subject. "What about the smashed GPS unit? Can we get anything from that?"

"It was damaged when Nate dropped it on the rocks where you found him, but the computer logged all of its movement up until then." Wickham switched to a different screen.

"Go back the entire day, let's see where he was before the jaguar followed him back to camp."

"Looks like he went north about a mile and a half that morning... thennnn...»

"Then *what*?" Jason inquired, puzzled at Toby's hesitation.

Wickham typed furiously at the holo-interface, trying fruitlessly to extract the missing data. "Well, the signal just disappears. That's odd."

"Disappears? *How*?"

"Normally this could only happen if there was some kind of interference messing with the signal, but there shouldn't have been any magnetic or electric interference that strong where he was." Then some new data finally popped up on the display and Wickham continued, "Ahh, *here* we go. Looks like an hour later the signal reappeared and he came back to camp—in a hurry, it would seem."

"Being chased by the jaguar."

"Yes, that would make sense given the timing of the pyramid breaches. As soon as he passes through the security field, the jaguar *and* our mystery frog-man show up within seconds. Then two minutes later the jaguar leaves, followed by the frog-man. And then...»

Wickham paused as he tried to make sense of the data, his brow curling up into a row of plump ridges.

Jason became impatient with the delay in Toby's response. "And then *what*?"

"Well... then Nathan leaves the camp and goes

north *again* to the same spot he was earlier, and when he gets there, the signal disappears again. None of this makes any sense. What the hell was your man up to out there?"

Jason had not yet offered every detail of the bizarre events Nate had fallen into, but he supposed there was no point in holding back now; he needed Toby's expertise to figure out what had really happened, or at least try to.

"I sent him to investigate a meteorite impact site at the request of the Brazilian Astronomical Society. As you're aware, our financiers are quite sympathetic to that organization, perhaps even more so than ours, so I was obliged to help."

"Let me guess. Antonio Perron and Alan Mercer."

"Yes, Tony and Mr. Mercer go way back... and Alan did insist I help Tony out."

"I should have known. Why don't you guys tell me these things? I could have sent gear with Nathan more suitable for this kind of thing than collecting bugs, had I known."

"We didn't know this was going to happen. Tony called me *after* Nate was already there. So, do you think a meteorite might generate the interference that messed with the GPS locator?" Jason wasn't ready yet to speak of Perron's belief that the meteorite Nate found was, in fact, the missing Brazilian helicopter.

"Well, that *might* explain it, but it's a long-shot. I imagine a good-sized meteorite *might* have had some magnetic or electrical interference that messed with the signal. You did check Nate for radioactivity, right?"

"No," Jason replied. It hadn't even crossed his mind to run such a test. But that might explain why the meteorite was still so hot after 72 hours on the ground — if it really was a meteorite.

"You might consider it. Whatever killed the GPS signal might have affected him as well."

"Right. I'll do that," Jason replied, then yawned. Toby could see the deep fatigue in Jason's posture.

"And maybe you should go home and get some sleep. You look like shit, old chap."

"I *feel* like shit... hardly slept in the last three days. Think I'll take that advice. But promise you'll call me the moment you find anything else unusual?"

"Yes, fine, I will. Now get out of here. I've got this, chief."

Jason had barely left the parking lot when Wickham rang in on his cell phone.

"Yes?" Jason yawned as he answered.

Wickham sounded very irritated. "Jason, if you expect me to help you figure this out, you need to tell me what *really* happened with Nathan out there. And I mean *everything*! What in bloody hell did he get himself into?"

"Why, what else have you found?"

"The GPS unit. I opened it up right after you left. It's been altered somehow. It's *amazing*; I've never seen anything like it."

"What do you mean, altered?"

"Well, for starters, the thing is smashed to bits, I mean it's totally demolished, as if he smashed it repeatedly against the rocks! I built it quite rugged, you know, and a mere fall onto a rock couldn't have caused this much damage. But some of the guts are still intact, and the most curious thing is that the uplink circuitry appears to have been completely rewired. And the graphics interface has been rewired, too."

"How is that possible? Why would Nate do that?"

«*Nate*? Are you *joking,* old man? Nate couldn't have done this. Hell, *I* couldn't have done this. Nobody I know could have done this! The circuits are all re-worked using nearly microscopic solder points. It's the most precise soldering I've ever seen."

"You must be joking, right? Listen to yourself, Toby—this all sounds preposterous. You're supposed to be the expert here. There has to be a more logical explanation."

"Do I sound like I'm joking? Why on bloody Earth would I make this up? I *am* the expert here, and I'm telling you exactly what I've found."

"Okay, okay, sorry... please continue."

"It's not just the precise solder joints that completely reconfigured the circuit board, it's the components themselves, the capacitors, resistors, diodes, and transistors — they've all been converted *internally* to perform different tasks. This is *impossible*... at least, it *should* be impossible. But here it is, sitting on my bloody desk. Jason, *what is going on here*?"

"I don't know, Toby... I honestly don't know.

Something odd did happen out there involving the meteorite. Nate says he blacked out and hit his head on a rock, and now seems to have developed amnesia about the whole episode. Then I'm told a Brazilian military chopper was lost while trying to find him, and there's no trace of it. That's all I know at the moment."

"Bloody hell." Wickham snorted in skepticism. "I'm not a fucking mushroom, Jason. You must have *some* ideas about what happened."

Jason hesitated, wanting to tell Toby of the helicopter's presumed fate; but not yet believing it himself, he elected to keep that mum for the moment. "Toby, I swear I will tell you everything as soon as I get some more information. I truly don't know what happened, but I *will* find out, and you'll be among the first to know, I promise."

"Fair enough. I'll do you the favor of not sharing this with anyone. Every government on the planet would love to study this GPS unit, I can assure you that!"

"Yes, absolutely, *please* keep a lid on this. I can't think straight right now, I'm exhausted. I'm going to get some sleep, and then I'll talk to Nate and try to get to the bottom of this. Stay cool, old chap, I'll be in touch."

CHAPTER 36

Tracie lay curled up on the sofa with Doo-Doo, staring blankly at the lifeless TV. There was no program on; every screen in the house had been altered by Dewey's little laser-beam thingy and didn't work normally anymore, so she couldn't binge-watch any of her favorite series to pass the excruciating hours. It had been almost twelve hours since Nate had left with Dewey, and she hadn't slept a wink. She was completely exhausted, but too anxious to sleep and afraid of taking a sleeping pill, lest she miss any communication from Nate.

She was grateful the entire episode had happened over her one weekend off per month, unsure that she could keep her shit together at work. In fact, she was sure that come Monday, she'd be calling in sick until Nate returned... assuming he returned at all. What if he didn't come back? What would she do? What would she tell everyone? She was terrified, and trembled at the thought.

When her cellphone rang, she leapt off the sofa like a frightened cat, sending a startled Doo-Doo tumbling onto the carpet. She answered excitedly, hoping it was a long-distance call from deep space. "*Hello*?"

"Hallo, Tracie?" It was Jason O'Rourke.

Oh God, please don't ask where Nate is! Tracie thought to herself, clamping her eyelids shut and wincing. She wasn't in any mood to talk to anyone, especially anyone from ARCA, and silently chastised herself for answering the phone before checking the Caller ID. *Of course he'll ask where Nate is, you idiot. Why else would he be calling on my phone? He can't reach Nate... nobody can.*

"Hello, Jason, how are you?" she managed, doing her best to conceal her anxiety.

"I'm well, thank you. Rather exhausted, I must confess, but in one piece. I trust you two are getting back to a normal life now that Nate is home safe and sound?"

"Oh yeah, normal as can be." Tracie chuckled sarcastically.

"That's wonderful. Is Nathan about? I really need to chat with him, and I can't get through on his phone."

"No, actually, he's gone for the rest of the weekend."

"I see. Where did he go? It's rather important I reach him."

"He's... fishing. He went fishing with a friend down in Sanibel. They usually go way out off-shore, that's probably why he doesn't have a signal."

Across the Atlantic on the other end of the call,

Jason frowned, thinking silently, *He gets home from a near-death experience in the Amazon, hasn't seen his wife in weeks... and he goes fishing?*

"Right then, well, I'm sorry for the bother. When you talk to him, please let him know that I'll be coming to the States this week, and I'll need to sit and have a talk with him while I'm there. I'll be by his office at the university on Tuesday. There are some new questions that have surfaced about what happened, and I'm hoping he can shed some light."

"You bet, I'll tell him. What kind of questions? I'm sure he'll ask."

"Oh, just more boring details. Bloody monotonous, you know, all this red tape, but I need to give a presentation to ARCA's board of investors in New York, and I'm still a little puzzled about what happened when he found the meteorite."

"Well, he hit his head pretty hard, Jason. I think he's probably told you all he can remember."

"I'm sure that's the case. I'm just hoping after a few days home, he might recall something else if I help him jar his memory. Perhaps not, but worth a try, eh?"

"I suppose, but please go easy on him; he's been through a lot."

"I will, I promise. Good day."

After hanging up, Tracie collapsed back onto the sofa and cried softly. Doo-Doo jumped into her arms and licked her face. She held him tight and sobbed, "That bastard better be home soon, Mr. Stinky, or they're going to have to lock me up in a padded room."

Back across the Atlantic, Jason's six-year-old daughter, Kimberly, found him in his den, staring at his phone. She hopped into his lap, giggling, and hugged his neck. "Daddy, why are you frowning, aren't you happy to see me?"

He didn't answer right away. He could only hang on Tracie's words… he was convinced she had been concealing something. *But what, and why*?

"What's wrong, Papa? Are you sad?" Kimberly insisted, the innocent curiosity in her tone prying a gentle smile out of Jason's frown. He momentarily snapped out of his angst over the matters at hand and gave his daughter a firm kiss on the forehead.

"Nothing for you to worry about, my pretty little peanut. Papa's just a bit tired, that's all."

"But you've been sleeping for hours. How can you still be tired?"

"You *are* a perceptive one, aren't you?"

"What does that mean?"

"Well, it means you're good at noticing what goes on around you, and that is a wonderful quality. But the truth is, Papa was only lying in bed for a while. I tried to sleep, but I have a lot on my mind."

"Like what?" Kimberly persisted, forcing a bigger smile and laughter.

"It's very complicated, Peanut. And nothing *you* need worry about at your tender age."

Kimberly changed the subject. "Must you go to America tomorrow? You just got back, and Mummy has a holiday planned for us this weekend. She's very upset, you know."

"I know, Angel, and I'm very sorry; but yes, I must go. I promise we'll all go on a holiday as soon as I get back next weekend. Now run along, Papa's got more work to do."

"Oh, all right," she conceded with a sigh "But I miss you so when you're gone. Please hurry back this time."

"I will, I promise. I always miss you as well… and your brother and Mummy too."

As soon as Kimberly left the room, Jason made another call, this time to ARCA's chairman, Alan Mercer. Mercer was a hugely successful venture-capitalist, a multi-faceted entrepreneur from New York considered to be one of the wealthiest individuals ever to live. With the foundation of his father's wealth as a launching pad, his formidable empire had come from decades of cunning and shrewd business deals, but in his heart he harbored a deep passion for the sciences, particularly biology, astrophysics, and cosmology, and he was well educated in all of these fields. To the world, he was recognized as equally philanthropic and self-serving, as he used his vast fortune and keen intellect to accomplish things that, at times, greatly benefited the population of the Earth. But at other times, his ridiculously expensive projects catered only to his own whims and desires.

Massive grants from Mercer and a few of his richest partners had been the primary source of ARCA's funding for years. Mercer and his group were also significant contributors to astronomical research groups, including the Brazilian Astronomical Society that Antonio Perron headed. Perron and Jason had first met each other at one of Mercer's lavish parties several years prior. The leverage Mercer held over ARCA was a sore spot for Jason; he hated feeling like Mercer's puppet at times, but it was a necessary evil as far as he was concerned. Having Mercer's deep pockets to tap into had allowed ARCA to move years ahead of any similar organization... and so Jason did Mercer's bidding with little question. Most people treated Mercer this way.

It was Mercer who had propagated and funded ARCA's going high-tech, using his own resources and tech companies to help develop the security pyramid and space-age survival gear that Nate Johnston had used in the Amazon. This had seemed odd to Jason, as the price tag was immense and there was really no monetary return on such investments, only the advancement of learning new things about the rainforests and contributing to scientific development with more efficiency and comfort. But Mercer had other motives that he did not speak of, and clearly never expected to make money from ARCA. He did, however, expect the funds and equipment to be used effectively and productively, and he held

Jason to high standards in those regards.

As head of ARCA, Jason was to provide a detailed accounting of every dollar spent to Mercer and his board. There would be a lot of explaining to do about the bill for Nate's adventures in Brazil. The expedition had been allocated a big chunk of money to begin with, and Jason had spent another fortune to go find Nate when he went missing, without permission to do so. For the past two days Mercer had been leaving Jason voicemails and e-mails with mounting questions on the episode, but Jason had not yet replied. He wanted to have some credible answers for Mercer before he did so, because Mercer hated to hear the words "I don't know."

And now Mercer had been informed there were allegations by the Brazilian Air Force that ARCA might have played a role in the loss of a rescue helicopter and its crew. Most concerning to Mercer was this bizarre meteorite that Nate had supposedly discovered, which now was in the possession of Antonio Perron at the Brazilian Astronomical Society's main complex in São Paolo. He had been trying to reach Perron as well to get more information, but like Jason, Perron had not returned any of his calls yet either, and this was most annoying to Mercer.

Jason was hoping to speak further with Nate and Perron before contacting Mercer, but he couldn't put it off any longer. He got through to Mercer's assistant and was only on hold for seconds before Mercer picked up, noticeably angry. "Jason, where the hell have you been, man? I've been trying to reach you for two days!"

"Yes, Alan, my apologies. The past 48 hours have been... interesting, to say the least."

"No shit, Jason. Tell me about it! The Brazilian government wants *me* to pay for a lost chopper and its crew, not to mention pending lawsuits from the crews' families, and I need Perron to start sharing data on this supposed meteorite Nate found, but I can't get *him* on the phone either! Why do I not know what's going on here yet? What the hell am I forking over all this money to you two for when you don't even return my calls? Can you please shed some light and get me up to speed on this?"

"I'm still sorting it out, but I hope to have some answers for you when I come in next week. Right now none of it makes much sense; that's why I haven't called back yet, Alan. I was hoping to have an explanation for everything once we connected, and... well, I just don't yet. It's all quite bizarre."

"Well, you should have been in touch with me from the start. I thought we were clear on things like this."

"With all due respect, Alan, things like this have never happened before."

"Okay, I get that, but from here on out I need to be in the loop on this every step forward. And why the hell is Tony being so quiet about this meteorite? No one here has heard *anything* from him since it was delivered to his labs. Who rightfully owns the damn thing, anyway? Have you figured that out yet? We found it, so can't we keep it?"

"I doubt it. Nathan did find it, and he was on ARCA's bankroll, but since it landed on Brazilian soil, it technically belongs to them. For the moment, I believe Perron has authority over it, unless the government steps in and takes it from him."

"If he still has it, then why is he not retuning my calls?"

"I don't know," Jason lied.

"Good Lord," Mercer muttered, his tone softening a bit. "Okay, I'll just keep trying to reach him, I suppose. I understand Nate has some amnesia about the whole episode, hit his head pretty hard. Will he be okay?"

"Yes. And I'm hoping a little time will help him remember more details. I'm going to visit him before I come see you next week."

"Excellent, bring him with you!"

"Pardon me?"

"You heard me/ Bring Professor Johnston to New York with you. I'd like to meet him."

"Alan, I... I don't think that's a good idea."

"Nonsense! Don't worry, I'll behave. I promise. I'd like to meet the man who's costing me all this money and trouble. Well, besides you, Jason."

Jason fell silent on the line.

"Lighten up, man, I'm kidding. Now that we're *finally* in contact, let's work through this thing."

"I'm sorry for the delay, Alan, I truly am. This

whole thing is a bloody mess. I will not rest until we figure it all out, and I promise to keep you informed."

"Yes, I know you will. I know you and your team are handling it as best you can under the circumstances. But there's a lot of eyes on me about this whole episode, especially with the missing helicopter. I'd like to get it all straightened out as quickly as possible, and speaking with Nate in person will help me feel like I'm doing all I can on this end. Besides, it will be an honor to meet him. I really admire the man's work."

"Well then, I'll see what I can do to get him on the plane with me and we'll see you Thursday."

"Excellent! And if you talk to Tony before I do, tell him to call me right away."

CHAPTER 37

N ate was sound asleep and dreaming of the rainforest, compliments of the sedatives Dewey had included in his habitat's liquid. As the ship approached the end of the gravity tunnel, Dewey discontinued the sedative and introduced a new agent to wake Nate.

Nate's awareness shifted from being in the rainforest to a narrow passageway that was lined with pipes and high-tech control panels, reminding him of things he'd seen once during a tour of a modern nuclear submarine, or maybe a sophisticated factory of some sort. He was surrounded by three brawny young men and an athletic woman, all clad in soldier's gear, brandishing some very impressive firearms. The soldiers began shooting sporadically at the walls of the passageway, which instantly came alive in a tangle of organic activity... serpentlike creatures that were hissing and lunging with menacing silver teeth.

Nate was completely startled. He panicked and tried to run, but he was unable to move quickly, his legs hampered in some kind of paralysis, like he was trying to run through a pool of thick syrup. He did briefly consider the possibility he was dreaming all this, but it seemed and felt very real. Then a woman's voice pierced through the gunfire, as if speaking over a walkie-talkie or intercom of some sort, barking frantic orders at the soldiers. Nate recognized the voice; it was Ripley. *Lieutenant Ripley? Sigourney Weaver?*

Nate now recognized what he was seeing: a scene from the movie *Aliens*, the second episode of the franchise and one of his favorite sci-fi flicks. But he'd never dreamt about it before, so it seemed very odd that he would leave his dream of the Amazon to come *here. And what was with the thick fluid he was floating in?*

Suddenly everything came rushing back. *Dewey! I'm still in Dewey's spaceship in the habitat! I'm in fucking outer space, watching the movie* Aliens*!*

Nate shook off the remaining cobwebs and looked forward through the habitat wall. He recognized the back of Dewey's floating chair, and above the chair he saw Dewey's eyes atop their stalks. Dewey looked as if he were mesmerized by the film, which continued to play all around the ship's interior in panoramic view. Nate located the holo-keyboard and typed a message. "Dewey, are we still in space?"

«YES. TRANSPORT IS NEARING THE END OF THE GRAVITY TUNNEL. SOON WE WILL REACH NEW

DESTINATION. DOES NATE FEEL REGENERATED?"

"Yes, I feel great. But what's up with this movie playing on the walls around us?"

«IT IS A RECORDED TRANSMISSION FROM EARTH, DEPICTING FICTITIOUS ALIEN LIFE FORMS CONFLICTING WITH HUMANS. DEWEY ENJOYS THIS FOR ENTERTAINMENT DURING GRAVITY TUNNEL TRAVEL."

Nate grinned as he read Dewey's message. *A real Alien watching our movies about fake aliens. Far out.* He typed some more. "Well, the food is so-so on this trip, though I must say the in-flight entertainment is excellent! But I've seen this movie many times already; can I see what's going on outside the ship?"

Dewey engaged the external viewer and the image instantly changed to the vast canvas of deep space, an ocean of black with endless points of light peppering the distance. With the glow of the sun no longer polluting the view, the stars seemed alive and far more brilliant than Nate could remember ever seeing before. There were also two massive nebulas visible, one on either side of their path. One was hourglass-shaped and crimson, with bright green and blue streaks extending from its center section. The other had no specific shape; it was spread out in sporadic puffs of swirling yellow and orange with countless twinkling points of light throughout. Nate knew that the nebulae must be at least several hundred light-years away, but they appeared massive and beautiful on the display as if he could reach out and touch them.

"Are we in a gravity tunnel now?"

"YES."

"Why can't I see the tunnel?"

"TUNNEL IS PASSING TOO QUICKLY TO BE VISIBLE. WHEN SHIP DECELERATES YOU WILL SEE IT."

"How fast are we going?"

«TUNNEL CREATES PATH BETWEEN TWO LARGE SOURCES OF GRAVITY. SECTIONS OF SPACE COLLAPSING OR EXPANDING INSIDE TUNNEL PROPELS INNERMOST SECTION WITH TRANSPORT TO 1,000,000 MULTIPLES OF SPEED OF LIGHT. TRANSPORT TRAVELS JUST UNDER SPEED OF LIGHT WITHIN TUNNEL.»

Dewey had briefly forgotten that he had decided not to divulge too much information to Nate about the technology of his ship. But he quickly dismissed any concerns; he was enjoying answering Nate's questions.

"We're going a million times the speed of light right now?"

"YES."

Nate felt weak and lightheaded as he pondered the concept of travelling this fast. He had never felt so vulnerable or fragile in his life. This kind of travel shouldn't be possible; it contradicted every law of physics he had ever heard.

"What if something goes wrong? Won't we be

pulverized?"

«YES, IF THERE IS A MALFUNCTION THE TRANS-PORT WILL IMMEDIATELY CEASE TO EXIST.»

"Great."

«WE ARE NOW APPROACHING OUR DESTINATION.»

Dewey plugged a few commands into the holo-displays. Nate felt a tingling sensation, and on the viewer he noticed a change in the space surrounding the ship. A pattern began to emerge, distorting the view of the distant stars like a weave of water spirals moving rapidly past the vessel; then everything became a blur of dull light. After a while, the spirals gradually slowed until Nate could see flashes of black space and stars, visible through open segments of the spiral pattern. When the transport had slowed to several thousand miles per second, it exited the gravity tunnel and Nate could once again see all the celestial sights that surrounded the ship. Directly ahead, a star was getting larger in the viewer, and shortly after Nate detected several planets, looking like small dots in orbit around the sun. *A solar system!*

"Dewey, this is just amazing. Where are we?"

«IN A LOCATION OF GALAXY: MILKY WAY FAR FROM EARTH. THERE IS A PLANET HERE WITH MUCH LIFE," Dewey announced, and then a holo-image of the Milky Way manifested on the inner wall of the habitat, with a green dot and red dot, a dashed line between them showing Nate Earth's location and where they were now.

The ship proceeded towards the star for a few more minutes, then changed course slightly to intercept an approaching planet, orbiting at what seemed to Nate a similar distance as the Earth to the Sun. Dewey navigated around the backside of the planet and docked with the local station, which the Aliens had placed there a bit over a million years ago when they had discovered this planet. To Nate's eyes, this station was identical to the one back home, behind Jupiter. But obviously there was no need to hide this one from its subject planet's inhabitants, as it was orbiting in plain view just beyond the outer atmosphere. They were close enough that Nate could see the geographic features of the planet below quite well.

It somewhat resembled Earth, with clouds, vast blue oceans, and several continental land masses. The continents were clearly vegetated, the surface appearing rough and somewhat fuzzy instead of smooth and rocky like the Moon or Mars. But the plant life of this planet was a patchwork of crimson and purple instead of green. There were also plentiful snow-capped mountain peaks peeking through the clouds. From this position, he also noticed three small moons beyond the station's orbit, two of which appeared to have blue oceans, the third looking dead and lifeless like Earth's sole Moon. Beyond the orbits of the moons there was a giant multi-colored ring, similar to Saturn's.

"This is so beautiful!" he typed.

"YES IT IS. DEWEY IS HAPPY TO SHARE THIS EXPERIENCE WITH NATE."

Nate remained on the ship in his habitat while Dewey entered the station. There, Dewey gathered coordinates and data about the planet's best landing locations from the station's memory banks, having disabled the ship's automatic synchronization functions and being very careful to erase all evidence of his unauthorized docking. There were no new missions scheduled to this planet at the moment; its life-forms had all been catalogued centuries ago, and none of his kind would return to study this part of the Milky Way for at least another thousand years. But he wanted to be sure that when they did, there would be no record of his having been there.

Moments later, Dewey returned to the ship and loaded new coordinates into the navigation computers. First, he took Nate on a tour of one of the planet's moons, dipping down near the surface and into the oceans and lakes to see some of the life-forms that thrived there up close. Some looked eerily similar to those of Earth, while others were bizarre and foreign to anything Nate had ever imagined.

"Dewey, this is amazing. Do you have all of these life-forms catalogued?"

"YES. OTHERS BEFORE DEWEY HAVE RECORDED MUCH LIFE IN THIS PLANETARY SYSTEM. DEWEY

HAS NEVER BEEN HERE BEFORE. DEWEY HAS ONLY SEEN CLONES OR HOLOGRAPHIC SIMULATIONS OF THESE LIFE-FORMS BEFORE.»

Nate had to remind himself that Dewey was a rookie explorer who had never left his own solar system until now. This fact had been unnerving when Dewey first proposed taking him on a gallivant about the Milky Way, but Dewey was handling the trip with such proficiency that it seemed implausible he had zero experience other than holo-simulated training, and Nate had completely forgotten about it. But the truth was they were both experiencing this adventure for the first time, and this pleased Nate and Dewey immensely. For both, there was something magical and intoxicating about the uniqueness of their adventure together, not to mention the miniscule odds that such a bonding between two species, separated by an entire Universe, could ever have happened in the first place.

On the second moon, Dewey and Nate observed a large winged creature hunting in the lower atmosphere. It had long, thick tentacles hanging underneath its disc-shaped body, with four sets of wings on its topside. The massive wings flapped gracefully as it hovered over a rocky mountain ledge that was crawling with orange crab-like creatures, each as big as a horse. The giant mountain crabs were grazing peacefully, meticulously searching nooks and crannies in the rocks for food with agile pincers, and were completely oblivious to the predator hovering above. After singling out a victim, the flying beast suddenly folded its wings above its body and dropped like a rock, its tentacles spreading out in the wind to reveal a large, pointed cone that protruded from its underside. The cone looked to be made of bone or tooth enamel, and when the predator landed right on top of the mountain crab, the hard point smashed the hapless creature's shell to bits. Then the dive-bombing cephalopod wrapped its tentacles around the mangled carcass, flapped its wings, and carried it off. The rest of the mountain crabs scattered for a moment, but then resumed their casual grazing as soon as the episode was over. They didn't seem to notice that another of the flying predators was approaching.

After witnessing several more fascinating life-forms on this moon, Dewey took the ship back to the host planet.

The planet's sky was blue like Earth's, but the clouds were very different—wispy swirls of pale green and yellow, twinkling as if someone had tossed handfuls of glitter about inside of them. Dewey slowed the ship and entered one of the clouds, and Nate could see the source of the twinkling: there were swarms of small flying creatures with shiny silver backs fluttering about inside. Their bodies were flat and hexagonal, with small heads at one end but no tail. Their six spindly limbs supported a kite-like fabric of skin, and they had what looked like small suction cups at the ends of their feet. Nate thought they resembled bats or flying squirrels with six legs. A few landed on the outer surface of the ship and crawled about using their suction-cup feet to hold on. As the vessel passed out of the cloud and continued downwards, the creatures released their grip and ascended back up towards the cloud on the updrafts rising from the planet surface.

«THESE ANIMALS HAVE LITTLE MASS. THEY RIDE UPDRAFTS INTO THE CLOUDS TO FEED ON NUTRIENTS IN THE ATMOSPHERE," Dewey commented. Then he brought the transport to a full stop, hovering beneath the clouds. "LOOK ABOVE US AND OBSERVE. THERE IS A PREDATOR APPROACHING TO FEED ON THE CLOUD DWELLERS.»

Nate leaned backwards into the habitat's purple fluid to see a massive silhouette move into view above the ship, blocking the star's glow as it lumbered overhead. Whatever it was, it was enormous, as big as a jumbo jet, Nate thought. It had a long, flat, wide body, with two broad wings across either side. It soared gracefully towards a cloud full of the shimmering creatures and its gaping mouth opened wide as it entered, taking in a huge gulp of the hapless prey. When the behemoth exited the cloud, puffs of green and yellow mist exited gill-like slits at either side of its monstrous head, sans the unfortunate little cloud-dwellers who were filtered out and swallowed by the hundreds.

"It's just like a whale or manta ray feeding on a school of krill, only in the sky," Nate typed.

"YES," Dewey agreed. "THE SIMILARITY IS FASCINATING."

Dewey and Nate both fell into a trance as they watched the sky-ray feed above the ship. So fixated on the creature were they that neither of them saw what was approaching from below. When the proximity sensors shot a warning alert through a holo-disc and straight into Dewey's brain, he turned one eye-set to see what the problem was, and immediately stiffened in his chair.

«NATE, PREPARE FOR AN IMPACT.»

Nate looked to see what Dewey was referring to. Directly beneath the ship was another of the sky-rays, its humongous mouth agape and headed directly towards the ship. There was no time for Dewey to react. Nate watched in horror as the beast engulfed the entire ship in its mouth. A jolt rippled through the fluid of the habitat as the creature shut its jaws around the transport, completely engulfing it.

Everything went pitch black inside the ship, except for the holo-displays.

The next few minutes were like a horrible nightmare to Nate. What had been a smooth, comfortable ride in the inertia- and gravity-stable environment of the habitat was now like being in a barrel that had just been tossed over a cliff. He bounced around the habitat as if it were being violently shaken. He caught a few glimpses of Dewey, barely visible in the glow of the holo-displays as he frantically punched commands into the stabilizer and nav systems, but it was obvious that there were malfunctions that he could not overcome quickly. Then Nate hit his head hard on the ceiling and felt himself begin to black out. The last thing he remembered was seeing a set of Dewey's eyes looking back at him from the cockpit viewer, and pain… a lot of pain.

CHAPTER 38

When Nate came to, he was floating askew in the habitat. His whole body ached, and his vision was blurred. He stayed motionless for a moment, trying to recall what had just happened, and then the whole episode of the big flying creature swallowing the ship came rushing back. He struggled to right himself and took a look around outside the habitat, frantically trying to see where Dewey was.

As his vision cleared, he realized the habitat was no longer inside the ship.

The habitat sat on the ground outside the ship, which was also on the ground. This was immediately concerning, as Nate had never seen Dewey's ship actually resting on the ground before now; it had always hovered a few feet above. He turned painfully, wincing, trying to get a better view of the surrounding area. The local star was shining brightly overhead, and Nate could see clearly in every direction.

The ship and habitat were sitting on a smooth beach of pale orange sand next to a shimmering aquamarine ocean. Inland off the beach, a thick jungle of strange-looking trees sloped upwards several miles into the distance, culminating at the base of a sprawling, snow-capped mountain range. The trees had thick black trunks and dark red branches with no leaves; rather, each branch had clumps of thick, spaghetti-like strands that were all slowly writhing and undulating in a moving mass, as if probing the air for nutrients. They reminded Nate of the sea anemones Tracie studied at the aquarium back home. The sky above was blue like that of Earth, sparsely peppered with the green and yellow shimmering clouds. Had it not been for the current predicament following the disaster in the sky, Nate would have thought this to be a perfect day on this alien world.

Then Nate turned to see what was in the opposite direction, and he saw Dewey.

Dewey was squatting in the sand a hundred feet up the beach next to a massive, dark mass of mangled flesh piled up on the shore. Nate assumed it must the remains of the flying beast that had tried to swallow the ship. It lay motionless, streaks of mustard-colored ichor oozing from various wounds in its gargantuan corpse. Indigenous scavengers were already starting to gather; there were droves of small crustacean-like creatures swarming about the carcass, nipping at it with claws and mandibles. Bizarre-looking flying things circled above like vultures, preparing to descend upon the feast. Nate could see the eyes of the expired beast, a line of them in a wide crest about its huge skull, each the size of a soccer-ball, black and lifeless.

Dewey was touching the fallen goliath with all four hands, and he was bowing towards it as if in prayer. He had kept one set of eyes focused on the habitat, and when he saw that Nate was awake, he rose from his squatting position in the sand and scurried over to check on him.

«NATE FRIEND, ARE YOU WELL? IS NATE IN ANY PAIN?" Dewey's message was a tremendous relief to Nate. He had feared the accident might have damaged some of Dewey's technology, including the ability to communicate. Then the holographic keyboard re-appeared in the liquid and Nate typed with shaky hands.

"I think I am okay. What happened? Why did that animal try to swallow the ship?"

"DEWEY SUSPECTS LIFE-FORM SAW CLOUDS REFLECTING ON SURFACE OF TRANSPORT AND BELIEVED TRANSPORT WAS A CLOUD. LIFE-FORM TRIED TO INGEST TRANSPORT TO FEED ON CLOUD-DWELLING CREATURES. LIFE-FORM WAS UNABLE TO DISLODGE TRANSPORT FROM THROAT AND FELL TO OCEAN. LIFE FORM PERISHED.»

"What were you doing to it just now?"

«DEWEY IS RESPONSIBLE FOR DEATH OF LIFE-FORM. DEWEY IS ASKING FOR FORGIVENESS AND REQUESTING THAT THE CREATOR CARE FOR SPIRIT OF LIFE-FORM.»

Dewey was visibly upset, his eyes changing into

a variety of mottled colors; his skin had turned pale gray with yellow streaks. Nate tried to console him. "I'm sure the Creator will forgive you. It was an accident. So was the helicopter on Earth. It's my fault, too, I interfered with your mission on Earth and asked you to bring me here. These are extraordinary things that you and I are doing, Dewey, and we have both been caught up in the excitement of it. We have both been a little reckless. We are both to blame."

Dewey's eyes turned solid purple. "NATE FRIEND IS VERY KIND. BUT DEWEY IS ASHAMED. DEWEY SHOULD NOT HAVE ALLOWED THESE THINGS TO HAPPEN. DEWEY HAS BEEN THE MOST CARELESS."

Nate changed the subject. "Is the ship okay?"

«NO, IT IS DAMAGED. REPAIRS ARE IN PROGRESS.»

Nate glanced at the ship and noticed that there were several silver spheres, like large ball-bearings, hovering around the vessel. Thin fans of blue light emitted by the spheres swept across the surface of the crippled craft.

"Will we be able to get back to Earth?" Nate typed nervously.

«YES, BUT REPAIRS WILL TAKE TIME.»

"How much time?"

«APPROXIMATELY 107 MINUTES. WOULD NATE LIKE TO EXIT HABITAT? ATMOSPHERE OF THIS PLANET CONTAINS SUFFICIENT LEVELS OF OXYGEN FOR HUMAN SURVIVAL. NO DANGEROUS COMPONENTS IN ATMOSPHERE. TEMPERATURE IS 86 DEGREES

FARENHEIT. RADIATION LEVEL IS NOT DANGEROUS. GRAVITY IS 40 PERCENT LESS THAN EARTH.»

"Sure, why not?"

Nate was a little frightened, but couldn't resist the temptation to explore this new world a bit without the encumbrance of his fish-bowl. Dewey sent a command through a holo-disc, and the habitat's lid opened. Nate felt the tingling sensation in his ribs as his body rose and began to exit the liquid. He had expected to go through a coughing fit to get the fluid out of his lungs, but to his amazement, the goop easily exited on its own and ran down his body, purposefully dripping back into the pool below. He took a deep breath. The air felt thick and tasted sweet, like syrup, and he started to speak.

"Dewey, that was...." Nate didn't complete the sentence. His words sounded like a chipmunk cartoon character's. *Must be this atmosphere, like breathing helium or something!*

"Well, whaddaya know!" Nate stated with a big grin, and then laughed hysterically at his whimsical new Munchkin voice. He grinned and began singing. "We represent the Lollipop Guild, the Lollipop Guild, the Lollipop Guild... follow the yellow brick road!"

Dewey watched Nate with concern, puzzled as much as fascinated by the sudden, strange behavior.

"PERHAPS THIS IS NOT A PRUDENT IDEA. THE ATMOSPHERE IS CAUSING NATE TO BECOME IRRATIONAL."

Nate didn't reply; he was above the habitat now,

and did not notice Dewey's message on the inner wall of the container below. When the energy field gently brought his feet down to the beach and released his full weight, he immediately experienced the sensation of being much lighter than he was on Earth. He tried to take a few steps, but flailed awkwardly as he bounced a few feet before stumbling to his knees. He stood and tried again, bouncing back and forth as he became better acquainted with how to maneuver in the lower gravity.

"I don't suppose you have any *clothes* I can wear?" Nate jokingly asked, feeling a bit foolish being naked, on top of speaking like a Munchkin.

"Graaaf-peooood-friiiiiiyj," Dewey responded through his blow-holes. His vocalizations were also higher-pitched than they had been on Earth. Nate realized that outside the habitat and with the ship under repair, there was no readily available surface for Dewey to display the words.

"I assume that was a no. Oh well, I guess nobody I know will see me here anyway." Nate sighed, gazing out at the pristine ocean. The water looked inviting compared to the purple goo he had lived in for the past forty-eight hours.

"Say, Dewey, is the seawater here safe for me to come in contact with?"

"Kweeeeerp!" Dewey exclaimed and made a pseudo thumbs-up with one of his hands, mimicking the gesture he had seen Nate make before.

"Okay, then, I feel a bit ripe… think I'll take a quick dip!"

Without hesitating, Nate bolted towards the water, leaping ten feet per stride through the shallow water towards an approaching wave. He took one final lunge and then planted both feet in the surf and launched himself into the air, soaring in a quasi-swan-dive over the wave's frothy crest into the smoother water behind it. This startled Dewey; he didn't think Nate was actually considering going out *into* the water. The water itself was safe. It was what lived in it that concerned Dewey.

As Nate frolicked in the waves, Dewey used a holo-disc to scan for life-forms. At first, the readings showed nothing overly alarming nearby; but moments later there appeared a very large creature, approaching from several thousand feet offshore, just below the surface. Dewey gazed out across the waves and caught a glimpse of two long, snake-like appendages that had risen from the water, moving towards shore at a steady pace. The giant antennae probed the air, swaying about randomly as they searched for the source of what had attracted them: the scent of the sky-ray's carcass. Dewey recognized the approaching animal from his studies back home, and was immediately concerned.

Nate had momentarily come back to shallower water, only to turn and leap towards another approaching wave. He was soon airborne in another swan-dive, but before he started to descend, Dewey shot an energy-beam from a holo-disc that engulfed Nate and suspended him in mid-air. Nate flailed as the beam pulled him back to shore and deposited him face first onto the sand at Dewey's feet.

"What was that for?" Nate wailed, picking himself up and spitting out orange sand, brushing more of it from his face and chest. Dewey pointed at the big antennae, now just a few hundred feet offshore and approaching fast. "Oh shit! What are those?"

Dewey didn't waste time trying to communicate. He grabbed Nate by the arms, squatted, and then leapt, launching himself and Nate high in the air and away from the water's edge. When they landed, Dewey leapt again, putting more distance between them and the approaching animal. From this safer vantage point, Dewey and Nate watched in awe as the water beneath the giant antennae began to swirl, and two enormous black eyes rose above the surface at the ends of massive stalks. Then the gargantuan beast launched itself completely out of the water in an explosion of spray and mist, soaring towards the beach and landing next to the sky-ray's carcass with a thud. The impact kicked up a cloud of sand, sending all the little scavengers that had been feasting on the carcass scattering back into their burrows. The new arrival quickly staked its claim, towering over the carcass and making blood-curdling snorting roars at the lesser creatures, warning them to stay in their holes and away from its meal.

When the sand settled, Nate and Dewey got a

better look at the big beast. It was covered in dark fur, matted down like a wet seal's coat, and it had a stocky, tapered torso. It stood about a hundred feet tall, slightly hunched over on a single, muscular leg with an enormous webbed foot the size of a blue whale's tail. Two massive arms draped from the creature's broad shoulders to the ground, and the beast used them like crutches to support its body along with its lone foot. At the end of each arm were two menacing, scythe-like claws, long and curved like those of a sloth, only far more lethal-looking. The claws curled upwards, flat against its forearms, so that the animal could support its bulk on calloused knuckles. Like Dewey, it had a fixed, bulbous head, to which were attached the two eye-stalks and the two large antennae. Most odd to Nate were the two tubular appendages, thick and serpentine like elephant's trunks, that stuck straight out from its chest. At the end of each trunk was a large mouth lined with sharp teeth.

Dewey remained calm, while Nate's heart was pounding; he wanted to get further away and retreat into the spaghetti trees, but Dewey held his arm firmly and the two stood their ground. The creature had seen them and it stared at them for a moment, but didn't seem overly interested or concerned by their presence. It was, however, curious about the ship and the habitat. It lumbered over to them and probed them with its antennae, but quickly became disinterested and moved back to the dead sky-ray. It unfolded its claws and sank them deep into the sky-ray's flesh, and then both its mouths began ripping massive chunks of meat from the carcass, swallowing them without chewing.

"It doesn't want us," Nate said with a tone of relief.

Dewey used a holo-disc beam to draw words in the sand.

«CORRECT. WE HAVE NOTHING TO FEAR FROM THIS LIFE-FORM AS LONG AS WE KEEP OUR DISTANCE. BUT ACCORDING TO MY ARCHIVES ON THIS PLANET, THERE ARE OTHER MEMBERS OF THIS GENUS THAT DWELL IN THE FOREST. THOSE WE MUST FEAR. NOW THAT THIS ONE IS FEEDING THEY MAY DETECT IT AND COME TO INVESTIGATE.»

"But if they just want to share their big brother's scraps, why do we need to worry? Won't they leave us alone?"

«NO. THE BIG ONE WILL ONLY EAT FROM THE DEAD ANIMAL. THE SMALLER ONES WILL EAT LIVING CREATURES AS WELL. THEY WILL CONSIDER US PREY.»

Just then, as if on cue, an eerie sound came echoing from the jungle behind them. It was a deep, guttural moan followed by a volley of high-pitched screeches. A few seconds later an identical call came from a different direction, then another, and another. Now the air was filled with howling and screeching, and Dewey quickly wrote another message in the sand.

«DEWEY MUST GET TO THE TRANSPORT NOW. NATE MUST RE-ENTER HABITAT NOW.»

Before Nate could respond, Dewey leapt, holding onto Nate's arms, and bounded towards the ship and habitat. When they reached the ship, Nate felt tingling in his ribs as Dewey used an energy-field to levitate him back into the habitat. As soon as he had slipped back into the liquid, the habitat's lid sealed above him. He wasted no time filling his lungs with the fluid and quickly typed a message to Dewey on the floating keyboard.

"Dewey, what's going on? What should I do?"

Dewey did not respond; he was walking around the ship doing something with a holo-disc. Nate watched nervously as the towering animal feeding on the carcass suddenly stopped ripping apart its meal and stood upright, its eyes and antennae scanning the perimeter of the woods at the edge of the beach. It was obviously agitated by the sounds coming from the trees.

"Aren't we a little too close to that thing?"

Dewey still didn't answer. He was using a holo-disc to check the status of repairs on the ship. The spheres that were fixing the broken craft were still buzzing about it like flies, not yet finished with their task. One of Dewey's discs then projected a proximity alert holo-display, and in the floating picture Nate could see a crescent of numerous purplish dots moving in on a solitary cyan dot...what he assumed was their position.

Dewey began pacing between the transport and Nate's habitat, methodically scanning the edge of the forest with all eyes. His eyes and his entire body changed to a uniform orange, blending him in with the colors of the sand. The spaghetti-trees at the edge of the beach began to rustle and sway as the howling and screeching grew louder. Then in an instant, the trees became still and the noise abruptly stopped, the beach becoming calm and peaceful for a moment.

The large beast took a deep gulp of air into its nostrils on the back of its head, then grunted noisily through both mouths and lumbered up the sand towards the forest. It stopped a hundred feet short of the trees and began pounding its massive, clawed fists into the sand, shaking the ground like an earthquake. It let out another deafening roar, which echoed off the cliffs in the distance, and then stood quiet and still in a defensive posture, as if ready to take on whatever was about to come out of the forest.

A moment of eerie silence passed, and then the spaghetti-tree forest erupted in a flurry of black fur, claws, and fangs. Countless animals bounded out of the woods. Aside from their single foot looking more like a monkey's than a duck's, and their nostrils being on their chests instead of atop their heads, they looked almost exactly like the large beast that had come from the ocean, only these were much smaller... about Dewey's size. Like a rabid pack of gorillas, they bounced and galloped across the beach on their knuckles and stubby legs, kicking up clouds of sand. Within seconds they'd reached the big one, who began slashing at them with its fangs and claws.

Nate was terrified. He felt completely helpless and vulnerable in the habitat. The animals were obviously well-organized, breaking off into four distinct groups, each moving towards a specific target: the large scavenger, the carcass, Dewey, and the habitat. The pack that came to the habitat hit it with enough force to roll it over several times. Nate sloshed back and forth in the liquid as the relentless beasts pushed the globe back and forth, slapping and poking at it with their claws and fanged mouths. Nate curled into a fetal position as he bounced and rolled off the habitat walls. He was relieved to see that the container seemed strong enough to ward off the onslaught, and the syrupy liquid at least prevented him from hitting the walls too hard. For the moment, he believed he would survive this, but he lost sight of Dewey and worried about his safety if he was still out in the open.

He hoped Dewey had managed to get back into the ship, but that was not the case. Dewey hadn't been able to reenter the ship while it was under repair, and beyond Nate's line of sight, he was fighting off the beasts as they gathered around him.

Nate shifted his focus to the big animal, which he *could* see looming high above the chaos on the beach. It didn't seem to be in any danger from its smaller cousins, its thick skin impervious to their claws and teeth. Those that tried to climb onto their big cousin to attack it were quickly dispatched. But the behemoth quickly gave up hope on chasing the smaller ones away from its meal. It did all it could to fend them away from the carcass, but there were just too many. In a last-ditch effort to salvage its meal, the big scavenger dug its claws into the sky-ray and dragged it down the beach towards the water. The smaller animals swarmed the carcass, plunging their own claws and teeth into the flesh, pulling with all their combined strength in a desperate tug-of-war. But their foe was too strong, and the shredded carcass soon slipped from their grip and disappeared beneath the waves in a swirl of froth and yellow blood. Not nearly as adapted to water as their ocean-dwelling kin, the disgruntled hunters retreated to join the others on the beach, who were feverishly attacking Dewey and the habitat.

So far, Dewey had managed to ward off the attacks, but without the additional firepower of the ship, he would soon be overcome—and the repair spheres weren't finished fixing the ship yet. If they didn't finish soon, he knew he might die. Bolts of energy from his holo-discs neutralized a good number of the predators, and he formed the digits of his hands and feet into sharp, rigid points, stabbing at others that got close enough. He also shot his defense spikes from his torso, trying to be as precise in aim as possible to penetrate vulnerable spots on the beasts' abdomens, but he had a limited number of spikes available before his body would need time to make more, so he had to use them sparingly. His defenses were successful so long as they lasted, but the sheer number of aggressors he faced was becoming overwhelming.

Meanwhile, the animals trying to get to Nate were getting frustrated. The habitat was impervious to their efforts, and one by one they gave up and turned on Dewey instead. Soon, none of the creatures were bothering with the habitat any longer, and Nate watched in horror as they formed a writhing mass of flailing limbs around Dewey, climbing over the bodies of their felled comrades to get at him.

Nate knew Dewey was losing control. He watched helplessly as the relentless beasts surged and piled in on his friend. Nate still couldn't see Dewey through the frenzy, but suddenly a purple-gray appendage came flying out above the mass of bodies, then another. *Those were arms, Dewey's arms!* Several of the rabid creatures chased after the arms and began fighting each other for bites, while the rest continued massing on Dewey. Nate's heart sank as he imagined Dewey being ripped apart and devoured by these monopod animals. Next came the grim realization that this was likely where he would die, entombed for eternity in a purple fish tank on the beach of a distant planet.

Dewey's holo-discs had run dry on power, and

he had used the last of his spikes. He was out of defensive options, save his two remaining arms and his feet, but those were inadequate to thwart the onslaught, and he was about to be completely overcome. Claws and teeth were lunging at him from all directions, and some managed to get a grip on one of his eye stalks, ripping and pulling until the stalk was separated from his head and quickly devoured.

Then, without warning, a loud hum pierced the air, startling the monopods and causing them to discontinue their attack. They all fell silent and stood upright, looking for the source of the sound. Nate heard it as well, and it sent vibrations through the liquid in his habitat that made his ears hurt. He then saw the ship slowly rise off the beach and hover several feet above the sand. The creatures went berserk, howling and pounding their fists into the ground. They moved away from Dewey and formed a ring around the floating ship, giving Nate his first glimpse of Dewey since the attack had begun. Nate could now see that his friend was still alive, but severely maimed and writhing painfully, barely able to stand.

Next, there was a deafening *ZAP*, like a massive clap of thunder that echoed into the mountains. Accompanying the startling noise came a network of bright-blue bolts of energy that radiated from the ship and targeted each of the creatures, instantly felling every one of them. In a matter of seconds, they were all collapsed in steaming heaps about the vessel.

Dewey collapsed into a squat, exhausted, and sat motionless for a moment. Nate feared he was dead, but then Dewey stood and slowly trudged over to the habitat. He peered in to see if Nate was intact, and a message appeared on the habitat wall.

«IS NATE DAMAGED?"

"I'm fine, but what about you? Your arms? Your eyes? Are you in pain?"

«DEWEY IS DAMAGED, BUT NOT LIFE-THREAT-ENINGLY. LIMBS AND EYES WILL REGENERATE. PAIN IS SEVERE BUT TOLERABLE. WE MUST GET INTO TRANSPORT NOW AND DEPART. MORE LIFE-FORMS ARE APPROACHING. DEWEY DOES NOT WISH TO HARM ANY MORE OF THEM.»

"Agreed. Let's get out of here."

Within minutes, the habitat was back in the cargo bay, and Dewey was strapped into his floating chair. Without hesitation, the ship lifted off the beach and headed for the upper atmosphere. Once docked at the station, Dewey made haste in programming a gravity tunnel back to Earth.

Nate watched the station, the planet, its moons and rings fade into the distance behind them as they shot into the gravity tunnel. He reflected on the incredibly dangerous things they had encountered, and how fortunate they were to be alive. He knew Dewey felt terrible, his pride hurt, and he felt sad and sorry for his Alien friend. Nate knew that Dewey had never intended to put them in any peril, but now he realized that even as technologically and intellectually advanced as Dewey was, he had miscalculated one huge variable: his own inexperience in dealing with the unexpected. Sure, he had seen this planet and its life-forms many times in holograms or clone displays and at the Intergalactic Zoo, and had probably flown countless missions in simulated scenarios, but always in controlled situations. Actually going to the planet, especially with a Human in tow, was an adventure Dewey had been ill-prepared for.

Nate tried to console his friend. "Dewey, thank you for showing me these things. I know you didn't mean for us to get into trouble. I am still very glad I came."

«NATE IS VERY KIND. NATE COULD HAVE PERISHED FROM DEWEY'S CARELESSNESS. DEWEY DID NOT EXPECT THESE THINGS TO OCCUR. DEWEY IS ASHAMED THAT LIFE-FORMS HAVE PERISHED DUE TO DEWEY'S MISTAKES.»

"Will you get into trouble for all of this?

«DEWEY WILL ERASE ALL EVIDENCE OF THIS ENCOUNTER. DEWEY MUST CONCEAL THESE ACTIONS. DEWEY DESERVES PUNISHMENT FOR BREAKING PROTOCOL, BUT DOES NOT WANT TO JEOPORDIZE FUTURE MISSIONS TO MILKY WAY. DEWEY WISHES TO RETURN TO EARTH AGAIN.»

Nate grinned as he replied, "Well, your secret is safe with me. And next time you're out this way, if you want to do this again, count me in! Let's just be a little more careful next time."

"AGREED. NOW NATE MUST SLEEP."

"No! Dewey, I'm too worked up. I don't want you to put me to sleep this time, please. If I get tired, I'll sleep on my own."

"AS YOU WISH."

So Nate stayed awake this time, conversing with Dewey about the experiences of the past 48 hours. Along the way, they also viewed clips from several movies and television programs, which Dewey had downloaded from the Earth Station's databanks, including an episode of *SpongeBob SquarePants*. "CAN NATE PLEASE EXPLAIN TO DEWEY THE SIGNIFICANCE OF THIS TRANSMISSION?" Dewey asked.

"It's children's entertainment. I have no children, so I'm not very familiar with it," Nate lied. He loved SpongeBob, and secretly watched it often when Tracie wasn't around. He expected Dewey to quickly move on to a more adult program, but he didn't, and he seemed quite amused by the cartoon.

Sharing the SpongeBob experience with Dewey brought back fond memories of binge-watching old Loony Tunes episodes with his grandfather when he was little. Nate and "Big Mart," as his grandfather was nicknamed, could sit around watching Bugs Bunny, Foghorn Leghorn, or the Roadrunner and Wile E. Coyote's shenanigans for hours, their guts aching from laughing so hard. And now he was having a similar moment with Dewey, who was watching intensely and hanging on every word of the dialogue. *A member of the most advanced species in the Universe has become a SpongeBob fan. Who would have guessed?*

Just then, the cartoon's story-line showed SpongeBob transporting a playful jellyfish in a glass jar with a metal lid on it, remotely resembling the habitat with Nate floating about inside. Nate grinned widely, unable to laugh out loud but deeply amused by the irony. Dewey found it entertaining as well, and he undulated with glee in his floating chair.

CHAPTER 39

I t was late Sunday afternoon in São Paolo, Brazil. Antonio Perron was working in the dimly-lit warehouse of the Brazilian Astronomy Institute, where supplies and spare parts were stored for use at the observatories he was in charge of. He paced nervously near the loading dock at the rear of the warehouse, where on the concrete floor in front of him was a heavy-duty flatbed cart used for moving heavy objects about the building... but none as heavy as the burden it bore at this moment.

Sitting on the cart, cradled by steel rails that had been crudely welded into place at Perron' direction, was the alleged meteorite Nate had found. The sheer weight of it had caused the bed of the cart to buckle, and the industrial-strength casters it rested on were bent outwards from the strain. Perron would have preferred hauling it up to the main lab on the third floor, but it was too heavy for the freight elevator, let alone the tile flooring. And so the orb had remained in the warehouse, and he had set up a makeshift lab there to study it.

Perron ran test after test on the sphere's

composition, trying relentlessly to find some evidence of its coming from deep space. But, as he had told Jason O'Rourke he suspected was the case, he kept coming to the conclusion that there was only one place where this thing could have originated: Earth. More specifically, a helicopter factory. Perron was quite sure of his theory now, but unsure how to report it. Until now he had managed to keep the Brazilian government and his colleagues in the dark, claiming he needed more time to study the meteorite before offering it up to the world's eyes. But pressure was building to provide details and let the thing be seen and studied by others, and he couldn't keep it to himself any longer. He somberly stared at it, trying to put together the words he would use to go public with his findings... that it was no meteorite, but rather what remained of the missing helicopter, including its crew, densely packed into a small sphere. There would be immediate outrage once the truth was revealed, especially since he had no clue how to explain what could have caused it.

Perron took a deep breath and pulled his phone out of his back pocket to initiate the disclosure process, but the sound of a truck approaching outside distracted him. The truck sounded as if it had pulled up to the dock rapidly, and Perron heard brakes squealing and gravel churning as the vehicle came to a halt. Next came multiple heavy footsteps, and then the small side door next to the larger dock doors burst open. A dozen heavily-armed men wearing black uniforms and ski-masks filed through the door and scattered through the warehouse, waving automatic rifles with laser sights in every direction.

Perron shouted at the men, demanding an explanation, but there was no response. They seemed oblivious to his presence, and remained silent as they purposefully moved about the room like a precision SWAT team. After sweeping the entire warehouse, several of the men surrounded the cart holding the sphere, and one approached Perron.

"Who are you? What do you want?" Perron insisted.

The hooded man didn't answer him as he approached and raised his weapon. The last thing Perron remembered was the butt of the rifle coming down on his forehead, then intense pain and blackness. When he awoke, he found himself in a hospital room. His head was aching and his ears ringing, but he could hear several of his associates from the Institute conversing in the hallway outside the room. He called out to them, and they came rushing in. "Antonio, thank God you are awake, we thought you might slip into a coma!" one of them exclaimed as the group surrounded the bed, laughing and smiling with relief. Perron feebly tried to sit up; but there was an IV in his left arm restricting his movement, and he was too weak to prop himself up on his right elbow, so he just fell back onto the pillow.

His mouth was dry, but he managed to speak in a shaky voice. "The sphere... the meteorite, is it safe?"

The men seemed puzzled that he was more concerned with the meteorite than his own health. One replied, "We don't know, it's *gone*. But you are okay, that is what matters!"

Perron felt a surge of adrenaline and he sat up, dragging the IV line with him. "Gone? Gone where? Who took it? Who were those soldiers?"

"They weren't soldiers, at least not from Brazil or anywhere in South America, as far as we can tell. Nobody knows who they were. They came in a large truck with a big forklift and broke through the security gate. Then they attacked you and stole the meteorite."

"And nobody knows where they went?"

"The truck was found yesterday, abandoned at a remote fishing boat dock in Iguape. They must have put the meteorite on a boat. They are gone without a trace. But you are lucky, my friend. They could have killed you."

Perron fell back onto his pillow and let out a deep sigh. "Yes, I suppose I am lucky. Thank you. Can someone please get me my cell phone?"

CHAPTER 40

I t was mid-afternoon in Tampa when Dewey's ship arrived back at Earth Station. Nate had finally fallen asleep several hours prior, from pure exhaustion this time, not requiring a sedative. Dewey planned to take him home in a few hours, as soon as it was dark enough over the Florida peninsula to avoid being seen. He was sure that Nate would be pleased to be done with the haphazard journey, so he made haste with the docking and immediately got to work modifying the sync protocols. Once he was satisfied that no record of the trip had been uploaded to the station data banks, he woke Nate and announced the plan.

«DEWEY WILL RETURN NATE TO EARTH AS SOON AS EARTH ROTATES TO PROPER POSITION.»

Nate was puzzled and disappointed. "I thought you were going to show me something on Mars that you wanted me to see?"

Dewey was equally puzzled by Nate's reply, and his eyes changed from green to brown. "DOES NATE NOT WISH TO RETURN HOME IMMEDIATELY? IS NATE NOT FRIGHTENED OF FURTHER EXPLORATION

WITH DEWEY?"

"Are we still in danger? Will Mars be dangerous?"

«NOT AS DANGEROUS AS PREVIOUS PLANET. ALL SYSTEMS ARE FUNCTIONING PROPERLY. THERE ARE NO AGGRESSIVE LIFE-FORMS ON MARS. NO LIFE-FORMS REMAIN ON THAT PLANET.»

"No life-forms *remain*? Was there life there before?"

"INTELLIGENT LIFE EITHER LIVED ON MARS OR VISITED THE PLANET PERHAPS 100 MILLION YEARS AGO. THERE IS EVIDENCE.»

"I'd love to see it."

"VERY WELL," Dewey replied, rather pleased Nate didn't wish to go home right away. Besides, it would be six hours before darkness fell on Florida. Plenty of time for a quick adventure on Mars.

Thirty minutes later, the ship entered a low orbit around Mars over its sunlit hemisphere, giving Nate a good view of the planet's geographic features. Then Dewey took manual control and headed down closer to the surface, navigating through the massive Mariner Valley. The ominous terrain reminded Nate of the Grand Canyon back home, only much larger... and redder.

Beyond the canyon, Dewey piloted across a vast, featureless plain, telling Nate it had once been an ocean bed. Then he took Nate to the Cydonia region of the northern hemisphere, peppered with a variety of scattered buttes and rocky mounds, and of course, pockmarked with the ubiquitous craters.

The ship descended low to the ground and headed to one of the mounds, slowing and then coming to a stop, hovering a few feet off the dusty surface near the mound's steep base. Nate was surprised when the viewers shut down and the cargo bay door spiraled open, flooding the ship's interior with reddish sunlight reflecting from the Martian landscape.

Dewey dismounted his chair and exited the ship, then levitated the habitat out of the cargo bay. Out in the Martian daylight, Nate got his first good look at Dewey in a while, and he was amazed to see that Dewey's missing arms were already starting to grow back, looking like young tree saplings sprouting from his upper torso. Dewey squatted and then leapt, landing squarely on top of the habitat's lid; and then the habitat began to float forward with Dewey riding it like a giant, globular surfboard. It traveled several hundred yards up the mound's sloped side, then stopped when they reached a vertical wall of rock, thirty feet tall and twice as wide.

"LOOK CLOSELY AT THE VERITICAL SURFACE. DOES NATE SEE THE DISPARITY IN THIS SURFACE AND THE REST OF THE MOUND?"

Dewey scurried to a specific spot on the wall and used his two good hands to brush red dust off a segment. As he cleared the dust away, Nate saw what appeared to be a metal surface with some sort of symbols engraved in it. "Dewey, what is that?" Nate typed.

"IT IS A MANUFACTURED STRUCTURE OF

UNKNOWN ORIGIN. IT IS MOSTLY BURIED BENEATH THE PLANETARY SURFACE EXCEPT FOR THIS MOUND, WHICH HAS BEEN COVERED IN ROCK AND DUST OVER MUCH TIME."

"A structure? What kind of structure? Who put it here?"

«WE DO NOT KNOW. IT IS TENS OF MILLIONS OF YEARS OLD. WE ARE UNABLE TO OPEN IT, AND OUR SCANNERS CANNOT SEE NOR PENETRATE IT."

"Tens of millions of years?"

"YES. THE STRUCTURE WAS HERE LONG BEFORE WE DISCOVERED THIS SOLAR SYSTEM 75 MILLION YEARS AGO. WE ONLY DISCOVERED IT RECENTLY BUT THE ROCK THAT HAS FORMED AROUND IT TELLS US ITS AGE."

"The whole mound is a metal structure?"

«YES, BUT THE ALLOY IS UNKNOWN AND THIS MOUND ONLY REPRESENTS A SMALL PORTION OF THE STRUCTURE. NINETY PERCENT OF THE STRUCTURE IS BURIED BENEATH THE SURFACE. IT IS ONE OF THREE IDENTICAL STRUCTURES WE HAVE DISCOVERED IN THIS SOLAR SYSTEM.»

"Why don't you guys dig the dirt and rock off of it to get a better look?"

"BECAUSE HUMANS WOULD THEN BE AWARE OF OUR ACTIVITY HERE."

"Yes, of course. But can't you at least get inside it somehow to study it?"

"NO. WE HAVE TRIED. IT IS IMPENETRABLE TO OUR TECHNOLOGY."

"What kind of intelligence would it take to make something your scientists can't figure out?"

"ONE SIGNIFICANTLY MORE ADVANCED THAN US."

"If they're so advanced, they must know you're here visiting their structure. Why haven't they tried to contact you?"

"UNKNOWN. IT IS THEORIZED THEY MAY NOT ELECT TO HAVE CONTACT WITH US JUST AS WE ARE INSTRUCTED TO AVOID CONTACT WITH HUMANS. OR PERHAPS THEY ARE A SPECIES THAT NO LONGER EXISTS AND THE STRUCTURES WERE ABANDONED LONG AGO."

"Where are the other two structures?"

«I WILL SHOW YOU. WE HAVE TIME TO VISIT ONE MORE BEFORE DEWEY RETURNS NATE TO HIS HOME."

Dewey returned the habitat to the ship, and soon they were airborne. As they gained altitude, Nate gazed directly down at the irregular dome of sand and rock that covered the alien structure. When it came into full view, he felt chills as he realized what he had not noticed on approach: *he had seen this before*. It was the "Face on Mars," infamous for its similarity to Human facial features when viewed from high above by unmanned probes. The theory that an ancient civilization had crafted the mountaintop into their own image had long been debunked as pure coincidence of shadows and geologic features playing tricks on the Human eye, but now Nate questioned it anew.

"I have seen this before. We call it the Face on Mars." Nate stated, wondering if Dewey might now provide some truth to it's being a face after all.

"WE ARE AWARE OF THIS. THE SURFACE OF THE BURIED DOME DOES BEAR THE IMAGE OF AN UNKNOWN BEING. THE IMAGE IS REFLECTED IN THE ROCK AND SOIL COVERING IT, BUT IT IS DISTORTED."

Dewey generated a holo-image to show Nate the true shape of the face atop the structure. The rock and sand had added to its proportions significantly through the millennia, giving it a somewhat Human appearance on the surface. But the image on the structure itself was definitely *not* Human. It looked to Nate more like the face of an insect.

"HERE IS WHERE THE SECOND STRUCTURE IS LOCATED."

The image of the Face on Mars vanished and Dewey put up an image of Venus. The graphic's perspective morphed, circling beneath the planet and then zooming in on an area near the south pole. Layers of the surface peeled away, showing the top of another gargantuan structure buried there. At the very center of its concave top was a dome, several miles in diameter, with an identical face to the one on the Mars structure. Nate was mesmerized by the images, dumbfounded that all of this had gone undetected by his own species, despite their fervent study of the solar system in recent decades. Of course, it was well under the ground...

When the image of the Venusian structure dissipated and Dewey re-engaged the external viewer, Nate suddenly realized the ship was approaching Earth.

"Dewey, why are we headed to Earth? I thought you were going to take me to see the third structure?"

"YES. DEWEY WILL NOW SHOW YOU THE THIRD STRUCTURE."

The third structure is on Earth! Nate realized.

Dewey took the ship to a spot high above the Indian Ocean, northwest of Australia and just south of the Indonesian islands. He hovered there a moment while the scanners located all Human activity in the area and plotted a trajectory to avoid it, and then the ship plunged downwards, effortlessly penetrating the water moments later. The light from the surface disappeared quickly as the ship dove deep, descending into the immense, pitch-black depths.

"Dewey, why are we here?" Nate typed.

«YOU CALL THIS BODY OF WATER: THE INDIAN OCEAN. WE ARE ABOVE THE AREA DESIGNATED: THE JAVA TRENCH. IT IS THE SECOND DEEPEST LOCATION IN ALL OF EARTH'S OCEANS.»

Nate was well aware of the Java Trench, second only to the Mariana Trench in depth. Tracie spoke of it often in her research. "Yes, I know of this place. But why are we here?"

"TO SEE THE THIRD STRUCTURE."

"It *is* on Earth?"

"YES."

How could we not know? Nate pondered, not believing something so huge could have gone undetected by modern humanity.

The ship plummeted into the trench for several more minutes, and when Dewey switched on the external lights, the viewer walls came alive with strange creatures, as strange as anything Nate had seen on the other planets he had visited these past two days. He was reminded of Tracie's ramblings that Humans actually knew less about the Earth's deepest oceans than they did about outer space, as he gazed at each bizarre fish, cephalopod, and crustacean that swam by.

"Tracie would have loved to see this."

When the floor of the trench came into view, Nate had expected to see the flat, smooth surface of a large butte that rose from the ocean floor, similar to the one on Mars. But the bottom was a smooth layer of sediment. The transport came to a halt several yards off the ocean floor, stirring up some of the sediment into a small cloud. "THE STRUCTURE IS DIRECTLY BENEATH US NOW."

"All I see is a smooth mud floor."

«THE STRUCTURE IS FAR BENEATH THE OCEAN FLOOR.»

Dewey generated a new holo-image into the habitat for Nate to see, this time showing a three-dimensional graphic of the structure's entire profile. Its domed top was identical to the ones on Mars and Venus, but now Nate could better see what was beneath the dome: a huge cylinder with a slightly tapered profile that narrowed at the bottom, buried several thousand feet beneath the ocean floor and continuing twenty miles deep into the Earth's crust. "Dewey, you didn't show me this view on Mars. Are all the structures cone-shaped like this?"

"YES, ALL THREE STRUCTURES ARE IDENTICAL."

"Did these structures all show up in our solar system at the same time?"

"THE DATA IS NOT CONCLUSIVE, BUT WE BELIEVE THE STRUCTURES ON EARTH AND MARS WERE PLACED MORE RECENTLY, WITHIN SEVERAL THOUSAND YEARS OF EACH OTHER. THE STRUC-TURE ON VENUS WE BELIEVE TO BE MUCH OLDER.»

"Any theories what they were for?"

"WE HAVE NO CONCLUSIVE THEORIES. WITHOUT KNOWING WHAT IS INSIDE THE STRUCTURES, IT IS IMPOSSIBLE TO DETERMINE THEIR PURPOSE."

Nate felt dizzy as he contemplated the meaning of what he was seeing. Not only had *another* intelligent species been visiting Earth's solar system millions of years ago, they were so advanced that even Dewey's species couldn't figure out their technology. And now he was the sole Human who knew the structures existed. Keeping this under his hat would be challenging.

As if he were reading Nate's mind, Dewey posted a new message.

«NATE FRIEND, IT IS VERY IMPORTANT TO DEW-EY THAT NATE NOT TELL OTHER HUMANS WHAT

DEWEY HAS SHOWN NATE. MUCH HARM CAN BE CAUSED IF THIS INFORMATION IS SHARED WITH OTHER HUMANS. PLEASE DO NOT TELL ANYONE WHAT YOU HAVE SEEN."

"I promise. I won't tell anyone."

"EXCEPT FOR TRACIE," Dewey continued "DEWEY UNDERSTANDS NATE MUST HAVE TRUST WITH MATE.»

"Thank you. I will make sure she does not tell anyone either." Nate paused, then resumed typing. "Dewey, I wish I could visit your home and meet your mate. I would have enjoyed that."

«THAT WOULD BE ENJOYABLE FOR DEWEY ALSO, BUT NOT POSSIBLE. IT IS TOO DANGEROUS FOR NATE TO GO TO PLANET OF DEWEY. IF NATE WERE DISCOVERED, NATE WOULD BE QUARANTINED AND NOT ALLOWED TO RETURN TO EARTH. NATE WOULD NOT BE ALLOWED TO LIVE WITH OUR HUMAN CLONES. NATE WOULD BE CONSIDERED A RISK FOR CONTAMINATING CLONES WITH KNOWLEDGE OF THEIR ORIGINS. NATE WOULD BE FORCED TO LIVE IN ISOLATION FOR REMAINDER OF LIFE CYCLE."

In the euphoria of the past two days' adventures, Nate had forgotten about the Human clones on Dewey's planet. "Dewey, how many of us have you cloned?"

«WE MAINTAIN MANY THOUSANDS OF HUMAN CLONES IN OUR RESEARCH AND DISPLAY HABITATS, ALONG WITH OTHER EARTH SPECIES. EACH EARTH HABITAT CONTAINS SPECIES ENGINEERED

TO REPRESENT DIFFERENT TIME-PERIODS IN EVOLUTION OF EARTH LIFE. MANY OTHER PLANETS IN UNIVERSE ARE ALSO REPRESENTED IN OTHER HABITATS.»

"They don't know where they came from or where they are?"

«NO. NONE OF THE HUMAN CLONES ARE EVER INFORMED OF THEIR ORIGINS AND NONE HAVE EVER SEEN US. THEY LIVE THEIR ENTIRE LIVES UN-AWARE OF OUR EXISTENCE.»

Nate understood the logic behind cloning Humans for study instead of abducting real ones. He even appreciated, to a degree, that the Aliens had taken that more "humane" route. But given the magnitude of what Dewey had just described, en-tire civilizations of Humans living in artificial worlds, completely oblivious as to the details of their ex-istence... he had no idea what to think or how to reply. As a scientist himself, he was fascinated and impressed. As a Human being, he was horrified. Instead of responding, he changed the subject.

"Dewey, I should go home to Tracie now."

«AGREED. IT IS TIME FOR BOTH DEWEY AND NATE TO RETURN TO OUR FAMILIES.»

CHAPTER 41

By Sunday evening, Tracie was neurotic with anticipation and fear. Dewey had said he would try to return Nate home by today, but it was getting late, and with each passing moment, her anxiety reached a new high.

The house was a wreck; she had barely slept and had been cramping, which she attributed to immobility and an overdose of stress and junk food, a departure from her usual disciplined diet and exercise habits. Having depleted most everything resembling nutrition from the fridge and pantry, she had scoured every cupboard for stashes of treats, leaving candy wrappers, empty chip bags and chocolate bar crumbs strewed about the kitchen and living room. She hadn't left the house at all since Dewey and Nate left, but was now expected to be back at work first thing tomorrow morning.

"No freaking way I'm going in tomorrow if he's not back yet!" she spoke out loud to Doo-Doo, who was pacing the kitchen floor while Tracie inhaled a bowl of Peanut Butter Captain Crunch... dry, as she was out of milk. Tracie also knew that Jason O'Rourke would be calling Monday, expecting to stop by and see Nate. She continued ranting to Doo-Doo, half laughing, half crying, "That son-of-a-bitch left us and got killed in outer space and now *I* have to make up some explanation of how he just disappeared from the face of the Earth! They're gonna lock me up and dig up the backyard for sure!"

Doo-Doo cocked his head and yipped, less concerned with Tracie's dilemma than with whether or not she intended to drop any Captain Crunch on the floor. Then came a crackling noise from the living room... *Oh my God, it's the TV*, Tracie realized, her eyes popping wide open. She dropped the bowl onto the counter, knocking cereal onto the floor that Doo-Doo quickly exploited. She ran into the living room to see that the TV had turned itself on and there was static on the screen. She braced herself on the back of an easy chair and held her breath as the static slowly congealed into an image. *There were letters appearing*.

"HONEY, I'M HOME!"

Tracie stumbled towards the TV and collapsed on the sofa, crying tears of relief and joy. Waves of emotional release paralyzed her for a moment, but as she regained her composure, she decided she wasn't about to miss the arrival. She had been too freaked out by Nate's leaving and stayed in the house when Nate and Dewey departed, but now she really wanted to see the spaceship and the device Dewey had constructed to keep Nate alive.

She wouldn't pass up the chance now. She quickly donned a pair of hiking boots, grabbed a flashlight from the garage, and exited through the sliding door in the kitchen. Doo-Doo wanted to go as well and bolted towards the open door, but Tracie slid the door shut before he could follow her through, leaving him spinning and yapping in incredulous protest.

Tracie glanced around to make sure there were no nosy neighbors watching her, and then headed into the woods behind the house. She knew exactly where the ship would land; she had found the clearing years ago when Doo-Doo had chased a flock of wild turkeys and she frantically went to retrieve him… and save him from being pecked to death. She ventured fifty feet into the trees before turning on the flashlight, using its shaft to swat away spider-webs that blocked her way. As squeamish as she normally was about spiders and bugs, she found herself quite unaffected by them now.

When Tracie broke free of the thick undergrowth and cypress trees into the grassy clearing, there was nothing there. No ship, no Dewey the Alien, no Nate. She pointed the flashlight into the sky above but saw nothing, only its narrow beam piercing the heavens like a thin spotlight. After poking around the clearing for a few minutes, she found Nate's clothes and shoes, neatly folded and stacked on a large cypress knee at the edge of the clearing. She let out a big sigh and sat on the root next to her husband's clothes, gazing at the sky.

Far above, as Dewey navigated the ship down through fifty thousand feet, he pulled up a holo-display with graphics of the landing site and its surroundings. A quick bio-scan highlighted every living creature in the area, revealing one Human female at the edge of the clearing. Dewey announced this discovery to Nate.

«THERE IS A FEMALE HUMAN AT THE DESIGNATED LANDING SITE. THERE IS NO HUMAN AT DWELLING OF NATE AND TRACIE. PERHAPS THE HUMAN AT THE LANDING SITE IS TRACIE.»

Nate typed, "She must have seen my message on the TV and came to meet us. Can you verify if it is her?"

"YES."

While Tracie scanned the sky for any sign of the approaching spaceship, a split-second flash of light blinded her as Dewey engaged the long-range viewer's auto-focus. She rubbed her eyes and saw dancing stars for several seconds before she could re-focus on the real stars above.

Dewey routed the magnified image into the cargo bay, and the panoramic scene of Tampa's city lights that Nate had been gazing at morphed into that of Tracie sitting on the cypress root, looking straight up at the sky. Nate shuddered, momentarily overcome as he gazed upon his wife, her forlorn face displayed larger than life on the cargo bay's wall. Her hair was a mess and her cheeks drenched in tears, and Nate felt his own tear ducts swell as he reached out, trying to touch her image; but the clear wall of the habitat stopped his hand. He could see the pain in her eyes, and he questioned his decision to have ever left her behind for this crazy adventure. *What trauma this must have caused her*. His heart ached, and he felt remorseful.

A message from Dewey superimposed itself over Tracie's image. "CONFIRMED. THE HUMAN AT THE LANDING SITE IS WIFE OF NATE, TRACIE.»

"No shit, Sherlock," Nate typed back, smiling towards the cockpit. Dewey hesitated as he deciphered Nate's sarcasm, then undulated with amusement in his floating chair.

Dewey slowed the ship as he maneuvered it directly above the clearing and began final descent. Tracie couldn't see it yet, and her neck was starting to ache from looking up, but she kept her eyes fixed on the sky. Finally, she thought she noticed a small distortion in the blackness. She stared closely at the spot where she had noticed the distortion, then realized something *was* moving, coming straight down towards the clearing. There was no sound.

As the object drew near, she thought it might be circular; but when it got closer, she realized it was more like two cones joined base-to-base, with a surface that was curved and reflective, like polished chrome. She could see the faint reflections of moonlit trees moving across the curves of the ship, but when she shined her flashlight at it, it didn't redirect the beam like a curved mirror would, as if the light were being absorbed by the shiny thing.

Now Tracie could see the size of the ship; it wasn't tiny, but it was much smaller than she had imagined, about the length of a semi-truck, and its smooth, featureless surface not at all what she expected. There were no lights, antennae, windows, engines, or anything... just a big, shiny, football-shaped thing floating silently down from the heavens.

Now she felt a slight vibration beneath her feet, and backed up into the trees a little, out of the clearing. Did they know she was there? Was she in danger from radiation or something hazardous from the ship's propulsion system? She hadn't considered this before, and became petrified with fear, second-guessing her decision to come, but she couldn't turn her gaze from the scene. She had to see this.

Tracie kept her flashlight trained on the craft as it gently descended below the tree-tops and into the center of the clearing. It came to a halt several feet off the ground and hovered, silent except for the faint hum, and then even that disappeared. She felt chills, and goosebumps erupted all over her body as a dim blue ring appeared on the ship's surface and the cockpit's circular hatch spiraled open. A bath of eerie light poured into the mist through the portal, and then Dewey's tentacle-like limbs appeared and pulled his body out of the ship like a giant spider squeezing itself through a hole.

Dewey hopped to the ground and stood upright, one set of eyes looking right at Tracie. She grinned nervously and waved, and Dewey held up a hand in acknowledgement. Tracie noticed something odd; two of Dewey's arms looked smaller than the others, not fully-developed.

"Is it safe for me to come closer?" she half-shouted across the clearing.

Dewey snorted a few unintelligible Alien words and then made a crude thumbs-up with one of his good hands, motioning for her to approach with the other. Tracie left the confines of the cypress trees and cautiously stepped into the clearing, speaking to Dewey apologetically with a shaky voice. "I'm... I'm sorry, I couldn't help it. I know you probably didn't want me to come out here, but I really wanted to see your ship. And I've been so worried about Nate, I had to come see if he's all right. Where is he?"

Before Tracie finished her sentence, a second ring of blue light appeared on the side of the transport, this one at the craft's fat middle section and much larger than the hatch Dewey had emerged from. As the cargo-bay door spiraled open, Tracie saw Nate's habitat for the first time. She gasped when she saw him, naked and motionless, suspended in the glowing purple fluid. At first she thought he was dead, but then Nate's eyes opened and his head turned towards her, a big toothy grin erupting when he saw her standing there. Tracie broke down in tears, collapsing to her knees as the habitat floated out of the ship and came to rest on the ground in front of her. She crawled to it and put her hands up to the curved, clear surface, and Nate moved through the goo to where she was and put his hands up to hers from the inside. He mouthed to her, "I love you."

"I love you too." Tracie began to bawl uncontrollably, but she was smiling now.

Dewey put a hand on Tracie's shoulder and gently urged her back, away from the habitat as its top opened. Nate began to float upwards, pulled by an energy field that levitated him out of the liquid and suspended him above for a moment while the fluid exited his lungs. He took a deep breath. The taste was thin and polluted compared to the syrupy, sweet air he had sampled on the sky-ray's planet, but never had a breath of air tasted so good to him.

Tracie felt as if she were dreaming, watching her naked husband float down to the ground with no visible assistance. Nate struck a mid-air pose mimicking a theatrical descent, like an awkward Superman descending from the sky to greet Lois Lane... sans cape and leotards. This made Tracie burst out laughing through her sobs. When his feet touched down, his knees buckled slightly and he wobbled a bit, momentarily readjusting to Earth's gravity, and then he stood upright and gazed into his wife's teary eyes, offering a wink of reassurance that he was okay.

"Hi sweetheart, what's for dinner? The food on that flight was *terrible*.»

Tracie smirked and shook her head, and then she lunged towards him and threw her arms around his neck, crying into his neck for a moment before she could manage to say anything. "You bastard, don't you *ever* do anything like this again."

"I won't, I promise. I'm so sorry, honey. I'm sorry that I left you like that. I know I shouldn't have gone, but I just couldn't resist."

"I know, I know," Tracie whispered between sobs. Then she grabbed Nate's uncovered genitals and dug her nails into his tenderest flesh, causing him to flinch and gasp.

"But if you *ever* do anything like that again, *I'll cut these off!*»

Nate blushed beet red, and chuckled nervously as Tracie's grip intensified. "Ahh… please, sweetheart, not in front of the Alien!"

Tracie laughed and then sighed, releasing her grip of death and returning to hugging Nate. He put his hands on her cheeks, pulling her head out of his chest so their eyes could meet. "Honey, the things I've seen — it was just amazing. I can't wait to tell you. Let's go home now."

"Okay, but put your clothes on first. I will *not* be seen by the neighbors dragging you naked out of the woods."

Dewey had left the two alone to have their reunion while he loaded the habitat back into the cargo bay and prepared the ship for departure. But he had kept one set of eyes and an ear trained on Nate and Tracie's emotional interaction, observing them with deep fascination. Back home, he and his colleagues had little opportunity to witness exchanges like this between Human couples. The clones lived under tightly controlled circumstances, and were never subjected to traumatizing events or separations for the sake of research; it was considered too cruel. Behavior like this had only been studied from a distance during missions to Earth, or from analyzing the Human broadcasts that dramatized such occasions. But in that medium, it was never clear where reality ended and fiction began, so there was much debate as to the reliability of the broadcasts as scientific evidence. This display between Nate and Tracie warmed Dewey's hearts, and he concluded that Humans on Earth *did*, in fact, have the capacity to miss one another when separated. They loved and cared for their family just as much as his own species did.

With the habitat stowed and the cargo bay door secured, Dewey approached Nate and Tracie and displayed a new message on the side of the ship. "DEWEY MUST LEAVE NOW. DEWEY IS HONORED TO HAVE MET NATE AND TRACIE AND DOO-DOO. DEWEY WILL ALWAYS BE FRIEND OF NATE AND TRACIE AND DOO-DOO. PLEASE REMEMBER DEWEY. PLEASE DO NOT TELL OTHER HUMANS OF DEWEY.»

Nate responded, "We won't, Dewey, we promise." Tracie nodded in acknowledgement. Nate continued, "And thank you, Dewey, for being our friend and taking me on the trip. I can't even begin to tell you what an incredible experience this has been."

"IT HAS BEEN A PLEASURABLE EXPERIENCE FOR

DEWEY AS WELL."

"Will we ever see or hear from you again?" Tracie asked.

«IT IS UNLIKELY BUT NOT IMPOSSIBLE. IF DEWEY IS CHOSEN FOR ADDITIONAL RESEARCH ON EARTH, DEWEY WILL ATTEMPT TO LOCATE NATE AND TRACIE. IT IS POSSIBLE THAT DEWEY MAY RETURN BEYOND LIFESPAN OF NATE AND TRACIE. WILL NATE AND TRACIE TEACH THEIR OFFSPRING OF DEWEY? SHOULD DEWEY CONTACT OFFSPRING OF NATE AND TRACIE IF NATE AND TRACIE ARE NO LONGER ALIVE?»

"Offspring?" Nate exclaimed, laughing. "Well, maybe. We've thought about kids. but haven't decided just yet."

Tracie's expression went blank, as if she'd suddenly come to a realization that had been staring her in the face but that she had not acknowledged. Dewey's eyes went from purple to green as he shot a puzzled look at Tracie. A new message appeared on the side of the transport. "WILL TRACIE NOT GIVE BIRTH TO AN OFFSPRING IN APPROXIMATELY SEVEN AND A HALF MONTHS? HAS DEWEY'S SCANNING DEVICE MALFUNCTIONED?"

Tracie became flushed and dizzy, breaking out in a cold sweat and grabbing Nate's arm to steady herself. "Oh my God! Nate, *we're pregnant*!»

"What?"

"I've been barfing and crying all over the place and having weird food cravings. I thought I was just freaked out over you going missing in the Amazon and then leaving me to go with Dewey, but now that I think about it... well, I 'm definitely showing signs of *being pregnant*.»

Nate grinned, looking up at Dewey for confirmation. "A baby...we're going to have a baby? Dewey, you can tell that she's pregnant? Are you sure?"

"YES, DEWEY IS CERTAIN."

As Dewey's words appeared on the ship's hull, so did a new image; a detailed graphic of the tiny fetus in Tracie's womb.

"TRACIE IS CARRYING A HEALTHY FETUS. THE OFFSPRING IS MALE.»

Tracie laughed out loud as she realized she was seeing the first picture of her unborn son. She playfully scolded Dewey. "Well thanks, pal, so much for ruining the surprise!"

"DEWEY APOLOGIZES. DID NATE AND TRACIE NOT WISH TO KNOW OF THEIR OFFSPRING?»

"No, don't apologize, it's quite okay," Nate said. "She's just kidding. It's humor."

Dewey still did not completely understand Human humor or sarcasm, but once he recognized it he was always amused, and now he undulated with glee.

Then Nate put his arm around Tracie and held her close to his side, addressing Dewey in a somber tone. "Dewey, it's going to be light in a few hours. You'd better go." His heart sank as he spoke the words. He felt as if he were sending away a life-long friend he'd never see again.

Dewey moved towards Nate and Tracie and extended his two good arms, his spindly digits spreading out in a fan. His eyes shifted to a deep crimson as he posted a new message. "FAREWELL, NATE AND TRACIE. DEWEY WILL NOT FORGET YOU. MAY THE CREATOR ALWAYS GRANT GOOD FORTUNE TO YOU."

Nate and Tracie each offered a hand, Dewey's long fingers wrapping completely around them and halfway up their forearms. The three shared a silent moment, relishing their inter-galactic entanglement of fingers, and then Dewey started to pull away. Nate let go of Dewey's hand, but Tracie firmed her grip and pulled Dewey back from his departure. Dewey looked at Tracie, his eyes turning orange, puzzled.

"WHAT IS IT, TRACIE?"

"Dewey, I almost forgot to ask you — how are we supposed to fix our TVs? Since you showed up, none of them work anymore."

CHAPTER 42

Dewey departed Earth immediately after saying goodbye to Nate and Tracie. In lieu of returning to their home himself to fix the televisions, he dispatched a pair of maintenance spheres, two of those Nate had seen repairing the ship when it had been damaged on the distant living planet. The spheres accompanied Nate and Tracie back to the house, floating silently behind them as they tromped through the woods. Once at the house, they quickly finished their task, returning the TVs' circuitry to their original configurations, and then parked themselves mid-air in front of the kitchen door.

"I think they want out," Tracie commented nonchalantly, as if this kind of thing were common. Grinning, Nate slid the door open and the spheres floated into the backyard, and then in an instant they shot off towards the heavens, in the direction Dewey had gone.

"We need to get one of those!" Tracie stated smugly, Nate nodding in agreement.

Exhausted and emotionally spent, they then

climbed the stairs arm-in-arm to the bedroom and flopped onto the bed fully clothed, teeth unbrushed, and soon passed out in each other's arms. Little Doo-Doo protested at the side of the bed, dissatisfied with the level of attention he had gotten from Nate after his return. Nate momentarily regained consciousness and leaned over the side of the bed, reaching out to scratch Doo-Doo behind the ears and under his tiny chin. "Sorry, Dew-man, Daddy's been a little distracted lately. I love you, you little shit."

Doo-Doo savored the attention, rotating his pointy little head so that Nate's massaging fingers could reach all his favorite spots. Nate leaned down and kissed him on the forehead and said, "Good night, little man," then rolled over to resume spooning his snoring wife. Doo-Doo let out a sigh of satisfaction and returned to Tracie's side of the bed, did a couple of three-sixties, and plopped onto his little doggie mattress. A tiny yawn later he curled up in a ball, falling asleep soon afterwards.

In the morning, Nate and Tracie rose briefly to brush their rotten breath away, let Doo-Doo out for a bio-break and feed him, and stayed up long enough for Tracie to call work and tell them she'd be in late. Then they returned to bed and spent the morning making love, despite Doo-Doo's occasional eruptions of protest. In the afterglow, they snuggled and spoke of the baby they now knew they were expecting, and Nate told her everything he'd seen and learned during his adventures with Dewey. He described to her everything in great detail, and Tracie barraged him with questions about every creature they had encountered, especially the aquatic ones.

Then Nate's cell-phone rang.

"I'll just let it go to voicemail. I can check the messages later... I must have dozens by now," Nate said, and resumed nuzzling Tracie's neck and stroking her hair.

But Tracie sat up and cringed, realizing she had forgotten to tell Nate that Jason O'Rourke had planned to visit. "Crap, I'll bet it's Jason! He's been calling me relentlessly looking for you, and he's coming here later today! He also said something about you going to New York with him to talk to ARCA's Board of Directors."

Nate pulled away from her, feeling suddenly panicked. "What! Honey, why didn't you *tell* me? What did you tell *him*?"

She cocked her head and gave him her best evil eye. "Cool it, mister! I guess I've been a bit *distracted*, so I forgot until just now. I'm sorry."

Nate felt foolish, and quickly dropped his attitude. "Yeah... yeah. I'm sorry, sweetheart, you're right. I guess I knew he would be calling... I was just hoping to avoid him for a while. This thing with the helicopter in Brazil looks pretty weird, so I'm sure they want some more answers out of me if they think they can get them. But I have classes to teach this week. I can't just go to New York."

"Well, I told him you were on a fishing trip all weekend and couldn't be reached by cell."

«*Fishing*? Since when do I go *fishing*?"

Tracie rolled her eyes, then leaned over to give him a long kiss on the lips before getting up and heading for the bathroom, talking back at him over her shoulder. "Since *you* decided to run off in a spaceship, leaving me here alone to make excuses for you, lover! Now it's your problem, not mine. You can figure out what lies *you* want to tell him and call him back. I have to get ready for work... I've got to talk to my staff and plan my maternity leave!"

The view of Tracie's bare behind shuffling into the bathroom mesmerized Nate. It always did. He felt so very lucky to have her. She was as beautiful as she was witty, and her sarcasm, as annoying as it could be sometimes, drove him wild with passion for her. He leaped from the bed and followed her into the walk-in shower. Lying to Jason could wait another thirty minutes.

An hour later, a glowing Tracie kissed Nate good-bye and left for the aquarium. On her way, she called her doctor's office and managed to get an appointment for Tuesday morning, thanks to a cancellation. Nate dressed and savored a cup of medium-roast, fresh from the Keurig, while listening to all the messages his phone had collected over the weekend.

Most of the voicemails were from Jason, the one from an hour ago announcing he had arrived in Orlando from London that morning and was headed to Tampa in a rental car. He wanted to visit with Nate as soon as possible to plan a trip to New York for a few days. Nate slurped his coffee, took a deep breath, and hit the return-call button.

⊷◉⊶

Jason was relieved to see Nate's name show up on the screen of his cell phone. "Hallo, old chap, how was the fishing?"

"It was excellent. I needed a little time away from things, so I spent a few days with a friend on his boat. There's no cell service out on the water. Sorry, I didn't realize you'd be coming to visit so soon, or I would have told you."

"No worries. I *have* been a bit frantic in trying to reach you, my apologies to your lovely wife, but all's good now. And you certainly deserved a bit of a holiday. But as you can imagine, Mercer and the board are asking me a lot of difficult questions, especially about the rather large amount of money I spent to come rescue you. And, of course, there's this mysterious helicopter that went missing. *That's* a bloody mess and a half, which no one seems to be able to explain. Needless to say, I could really use more of your input as we investigate these matters."

"Sure, sure, of course. But Jason, I've told you everything I can remember, and I have lectures at the University this week. I've already been gone a few weeks; I'm not sure I can get away with taking more time off right now."

"Yes, I realize that, but the immediate future of ARCA depends on this meeting going well. You know that Mercer's group is, by far, our largest contributor. I fear we'll lose that funding if I can't explain this properly. Even if you can't add anything new, it would really help if you were just there to give them an accounting in your own words. Besides, Mercer is a bit of a fan of yours; he really wants to meet you. Can you possibly get your classes covered for just one more week?"

Nate realized he wasn't getting out of this easily. And Jason *was* right; the responsible thing to do was to go to New York with him and help explain it all, or at least *appear* to help. "Okay, okay," he agreed with a sigh. "I'm sorry I can't see you today — I need a bit more time to get my act together — but you can come by the office tomorrow morning. I'll talk to the dean and explain to him that I need to extend my leave. I'm sure I can get my teaching assistant to conduct the classes."

"Excellent! I'm at the Marriot Bayside tonight. I'll be by your office first thing in the morning, and we can make the flight arrangements to New York."

"Actually, you'd better make it late morning. I'm taking Tracie to the doctor in the morning — I have to pick her up at work, then get her back afterwards. Why don't you come in around ten-thirty?"

CHAPTER 43

Dewey's first stop after leaving Earth would be the Earth Station behind Jupiter. There, he would triple-check that he had thoroughly erased all evidence of his wrongdoings from the ship's and the station's data banks. There could be no record of his close contact with Humans and the other things that had happened, especially his carelessness in causing the deaths of those Humans in the Amazon and the sky-ray and monopods on the planet he and Nate had visited.

He felt deep remorse for these tragedies, although the men in the helicopter *had* been reckless and tried to destroy his ship unprovoked, putting Nate in great peril as well... so he partially forgave himself for that incident but felt horrible for their families. The sky-ray's death, on the other hand, could have easily been avoided. He should have considered the possibility that one might mistake the reflections on the ship for a cloud full of prey and try to ingest it. If he had been paying more attention to the proximity sensors, he could have adjusted the ship's trajectory to prevent such a mishap. Instead, he had been too distracted with entertaining Nate, and the poor beast had choked on the ship.

Despite all that, Dewey could not help but feel that it had, perhaps, all been worth it, the loss of life simply a stiff price paid for the chance to interact with real Humans... and that made him feel even more ashamed. *All* life was precious. Being responsible for these terrible things, regardless of any perceived justification, went against every grain of his being. Yet he was still glad that he had dismissed protocol and gone on the adventure with Nate. It *had* been such a wonderful adventure, one beyond his wildest dreams. Besides, there was nothing he could do to change any of it now, so he did his best to clear his mind of guilt and focus on erasing his tracks and getting home safely.

As the ship sped past the Moon, the spheres Dewey had left behind to fix Nate and Tracie's TVs caught up to it. Dewey didn't want to stop to open the cargo bay door and let the spheres back in, so he instructed them to just follow the ship to the station. Half an hour or so later, the ship slowed to dock with the station, and Dewey stared one last time at a holo-image of Nate, Tracie, and Doo-Doo standing in their kitchen. He emblazoned the picture into his minds, and then, before it could be downloaded to the station, he erased it from his holo-discs forever, along with every other image and record that might incriminate him.

Dewey wasted no time after docking. He quickly

dismantled Nate's habitat and replaced all its components into the station's spare-parts inventory, jettisoning the remaining fluid out onto space, as it would contain traces of Nate's DNA. Then he double-checked that all data involving anything but his core mission had been expunged, and plotted a course back to the Central Station near the black hole at the heart of the Milky Way. Within several hours, he would arrive there and generate the gravity tunnel that would take him home, 45 million light-years away.

CHAPTER 44

Tuesday morning, Nate picked Tracie up at the aquarium and chauffeured her to her doctor's appointment. A few tests later, it was confirmed that she was almost six weeks pregnant. She was terrified, yet giddy with delight, unable to resist poking some fun at Nate as he drove her back to work. "Well, stud, I guess you had a little containment problem that night before you left for London!"

"I don't have containment problems, my dear. Are you sure it wasn't the mailman?"

"No, it couldn't have been. I dumped him for the pool guy three months ago."

"We don't have a pool."

"We don't need one."

The two laughed to the point of tears, then chatted about how their lives would soon change dramatically. They had briefly discussed having children when they'd gotten engaged, but since then had shelved the subject, assuming they would wait until the time was right. Neither had minded prolonging the delay, both equally apprehensive about managing their careers with a baby in the mix. But now, to their surprise, those fears had quickly faded with the affirmation of Tracie's pregnancy.

They also admitted to each other that Dewey the Alien had played a significant role in their new-found comfort with parenthood. Meeting him had given them a whole new outlook on life, reinforcing how unique and precious it is to be alive and self-aware in a Universe full of life in every conceivable form. Suspecting there's abundant life beyond Earth was one thing; *knowing* so brought them a whole new perspective as to the grand scheme of things.

Nate kissed his glowing wife goodbye and was in his office at the University by ten. By ten-thirty, he had arranged with the Dean and his TA for him to take the rest of the week off, so he could accompany Jason O'Rourke to New York. As luck would have it, aside from being ARCA's top contributor, Alan Mercer was also a significant donor to the University's College of Sciences. Nate easily leveraged this into justifying the additional time off.

At ten-forty-five, Jason popped his head through the door of Nate's office, where he found Nate waiting for him, engrossed in a book on astrophysics. "Hallo! Since when are you interested in things that don't crawl around in the forest?" Jason inquired with a puzzled tone as he entered the room.

Nate abruptly shut the book, tossed it onto the credenza behind him, and rose to greet Jason with a firm handshake. "Well, having to be rescued from a meteorite impact in the Amazon does pique a person's interest in such things," Nathan replied with a grin. "But it's just a mild curiosity. I think I'll stick to bugs and spiders."

"I'm with you on that one," Jason chuckled. "But ARCA has been under pressure from Mercer to branch out into stuff like that, you know, studying space and the possibility of extraterrestrial life and such. I keep telling him it's just not what we do... ARCA exists to study life on *this* world, not speculate about life on other planets that we'll likely never be able to see in person, at least not in our lifetimes. Besides, he has Antonio and others like him around the world to do that for him."

Nate thought of many ways he could reply to this, but kept silent, nodding in agreement.

"So," Jason continued, "how did it go with the Dean? Are you all right for a few more days off to go to New York with me?"

"Yup. It was a piece of cake. In fact, I think the Dean would have gladly come along and crawled right up Mercer's ass had we invited him."

Jason shook his head, chuckling. "Yes, Mercer does have a way of endearing himself to certain people."

"That he does. I think it's called a *cash enema*.»

The two men laughed, then caught up on small talk. Nate told Jason of Tracie's pregnancy, and Jason spoke of his children and how much Nate would enjoy starting a family. Then Jason's tone got serious, and they got down to business. "Nathan, I don't have to tell you that Mercer and his cronies are quite mystified as to what happened down there, as am I. We blew a shitload of their money getting you out, on top of what had already been spent on the expedition, and the mission was a bit short on results because of lost time. All *my* responsibility, of course, but I really need you there to back me up. I really appreciate your coming along."

"No problem, I'm happy to help. But I don't know that they're going to be any more enlightened with my report. I'm sorry, Jason, but I just don't remember much other than finding the meteorite and then falling on the rocks."

"Do you, by chance, remember being attacked by an animal? Perhaps a jaguar back at the camp? The security fence sensors recorded a large four-legged creature passing through while you were there."

The question caught Nate off-guard, but he was getting accustomed to rapidly fabricating stories. He responded with confidence. "My God, I *did* forget to mention that! I guess I didn't think it was relevant. There *was* a jaguar. It had been stalking me since I got there, but the first time it tried to get me, the pyramid zapped it good and it ran off. I didn't think it would try again, but it did. It came through behind me so fast I didn't have time to raise the power on the shield." *If the shield recorded the jaguar, it must also have detected Dewey coming through the pyramid,* Nate thought, silently panicking. He decided to come up with a quick explanation before Jason could ask about it. "If it weren't for some curious local tribesmen in the area, it might have killed me. They showed up just as the jaguar was attacking. One shot a blow-dart at it, and it ran off."

Jason frowned. This explanation did make sense, except for the fact that the images of what came through the shield besides the jaguar hadn't resembled anything Human. He leaned forward, checking behind him to see that no one was near the office door before speaking again in a soft voice. "Do you remember anything curious about your GPS unit?"

Nate panicked more. What could they have gotten from the GPS unit? He was sure it had been smashed beyond repair on the rocks, helped along by his whacking it on them a few times with all his might. He kept a good poker face. "Curious? No, I don't recall anything. What do you mean by 'curious'?"

"Well, according to the satellite logs, it seems to have become inop when you got near the meteorite. And, well... it was... sort of rewired."

"Rewired?" Nate tried to sound shocked and surprised.

"Yes. And what's most odd is the *way* it was rewired. As if it were converted to a different sort of device altogether, using methods we don't recognize. We're not aware of any technology that makes micro-welds and connections like that, or that can change the internal structure of capacitors and other internal components. It's a complete mystery."

Nate felt mildly relieved. ARCA knew the GPS had been altered, but they didn't know why or how. He manifested his best puzzled look and continued to act startled and naive. "Wow, that's really bizarre. I don't know what to tell you, but *I* certainly didn't do it, and I can't imagine who did. It couldn't have happened in the rainforest; I had it with me the whole time. It must have come that way from the manufacturer. Maybe they gave us the wrong model?"

Jason shook his head. "No, no... Toby checked with them, and they don't make a model like this. In fact, one of Mercer's companies made it."

"That figures. Well, then, maybe Toby thought it came from Mercer's company, but we got it from someone else?"

"No, we checked that, and that's just it — *nobody* makes a model like this. We're not even sure what the modifications are supposed to *do*. A receiver of some type, we think, but not like anything we've ever seen before."

"Where's the unit now?"

"Right here." Jason proclaimed, patting the side of his briefcase. "Mercer insisted I bring it to him. I imagine he'll have his own people take a look, but I doubt they'll come to any conclusions beyond what Toby found. Toby knows his stuff." Then Jason changed the subject. "Say, time's getting away from us here. May I use your laptop to get our flights booked? I'd use my phone app, but it will be quicker if I can use a full-size keyboard... my fat fingers struggle with these stupid little screens."

"Sure, help yourself." Nate said, standing and motioning for Jason to have a seat at his desk.

Jason slipped into Nate's chair and logged in to ARCA's travel site, booking himself and Nate to New York on the first flight out in the morning. Nate paced about the office, twitching his fingers nervously and staring at Jason's briefcase on the floor, plotting how he might get ahold of the GPS unit and dispose of it without Jason knowing.

CHAPTER 45

As the gravity tunnel dissipated and Dewey's trip neared its end, holo-displays filled the cockpit with graphics of his native solar system and the ship's plotted trajectory to its final destination. His hearts swelled with relief and joy at the sight of the Purple Planet on the viewer, still just a bright dot in the distance but growing rapidly until it filled the ship with its comforting lavender glow. Orbiting around from the dark side of the planet, the Exploration Ministry's Launching Station came into view, and the ship slowed to final approach speed.

As soon as the ship had exited the gravity tunnel, communication was possible. Its systems automatically synched up with those of the Ministry Network, broadcasting news of Dewey's return. Within moments, his brains were bombarded with messages coming in through his holo-disks. The majority were from the Mission Retrieval Unit, preparing him for docking and decontamination procedures. The Medical Technician sent an urgent inquiry as to his physical well-being, as his bio-scan indicated there had been some form of severe injury during the mission.

But then came a communique from his mate and off-spring, expressing their joy for his return, and finally, his Mentor, who simply stated, "Welcome home, my young Apprentice. I will come to the Station immediately to greet you when you dock."

Then a holo-display alerted Dewey that the ship's master computer had received an odd signal that it did not recognize as part of normal protocol, and was analyzing it to determine its purpose and origin. Dewey didn't recognize it either, but the computer soon reassured him it was a routine scan that went directly into the ship's and his holo-disks' data banks. The security codes were confirmed and accepted, so he assumed it must be a newly implemented systems check for returning missions, one he had not been made aware of during his training, so he did not inquire about it.

On previous missions, as Dewey understood it, the databanks were not scanned until the returning ship had completed docking and decontamination. Apparently, this was now being done prior to those actions, and he observed nervously as the unexpected scan probed through the logs. If he had not been thorough in erasing all records of his encounter with Nate, it would soon be known by all. After twenty seconds, the scan ceased, and the signal that carried it disappeared from the ship's uplink system. Dewey waited anxiously for a message that inquired about anything unusual in the mission's logs. None came, and he felt a wave of relief.

The ship slowed to a crawl as it neared the station, entering and then coming to a halt inside the huge funnel that tapered down into the receiving chamber. The aperture at the bottom of the funnel opened and an energy field gripped the ship, lowering it through the containment field and into the chamber, after which the aperture sealed and all the technicians and scientists who had partaken in Dewey's departure converged on the vessel once again. The cockpit portal opened and Dewey emerged to a ruckus of audible cheers, his eyes beaming blue. The Medical Technician approached him first, alarmed at why two of his arms and a pair of eyes had been required to fully regenerate. The MedTech reached for the two smaller, brand-new appendages, feeling them and scanning them with his holo-discs.

"When I inquired about your health status, you did not mention having lost two limbs and an eye-pair! How did this happen?"

"An Earth creature, a large feline carnivore called a jaguar. It caught me off-guard and ripped my arms and eyes off before I could incapacitate it. I am fine; there is no need for concern."

"The arms are regenerating properly, but why was this not mentioned it in your log? The Bio Unit must have malfunctioned."

Dewey panicked silently; he had not thought of this when he erased the record of his run-in with the creatures that dismembered him.   Then a private message came silently through one of Dewey's holo-disc. "The Medical Technician is correct. The Bio Unit's log should have recorded such severe injuries. It is very odd that it did not." It was from his Mentor, and he felt her presence in the chamber.

Dewey raised a set of eyes and telescoped his vision, pivoting slowly to scan the vast room. He located her, emerging from an interstation transport bay, two High Council members of the Exploration Ministry walking beside her in his direction. This was the moment he was most apprehensive about. If any conclusive record of his disobedience had been discovered in the database scans, something he had missed, he would hear about it very soon now.

Dewey pushed his way through the technicians that were unloading the Earth specimens he had collected from the ship's cargo bay, then scampered across the chamber to greet his Mentor and the Ministry members. As the group converged, all held out a hand, digits extended to intertwine with Dewey's. "Mentor, Councilors, it is good to see you. I gathered many new specimens; I think you will be pleased," Dewey stated audibly.

"Good work. I'm sure we will all be most pleased," the Mentor replied, her eyes changing to mottled black and yellow.

The Councilors congratulated Dewey, and then eagerly scurried off to inspect the growing stack of specimen containers, leaving Dewey alone with the Mentor. Dewey felt a wave of relief that they had not mentioned anything about any strange readings from the scans; it would appear he had successfully erased any evidence of his wrong-doings. But the Mentor's eyes changed to dark red, and she sent Dewey another private message.

"Did you encounter any Humans?"

The abruptness and directness of the question caught Dewey off-guard, but he had prepared himself for this. As painful as it was, he lied to her. "No, Mentor, there were no Humans in the rainforest. But I did see the lights of their cities as I approached Earth. It was exciting to be so close, but frustrating to not get a closer look at them."

There was a moment of deafening silence from his elder that made him nervous. She was motionless, staring at him with all eight eyes now. Had she believed him? It felt so foreign and uncomfortable to deceive her. He had never lied to anyone before, let alone the person he trusted most outside of his immediate family. But he knew if he wanted to be allowed to return to Earth again, he must maintain his composure and not reveal what had happened.

Finally, she replied. "I agree; it is a shame that you were not authorized to study them up close on your first mission. But that has been the case for all of us who are fortunate enough to be selected for Earth study."

"Yes, I am very fortunate to have been chosen. My disappointment does not overshadow my gratitude."

"I'm sure it doesn't. I taught you as best I could to manage such emotions. But if, say, by pure accident, you *had* encountered Humans on this assignment, it would be in your best interest to conceal that fact. Otherwise, there would be an extensive inquiry by the Ministry Tribunal and it would put your future advancement in jeopardy. It would be most disappointing for you, and me as well, if you were delayed or permanently denied returning to Earth."

Dewey recoiled his eyes, the puzzling words catching him off-guard. But he responded quickly and confidently. "I would certainly not wish to be delayed or denied. But, as I said, I saw no Humans."

"So be it. I am simply stating that if you *had*, it would be best to not reveal it to anyone."

Now Dewey was very confused. Did she know that he had encountered Humans, or was she just insinuating that she would condone his concealing it if he had? Either way, it now seemed that she was not as opposed to unauthorized contact as he had previously thought. "You would suggest that I lie to the Ministry?" he asked.

«*Lie* is a strong word. I am saying that in such a circumstance, I would simply consider not revealing the complete truth. That is, unless the complete truth was something you felt was necessary for the good of all of us."

Dewey's eyes turned from dark green to bright red. *She knows something... but how?* The elder noticed his discomfort and continued. "Young one, it was obvious to me before you left that you were highly motivated to study Humans up close, and that you felt you were ready for such a task regardless of your experience level."

"Yes, that is true, but I do not wish to defy protocol. It was... it *is* never my intention."

"Whether you wish to defy protocol or not is irrelevant. One can still defy protocol while not truly wishing to do so, especially if the protocol is so restrictive that it contradicts what is in one's hearts. Can you identify with such internal conflict?"

"I can," Dewey admitted, feeling as if any moment she was about to call him out. But he was not ready to concede yet. "But Mentor, I have not defied protocol."

"Good. That is the proper answer in this circumstance. You must maintain that position. Do you understand?"

"Of course, Mentor."

She does know! Dewey was convinced of this now, and was struggling to keep his composure. But if he had been discovered, he could not understand why he wasn't being confronted more directly with his lies. If the scans *had* revealed his breaking protocol— found something he had missed—*then why hadn't he been questioned by the Ministry members already*? Surely immediate action would have been taken if he had been caught doing something so blatantly defiant. Keeping two eyes focused on the Mentor, he used the other six to scan the chamber and see if anyone else was near enough to sense his tension. No one was. Everyone else was busy studying the ship and the new Earth specimens. None seemed overly interested in the private conversation he was having with his teacher. *Maybe only she knows? Perhaps the Ministry is not aware!*

The Mentor had sensed his angst, and she placed a hand on his chest. "Are you well? You seem anxious and preoccupied." Dewey returned all eyes to her. "Why are you so tense? Did, perhaps, you break protocol on Earth after all?"

Dewey wanted to confess everything to her now, come clean of his guilt. But he just couldn't push himself over that edge yet. Instead he turned the question back to her: "Mentor, did you ever break protocol on Earth?"

She retracted her hand and remained silent for a moment, her eyes turning pale yellow, then said, "I was always as eager to study real Humans as you are. You are aware of how many missions to Earth I was entrusted with, and on each one I always followed protocol precisely. I kept my distance from them on my first three trips, as instructed. On subsequent missions, when I was finally authorized to study them up close, I was very careful not to make myself known to them. I never broke these rules... until my final mission."

"What happened?"

Now it was the Mentor who nervously scanned the room to make sure nobody was nearby or coming their way.

"I was collecting DNA samples for cloning. I wanted desperately to try to communicate with the subjects. It was very tempting, so much so that I agonized over it, but I never did. I was too afraid of the consequences if I were caught."

"I don't understand. If you never broke protocol, then what are you referring to?"

"I never broke protocol until something went very wrong on my final mission. I didn't plan it, nor did I intend for it to happen. A young male I was harvesting DNA from awoke during the procedure. I know I sedated him adequately, but somehow, he did not react to the sedation like other Humans, and he woke before I had finished. Not only did he wake, but he was immediately alert and aware of my presence."

"But that's impossible! Our Human sedative is engineered to be flawless on any subject."

"Apparently not, as what I'm telling you truly happened. And when he woke up and looked into my eyes, I felt suddenly connected with this Human child in a way I cannot describe, nor could I have predicted. I was not prepared for such a thing, and I found myself completely unable to follow protocol and dispatch the boy. It just didn't feel right... so I let him live."

"Did you communicate with the Human child?"

"Yes, and it was astonishing. This tiny Human was incredibly intelligent... much more so, I believe, than most Human children. He was able to speak of things beyond the comprehension of many adult Humans we have studied. And he did not fear me whatsoever."

"How was he able to understand your speech?"

"I used a holo-disc to illuminate words in his

language on a fallen tree trunk. He would answer my questions and ask me many in return, understanding most of my replies with ease. Since then, I have regretted that I did not break the rules prior to that and attempt communication with others I had encountered."

Dewey was stunned. "Why are you telling me this now? Why did you not mention this before I departed for Earth?"

"Believe me, I wanted to. I have come to realize that the Ministry's policy of remaining unknown to the Humans is outdated and counterproductive. We should be communicating with them, and this needs to begin with our new generations of Explorers like yourself. But I wanted you to pursue such rebellious thinking on your own accord, not by me suggesting or encouraging it. If the Council were to find out I had fostered such ideas in my top student, both our careers would be in jeopardy."

"I would never have told them if you had. You could have trusted me."

"Yes, I know this. I do trust you. But still, I could not take such a risk. Besides, only the right kind of Explorer will be able to handle such acts of defiance carefully enough to avoid doing irreversible damage. I had to be sure you were of the caliber and mindset to be such an Explorer, and only once you had been to Earth on your first mission could we both know how well you might handle such responsibility."

Dewey could not contain himself any longer. "You

know what happened, don't you, Mentor? You must know, or you would not be saying these things to me now."

She did not reply, and her lack of any immediate denial was proof enough. Then it struck him: the odd scan was not a routine Ministry Systems check... *she must have sent it!* "You sent that unscheduled scan. It wasn't from the Ministry. They don't know. Only you know what really happened."

"Yes, I sent the scan signal concealed in my greeting. It was undetected by the Ministry."

"But I was sure I had erased everything from the ship's databanks, as well as my holo-discs. What did you find?"

"The ship and your disks were clean; you succeeded in that regard. What you failed to realize in your inexperience is that the ship's utility-spheres each contain independent memory banks, in which they record all their activity during a mission; and although they do synch up with the main databases, this does not happen in reverse. Their data stays intact until it is manually erased or changed. This is done as a security measure in case the ship was severely damaged and the data banks become irretrievable. Sometimes the data on the spheres can be useful in determining what went wrong."

"And they recorded every task I commanded them to do." Dewey was embarrassed not to have thought of this. It was not in his training, as there had been no need for him to know.

"Yes," The Mentor confirmed his assumption. "Despite your erasing all incriminating evidence from the ship and your holo-discs, the spheres still held records of how they constructed a bio-liquid habitat for transporting a Human in the cargo bay, and how they repaired the transport when it was damaged after an impact. Then, most odd, was the record of two spheres having repaired several Human devices... I believe the ones that receive and display their audio-visual transmissions. Televisions, they call them? I can only assume from this evidence that you did, in fact, come into close contact with at least one Human, possibly several."

Dewey was ashamed and embarrassed at his carelessness. "If you know this, then the Ministry will be discovering it themselves when they inspect the spheres."

"They do not know, nor will they unless you tell them. I took the liberty of synchronizing the data on the spheres with that of the ship and your holo-discs. If you were to confess, I would be considered just as guilty, as I am now your accomplice in this matter."

Dewey could not believe his good fortune. His fondness and admiration for his Mentor increased a hundredfold at that instant.

"I cannot begin to tell you how grateful I am for this. But I am ashamed of my carelessness. There was unnecessary loss of life because of what I did."

The Mentor's eyes turned black. This was not good news. The sphere's databanks held nothing about any loss of life, only of their own activity. "Human life was lost?"

"Yes. Three Humans on Earth, and numerous animals on Planet 678329 of the Milky Way galaxy died because of my mistakes. I tried to be careful, but some Humans attacked the ship with one of their flying devices. If I had not engaged the defense systems and it had not neutralized them, the ship might have been damaged."

"And the animals on 678329? What happened to them? And why were you there in the first place?"

"I don't know where to begin explaining everything that happened. I experienced some amazing things, but the loss of life was a terrible mistake, completely my fault. I feel unbearable guilt for this."

"You can tell me the details later; I don't need to know everything right now. The unnecessary loss of life is tragic and alarming, and I am disappointed in you for not preventing it. But in the larger scope of things, I hope it will have been a valuable lesson to you in how you conduct yourself during future missions, especially if you come in contact with Humans."

"Mentor, I am perplexed that you are not angrier with me."

"I am saddened by your carelessness, but my anger is directed towards myself. I knew that you would not be able to resist defying protocol given the right opportunity. I should have trained you as if it were going to happen."

"And you are suggesting that I should again defy

protocol and make contact with Humans on future missions?"

"Yes. I do want you to contact Humans again if you go back to Earth. Our rules are obsolete and counterproductive. We have already communicated with the cetaceans, but their capacity to interact with us is limited by their physical nature and their refusal to progress into a technology-based society. I believe the Creator meant for us to communicate with the Humans, despite their sometimes destructive and selfish ways, which could complicate such interaction."

"They are not all that way, Mentor. I have witnessed compassion and caring equal to our own."

"So have I, but it was a long time ago. I am eager to hear about all your experiences later. Did you by chance review any of the new data the Earth Station recorded since the last mission? Are there any significant new developments in their space-travel capabilities?"

"They are making progress, but it has slowed due to recent shortfalls in their currency-based economic systems. The general public has not been willing to fund progress at the full potential of their scientist's capabilities."

"Will they still explore the fourth planet in coming years, as we have suspected?"

"Yes. I am certain of it. They have sent numerous probes to the planet's surface, and a manned mission is imminent within several years."

"Have the probes discovered the structure?"

"Not yet. They have detected the rocky mound covering the center of its top, but are convinced it is a natural feature of the planet surface. They do not suspect there is anything unusual beneath the mound."

"Is there progress in deep ocean exploration?"

"Yes, but I do not believe they will find the structure in the deep trench anytime soon. It is more likely they will find the one on the fourth planet first."

The Mentor's eyes shifted to mottled black and purple.

"Eventually they will discover both. I believe we should be in contact with them before that happens. I believe there is much to fear from the structures, or whoever put them there should they return one day, and the Humans should be warned."

Dewey's eyes shifted to light gray, and he felt compelled to add another confession to the conversation. "Mentor, I revealed the structures on Mars and Earth to a Human."

The Mentor did not reply, but her eyes changed to bright blue and her limbs quivered.

"I should tell you everything."

"That is enough for now; my old hearts need a rest. And you have to go to the Ministry Council and get debriefed. We will continue this conversation tomorrow."

By now, the Councilors had concluded their inspection of Dewey's harvest from Earth, and they scampered across the chamber back to where Dewey and the Mentor were having their private conversation. They announced it was time to escort Dewey back to the planet's surface for his debriefing. There, a panel of senior scientists would review his bounty and data entries to determine the mission's overall success, and assess whether he qualified for future trips back to Earth. The Mentor was not allowed to be a part of this panel. Mentors and their Apprentices often shared deep friendships and loyalties, and the decision to send Explorers back to Earth was to be purely unbiased, based solely on the achievements of their first missions.

As Dewey accompanied the Councilors to their waiting ship, he turned one set of eyes back towards the Mentor. He shot her an appreciative glance, his eyes turning bright purple, and he sent her a private message. "Thank you for everything. I will tell you all that happened soon."

The Mentor said nothing in return, but held up two hands with all fingers spread into a large fan pattern...the Alien gesture for "Good luck."

CHAPTER 46

By late Wednesday afternoon, Nate and Jason were in an Uber, crawling through rush-hour traffic towards lower Manhattan from La Guardia Airport. The flight had been eventless, but the GPS unit in Jason's briefcase had raised quite a stir getting through security at Tampa International.

As Jason waited in the TSA Pre-Check line, a K-9 detail went berserk when the dog sniffed at his briefcase, causing it to be quickly confiscated and removed to a secure area. Jason was also detained for a thorough and very personal search. Upon further inspection of the case's contents, the K-9 singled out the partially-smashed GPS unit, encased in a large zip-lock bag, and the confused beagle wagged its tail erratically, whimpering and howling as if not sure what it was smelling; this scent was like nothing it had ever encountered before. The TSA agents could not find anything threatening about the GPS unit, nor anything dangerous in Jason's shoes or underwear, so the briefcase and all its contents were returned, apologies were given and accepted, and he was allowed to pass just in time to join Nate for boarding.

Nate was also held up in security. As he passed through the body scan unit, the alarm went haywire, yet there was nothing under his clothes showing up on the screens. He had removed all metal objects before entering the X-ray chamber, and shrugged at the agent when asked if there was anything left to shed before passing through again. The second pass yielded the same result, so Nate too was escorted to a private room and treated to the same intimate rubber-gloved treatment Jason had so thoroughly enjoyed. As the metal-detecting wand was passed over his body, it shrieked loudly when it passed across his left arm, at the exact spot where Dewey had implanted the locator device.

"Do you have a metal pin in your arm, sir?" the agent had inquired.

"Well… yes, I guess I do!"

"You should have mentioned that before going through the scanner, sir. You are free to go."

"Yeah, I forgot. Sorry about that."

Nate had been relieved to see that Jason was distracted with his own security search, and so he had not heard Nate fib to the TSA agent about the pin in his arm. *One less thing I have to lie to Jason and Alan about!*

The Uber eventually reached the bustling mayhem of New York's business district, delivering Nate and Jason to Mercer Tower, where a number of Alan Mercer's companies were based, and where ARCA's

Board of directors convened. The two rode the elevator to the thirty-seventh floor, where they were greeted by a smiling, stunningly beautiful young woman in business attire. Prancing like a runway fashion queen, she escorted them to a lavish boardroom with a breathtaking view of the city's sprawling skyline.

At the far corner of the room, Alan Mercer was sitting at the elliptical conference table conversing with four other men. Mercer was in his early seventies, but the only sign of his true age were the occasional strands of silvery gray in his brown hair, his physique and complexion that of a much younger man. The other board-members were less youthful in their appearance and demeanor. All were dressed in what Nate believed must very expensive suits, making him feel seriously underdressed in his khakis, white oxford, and corduroy blazer.

"Jason, Professor Johnston, thank you for coming!" Mercer greeted them cheerfully, rising and walking towards them with open arms. He offered them each a firm handshake, and then introduced them to the board. "Gentlemen, you all know Jason O'Rourke, of course, and may I present Professor Nathan Johnston. Nate, this is Jack Porter, Larry Hunter, Ronald Pierce, and Bryce Eckerd, my top financial and intellectual partners on numerous private endeavors, not the least of which is ARCA."

Nate and Jason shook hands with each, then everyone sat down at the huge table, engaging in chit-chat about their involvements in the world's scientific communities, and how each had been recruited into Mercer's various doings about the globe. And then the pretty young receptionist entered the room again and announced another guest.

"Mr. Mercer, gentlemen, Mr. Perron is here. He's freshening up in the washroom and will be in momentarily."

"Tony's here?" Jason asked, glancing at Mercer.

"Yes," Mercer replied, "I asked him to be here for this meeting. I thought it pertinent, given his indirect involvement."

"I see. Well, it will be good to see him again," Jason said, trying to hide his surprise and concern at Perron's unexpected presence. "Gentlemen, please excuse me a moment? Now that it's been mentioned, I could use a restroom break as well before we commence."

Jason found Perron stalling in the posh executive washroom, staring at himself in the mirror, trying to reel in the anxiety he had felt ever since Mercer had summoned him to New York. He had hoped to have some clues as to the whereabouts of the stolen sphere and who the men were that stole it before reporting to ARCA's board, as he had not yet informed Mercer nor Jason of this event. But he had no answers yet, only more questions.

"Tony! I had no idea we'd be seeing you at this meeting," Jason said as he entered.

"Oh, I wouldn't miss this for anything," Antonio

said sarcastically.

Jason immediately noticed the bandage covering a large portion of Perron's head. "My God, man, what on Earth happened to your head? Are you okay?

"It's gone, Jason," Perron replied quietly.

"What's gone?"

"The meteorite... the sphere... the helicopter remains, if *that* theory of mine is correct. It's gone."

"What do you mean, *gone*?"

"It was stolen. A bunch of armed men stormed in, knocked me out, and took it out of the country by truck and boat. We don't know who they were or where they went. It's just gone."

"Armed men? Are you *kidding* me?"

"I wish I were. And the way it was taken... Jason, I tell you, this was like a precise military operation. These men were highly trained and well-equipped. And it was expensive... cost someone a lot of money."

Jason scanned the room to see if he could detect any listening devices, knowing fully well that if there were any, he probably couldn't see them anyway. He leaned in toward Perron and whispered, "Does Mercer know about your theory?"

"No, not yet. I was hoping to have some better answers before I mentioned it, but it's all still a big mystery, and now it's gone altogether, so we may never know for sure."

"Tony, I think it might be best that we keep that theory amongst ourselves for now."

"I agree, but...»

Perron didn't have a chance to finish his response, as Mercer himself burst into the washroom. "Antonio, come in and meet everyone! Jason can't have you all to himself! Shit, what happened to your head?"

"I had a little accident. I'll be fine, it was just a minor concussion and a few stitches."

The three men returned to the boardroom, and Mercer introduced Perron to everyone. "Gentlemen, I invited Antonio to join us today so we can get some input from his perspective on this odd episode."

For the next two hours, Nate, Jason, and Perron presented their recollections of the events in Brazil and answered a barrage of questions, Nate being very careful to keep his fictitious answers as identical as he could to all previous testimony. When the subject of the GPS unit came up, Jason took the contraption out of his briefcase and offered it to the group for inspection. Nate cringed. He had hoped to somehow steal it from Jason and make it disappear, but had never had the opportunity. Jason had kept his briefcase by his side at every moment.

Jason showed the group enlarged photos of the unit's altered microcircuits, which drew blank stares of amazement from those that understood electronics well enough to know that what they were seeing was something extraordinary and inexplicable. New, microscopic circuits had somehow been manifested with absolute precision into the unit's components, as if transformed to perform new tasks. Not even the most advanced microchip manufacturers were able to alter existing circuits like this, to anyone's knowledge... save Mercer, but he remained silent.

Nate continued to plead ignorance on the GPS modifications, saying that *he* certainly couldn't have done it, so it must have been that way when it left ARCA's facility in London. But Jason countered that theory. "Toby certainly didn't do it. He's very good, but not that good."

"Well *someone* did it, so who the hell was it, then?" Eckerd demanded. "This makes no sense! We need answers."

Jason continued, "Toby also sent these pictures to the manufacturer that makes these for us, and they said they couldn't have done this even if they tried... in fact, they're asking me if they can buy it back. I suspect they would like to reverse-engineer it to see if a competitor has somehow surpassed their technology. Alan, it *is* one of your companies that we get these from, Addi-Comp Technologies, so I'll let you make that call."

"That's not going to happen." Mercer said immediately, grabbing the GPS off the table and putting it into *his* briefcase and placing that at the foot of his chair. "I'll be hanging on to it for now and explain it to Addi-Comp. I want my own labs to examine it first."

Nate silently cringed, doing his best to hide his horror as Mercer confiscated the GPS. Then Mercer asked about the meteorite, and everyone turned to Perron.

"Yes… the meteorite." Perron dropped his eyes to the table, unable to meet anyone's stare as he bore the bad news. "I am embarrassed to tell you, the meteorite has been stolen, and I have no idea where it is now. In fact, I lied to you, Alan… my injury was not an accident. I was assaulted by a group of men as they were taking the meteorite."

"My God, Antonio," Mercer responded. "Why didn't you tell me sooner?"

"It only happened a few days ago. I was in the hospital for a while, and pretty drugged up, so I haven't had much time to look into it further. I had hoped to have some news from the police on where the meteorite might be, but it has disappeared without a trace," Perron offered apologetically, and then he described to everyone how the group of armed men had executed their well-choreographed robbery.

Mercer and the Board acted only mildly shocked to hear this, offering their sympathy to Perron for his suffering through the assault — but Perron thought it odd that they showed surprisingly little outrage over such a violent act.

Jason and Nate were equally puzzled by the Board's calm response, but they were also re-lieved that they were not getting lambasted for the amount of money the entire episode had cost with very little to show for it. Nate had collected only a small number of new specimens from the rainforest, and Perron now had no meteorite to study further. Jason was further relieved that Perron had kept his word, and didn't offer up his theory that the stolen meteorite was, in fact, the Brazilian military's missing helicopter.

After another half-hour of questions from Mercer and the Board, the session concluded with a closing statement from Mercer, who stood to deliver his thoughts.

"Well, gentlemen, this is certainly frustrating and quite mysterious. I had hoped to get to the bottom of all this today, but it seems we have raised more questions than we have answered. Much about this whole episode will have to remain a mystery until some more facts surface, *if* they ever do. I heard nothing here today that will help the Brazilian government find their missing helicopter crew, but I will offer them any assistance that they feel might be useful. Meanwhile, I will use my resources to study the GPS unit's alterations, and to find out who is responsible for Tony's injuries and stealing the meteorite. Aside from those curiosities, it was pure coincidence that the meteorite hit so close to the campsite. Tony's folks were right to ask ARCA to have Nate find the impact site; we ask this kind of cooperation from all organizations that we fund. And Nate's subsequent mishap at the site was nothing but an unfortunate accident, nothing any of us could have foreseen. Under the circumstances, I can identify no misconduct or misappropriation of funds by ARCA in its expedient retrieval of Professor Johnston. Indeed, it was a good call to get him out immediately, no matter the cost, Jason. He might have died there otherwise. But... the GPS modifications, missing helicopter, and now, it seems, the missing meteorite are rather serious things we must investigate further. I would ask that all of you and your organizations work with me as needed to get to the bottom of these things."

The men all agreed, shook hands. and said their farewells to Mercer and the Board. Then the pretty receptionist escorted them out of the boardroom and back down the long hallway to the elevators, all three of them silent.

Back in the boardroom, once the doors had shut and locked, all smiles disappeared from Mercer and his partners. "Why didn't Perron mention that the meteorite was composed of the exact elements found in the missing helicopter?" asked Eckerd. "He had it long enough to run plenty of tests; he *had* to know, or at least suspect there was something extremely odd about it."

"Perhaps we should have asked, as I suggested," Hunter exclaimed. "We *should* have asked. Put him on the fucking spot!"

"Dammit, Larry, we couldn't ask, now could we?" Mercer stated angrily. "If we had asked, they would realize that *we* have it. We can't risk them finding out we're the ones who stole it. The idiot in charge of that op almost killed Perron!"

"Do any of you really believe Johnston can't remember anything?" Porter questioned the group.

"Of course not, he's fucking lying through his teeth. He's hiding something," Hunter said. The rest nodded in agreement.

"Well, at least now we have the meteorite *and* the GPS unit. Do you think your people can get to the bottom of this?" Pierce directed his question at Mercer.

All fell silent, and eyes shifted to Mercer. Mercer stared down at the table for a moment, rubbing his jaw with the thumb and index finger of his right hand. He lifted his eyes and looked about at the group, then spoke confidently. "Yes," he stated. "Rest assured, gentlemen, I will not stop until I find out what the hell really happened in the Amazon last week. And I already have a pretty good idea."

CHAPTER 47

Nate, Jason, and Perron sat quietly as Mercer's limo took them back to their hotel, none of them quite sure how to interpret Mercer's curiously calm reaction to Perron's story... or the fact that Nate had failed to remember any additional details of the incident in the Amazon.

Jason had expected to receive a harsh grilling on his exorbitant use of ARCA funds to rescue Nate, not to mention the heat ARCA was facing over the missing Brazilian helicopter and its crew. Nate had been sure he was going to be relentlessly questioned and pressured into a contradictory statement that might jeopardize his ruse, and Perron had feared losing his generous funding once Mercer learned the meteorite had been stolen under his watch. But none of these things had happened; Mercer had sent them on their way without any reprimand whatsoever.

Over dinner, at Jason's strong insistence, Perron reluctantly shared with Nate his theory about the alleged meteorite actually being the helicopter's remains. Jason explained to Nate that although he and Perron had originally felt it best they not share this theory with anyone until they could prove it, he now hoped it might help jar Nate's memory, perhaps revealing some insight as to how such a catastrophic thing might have happened. Mercer was certainly motivated to get to the bottom of the missing meteorite, and with his vast resources, chances were he *would* find it... and then, if Perron's theory were true, all hell would break loose. It would be far better if Jason and Perron could find some answers before Mercer's people discovered too much, and be prepared for the fallout.

But Nate offered no such satisfaction. Instead, he held character, pretended to be thoroughly shocked, and said he had no idea how such an ex-traordinary thing could be even remotely possible. With acting skills worthy of an Oscar, he debated the matter, selling completely the notion that he considered the idea ridiculous... that an entire he-licopter and its crew could *not* be reduced to the size of a yoga ball out in the middle of the rainfor-est. There had to be another explanation, though none of them could think of one.

On the inside, Nate felt terrible that he had to keep the truth from them. These were good men and trusted friends, who had gone to great lengths to rescue him in the forest. Lying to them made his guts ache, but he wasn't about to break his prom-ise to Dewey—that insanely unique pact between two beings from opposite sides of the Universe.

Regardless of any potential implications or consequences of remaining silent or outright lying, Nate felt a great deal of responsibility in honoring his intergalactic agreement.

The following morning, when their sedan arrived at the airport, the three men vowed to stay in touch in case anything new surfaced, and then each went their separate ways to catch a flight home. It was late that night when Nate arrived home and found that Tracie was in bed but still awake watching a movie—a remake of H.G. Wells' *War of the Worlds*, featuring Tom Cruise as the resilient Human that must fend off the vicious invaders in order to survive annihilation and save his children. She hated Tom Cruise, had always thought him pompous and arrogant, and thus refused to patronize his work; but in this case she was transfixed on the story and could not turn it off.

"Hi babe!" Tracie greeted Nate with a toothy grin, relieved that he was finally home.

Nate sneered playfully, poking fun at her choice in entertainment. "Really, honey? *War of The Worlds?* Tom Cruise?"

"Yeah, I know, right? Since when am I into this kind of shit?"

"'Shit' is right. I used to love those kinds of movies. But now, after meeting Dewey, I don't think I can stomach them. Aliens just aren't evil like that."

"Chill, Professor!" Tracy scolded, throwing a pillow at Nate. "It's just a movie, you dork. I *know*

Dewey's kind isn't evil, but that doesn't mean others aren't. What about the ones who put the structures on Mars and at the bottom of the Java Trench? How do we know *they* aren't evil? Maybe those things are weapons, and they'll come back to use them against us them someday, just like in this movie."

"I doubt it. Those things have been abandoned for a hundred million years."

"I hope you're right. Pretty freaky, though, that we're the only people on Earth that even know they're there."

"Yeah. Pretty cool, isn't it?" Nate smiled and winked at Tracie. Tracie turned the TV off.

"Come to bed, baby."

Nate disrobed, cleaned up, and climbed into bed. He snuggled up to his wife and rubbed his hand on her belly. "How's our little friend?"

"Hungry! You wouldn't believe how much I've been eating. Don't squeeze too hard, I'll barf on you."

Nate laughed out loud and loosened his grip on her.

"So, how did it go with Mercer?" Tracie asked.

"As well as could be expected, I guess. You'd have been proud of me; I didn't know I could be such a good actor. I snowed them pretty good. Antonio Perron was there, too. He did some tests on the meteorite... well, what everyone thinks is a meteorite, and he's very suspicious. His initial tests showed it was composed of exactly the same materials as the missing helicopter."

«So… he knows?"

"He knows something happened, but he didn't tell Mercer and the board, only me and Jason. He's pretty sure the meteorite *is* the helicopter, but it gets worse: the meteorite was stolen from his lab. Now no one knows where it is."

"What! Stolen? Who the heck steals a meteorite?"

"Don't know for sure. They *are* worth a lot of money to the right people, but I don't think it was taken for profit. I think someone suspects there's something different about it, and that someone wanted to have it for themselves. Whoever it was, they were well-organized, with modern weapons, gear, and masks, like a high-tech SWAT-team. Tony was hit pretty hard with a rifle butt, so hard he had to be hospitalized."

"Nobody knows who it might have been?"

"Nobody's admitting it if they do. But I have my suspicions."

"Mercer?"

"Yup. He and his pals have the money and the resources. And they love mysterious shit like this. My money says they have it."

"Well, let *them* figure it out. Time for *you* to move on and go back to being a boring biology professor… and a daddy, okay?"

"Okay. Boring sounds really good. And daddy

sounds *great,*" Nate whispered, then kissed his wife and turned off the light. Before consciousness faded, his last thought was of Dewey. He wondered what Dewey was doing at that moment, far across the Universe.

CHAPTER 48

At the same time Nate was answering Mercer's questions in New York, Dewey was facing his own inquisition, although his was far more thorough. He had been escorted by his Mentor and several Exploration Ministry Delegates from the orbiting station back to the planet's surface and directly to Ministry headquarters, nestled in the heart of the Prime City Complex.

Dewey spent many hours in the debriefing chamber, answering thousands of questions from dozens of members from the Science and Exploration Ministries. The preserved specimens he had collected in the Amazon were displayed about the chamber, and each was admired and examined closely, especially by the Cloning Technicians who would soon use the animals' DNA to replicate live samples for the Zoo's Earth Habitats. It wasn't until that moment that Dewey actually took any time to appreciate the fruits of his harvest. He had been so distracted by his encounter with Nate and Tracie, and so consumed with returning home without these events being discovered, that he had not paid much attention to how truly fascinating the creatures he had captured were.

All data retrieved from the ship, its utility-spheres, and Dewey's holo-discs was cross- examined for discrepancies, and Dewey felt immeasurable relief when everything correlated perfectly — thanks in no small part to his Mentor. He silently thanked the Creator that she had helped him. He still had no idea how she had managed to do that undetected, but if she hadn't, it would have been disastrous for him. He would have been disgraced by the Ministry and reassigned to another, probably nonessential profession, never to return to Earth again. Instead, the Ministry praised his successful mission, acknowledged him as qualified for future missions to Earth, and finally dismissed him to go home to his family.

Dewey's mate and two offspring were waiting for him at the Ministry's transport bay. Their reunion was emotional, the four of them intertwining their digits in a spaghetti-like mass of writhing fingers, their eyes changing colors randomly. They boarded a planetary transport and soon were speeding across the purple sky towards their home, halfway around the planet.

Dewey was never happier in his life than he was at this moment, surrounded by his precious family. He told them of the new creatures he had collected from Earth's rainforest, displaying images of them and other scenes from the Amazon about the transport's interior. But he did not mention Nate, Tracie, nor his adventures beyond the limits of his authority. He did not want his children to hear of these things… at least not yet.

That night, in the privacy of their sleeping chamber before the offspring came to sleep, Dewey engaged his mate in a private conversation through the discreet holo-disc channel that only the two of them shared. He told her of Nate and Tracie, and all that had happened. He described how his Mentor had discovered his actions and helped to cover them up, and he expressed how he had a newly fueled appreciation for the Humans and their role in the Creator's plan for the Universe.

Dewey's mate was, of course, shocked by all this. But as the shock wore off, she felt great excitement in being so exclusively privy to such an incredible story, and fortunate to be mated to the only Explorer who, to their knowledge, had ever been on such an adventure. She promised to never reveal what he had told her to anyone. For the next hour, Dewey answered the many questions she had about his encounters. Then she changed the subject.

"Mate, while you were on Earth, my body began to produce a new egg."

"That is wonderful news!" It was pitch-black in the sleeping chamber, but had it been illuminated, Dewey's eyes would have appeared bright purple. His hearts raced and his brains were filled with thoughts of the reproductive process he would participate in over the next several weeks. When the egg reached the proper stage, in about four months, he and his mate would go to the shore of a nearby purple ocean, the very same beach where their parents, and thousands of generations before them, had taken their eggs for the final gestation period.

At the beach, they would be joined by other Alien couples, trumpeting a symphony of wailing sounds from their blow-holes, calling out across the purple waves. Soon, a gargantuan, disc-shaped ocean creature, five hundred feet in diameter, would be attracted to the noise and surface as close to the shore as its behemoth body would allow. When the beast arrived, the Aliens would scamper into the surf and swim out to greet it.

When the expecting parents reached the creature, they would clamber onto its rubbery back and the females would each meticulously choose a spot to lay her single egg, secreting a sticky white substance that firmly attached the egg to the giant's skin. Once each egg was surely fastened, the males would squat onto them and deposit their sperm.

After all eggs were secured and fertilized, the parents would leap back into the ocean and swim to shore, by which time a new group of Aliens would be gathered on the beach. These were the most elderly members of the species, whose days in this world had come to an end. They would be surrounded by their families and friends on the beach, and would warmly greet the returning couples and say their goodbyes to everyone before swimming out to the egg-host beast, its cavernous mouth now agape and waiting for them just beyond the surf. The senior Aliens would willingly and joyfully swim directly in, feeding themselves to the hungry creature without hesitation.

This symbiotic relationship between the Aliens and the giant egg-hosts had existed for many millions of years, since before the Aliens themselves had crawled from the oceans and evolved into land-dwellers. The mineral-rich ocean, as well as secretions from the creature's skin, contained unique nutrients that were essential to the final development of Alien embryos. Likewise, the Aliens' flesh had always been a required food for the big animals, containing compounds vital to their survival that were not found in any other ocean prey. Many attempts had been made by Alien scientists to artificially recreate the conditions by which the eggs could complete their gestation, as well as to nourish the goliath beasts and prevent their extinction. But none had ever been as effective as what nature had engineered.

And so, it had always remained that the eldest Aliens, when close to dying of natural causes, offered themselves as food to the egg-hosts. This was their ultimate and final sacrifice to the prolongation of both species, and it was a great honor for Aliens to end their physical life this way. In return, the grateful egg-hosts fed the eggs and protected them from predators, who would not dare try to eat them from the host's back, lest they be ripped to shreds by retractable, razor-sharp spines that would be brandished with lethal force in any attack.

The eggs would stay attached to the animal's back for three years; then the offspring would hatch and swim to shore to meet their parents, who would be waiting for them on the beach. Genetic markers unique to each family would make it easy for the parents and offspring to find each other.

Dewey felt a wave of gratitude as he thought of these events to come. He looked forward to becoming a parent for the third time, and he silently thanked the Creator for the opportunity, as well as for returning him safely to his home... so far, without any apparent repercussions from his rogue actions on Earth. He also thanked the Creator for the Mentor's unexpected acceptance of his forbidden liaison with a Human, and her help in covering his tracks after he had been so careless in doing so himself.

Completely content and exhausted, he began to shut down all four brains for some much-needed sleep. As he faded from consciousness, his final thoughts were of Nate. He wondered what his new Human friend was doing at that very moment back on Earth.

CHAPTER 49

As Dewey and Nate settled back into their lives on their respective planets, something peculiar was happening near Mars.

Several hundred miles above the Red Planet's north pole, undetected by any Human technology or the sensors on the Aliens' Earth Station, a passage from deep within the Milky Way opened suddenly. This portal's appearance was quite different from the gravity tunnels Dewey's species used. It had no surface symmetry or weaving patterns of shifting energy and space; rather it appeared as a translucent distortion, like a tube constructed of rippling water. Moments later, a vessel emerged.

The ship resembled an asymmetrical mushroom, a hundred meters long. Its surface was irregular, its color translucent amber, making the craft look like a giant globule of hardened tree sap. It descended, orbiting the planet once before coming to a stationary position directly above the rocky butte that hid the ancient structure Dewey had shown Nate. Inside the ship, its occupants created a data-link between their vessel and the huge device below, which for millions of years had lain dormant beneath the Martian land-scape but now started to come to life.

These extraterrestrials were quite large com-pared to Humans and Dewey's species. They were insectoid, somewhat resembling twelve-foot tall, wingless waterbugs with broad paddles attached to the ends of their four swimming legs. Their upper torsos featured two large, spiked legs and, just be-neath that, four smaller appendages emerging from their chests, sporting numerous finger-like digits at the ends. The interior of their scout ship was com-pletely flooded with water, and as they gracefully maneuvered about with their various limbs, they communicated with clicking sounds.

"The third unit is uncompromised and working properly, but it appears someone has tried to enter it several times in the past few thousand years," one reported to the other.

"Could this have been done by a life-form from the third planet or the fifth planet's moon?"

"According to sensor readings, the fifth planet life still has no technology, but it looks as if a species of bipeds on the third planet does now have space travel. It was either them, or an unknown species has visited from another solar system."

As additional long-range sensor readings came in, the Waterbug scouts learned of the Aliens' un-manned Earth Station behind Jupiter, and assumed that whatever species had put it there was responsi-ble for disturbing the third unit. The readings coming from the third planet showed copious amounts of technology in use there by the bipedal land-species that had recently evolved, but these technologies were quite primitive in comparison to the station behind the fifth planet, and it was improbable that anyone from the third planet had made it as far as the fourth planet just yet, aside from the simple probes, rovers, and artificial satellites found there.

The Scouts then took their ship to Earth, eager to inspect the second unit and make sure no one had tried to compromise it as well. The ship would not be discovered by the bipeds' radar technologies, but they could be seen by telescopic devices if they came too close in the daylight; so, like Dewey had done, they waited for the Earth's rotation to position properly, and then descended to their target in the dark of night. The vessel's nose elongated itself, making it more arrow-shaped, thus more hydrodynamic, and then it plummeted through the atmosphere without creating a heat trail, headed straight towards the Indian Ocean. When it impacted, it slipped effortlessly into the water directly above the deepest part of the Java Trench, shooting straight down into the trench until it was positioned above the buried unit. Readings indicated that the unit was in proper working order, but, like the unit on Mars, there was evidence that someone had found it and tried, unsuccessfully, to penetrate it.

After completing their inspection of the unit, the Waterbug scouts left the Indian Ocean and entered a high orbit around Earth, gathering as much intelligence on its inhabitants as they could. This planet had exploded with life since the three units had been placed in this system, at which time life on the second, third, and fourth planets had been primordial and just beginning to develop in earnest. They studied, with great interest, the reasonably intelligent bipeds that had evolved to govern this world… "Humans," they called themselves.

These Humans had become advanced enough to leave the boundaries of their planet's gravity and visit its solitary moon, and had sent numerous drone vehicles to explore other planets throughout the system. Scans of their latest technologies revealed they were planning to soon venture further out, to begin visiting the fourth planet with manned missions. But that had not yet been accomplished. There was no evidence that the Humans had any knowledge of the Aliens' Earth Station, nor of any of the Waterbugs' Extraction Units.

The Scouts finished their observations of Earth, then moved on to inspect the unit buried on the second planet and assess the situation there. There was no water remaining there, and thus no life; the planet had suffered a runaway greenhouse event, and the unit had suffered significant damage during the planet's violent geographic evolution, so it was quickly dismissed as a loss. The life on the fifth planet's moon, which was a surprise bonus, might someday replace the losses on Venus and Mars.

Their tasks complete, the scouts returned to Mars to conclude their mission. They summoned the passage and promptly entered, speeding back to their home at the far side of the Milky Way at a speed that even Dewey's kind would find astonishing.

Along the way, the scouts prepared their report to deliver to their superiors. In it, they indicated that one of the three potential harvest planets in this system had ripened perfectly over the past hundred million years, and a fourth, also rich with life, had emerged unexpectedly. There was a land species, *Humans,* on the third planet that had developed advanced technology, but this would be of no consequence to the harvest other than a minor annoyance if they put up any resistance. What *was* of great concern, however, was the evidence of an unidentified species that had been visiting the system from parts unknown. *Their* technology was formidable, and they had discovered and tried to tamper with at least two of the units.

This would all be taken into consideration by the Waterbug leaders before any harvest operation would begin, but none of these concerns would stop it from proceeding. Long-term survival of their species was all that mattered, and the harvests were crucial to that cause.

To Be Continued...